# PRAISE FOR LOVE AND MAYHEM

'An absolutely stunning debut nove[l] ... love. It is just very well-written' Paul [...]

'A twisted tale of love set in a darke[r ...] and persuasive [characters] ... and w[hispers ...] – to come' Daneet Steffens, *Time Out*

'The novel is so full of insight and genuine innovation in form and content. I think it captures brilliantly all the nuances of passion, and the way that passion can sweep away the more rational side of us. Very sobering and moving' Alain de Botton, author of *Status Anxiety* and *The Consolations of Philosophy*

'As visceral a tale of love, sex and human emotion as you are ever likely to read ... the book is both dangerous and heart-stopping. Powerful, modern and moving, *Love And Mayhem* is as much a work of art as it is a work of literature' *The Magazine*

'The writing is swift and clean, the novel a solid and emotionally mature piece' Ashley Stokes, *Guardian* and *Times Literary Supplement* critic

'Bold and yet subtle on the same page, a useful balancing act, delivered with panache and sincerity' *Book Mark*

'The writing is tight ... painting London in a menacing half-light [and] Taussig's assertion that this was inspired by his own experiences adds a further edge to proceedings' Kingsley Marshall, *Notion*

'One of the best books of 2005, a book full of emotions and paradoxes which will excite the reader' *European Radio*

'This is a consistently well-written piece with an intensity which suits the mood of the narrative perfectly. An excellent debut, Taussig's second novel is due out next year, and I for one can't wait to read it' Elena Botterill, *Nottingham Evening Post*

'His rapid, urgent style and descriptive powers keep the reader in play, [and] the excellent sense of place deriving from the London background is a real strength, and there is conviction too, in the reasons for the final outcome' Margaret Laird, *Society Today*

'Sexy, edgy, maybe a bit mad, certainly disturbing, darkish but thought-provoking' *Ladsmag*

'An interesting and thought-provoking debut novel ... Taussig gives some humanity to characters of the street and leaves us questioning society as a whole. And that is something of note' Mike Henning, *This is…*

'Nick Taussig's debut shows a rare insight into a breathless relationship and the perilous path it can take' Hayley Whitlock, *The Book Place*

'A compelling read ... a darkly powerful story of love and its ability to destroy' James Cocks, *Vstudent*

# A NOTE ABOUT THE AUTHOR

Nick Taussig was born in 1973. He lives in London. He studied literature and philosophy at the University of Durham, where he obtained a First, then went on to acquire a Master's in Russian literature from the University of London. This is his first novel. He has co-written a feature film called *Just Left of Heaven*, which is due to star Peter Mullan. He is currently writing his second novel, which will be published in autumn 2006.

# LOVE AND MAYHEM

A novel by Nick Taussig

BOOKS

REVOLVER BOOKS
10 Lambton Place, London W11 2SH
www.revolverbooks.com

Revolver Entertainment Ltd, Registered Offices: Craven House, 16 Northumberland Avenue, London WC2N 5AP

Published by Revolver Books, a division of Revolver Entertainment Ltd

Copyright © 2006 by Nick Taussig
All rights reserved

The right of Nick Taussig to be identified as author of this work has been asserted by him in accordance with the Copyright, Designs and Patents Act, 1988

A CIP Catalogue record for this book is available from the British Library

ISBN: 0-9549407-7-6

Designed and typeset by Perfect Bound Ltd
Jacket design © Revolver Entertainment
Printed and Bound in Great Britain by Bookmarque Ltd, Croydon, Surrey.

Without limiting the rights under copyright reserved above, no part of this publication may be reproduced, stored in or introduced into a retrieval system, or transmitted, in any form, or by any means (electronic, mechanical, photocopying, recording, or otherwise), without the prior written permission of both the copyright owner and the above publisher of this book.

The scanning, uploading, and distribution of this book via the Internet or via any other means without the permission of the publisher is illegal and punishable by law. Please purchase only authorised electronic editions, and do not participate in or encourage electronic piracy of copyrighted materials. Your support of the author's rights is appreciated.

**FOR MY MOTHER AND FATHER, WITH LOVE**

## ACKNOWLEDGEMENTS

For his determined and ceaseless support and advice in the writing of this, my deepest gratitude to Justin Marciano; and to Lauren McCarthy, without whom this book would never have been written.

I would also like to thank Ashley Stokes for his editorial acumen and wisdom: I would have been lost without him.

I am indebted to the following people, whose thoughts, comments and words of encouragement along the way were invaluable: Danny Hansford, Paul Carter, Maria O'Connor, Jezz Vernon, Natascia Phillips, Carly Morrell, Tom Clark, Sharon Lougher, Martin Willis, Jill Crombie, Rhinal Patel, Christine Rose, Simon Hammerson, Michelle Taylor, Tessa McWatt, Leslie Mapp, Gilly Reeder, Emma Lindsey, Sarah Mitchell, Adam Connors, Emily Jeremiah, Annie McCulloch, Ursula Darrell, Shelley Silas, Helen Corner, Katie Scarfe, Abby Browde, Tess Masters and Kelley Harron.

Many thanks to Rebecca de Saintonge and Patsy Trench of the Literary Consultancy, and Steven Williams, Tony Mulliken, Sophie Ransom and Amelia Rowland of Midas PR.

And finally, grateful acknowledgement is given to the following authors and their works: *Love and Will* by Rollo May, *An Unquiet Mind* by Kay Redfield Jamison, *Essays in Love* by Alain de Botton, *From Pain to Violence* by Felicity de Zulueta, *The Outsider* by Colin Wilson and *The Rebel* by Albert Camus.

'The individual has manifold shadows, all of which resemble him, and from time to time have equal claim to be the man himself.'
*Sören Kierkegaard*

## CONTENTS

**I  LOVING CATHERINE**    1

**II  LOVING JACK**    103

**III  LOVING ONE ANOTHER**    221

# I

# LOVING CATHERINE

# 1

**BEING ALONE** has become a habit for him, and one which he has begun to fear he will never break. It has only been half an hour since he arrived, and yet already, he has had enough.

Jack sits in the corner of the room and observes the scene: there is a big dining table, which supports a lavish banquet of food, and a dozen or so people, mostly couples, sit round it; then more people, about the same number, mill around in the adjoining room. No one eats anything: everyone just chatters frantically. Yes, it is one of those evenings fuelled by cocaine. Jack does not want to be here, but he has promised Sam he would make the effort.

He watches a faceless couple get up from the table. The young man and woman make what they consider to be a clandestine visit to the bathroom: but in truth, there is nothing secret about this excursion. Jack then turns his attention to a debate going on beside him about the woes of corporate globalisation. Four or five people are involved. He does not see the point in participating, as they are not actually listening to one another's different arguments. The cocaine has convinced each of them there is only one valid point of view, and that is his or her own.

A woman sits in the opposite corner. Like Jack, she says nothing, just observes the scene. And like him, she looks a little lost. He wonders if she is here with anyone. She wears a gold blouse, hanging loose over her front, supported by two ties on her back. Jack watches as she rotates her body slightly. As she slides her hips on the chair, the smooth pale skin of her bare back becomes visible. Then he focuses on the woman's mouth, her lips coated with deep red lipstick. She is beautiful, he thinks, as he lets his gaze settle on her. She sips slowly from her glass of wine. Jack looks at her hand. She wears gold nail varnish, which resembles a kind of pale lacquer, shiny but refined. He catches the glint of her white teeth between the vibrant red of her lips. Then she looks over at him, and holds his stare. He looks away. She smiles confidently out of the corner of her mouth. Jack is now desperate to talk to her but he does not have the courage.

He continues to look over at her – he cannot stop himself – but he is sure she is not really interested in him. How can she be? he asks himself. He is not right for her. He is probably not tall enough, not handsome enough, and certainly not well-dressed enough. She is simply too beautiful. This last year, Jack has reasoned his way into a corner of romantic apathy, and his sex drive has waned to the point of extinction.

Jack gets up from the table and shuffles awkwardly towards the kitchen. He creeps inside and nervously pushes the door to. Enough. There is no point in saying anything to her. He will have one more quick drink, then go. He reaches for the refrigerator handle and pulls the door open. He suddenly feels the touch of soft skin on his hand and a woman's voice whisper into his ear, 'Hi.' He swings round. It is her. 'Hi,' she says again, 'what are you doing?'

'I'm… I'm… getting a drink,' Jack replies.

'You look about as comfortable here as I do,' she says playfully as he struggles with the fridge door.

'Yeah… Sam's a dear friend of mine, but I don't really know many people here and… well…' Jack speaks fast, struggling to get his words out.

'Neither do I. My flat mate, Genevieve, knows Sam. I'm a friend of a friend shall we say. I don't really know anyone here either.'

'Right…' he mumbles, as she closes the kitchen door, then walks past him towards the worktop next to the sink. Jack follows the sway of her hips and admires her legs, partially visible through her thin silk skirt. She turns to face him. Her eyes scan his body. 'We seemed to be the only people in the room not saying anything,' he goes on.

'Not talking bullshit you mean!'

'Well yes…' he replies, taken aback.

'I feel like doing something else,' she says excitedly. 'Do you?'

'Excuse me?'

'You heard me.'

'Can I…' Jack dithers, 'get you a drink?'

'I've got one already,' she says, holding up her glass. 'And I wouldn't class that as doing something else.'

'Sorry… I don't know what you mean?'

'I'd rather get out of here.'

'Oh right… sorry,' Jack says and looks down at the floor.

'What are you apologising for?'

'I… I don't know.'

She smiles at him. He smiles back, then looks away when she holds his stare.

'You're shy, aren't you?' she asks matter-of-factly.

'Yeah…'

'You're not very good at answering questions either,' she goes on.

'I…'

'And you often get the wrong end of the stick.'

'What d'you mean?'

'I wasn't planning to get out of here on my own. I asked if you wanted to do something else *with* me.'

'Right…'

'Well then?' She waits for him to answer, but all Jack can do is smile at her. 'Come on,' she continues, 'let's go.'

'Where to?'

'We'll think of somewhere,' she says as she takes his hand and leads him out of the kitchen.

They leave immediately. She flags down the first taxi she sees, and gives the driver swift instructions to take them back to her flat. Before Jack has a chance to query her choice of destination, she leans over and kisses him. Jack cannot quite believe what is happening. Neither one of them says anything during the journey home. They are only interested in exploring one another's lips.

When they pull up outside the flat, she thrusts a note in the driver's hand and bundles Jack out of the cab. She leads him to the front door, pushes him inside. She forces him up against the wall in the hallway, gropes his crotch. Jack pulls her hand away. 'I need a drink of something,' he says.

'No you don't,' she replies, kissing him, coaxing him towards her bedroom. Inside, she starts to undress him.

'Can we slow down a little bit?' he asks.

'It's okay,' she whispers, pushing him onto the bed and running her hands over his bare chest. She takes off his trousers and boxer shorts simultaneously. He is hard, but feels uncomfortable. She takes him in her mouth. He does not want this, pushes her head away.

She removes her mouth and makes her way up his torso until her face meets his. Then she opens her eyes and stares at him. They are deep brown. There is a softness to them, which surprises him. He relaxes. 'I need this… need you,' she mumbles, then kisses him gently on the lips. And he puts his arms around her and holds her tight.

She sits up and her thick black hair falls straight down around her shoulders as she arches her neck back. Unties her blouse. It falls onto Jack's stomach. She takes his hands and puts them to her breasts. Starts to gyrate on top of him, becoming excited. Her brown eyes dart wildly at him between strands of tangled hair. Her breath becomes heavier. She hitches up her skirt, stands up, pulls off her knickers. Puts her middle and index finger to her mouth, wets them with saliva, inserts them in her vagina. Then she grabs his erect penis in her hand, and squatting on top of him, slides it inside of her.

They stare intently at one another as they start to have sex. Jack's look is slightly perplexed, hers powerful, impossible to articulate. But he likes it that she takes charge.

Soon, it feels wonderful, him inside her. He is not inept with her, having the kind of clumsy sex he has experienced before. Rather he feels liberated, does not feel like he has to hide himself from her. He forgets the whole world while she pushes away on top of him.

'I want you to come inside me, come…' she pleads with Jack as she reaches orgasm, her eyes still fixed on his, staring at him, searchingly. He is not wearing a condom. He should pull out. 'It's okay, just come,' she continues, sensing his concern.

Her hips move so fast now, her breathing distinguished by short, noisy sucks and puffs. And then finally she slows, just as he does. Both of them twitch, shudder, and as she says, 'I'm coming…' so does Jack.

Afterwards, they lie naked on her four-poster cast-iron bed, entwined in one another's bodies, whispering to each other, the pink sheets crumpled up on the hardwood varnished floor. Jack admires the dark hue of her skin, so smooth when he touches it. In the dark of the room, it appears to belong to an Asian not a European woman. Then he peers through the part open drawer of her bedside table and catches sight of a red velvet-bound book. 'What's that?' he says, pointing to it as he begins to speculate about its contents.

'That's my journal,' she says as she rolls over and closes the drawer firmly.

'Is that where you put all your secrets?'

'Yeah… something like that.'

'I'm intrigued.'

'I bet you are.'

'D'you make a habit of this?'

'Of what?'

'Seducing younger men.'

'Yes.'

'And they're all in there,' he says, motioning to it again.

'Never read my journal…' she murmurs.

Then he stares at a photograph of Marlene Dietrich – mounted in an old, ornate gold frame – as the temptress in von Sternberg's *The Devil is a Woman*. 'That's quite a picture,' he says.

'Yes it is, isn't it,' she replies, admiring Dietrich's sexually dominant grin.

'I don't even know your name?'

'It's Catherine… Catherine Ramirez,' she says.

Jack feels himself floating when he leaves her flat the following morning. As he walks down her tree-lined street, which is adorned with summer flowers and foliage, he imagines he is entering a magical world; everything appears vibrant and bright even though it is a cloudy day. Before he reaches the end of the street, he misses her already and longs to see her again.

They meet some twelve hours later and have sex.

The next few days assume this dreamy and intoxicating pattern. He sits at work, thinking about Catherine all the time, and struggles to perform any action that does not involve her in some way.

'Your desk is becoming bloody chaotic!' Sam says to Jack while he is on the phone to Catherine. Up until now, he has always kept it in impeccable order, perpetually driven by the monotonous compulsion to tidy it at any available opportunity. Now, manuscripts, articles and Post-it notes are strewn across it; polystyrene cups and coffee spills litter and smear its surface. Sam leans over him, his tall, bulky frame pressing against the back of Jack's chair and squeezing him against his desk as he tries to locate a piece Jack is meant to have edited for the next issue. 'What's happened to you?' he continues.

Jack puts his hand over the mouthpiece and answers, 'I couldn't be better, really.'

'And where d'you get to the other night?'

'Oh, I left a bit early.'

'Okay,' Sam mumbles as he finds what he is looking for, then stomps off, his shock of brown unkempt hair and creased linen suit seeming to confirm his frustration.

Jack hangs up feeling breathless and elated. He looks at his desk. Should he tidy it? he wonders. No, why should he. He suddenly does not care anymore. And what about his other editorial work for the magazine and his freelance contributions? Well, he does not really need to submit anything until next month, he tells himself. Why work when he does not have to? For the first time in his life, he wants to be reckless with his professional life, yes, think about it less, make these beautiful moments with Catherine matter.

Close to the end of the day, Sam hands him a novel to review. Jack reads the back blurb. It is tragic and melancholic, his usual fodder. 'You got something a bit lighter?' he asks.

'What?' Sam replies. 'It's dark. That's why I bloody gave it to you. I thought it'd be a treat.'

'I'd rather not,' Jack says.

'You got something else in mind then?' Sam asks, sounding rather put out.

'I took a book off your shelf yesterday?'
'Nosing around in my office again?'
'Something like that.'
'Which one?'
'*The Purity of Love.*'
'Leonard Gold at his best.'
'I thought it might be good as a "Classic of the Month"?'
'We've done it already.'
'You sure?'
'Yes.'

'Shame, I would love to have written about it,' Jack says. After he and Catherine had sex last night, he was unable to sleep. He simply felt too euphoric. And so he picked up *The Purity of Love*, and then could not put it down, despite the fact that he had to be in the office early. He read the whole thing, all one hundred and eighty pages, and ended up not getting to sleep till very late. The book tells the story of a man who loses his wife. It follows the protagonist through his grief, step by step. And as it nears the end, the reader slowly becomes confident that he will overcome his grief and find love again. In the book, grief is depicted as a tragic and desperate emotional state that nevertheless passes with time and courage. And the protagonist is ennobled through his suffering. He comes to love his dead wife more deeply, but at the same time accepts that he must get on with his life, find someone else to love, and that she would not begrudge him this. For this is what she would have wanted him to do: to cherish life to the very end just as she had done. It is an exquisite story of love, loss and hope, as Jack sees it, and he also admires the way it is written – sparse, concise, beautiful prose. Jack continues, 'You know, I wouldn't mind hanging on to it for a bit. I'd like to read it again.'

'Sure,' Sam replies.

'Look, I've got to leave a bit early today,' Jack says, glancing at his watch.

'Where you off to?'

'I'll tell you tomorrow okay. I'd better go.'

'What now?'

'Yeah, if that's okay?' Jack says, and before Sam even has time to answer him, he grabs his jacket from the back of his chair and hurries out of the office. Sam and his other work colleagues are left to ponder this dramatic change in him.

He heads for the florist. Jack plans to buy Catherine a big bouquet of lilies: last night, she told him the lily was her favourite flower. He is not sure what it is about Catherine that makes him feel the way he does: he hardly knows her. But he is happy, for the first time in ages. Perhaps it is simply too early to articulate why, he wonders. At thirty-three, she is four years older than him. Maybe it is this? She is more mature, wiser.

He walks fast now, feels light, as he nears his destination. Jack considers whether this is the start of an everlasting love: his romantic musings and fantasies have their own momentum now, and are not based on observable reality but rather what he wants to feel, to experience. He is aware of this, but he does not want to moderate his feelings, no. For the first time in his life, he feels vivid, susceptible. It is as if Catherine has all of a sudden woken him up. His years of restless academic achievement – an Honours degree, a Master's degree and his published writings – pale into insignificance next to his feelings for her. And his intellectual drive to extend himself to an ideology, a concept, a principle, an essay, a piece of fiction now seems less important than his need to reach out to another person, a woman, Catherine.

White lilies or pink ones, ten flowers in each bunch. Both possess an equal beauty. He sniffs at them. He is tired of listening to that rational, cynical part of him, the inner voice that expresses caution and ambivalence. No, he has found something to believe in now, he tells himself. 'I'll have one of each please,' he concludes.

At the end of their first week together, Jack barges into Sam's office. He is desperate to tell him about her. 'Catherine's incredible!' he announces.

'What?' Sam asks, looking up from his desk.

'There's something about her.'

'Who?'

'Catherine Ramirez… your friend Genevieve's friend.'

'Yes, she's quite something? I wish I'd had more time to talk to her,' Sam says and looks to Jack, who is just grinning, looking pleased with himself. He continues, 'What?' But Jack still says nothing, just smiles broadly. 'You didn't?' Sam goes on, sounding almost unable to even comprehend what his friend's expression suggests.

'I can't believe it myself,' Jack speaks finally.

'Really?'

'Yes.'

'My God, I didn't think you had it in you. You're going to have to tell me all after work,' Sam says excitedly. 'I told you it was worth coming last weekend,' he goes on, then waits for Jack's reply, but again, all Jack can do is look at him rather serenely, and communicate nothing more than his current state of mind these past few days, a kind of perfect contentment. Sam continues, 'It looks like you've fallen for her in a big way?'

'I have.'

'Look, just be careful alright.'

'What you talking about?'

'You know what I mean?'

'No.'

'Look, I'm really happy for you. It's been a long time since you met someone – in fact we'd all bloody given up on you, thought you were becoming a monk – but just don't rush into anything.'

'Course I won't!' Jack insists as he turns to leave Sam's office.

'We'll go for a pint this evening, yeah, and you can tell me about her?'

'Okay,' Jack replies and closes the door behind him.

Catherine telephones Jack at the office later that day. 'Jack, I want to go away.' She has just finished another production. She directs short films and documentaries.

'When?' he asks.

'Now… today. You free?'

'Well… yes, I suppose I could…' he replies. They have just gone to print on the August edition, which gives him ample time to prepare for September's. *Detritus* is a small monthly magazine that covers a wide spectrum of interests including world affairs and politics, literature and the arts. He is confident that the chief editor, Sarah Winterson, will not have any objections. And his drink with Sam, well it can wait, it will have to. 'But for how long?' Jack asks.

'I've got one week off.'

'Where d'you want to go?'

'Anywhere. Just away from here.'

'Okay…'

'I'll call you in an hour, okay,' Catherine says, and hangs up the phone.

Jack throws his hands behind his head and leans back in his chair, then stares at the ceiling and tries to imagine what she is about to go and do.

# 2

**THEY ARRIVE** in Casablanca in the afternoon and find an old, elegant French colonial hotel with grand chandeliers, hand-painted murals on the walls and marble staircases lined with arabesque rugs.

In their room, Catherine immediately decides to get drunk. She perches on the edge of the bed, takes a miniature bottle of vodka from the mini bar and downs it. It is ice cold as it hits the back of her throat and makes her shudder as she swallows. Then she reaches for another one, unscrews the cap and puts it to her mouth as she lies back on the bed. It is empty by the time she is horizontal. 'Jack, I'm sure that if I drink a few more of these,' she says, pointing clumsily to the remaining bottles on the top shelf of the refrigerator door, 'it will get rid of my stuffy nose. It's a potent decongestant, you know.'

'Yeah, but only if you're planning to sniff the stuff,' Jack replies. 'Drinking lots of vodka will provide short-term relief but a long-term hangover, trust me.'

'Oh don't be such a party pooper,' she says, smiling at him mischievously as he strokes her leg. Catherine suddenly wonders if it was a good idea to go away with Jack. But then he looks at her that way again, those green eyes of his staring longingly, strongly. They make her feel a bit weak and giddy. No man has looked at her this way in a long time. She realises this. Catherine likes his broad shoulders and his short messy crop of light brown hair. He is slightly unshaven. He looks rugged but also refined, with his corduroys and his smart baggy shirt. And she likes his voice, a wonderfully deep voice. It makes him sound distinguished.

In the evening, Catherine stumbles downstairs wearing a slinky long black dress, treading her heels on its tassels. They have dinner in the hotel's empty ballroom, painted all gold and embellished with opulent marble and mahogany furnishings. Their table glitters with beeswax under the glass chandelier. An elderly Moroccan man holds a violin to his chin and adversely plays out a Paganini concerto with a series of lazy pizzicatos that makes her feel like they are in nineteenth-century Western Europe rather than contemporary post-colonial North Africa.

Back in their bedroom, they have sex on the balcony. Jack leans against a brass railing, put his arms around Catherine's bare waist and lifts her onto him as a golden minaret sparkles in an indigo sky. Old Muslim men in the opposing buildings look on with a contradictory mixture of fervent religious judgment and candid intrigue. Then without warning, she releases one of her arms from behind his neck and waves at one of them. She and Jack instantly lose their balance and fall to the floor in a giggling heap, her warm legs entangled with his underneath in the hot, damp North African air; the sweat below her breasts dripping onto his forehead. Hidden from view, they continue to have sex on the stone floor until they are exhausted.

Catherine does not fall asleep right away but stares at Jack's naked body and thinks about what she has just been through with him. She has had many lovers and has never really allowed these brief affairs to develop into anything more. In fact, her romantic history has a near adolescent quality, she now thinks, unsettled and confused, colourful splashes of excitement on a large canvas of solitude. According to her experience, love is an unsustainable emotion, ephemeral in nature and unpredictable. And so, lacking faith in committed and meaningful relationships, she has become a slave to the modern virtues of casual sex. This is sex as a physical pursuit, a technique to master, a hobby that requires very little commitment: all she has to do is meet a man, have sex with him, then leave him. She is not required to share anything more than her body. In fact, Catherine has got used to it this way, as something anonymous, detached, focused on the act itself: the raw, natural energy of sexual desire, that is all. And she no longer wants to feel close to the man she fucks. As far as she is concerned, there is almost something more real about an anonymous exchange between two people: they experience one another in the present moment as two yearning and desperate individuals in need of sexual fulfilment and some degree of intimacy. Jack is not her usual type: he is not as handsome as many of her past lovers. And he is rather awkward, intense. But he looked at her in the most profound way when they first had sex, as if he had suddenly discovered something wonderful, true, beautiful. Catherine knows she feels more for Jack than she usually does when she fucks someone: in fact it almost scares her. Oh, she knows what she used to tell herself all those years ago when a new man was inside her: she could spin herself a yarn, make herself believe there really was something more to this man than the one before. But more often than not, this sense turned out to be nothing more than lust's illusion. But with Jack, there does seem to be something more, even though she does not know if she wants it. It felt different again the second time they had sex, and the third. Catherine thought it would not, and imagined she would feel less for him. But she did not. She still wanted Jack to fuck her. It still felt great. No, she rebukes herself suddenly, turning away from him now, no longer wanting to look at him. She must not imagine some kind of future with Jack. It will only prove to be another false fairytale, she thinks. And she dares not lose her mind again. Catherine closes her eyes.

## LOVE AND MAYHEM

In the morning, she wakes up to the mystical sound of the *muezzin*. Catherine cannot see anything in the dark of the room. The spiritual cry seems to emanate from nowhere. She lies there and listens to it with a deep fascination as it reverberates around the walls of the bedroom, imagining many Muslim men rising from their beds in preparation for early morning prayer. She remembers what Jack said to her yesterday evening, when they heard it for the first time: it did not make him wince like the noise of English church bells, which always sounded almost hollow to him, as if they communicated nothing but an irritating clang. She laughed when he said this, and she chuckles again now. Catherine stares at the dark reflection of the net curtain, which seems to cast a shimmering spider's web across the floor, then sniffs the air; the room smells of sand and incense.

She listens to Jack softly breathing. Catherine tugs at his arm, warm and sleepy as the *muezzin* fades. For a moment, there is a delicious silence in the room, so distinct to her after London's persistent early morning clatter and hum. She watches him as he gets up and slides across the cold marble floor to the bathroom.

They are too excited to lie in bed anymore. She and Jack hire a car and head south from Casablanca towards Marrakech. The drive out of Humphrey Bogart's city is spectacular. They set off at sunrise. The night rain forms a sparkling mist as the early morning sun pushes past the moon. 'Thank you, God. The sun's taking off his pyjamas and getting ready for a lovely day,' Catherine says, mimicking her mother's subtle Gaelic drawl. She drapes her arm over Jack's shoulder and rests her head on his chest. She goes on, 'That's what my mother used to say to me when she was happy in the morning.'

The roads soak up the night's supply of moisture and market traders prepare their stalls after their morning prayer. As the morning mist lifts, she and Jack see young children playing football in discreet cobble-stone alleyways; old men feeding their mules; and Muslim women draped in black carrying large wicker baskets of freshly baked bread on their heads. People, animals and vehicles swarm through the streets: donkeys walking alongside brand new Mercedes and wealthy American tourists – weighed down with photographic equipment – brushing bodies with child beggars and old lepers slumped on the pavement.

Nearing the edge of the city, the hubbub becomes quieter as people and buildings become fewer. The landscape opens out, and she and Jack enter a raw and barren desert. The roads, straight and flat, go on and on, seeming to merge into the desert until the man-made road is barely traceable. This sense of space disorientates Catherine. She is used to the claustrophobia of London that often feels like a giant tin of sardines. Morocco does not possess the vast range of a country like America, and yet it feels more spacious. It has not been given a First World structure and design, perfectly farmed land forming a carefully constructed man-made passage between two cities, like the road journey she took a few years before from Los Angeles to Phoenix. The passage to Marrakech is different: small towns crop up along the way but they seem incidental. In short, the absence of Western design makes it feel more emancipated.

As they drive down, sometimes they do not pass another vehicle for fifty miles. She and Jack point out to each other the few things they see: small desert paths; a lone farmer with a herd of goats; the occasional young boy or girl sitting on the roadside trying to sell a handful of fresh vegetables and herbs in exchange for a few Moroccan *diram* or an American brand cigarette.

When they drive past a particular young girl who appears to be crying, Catherine insists that Jack stop the car. He pulls over and she hurries back down the road to the girl; she cannot be more than eight or nine years old. Catherine kneels beside her. *'Qu'est-il arrivé? Qu'est-ce qu'il y a?'* she asks.

The girl is hesitant at first – almost suspicious of Catherine's concern

– and flinches when she goes to put her arm on her shoulder and comfort her. Catherine continues, *'Hé, ne pas pleurer. S'il vous plait ne pleurer pas.'*

And with these words, the girl puts her face to Catherine's chest, and Catherine strokes her hair and kisses her head as she weeps. When the girl finally stops crying, Catherine is reluctant to leave her there and asks where she lives. The girl says nothing. Catherine turns to Jack. 'We can take her back to her home… we should do that,' she appeals to him.

*'Non… non, je suis bien,'* the girl insists, *'vraiment… vraiment.'* But it is obvious she is not okay, that something is wrong. *'Au revoir, madamoiselle, au revoir… et merci,'* she continues through tears as she scurries off down a dirt track off the roadside, which seems to lead to a small stone house some way off in the distance.

*'C'est là-bas… où tu habites?'* Catherine says, pointing to the house. But the girl does not answer.

'That must be where she lives,' Jack says.

Catherine runs after her, takes the girl by the shoulder, and forces her to stop. She thrusts a twenty-*diram* note in her hand. The girl looks at Catherine like she is mad, pecks her on the cheek, then presents her with some coriander stems; she offers them like a magnificent bouquet of flowers. And with this offering, she hurries off down the track.

'That's all I could give her Jack… just bloody money,' Catherine says despondently as she walks back to the car.

They arrive in Marrakech at sunset as the sky burns fiery orange. As they park the car outside the walls of the Old City, a distinguished-looking man with a thick black moustache confronts them. 'My name is Abdullah,' he proudly introduces himself. 'Let me show you round this wonderful city of mine. How long are you here for?'

'It's okay, we leave tomorrow morning for the Atlas Mountains, but thank you anyway,' Catherine fires back. She wants her and Jack to go it alone, to discover things rather than be shown them by someone else.

Catherine knows that he admires this about her, her fierce independence. She told Jack at Gatwick airport that they were adventurers not holidaymakers: they had their Lonely Planet guidebook, the romantic image of themselves as travellers with savvy and experience, and their combined worldly wisdom. She even joked when they were getting on the plane, 'What else do Lara Croft and her lover truly need?'

However, Abdullah is very perceptive and seeks to reassure them. 'I won't smother you or rip you off, okay,' he says, 'but if you only have one evening to take in Marrakech, you'd definitely benefit from a resident's knowledge.' He is very charismatic and charming, and his proposed tour is only two hours long. How can they refuse him? And so Catherine relents.

Abdullah takes them on his quick-fire junket round the city, which includes snake charmers, charlatan healers and pushy stall owners, and afterwards, he joins Catherine and Jack for dinner in *Jame 'el Fna*. They talk late into the night, and during those periods of the conversation when Jack and Abdullah find common ground and talk steadily to one another, Catherine sits there lost in thought about the young girl on the side of the road, and what might have upset her so much.

After the vivacious Abdullah has left, she and Jack watch the square slowly empty. The battalions of food-sellers are the last people to leave: the business of packing up their mobile kitchens is long and arduous. Finally, the square is deserted, except for an elderly Muslim woman who sits on a balcony above and peers at Catherine and Jack through her black veil. The meaty and spicy air becomes less pungent. 'It's so quiet now, so peaceful,' Catherine says. 'When we were driving through the desert, sometimes we couldn't see anyone… hear anything. When I was a child, I always dreamed of living in the English countryside, on a farm in the middle of nowhere, with animals beside me.'

'Yes, I've always wanted that as well. I'd love to move out of London someday,' Jack replies.

## LOVE AND MAYHEM

'I thought about doing it a couple of years ago but I wasn't established enough in my career. When I make my first feature, I could make the move then if I still wanted to. I could even move here, away from England, somewhere completely different. Yes… a totally new way of life…' she says excitedly, and Jack is silent.

Catherine has always been restless, she knows this, has always carried inside her an unrelenting desire to witness a different mode of existence, to experience another way of living other than the one she is so accustomed to, which continues to frustrate her to the point of despair. She looks up at the night sky now, a strong dark blue, and thinks of what she did when she left home all those years ago. She embarked on a new life away from her mother with a kind of youthful romanticism. 'You know, I was eighteen when I started my first job,' she says. 'The pay was awful, and I had just enough to pay the rent, feed myself and get blind drunk a few nights a week. But even then, with so little money, I'd always try and get away somewhere.'

'Where did you go?' Jack asks.

'I loved Devon, Cornwall and Wiltshire… I still do. And the Cotswolds, yes. I've always been like this, you see, in need of getting away. It was hard back then, but I loved the freedom I had. I felt like I was on the start of a great adventure. And when I began to earn a bit more, I started to take trips abroad on shoestring budgets, staying in hostels or dingy hotels. I didn't care. These trips made me feel so exhilarated. My heart would always beat fast when I walked out of the airport. And still to this day, when I'm away from home, I feel freer,' Catherine says, then takes a deep breath. She exhales slowly, smiles, has not felt like this for some time, anxiety gone, so relaxed and in control. Life is suddenly easier. She does not feel the panic to constantly be doing things, keeping busy, and scrawling endless dates and appointments in her diary. London often makes her feel trapped, smothered, and she craves solitude. She continues, 'I could stay here, Jack… for a long time.

I could if I really wanted to, couldn't I? I mean, I'm free to, aren't I?'

'Yes you are,' he says kissing her, 'though I might have a few objections.'

'I love it here. It doesn't make me feel hollow. Why can't I choose a different life… do something else… find a place that suits me? Maybe I don't because I'm just lazy?'

Jack looks at her adoringly as she whips up the idyllic scenario in her mind and starts to create a new life for herself. He muses, 'I think it's more about finding happiness in…'

'Don't Jack!' she says, anticipating his train of thought.

'What?' he asks.

'I know what you're going to say. But… you know what I mean.'

Perhaps this is what would suit her best, she thinks, life in another country, and only then would she be happy and peaceful. Jack told Catherine earlier that he is also weary of England, which in comparison to Morocco seems a soulless country, its people 'blinded by a capitalist ethos with rigid scientific foundations'. He can at times sound like a dreadful intellectual, but she rather likes this about him: he needs to have a theory about everything. He likes to write, he told her, but has felt uninspired for a long time; reviews are all he can muster at the moment. This guiding principle, Jack went on, a kind of 'hard-nosed and bitter rationalism', frowns upon the very notion of faith. According to him, the belief in some kind of divine providence or fate is now construed by the majority in England as an irrational device, an emotional crutch needlessly explored and used by those unfortunate people who need something more than experiential reality. However, the Moroccan people seem to be imbued with the vitality of a common belief, a universal truth, Jack said. This is not so much the faith of Islam as a collective consciousness, a strong and magical spirit that binds them together, as a community, a people. Catherine agreed with his assessment up to a point, even though it bordered on orientalism. But he had been very honest with her about why he felt this way. He was a Jew by blood alone, he told her. His father, Theo Stoltz, had brought him up on a staple diet of atheism and existentialism. The God of the *Torah*, the powerful and wise old man with the grey beard as Jack imagined him as a young child, was firmly rejected as a myth, a superstition, an illusory concept. Throughout his Godless childhood, an analytical mind was revered and blind faith dismissed. And so Jack was left to find his own way in a country where Christianity was slowly dying, only to be replaced by a dangerous agnosticism, a kind of uncertain faith in nothing, where rational curiosity alone is enough.

Catherine leans over now and licks Jack's cheek, taking a residue of saliva back in her mouth as she withdraws her tongue. Jack licks her back like a soppy dog.

The next morning, they drive out of Marrakech. They head up the Ourika Valley towards Oukamiden: a small village situated high up in the Atlas Mountains. En route, they pass by a group of small children who run beside their slow-moving car, which creeps up the steep mountain roads with its low cylinder capacity. The children heckle Jack and her in Arabic through the open car window, demanding money and food: '*diram*' is the only word Catherine hears clearly through their jabbering tongues.

They arrive at the mountain's peak to find a deserted ski resort town, which has shut down in the summer months. They check into a hotel that resembles a giant Swiss chalet. The concierge informs them that the black run ski lift, a relic from a prosperous European ski resort, runs every two hours. He exclaims, '*Allez, mes amis! C'est magnifique!*'

She and Jack reach the top and clumsily dismount the bucket seats without a pair of skis to propel them to safety. They duck down to avoid getting hit by the next row of ski chairs and collapse in a slapstick heap on the snow. They stare up towards the heavens to see a dramatic blue belt of sky pushing upwards a barrage of buoyant white fluffy clouds.

Then they cast their gaze down at the row of mountain peaks right in front of them, which looks like a giant sleeping body, the body of a voluptuous woman.

Jack takes her face in his hands and says, 'I've fallen in love with you, Catherine.' When he speaks these words, he sounds very conscious how hollow they might sound.

Catherine smiles at him as he holds her face and rebuffs, 'Don't say that Jack, you sound ridiculous! We've only been together ten days. It's just your libido talking… it's just chemical. Don't be fooled by it.'

'But the love feels real enough to me. I've had a permanent ache deep in my belly ever since I met you!'

'Jack, it's infatuation, lust… but please don't call it love.' Why should she believe his proclamation, she asks herself: it seems more reminiscent of the superficial pronouncements and simple obsession of a schoolboy who falls out of love as fast as he has fallen in love. 'You'll have a crush on another girl next week,' she adds. She does not want to be loved by Jack just because he happens to be having sex with her. If he loves her for this reason alone, because she fulfils his need for sex, then this is not love. She knows this more than most. According to this scenario, he will continue to have sex with her up until the point that he becomes bored, when he will finally realise that he does not love her after all, and then will leave her and find another woman to have sex with and profess his illusory love to.

'It's not just the sex,' Jack persists, '… it's so much more than that for me, really Catherine.'

'Love, Jack, is when you love all of me, not just my cunt!' she demands. He is silent. Catherine wants to believe that real, lasting love is possible, and yet she has never experienced it, or rather, she has not let herself experience it. She is very aware of the illusion of love that the libido creates. It can dupe two reasonable, intelligent and free-thinking people into believing that they are in love, when in fact, what they are experiencing is nothing of the kind. Jack knew almost nothing about her when they first had sex together. That night, they had been able to tell enough from one another's faces and bodies, which according to Catherine presented far more intriguing and compelling stories than the humdrum exchange of bland and often meaningless autobiographical monologues. Indeed it is quite possible, she thinks, that he has fallen in love with her precisely because he knows so little about her. She concludes softly, 'Jack I'm sorry, but please don't say anymore, not yet. Wait… just wait.'

They return to London on a warm summer's evening. Catherine does not know where their relationship will go from here. There is silence in the back of the cab as the driver turns into Catherine's street. When the car pulls up, Jack takes Catherine's bag and walks her to the front door. 'I've had a wonderful time, thank you,' he says.

'Me too…' she answers, 'I need to get some sleep. We haven't had much of it these last two weeks.'

'I won't ask if I can come in,' he says.

'You working tomorrow?'

'Yeah I'm due in the office first thing, but that's not why I said this.'

'Why then?' she asks.

'Because I know you think we've spent too much time together already,' he says flatly, and with these words she begins to laugh. 'And that might lead to emotional attachment, God forbid!'

'Yes, let's make sure we just fuck. We want nothing more than this. Fucking is everything, and all else is nothing,' she says playfully as she strokes his groin then closes the door behind her.

# 3

**WHEN JACK** gets back to his flat, he ambles into his living room and slumps on the sofa in a state of deep contentment; Catherine occupies all of his dreamy consciousness. As he closes his eyes and drifts off to sleep, he hopes that this feeling will persist for as long as possible.

The next morning, he still feels high. Jack makes his way to the bus stop. He always enjoys the short bus ride from Shepherd's Bush to Notting Hill: it is his ten minutes of quiet time before the mayhem of the office. In spite of the bustle of fellow commuters, the throb of the bus's engine, the tooting of car horns and the screeching of taxi brakes, he is able to slip effortlessly into his own private world, to steadfastly drown out all commuter noise and intrusion as if he is entering his own cocoon.

The bus he gets on is packed. He scans the bottom deck for an empty seat, then goes upstairs. As he reaches the top, he glances round and spots a vacant aisle seat two from the back. He sits down and almost immediately finds himself drifting into warm reflections about his time with Catherine in Morocco. The passenger sitting next to him suddenly grasps the seat rail in front with both hands and begins to rock to and fro in his seat. This action is accompanied by a hypnotic hum, as if it is some kind of alcoholic's mantra; Jack smells the stale stench of beer coming from his mouth. The man is in his mid-fifties, with a mass of wild grey hair and a thick black beard with streaks of grey. He is stocky, thick set, big. He has a rugged, pock-marked and leathery complexion, which looks like it has suffered years of abuse and neglect as a result of heavy drinking and exposure to the winter elements. He wears an old threadbare tweed jacket, a check shirt and a grubby pair of trousers. There is a plastic bag full of books and newspaper cuttings between his legs.

Jack has encountered this man a few times before; he is difficult to miss. The last time was a few months ago, in Notting Hill not Shepherd's Bush: Jack was getting off the bus as he was getting on. He remembers this because the man almost knocked him over. Jack had to grab hold of his shoulder to stop himself falling. The man clasped his arm, he had big hands, wore an old gold wedding ring. Jack looked at him closely then, searchingly, but the man did not reciprocate his observation. He just hurried away, as if fleeing the scene of a crime, and Jack was left to wonder how he might have ended up this way, so broken and destitute. He recalled that he talked to Sam about him the night it happened, who typically ridiculed him for his fascination with desperate strangers. It is his 'little idiosyncrasy': this is how Sam referred to it. Now, seated next to the man, Jack begins to speculate again about his fate. He finds himself, rather uncomfortably, staring at the man in the frankly curious manner of a small child observing a strange spectacle – an exposure of the tragic side of life, someone condemned to a life of eccentric pursuits and painful neuroses – something he must fathom. The man does not seem conscious of his inquiry as he continues to rock and hum.

The bus goes over the roundabout onto Holland Park Avenue. The man takes his wrist, pulls up his jacket and shirt-sleeve to reveal a tattoo, and begins to scratch it. Jack tries to discern the symbol on his arm: he cannot make out what it is. The humming stops and the man begins to mumble to himself, quietly at first, then much louder. 'I loved her… I did. She made life beautiful… wonderful.' He has a deep, distinguished voice. 'She's gone. What's there without her?' Then he clasps the seat rail, cocks his head sideways, stares hard at Jack and continues, 'What indeed!'

The man breathes heavily. Jack does not know what to do. Should he meet his stare? he wonders. But the man might do something, lash out at him. Jack's inclination is just to get up, pretend he has not heard the man and go down to the lower deck. But how can he not have heard him? The whole upper deck must have done when he lost it a moment ago. The man's breathing then starts to calm. Jack turns his head slightly to look at him and sees the pained expression on his face soften as the deep lines from his nostrils to the corners of his mouth become less pronounced. He nods at Jack, then turns away.

Jack feels that he should say something to him but he does not know what. He tries to anticipate what he will do or say next. The man removes one of his brogues, brings his knee up to his chest and clenches his foot: large blisters sit on the tops of three individual toes. They look very sore; he dares not tamper with them through fear that they will cause him even more discomfort. He cautiously inserts his middle finger in a gap between two of his toes and rubs frenetically in a bid to calm and to satisfy his itchy feet. He repeats this exercise between all his toes. Jack does not want to intrude upon this private ceremony despite his natural aversion to public chiropody and the noxious smell of his feet. Nevertheless it ends as brusquely as it began. The man puts his sock back on his foot, pulls his knee right up to his chest, and then lowers it to the point where it rests parallel with his other leg. He puts his old shoe in his lap. He begins to mumble again, 'It's real… my suffering… everyone's suffering,' then shouts out loud, 'Look around you… it's everywhere!'

This statement is expressed with such conviction that it resounds throughout the entire upper deck: it contains an almost profound sense of despair, Jack thinks, the enigmatic look in the man's eye seeming to oscillate between a sadness for himself and a sadness for the whole world. All the passengers are silent. At this moment, the man represents the dark corner where everyone does not want to look. A mocking laugh comes from the front of the deck. However, it does not last long. The eerie silence drowns it out.

Jack knows he is not able to console the man in his distress. His moral inclination to try and empathise with him, at this moment, appears inappropriate, trite – even vacuous. Jack senses that he has nurtured his suffering, has firmly attached himself to it, to the extent that it now forms an integral part of his psyche which, in one way at least, seems to perversely justify the drunk and destitute life he now leads. Perhaps he has resolved never again to experience the loss of a loved one, Jack wonders. Did she die or leave him? No matter which scenario, it seems to Jack that he would rather be alone now for the rest of his life.

The bus groans to a halt at the top of Holland Park Avenue, just before Notting Hill Gate. The man grabs his battered brogue, gestures to Jack that he wants to get off the bus and staggers to his feet. He clumsily makes his way down the winding stairs; Jack hears his heavy footsteps. When he reaches the bottom, Jack hears a commotion. He looks out of the window to see the man sprawled on the pavement; he drags himself to his feet as bewildered passengers look on, not sure whether to pity or ignore him. He seems to be oblivious to their empty stares. He looks up at Jack through the window. Jack stares at him, looking for something compassionate and meaningful to communicate to him but only finding a small smile. The man walks off.

When Jack gets to the office, he finds it very difficult to concentrate during his first meeting. He cannot get the man out of his head. He is desperate to know what exactly happened to him and wonders whether it is possible to love someone too much. His thoughts rapidly become obsessive.

Jack leaves the office at midday: he has to get out, go somewhere that will help him clear his head. He fobs off Sarah, telling her that he has a bout of flu coming on and needs to get home to bed. He decides to head for the East End: he has not been for some time. Jack often used to make Sunday excursions there; it had become the perfect weekend activity for a lonely bachelor. He started off by going to Columbia Flower Market, then headed over to Victoria Park in Bethnal Green – where he found a quiet bench and read for a few hours – and finally, made his way for Sunday roast at the Blind Beggar on the corner of Cambridge Heath Road and Mile End Road or traditional Pakistani cuisine in a canteen on Brick Lane. He looks at his watch now: it is midday. He will eat early.

As he walks down Brick Lane, Jack encounters hordes of Muslims streaming out of the mosque. The worshippers mingle in the middle of the street, seeming oblivious to the traffic after prayer, their faith taking precedence over the Highway Code. He watches them for a while, picking out individual men in the crowd and studying their bearded faces, trying to ascertain which of them are in love and which of them have lost love. He finds himself looking at every one of them as the potential victim of loss. However, these men, if one or more of them has indeed lost someone, can call on the love of *Allah* if not the love of a woman, Jack thinks. This is something that the man on the bus does not seem to have recourse to. And he neither.

In the canteen, Jack places his order – chicken curry and *chapati* – then heads for the toilet. He walks down a pokey corridor with peeling plaster walls towards a staircase. He looks at the man in front of him. First, he focuses on the baggy cotton folds of his *shalwar*, which are frayed at the bottoms and make him look like a dwarf circus clown: they part-conceal his skinny-looking legs. Second, he admires his immaculately pressed white *kurta* that gives him an air of spiritual authority. As the man continues upstairs to find a quiet place to pray, Jack stops at a storage door on a latch; the sign on it reads 'Men's Cloakroom' in decorative gold lettering, as if announcing an opulent lavatorial space. He climbs inside what immediately feels like a claustrophobic chasm and looks down at an old toilet pan that can barely fit inside the oversized cupboard. He becomes breathless as he struggles to unzip his trousers and the man on the bus comes to his mind again the more frustrated he gets. He urinates as fast as he can, while staring at a clump of mould encasing the toilet cistern, then escapes the constrictive space.

Jack returns to the canteen area and takes a seat at the back: the walls are covered with kitsch, cartoon-like posters of Asian champion wrestlers, curiously juxtaposed by delicate water-colour prints depicting rural England. Hungry men sit round him, munching on their food and sniffing hard between mouthfuls: the curry is hot and spicy. He still finds it hard not to contemplate the man's fate. He pours himself a glass of water from a stainless steel jug, wetting his mouth before he begins to eat. But eating is a strain as well: he just does not feel very hungry. He pulls out his notebook and begins to write, trying to recall in meticulous detail his encounter on the bus this morning.

He begins to speculate about the details of the man's loss: a wife, a daughter, a lover, a friend … Jack does not know. He wears a wedding ring. Then he must have lost either his wife or daughter, Jack reasons. It is the former, he thinks, there was passion in his voice. When did she die, what was she like? Jack sits there all afternoon and late into the evening writing frantically. This man has inspired something in him. He feels the urge to write again.

# 4

**SHE AND JACK** walk down a narrow open-plan floor, old wooden tables and chairs packed together to accommodate as many diners as possible. Catherine recognises Sam sitting at a table by some stairs. She remembers him, though not very well, from the party he held: that night, almost as soon as they shook hands, he was dragged away to be introduced to someone else. But now, Sam appears to be in no hurry at all as he slowly gets to his feet and raises his hand to greet her. And as she and Jack approach his table, Bill (whom Catherine met over a quick drink about a week after she and Jack got back from Morocco) stands up as well. It strikes her how different the two of them look. Bill is Sam's physical opposite, short and wiry. Sam kisses her on the cheek, and Bill follows suit.

The women at the table, Nathalie and Jude, are rather less welcoming. Catherine leans over and shakes hands with both of them. The appearance of Nathalie surprises her. She reveals herself to be tall and stocky when she stands up. She wears a black leather skirt and a skin-tight red vest, which accentuates her large biceps. Nathalie looks like she would utterly dominate Bill in bed. This is probably why she is with him, Catherine thinks, and he with her. Jude is waif-like and gracious-looking, wears an elegant blue dress, and manages a smile. She has the 'pure' looks of Genevieve – this is how Catherine refers to them – so beautiful she has always thought: a pale complexion, an elegant narrow face, small freckles on her nose and cheeks, long skinny legs. Catherine does not judge herself to be beautiful, God no. She has the kind of looks that men go wild about, but only because they want to get her into bed, fuck her. Genevieve, conversely, is jealous of Catherine for this, for which Catherine has never understood why. Men are always more affectionate with Catherine than women are. She believes that this is because they can usually sense what she is about, a woman who likes to fuck, and respond accordingly: men are rather predictable in this respect.

Catherine glances up at the ceiling as she sits down; ivy hangs from the bare brick walls, which creeps down from a large skylight in the middle of the room. She feels that the restaurant – an Italian – has the illusion of an old Tuscan courtyard, save the view of a grey British high street when she looks to her right. So here she is … lunch with Jack's friends, the concession she made him after so adamantly refusing to meet his parents. And she knows precisely how excited he is about this lunch. He told Catherine he is sure they will all love her. Well, it seems he is wrong about this already if Nathalie and Jude's first impressions are anything to go by. Oh, but she could not refuse him: Jack makes her feel so special, as if she is the only woman in the world. In fact, he often seems to only notice her; there might be other beautiful women around, but he does not even look at them. Also, he said he wants his friends to appreciate just how amazing she is. This made her laugh. Will they immediately understand why Jack feels the way he does, and like him, will they sit there in adoration? Of course not! His friends will experience her from a different perspective. They might all end up liking her by the end of the meal, but their feelings will most likely not extend beyond a certain level of warmth and affection. They will not feel what Jack does, will not be able to gauge the depth of his feelings. To this extent, all lovers are isolated, Catherine thinks.

A frenetic and vociferous waiter takes their order. He flirts with Catherine as he reads out the chef's specials in his most romantic and flowery Italian, much to the annoyance of Nathalie. Another waiter darts between the surrounding tables, shouting orders across the floor towards the kitchen. The conversation quickly splits between the men at the table and the women. While Sam discusses with Bill and Jack his ideas for setting up in business on his own, Nathalie and Jude discuss a feature in the latest edition of *Cosmopolitan* magazine, which asks a group of ambitious young women whether they value their careers more than their love lives. Catherine holds a particular dislike for this kind of magazine journalism, regards it as utterly inane and vacuous. But she will not express this opinion, does not want to cause a scene. She will just be quiet.

'Sam sometimes accuses me of putting my work before him. He says I can sometimes be obsessive about it, too ambitious,' Jude says rather earnestly. 'But I don't mean to be.'

'He would say that,' Nathalie responds aggressively. 'He should try working for a big law firm and see how he handles it. As a woman, you have to be dedicated if you want to get ahead. We've no choice!'

'Yes, maybe you're right,' Jude says, not entirely sure whether she should agree with her friend's strident gender position. 'Jack works very hard, doesn't he?' she continues, turning to Catherine now, trying to involve her in the conversation.

'Well yes...' she goes to speak as Jack looks over at her.

But Nathalie interrupts her and continues to direct the conversation at Jude, 'And anyway, you're earning almost double what he earns now,' she presses on. 'And they'll make you a partner next year. Sam should hardly be complaining. You're the main breadwinner now!'

'Yes,' Jude replies quietly, trying to pacify Nathalie, and again turning to Catherine. 'You were saying...'

'Yes... well, I think Jack does work quite hard,' Catherine goes on rather reluctantly, 'but it's difficult to gauge because of what he does... work and personal life merge, are often one and the same thing. It's like what I do...'

'Yes, Bill told me,' Nathalie says dismissively, finally acknowledging Catherine's presence at the table, 'but what d'you think about what I said before?'

'Which bit are you referring to?' Catherine asks quietly, trying to maintain her composure.

'Weren't you listening to what we were talking about?' Nathalie fires back.

'Nathalie?' Jude interrupts, appealing to her to be less confrontational.

'Yes I was,' Catherine says slowly, struggling to remain calm as she glances at Jack and catches his eye, 'but you said quite a few things and I was just trying to establish which of them you were asking me about?'

'That women have to prioritise work more than men do if they want to be successful,' Nathalie says impatiently.

'I don't think you can generalise.'

'Why not?' Nathalie continues, now sounding utterly unwilling to compromise on this let alone anything.

'I think it depends upon the individual career. The film and television industry has not discriminated against me. Far from it, I sometimes think my sexuality has helped me get a job.'

'I bet it has!' Nathalie quips.

And the table is suddenly silent. Catherine glares at Nathalie, and neither Jack nor Bill is sure what to do. Jude and Sam look uncomfortably at one another. All of a sudden, Catherine bends double over the table and thrusts her arms forward; a glass smashes on the floor. She groans in pain, then clutches her stomach. A bearded and bespectacled man sitting on the next table jumps up out of his chair and dashes over to her side with the apparent authority of a doctor. He looks demandingly at Jack and asks, 'Is she alright?'

Jack leans beside her and holds her hand. 'Catherine? Catherine?' he says, his voice full of worry.

'It hurts,' she mumbles.

'What is it?' Bill says to Jack.

'I don't know,' he replies. 'What d'you want me to do?' he asks her.

'Let me go to the toilet,' she mutters.

'Where is it?' Bill inquires.

'It's right here, just down these stairs,' Nathalie says, pointing to her right.

Catherine gets up and, clutching her stomach, shuffles down the stairs.

'Go with her, Jack!' Jude instructs him, as the bearded man on the neighbouring table returns redundantly to his seat.

'Is she going to be okay?' Sam frets as Jack stands up and follows Catherine.

No one at the table answers him.

When Catherine is confident that she is out of public view from all the diners in the restaurant, she stands upright, holds her head high and turns round to look at Jack. She shoots him a mischievous smile, which conveys a real satisfaction with her naughty self, her little game of make-believe. Even though Jack is partly furious with her, Catherine can see this on his face – to feign ill health is not a laughing matter, she knows this, particularly when it is clear to her just how concerned he was, and everyone else still is, for her welfare – she knows that he will also forgive her. For this act of hers cuts through all the crap: the crap of Nathalie's antagonism and the crap of meeting a new lover's friends, where she is deliberately on display – as the new girl – and consequently, is required to be on her best behaviour. Catherine wonders whether Jack might have suspected before that she would be driven to challenge such a staged encounter if she were provoked. For when she smiled at him just now and exposed her charade – and his own for dragging her there – he seemed to almost instantly pardon her. And she knows what power her smile holds over him. It makes him weak with desire.

Jack winks back at her now as Catherine strides confidently into the men's toilets. He pauses for a moment in the corridor, then walks inside. There is a man in a suit and tie, standing by the basin, looking with devilish intrigue at his reflection in the mirror as he zips up his trousers. The man gestures toward the end cubicle. Catherine's head peers out from behind the door. Jack walks towards her. She turns round and waits for him. Naked, she bends over the toilet pan, hands on the cistern, her salmon-pink dress lying crumpled on the floor beneath her feet. 'Fuck me, Jack… fill me up!' she says to him as he steps inside the cubicle.

He penetrates her slowly, kisses her, his lips are cold and fresh. They know that the man standing by the mirror will not leave … his sexual curiosity will not permit it: he simply has to stay to hear the show. She and Jack start to breathe harder, louder, and as both of them near the point of climax, they become oblivious to their public environment, the man outside and all the people dining upstairs. Finally, they scream as they come together. Jack collapses on the floor … Catherine sits on the toilet, spread-eagled, grinning to herself. Then they hear the man's feet shuffle across the tiled floor as he tries to make his exit as discreet as possible. Laughter immediately rises in both of them, which rapidly bursts into a fit of hysterical giggles.

Jack leaves the cubicle first, and tidies himself in the mirror before heading back up to the restaurant floor. Catherine waits. She will follow him shortly. She wets her face with cold water, sweeps her hair back, studies her reflection. Only then does she make her way upstairs. As she nears the top, she hears Jude ask anxiously, 'Are you sure?' and Jack reply, 'Yes, she's fine,' and Bill press him further, 'But she seemed to be in a lot of pain?' and Jack reassure them with the words, 'Really she's alright… really.' Catherine stops, hesitates to go any further just yet. She is still out of view of all the diners in the restaurant. She should not have done what she just did, she tells herself now, it was damn selfish and irresponsible. She must not let her sexual desires dominate her in this manner. She simply cannot yield to them so easily. Her madness has taught her self-criticism, and a violent one at that. She listens as they continue to question Jack about her. 'What was it?' Sam asks. 'Stomach cramps. She gets them from time to time,' Jack replies. And then there is silence. Catherine wonders whether she should just hurry up the remainder of the stairs and confess to them all, be done with it. No, she cannot. Just as she goes to complete her journey, she hears Jude say to Jack, 'You know, you two look great together, you really do. You seem… well, so in love…' and Sam confirm this sentiment with the words, 'Yes you do, you both look smitten with one another.' Catherine is compelled to wait where she is and listen, just listen. Then it is Bill's turn to speak as he says, 'She looks Southern European, Spanish maybe. Where's she from again?' and Jack answer, 'Her mother's Irish Catholic… and…' now she hears him struggle to fully answer Bill's question as his friend pushes him further with, 'And her father?' But all Jack can do, because she has told him so little, is mutter impatiently, 'I was just getting to that. Well… her surname is Ramirez.' Bill immediately follows this revelation with, 'I was right, Spanish. I knew she had some Hispanic blood in her.' Then it is Jude's turn to speak again as she says, 'She's very beautiful…' Nathalie has not said a word, Catherine realises, as Jack responds with, 'That's what my father told me. He saw a photograph of Catherine for the first time last week and couldn't keep his eyes off her.' 'Theo and Ruth haven't met her yet?' Jude inquires now. 'No, I don't think she's ready to meet the parents,' Jack replies. Catherine knows she should not be doing this: their conversation is not intended for her scrutiny, certainly not in this manner anyhow. But she feels compelled to hear a bit more. Nathalie finally speaks. 'Well it's been a few months now. I don't see why not,' she says. And Jack is quick to defend her with the words, 'I think she wants to take things one day at a time, you know.' But Nathalie has posed the question in Jack's mind again now, and he confesses, 'But I'd really like them to meet her… yes.' Catherine knows he really wants this. 'What d'you know about her parents?' Jude then asks. 'She doesn't really speak about them. She's told me very little, apart from the fact that they're not together anymore.' There is uncertainty round the table now; Catherine has become obscure, questionable, which Bill captures with the closing remark, 'Sensitive subject, I suppose.' Enough, Catherine finally tells herself, as she hurries up the final few stairs into view.

Jude is the first to see her as she says, 'Catherine, are you okay? You look rather pale, your eyes are bloodshot.'

'No, I'm feeling a lot better now, thank you,' Catherine replies as Jack takes her hand, kisses her cheek, then puts his arm round her waist and holds her tight, clinging to Catherine as if he has just been reunited with her after a long time apart.

# 5

**JACK OPENS** his eyes to see Catherine leaning over him and gently shaking his shoulder. 'Are you okay?' he mumbles through his sleepy mouth.

'Yeah, just can't sleep,' she replies. He notices that she always has difficulty sleeping when she has drunk a lot. She continues, 'I've been trying all night.'

'What time is it?' he asks.

'Early. Listen… I've got a bit of a crazy idea. Let's go to the park and see the deer.'

Jack rolls onto his back and looks at his watch. 'What… now?'

'Yes.'

'Catherine… it's five o'clock in the morning. It's a Sunday. And anyway, it's not going to be open.'

'But it will be in two hours or so. They open the gates at sunrise.'

'You sure you're okay?'

'Yeah I'm fine. Why shouldn't I be?'

'Because you want to go to the park in the middle of the night.'

'Look, I just can't sleep, that's all… and it's not the middle of the night any more, it's early morning.'

'In my book, it's still night.'

'Morning begins at five.'

'Who says?'

'Me'

'Okay.'

'It's amazing this time of the morning, really,' Catherine enthuses. 'It's so beautiful you could be anywhere.'

He is silent: still half-asleep, his mind works slowly to formulate a decision. 'Okay then, let's go,' he says finally.

It is a cold autumnal morning. They walk through the early morning mist. Jack feels the space around him as he and Catherine admire the shape of the land and listen to the deer groan as they wake from their deep slumber; during these early morning hours, they sound like Jurassic, prehistoric beasts. Like Catherine, he loves to feel lost in big open spaces.

When they finish walking, they find a secluded spot in a small patch of dense woodland and make love. It is 'love' for Jack even though he knows it is not for Catherine. She still views it as just sex. He wonders when it will be for her as it is for him. He hopes soon. Leaves rustle beneath them as they roll around on the muddy ground, entwined in one another's arms. Neither of them cares about the state their clothes will be in once they are finished.

'I'm coming…' Catherine screams as a crow caws violently, operatically.

She rolls off him onto her back, as her orgasm wanes, and lies there staring up at the sky. 'Look how blue it is, Jack. It's amazing. When it looks like that – it almost makes me want to cry.

Sometimes I wish I could fly… just lose myself in it.'

'I know what you mean,' he replies as he watches her twirl strands of her hair around her middle finger. He loves it when Catherine does this, just as he loves the way she frowns and screws up her face – as if she is a contortionist – when confronted with a problem. She remains everything in a woman and a lover that he has ever wanted. He sees in her so many of the qualities that he does not possess. And he realises that though he has not been able to find love in his own self-image, he has found it in his image of Catherine. And it is wonderful.

They both lie there, silent, listening to one another's breath.

'Thanks for coming with me,' she says.

'I've been meaning to ask you. It's my mother's sixtieth pretty soon… and I'd like you to come.'

'When is it?'

'Seventh November. It's a Thursday, I think.'

'I might be busy with work.'

'That's why I'm telling you so soon,' Jack says. He knows she is extremely committed to her work.

'It's only a month away.'

'That's an eternity for you!'

'But if I have a job on, then I must work.'

Jack sits up, frustrated, unwilling to allow Catherine to find an excuse. This is sufficient notice for her, he is sure. He is not being unreasonable. He is familiar enough with her working life by now, after three months. She is busy for weeks, then does nothing, short, sharp bursts of intense work, which always seem to be followed by winding down periods, in which she is given the time and space to gather herself in between productions. Jack presses her. 'Okay, but assuming you haven't, then you can make it?' Catherine is silent as he looks down at her expectantly. He continues, this time irately,

'It's just dinner for heaven's sake. I'm not asking you to bloody marry me!'

'I need some time to think about it,' Catherine says as she rises to meet his stare.

'What are you talking about? It's only a dinner.'

'Jack, it's not only a dinner,' she insists, now getting to her feet.

'I don't know why you're making such a big deal about this?'

'You're the one who wants to make a big deal.'

'What are you talking about?'

'Out of us, Jack… you're trying to make a big deal out of us!' she shouts. 'Look, I don't want this…' she goes on, then turns away so she does not have to look at him.

'Don't want what?' he asks her rather desperately, also getting to his feet.

'This… what this is becoming. You and I. You know what I want!' she states determinedly. Catherine turns to face him and continues, 'I've told you. It's the way we've been up until now. Both of us free to do what the hell we want… for there to be no bloody obligation, attachment, need…'

'But can we really carry on like this?'

'I don't see why not. We meet, we laugh, we talk, we fuck… we enjoy one another when we see each other, from day to day, that's it.'

'But what about me… what I want?' Jack demands. 'I don't know if you're just selfish, scared… or a bit crazy.' And with this final word, Catherine raises a smile. 'Okay, I know you're crazy,' he says, smiling back at her, 'but seriously, I feel as though you're keeping so much from me… and that this hidden part of you wants more than what we have at the moment.'

'Jack, if this part of me does want more, then I'll tell you. But at the moment, it doesn't.'

'It's strange… I know I should stop seeing you right now, I can see the warning signs, but I don't care. I just can't imagine life without you.'

'Enough Jack… enough. Let's not talk about it anymore,' she says as she walks out of the woodland, back into the large expanse of open land, to admire the panorama once more. And Jack stays where he is, overshadowed by trees, and watches her as she holds her head high and, arms wrapped round her chest, shivers slightly in the morning cold.

# 6

**JACK AND SAM** leave the office together. They decide to stop off for a drink on the way to the station. Jack is due to meet Catherine but has some time to kill, and he is eager for Sam to hear all about what he has started writing. Jack has been on at him about it for a number of weeks now, but Sam has been too busy with work to talk: he is preparing to leave his post at *Detritus* and set up his own small publishing house.

They go to their local, sit down at the bar. Jack proceeds, first of all, to tell Sam about his encounter with the man on the bus. But Sam interrupts him almost immediately, telling him that he has heard this story already and asking what on earth this has to do with what he is writing. Yes, Jack concedes, he did tell Sam about the time before, when the man almost knocked him over, but something else happened this time, he now stresses, which has given him the impetus to write. Catherine was intrigued, and he should be as well, Jack stresses to him. Sam seizes this opportunity to question him again about his 'little idiosyncrasy', asking Jack whether he has now gone so far as to invite this desperate stranger into his home. But Jack promptly tells him to shut up, then gets on with the business of telling Sam what happened that morning on the bus.

'So is it about him then?' Sam asks Jack when he has finished.

'Well no… not him specifically…' Jack replies uncertainly.

'Why d'you tell me about him then?'

'Well… it relates to him.' Now that he has finally told the story to Sam, he suddenly feels unsure about what he is writing.

'What does?'

'I'm…'

'Yes?' Sam inquires, becoming impatient with Jack.

But he says nothing, feels rather embarrassed, then eventually blurts out, 'Love, Sam,' speaking this word and voicing his friend's name as if making a terrible confession.

'What?' Sam asks with bemusement, and Jack is silent. 'Love?' he inquires.

'Yes,' Jack says, hoping that his friend will provide him with clarity of idea and purpose once more. All the reading and noting he has done so far, and it now seems all in vain.

'And?'

'That's what I've started writing about.'

'My God, she's really got to you, hasn't she!' Sam says derisively. 'Or he has?'

'Very funny.'

'So what about it?'

'Well… how it affects us,' Jack answers unconvincingly.

'Hardly groundbreaking stuff!' Sam rebuffs as Jack is quickly made to realise he has no real thesis, structure or format in mind. He has merely got over-excited, because of what he has been going through with Catherine, because he got back the urge to write, yes. What was he thinking? he asks himself angrily.

'But look at how this man was affected by it!' Jack says, looking to counter his own frustration and Sam's scepticism. He saw something in him, he knows he did, but he cannot articulate it, not now anyhow.

'Okay,' Sam acknowledges him coolly, as if suddenly trying to pacify him. 'But what are you going to say?'

'I was thinking about a collection of essays?'

'*Love* according to Jack Stoltz. So you plan to be the next Roland Barthes?' Sam says sarcastically, continuing to challenge his friend, which forces Jack to accept that, at the moment, it will not be this – a book of his own ideas – but rather just the recycled opinions of others. Sam goes on, 'Bloody hell, you're getting in deep there. Be careful, they might just tear you to shreds.'

'The critics, yes. And I of all people should know that shouldn't I.' Jack has not even stopped to think of them, rather ironically. Yes, they would be the first to consign his project to the scrap heap. He has been hard on other works of a similar nature, by critics who want to write the big book but end up producing something full of 'abstract propositions' and 'self-indulgences'.

'It'd be your come-uppance.'

'Thanks!' Jack replies dryly.

'What you're proposing is an enormous undertaking, and you should know that more than anyone else,' Sam insists. He is right about this, Jack thinks. He continues, 'Zygmunt Bauman didn't get there until his late seventies, and look at the size of his intellect.'

'Carol Gilligan got there sooner.'

'Yes but look at the size of hers!' Sam quips.

'Okay, so you're not a Gilligan fan,' Jack responds. 'Look, my desire to write something now is more about what I'm going through at the moment,' he says rather earnestly to Sam, 'about how I'm feeling.' At least he has got this from their conversation, Jack thinks, this bit of self-awareness, if nothing else.

'You mean you're getting laid more than any of us.'

'Yeah that,' Jack concedes, smiling to himself, 'but also because I'm…'

'In love,' Sam says bluntly. 'Yes, I've gathered Jack, as we all have.'

'Alright smart-arse, and there's no need to make it sound like a bloody affliction!'

'I'm really happy for you, you know that. We all are. I just don't want you to waste your time with something if you don't know where you're bloody going with it. I mean… you still haven't answered my question. Have you got anything new and interesting to say?'

'I told you, I need to get into it first. There's a hell of a lot of work to do, you said that yourself.'

'But you must have some ideas already?'

Jack sighs, shakes his head. 'I've got to say, I was expecting a little more support from you.' But he knows that, were he in Sam's shoes now, he would be just as tough as Sam is being.

'Know what you want to write, Jack. There's been a hell of a lot of books on love. I don't need to tell you that. I just don't want you to run before you can walk. You've got a lot of ability and you'd have no trouble applying yourself to the task, but think it through first. Don't just dive in because that's how you feel at the moment, because you're suddenly all loved up. You might just waste a few years if you do it this way, on a whim.'

'Why the hell not though!' Jack insists, now sounding rather petulant. 'You know, Sam, this is when I hate the ordered, structured world of literature and academia… when I hate how a piece of work is, and must be, judged. The excessive importance attached to critical method, the tiresome consideration of conflicting ideas, the fucking pedantic adherence to academic language. Sometimes all of it infuriates me, even though I make a bloody living out of it. Why can't I just write something because I want to, because I feel like it? Does what I write need to be published, and would it necessarily make it any better if it was? And why should I give a toss about how my work is judged anyway!'

'You sound like a fucking adolescent, Jack. Come on, be serious! You're an editor, a critic, an intellectual. Of course you bloody care about these things... about the quality of your work, and how people will judge it. You don't just write for yourself, you write to be read! Why do it otherwise, unless you just want to get off on yourself that is!'

'No, but need I, should I really care about how people respond to it?' Jack asks, though he already holds the answer to this question. He would care deeply, of course he would. He always has, always will. But he goes on, 'I mean... it's a serious question Sam. Should my principal motivation be to get published... or just be to write, because I want to, need to? That's what I'm saying. That's the point!' he demands. Sam does not respond. Jack continues, 'Okay, look... I don't know where I'm going with it yet, and I might sound pretty foolish and naïve, granted, not least because I plan to dedicate all this bloody time and work to it, but it's just something I want to do at the moment, that I feel passionate about.'

'And this is?'

'I've told you, Sam!' Jack snaps back, losing his temper. 'It's love. I mean... what the fuck is it, this thing... huh?' he shouts. 'I mean... it eluded me for long enough, didn't it!'

Sam sits back in his chair and both men are silent. Then Jack shakes his head from side to side as it dawns on him how he probably just sounded, too damn self-interested and heartfelt as always. Thank God Sam knows him well enough by now, Jack thinks. 'Look, the last thing I want to do is rubbish it,' Sam says. 'Christ, you can write about whatever you want. American capitalism, Theravada Buddhism, anything...'

'Well, thanks for your blessing!'

'Alright Jack, now it's you who's taking the piss.'

'Sorry.'

'Okay, so who've you read so far?' Sam asks, now striving to sound a little more supportive and enthusiastic.

'I've still got a lot to get through. I started with Plato and Aristotle, I'm still on them, then I'm going to tackle Freud and Jung. There's a lot there… I…' Jack says, sounding somewhat overwhelmed by the task he has set himself.

'From philosophy to psychology. You know, now that you're in love, I'm expecting an idyllic thesis.'

'I'd like that. You know, I want to produce something hopeful.'

'Listen, be careful you don't tread old ground. There's been so much already on the ones you've just mentioned.'

'I'm hoping that all their wisdom and insight will rub off on me,' Jack says with a smile.

'And what about taking in some Eastern thought? That's very popular at the moment. There's Confucius, Lao-tzu, Wu Ti… quite a few others as well. It'll give any publisher an angle, something different to work with.'

'You mean you'd like something different to work with, if you ever deemed it worthy of publication that is?'

'Well yes, naturally… assuming I can get it off the ground.'

'I'd thought about this you know, but it'll mean a lot more work.'

'Look, aside from what happens with my venture, I'd give it some thought. Unfortunately, publishers must think in terms of product, and you must make it easy for them to sell this product. Sadly, my dear fellow, you're not going to get it published any other way. And you've got to make a proper living some way!'

'Maybe you're right?'

'Look, it doesn't have to be what I said… Just make it bold. You need something that will distinguish your book. Don't play safe. Find a new source of inspiration. It could be from lesser known writers or thinkers.'

'Yes,' Jack says. 'You know, ever since I met Catherine, I've started to believe in…'

Sam interrupts him, 'My God, you're starting to sound like a bloody evangelist now.'

'Sorry, I'm sure I must sound like a right prat. I don't mean to bore you, it's just that… I don't think it's only the stuff of great fiction, you know. It's real… it's…' he searches for the appropriate adjective but cannot find it, then continues, 'I'm amazed by what I've felt these past few months. Me, of all people… the old cynic, the one who'd almost given up on it all. You know… it's funny that Catherine, for all her resistance to it, her reluctance to believe in it… has made me full of it.'

'Yep, couldn't agree more!' Sam quips.

'God, I walked into that one,' Jack admits. 'No, but really, I'm determined to come up with something optimistic. I've got to… I feel as though I owe it to Catherine. Maybe this is what it'll take to get her to believe in it?'

'What d'you mean?' Sam inquires, sitting back in his chair and looking pensively at his friend.

'Well… I've told you about this already, you know…' Jack says rather uncomfortably.

'Not really,' Sam replies, to which Jack does not respond. 'Her wariness to fall in love, you mean?' he goes on, asking this question forcefully.

'Yes.'

Sam is silent, then speaks quickly, as if unable to contain himself. 'Jack, how much d'you really know about Catherine?'

'You've asked me this before,' Jack replies.

'Yes, well… the relationship seems one-sided at the moment. You're mad about her, give her everything and yet she's…'

'She's what, Sam?' Jack interrupts him. 'I mean… where's this come from? You've been down on her from the start.'

'Jack, I haven't… it's just that…'

'What?'

'Look, I just want you to be happy, that's all. Forget it, okay. I don't want to ruin our friendship over this.'

'I better get out of here,' Jack says, standing up to leave.

'I didn't want to upset you,' Sam appeals to him, 'it's just that I felt I should say something.'

'You're entitled to say what you think,' Jack replies. 'Look, I'm not leaving in a strop. We'll talk about it some other time. I've just got to go, right now, otherwise I'll be late.'

'You go then.' And with these final words from Sam, Jack darts out of the pub.

Jack heads into the underground, and takes the train to Victoria. He is due to meet Catherine in a pub opposite Westminster Theatre. He has been given two complimentary tickets for a new play, which he is sure Catherine will love. As he walks out of the station, he notices it is an uncharacteristically warm evening for October. The sky is clear; stars are visible, glowing bright in a dark blue sky.

As he nears his destination, his phone rings and he answers it. 'Hi, it's me,' Catherine says. 'Look, I'm not going to be able to make it. I'm really sorry but I just can't get away.'

'It doesn't start for another forty minutes. We don't have to have that drink first. Just meet me inside the theatre, at the box office.'

'Jack, I'm going to be here late. We had a bad day today and didn't get nearly enough done.'

'Oh but you can't miss…'

She interrupts, 'I'm going to have to stay on to catch up. I've got no choice.'

'Right… okay,' he says frustratedly. 'Look, just call me in the morning. I miss you, and…'

'Yes, I'll call you then. Got to go, bye,' she says brusquely and hangs up the phone.

He is not sure what to do now. Jack is not that bothered about seeing the play, it was more for Catherine's benefit, and so wanders aimlessly down Victoria Street, soon coming to Westminster Cathedral. He thinks about what Sam just said to him and wonders whether he should indeed be more careful. He is doing all the running, he knows this.

Jack walks into the square and looks up at the cathedral, its imposing red brick structure and enormous tower illuminated by exterior lighting. The massive building looms down on Victoria's residents, casting its powerful God-fearing glare over the Westminster skyline. He fumbles in his pocket for the cigarette Sam gave him. He always likes to smoke when he has had a drink or two. But he does not have a light. It is only half past seven and yet the streets are quiet. Jack spies two men lying in the porch of an office block and notices that one of them is smoking. He approaches them, and as he gets closer, sees that they are both drinking from bottles wrapped in plastic bags. They are young, no more than twenty or twenty-one, and lie in grubby sleeping bags, their backs propped up against a graffiti-scrawled brick wall, their heads nestled into dirty, threadbare blankets. The smaller of the two rangy men is smoking. 'Can I borrow a light please?' Jack asks as he kneels down on one knee right in front of him.

The larger of the two looks at Jack threateningly with his baby-face and bulbous red nose. Then the smaller one pulls out a silver Zippo, grabs Jack's jumper and pulls him close to his scabby, bruised face. *'If u 'ad sum gear or anutha' bifter for me mate 'ere, den we migh' give yer a spark,'* he threatens.

Jack instinctively grabs the young man's hand in self-defence and forces him to release his grip on his jumper; he squeezes his hand as hard as he can, the young man flinches in pain, then lashes out with his head. *'Yer cunt, yer fookin' cunt. I'm gonna fookin' drop yer,'* the young man screams, butting Jack hard on the top of the nose.

Jack loses his balance, staggers backwards and falls flat on his back. Before he can get up, both men lunge at him on the floor, punching and scuffing like two rabid dogs.

*'Get 'is fookin' moolah,'* the larger of the two shouts as he grabs Jack's head and forces it against the pavement.

Then his accomplice produces a knife and holds it to Jack's neck. *'I'm gonna fookin' slice yer, cunt, make yer bleed!'* he says as he grabs Jack by the belt and searches for his wallet in his back pocket.

'Leave him alone!' a deep, commanding voice shouts from behind them.

The smaller of the two men turns round, then immediately pulls the knife away. *'I wanted to fookin' kill yer!'* he says to Jack as he scrambles to his feet.

Jack looks up to see the figure of a man hurrying towards them. He is big but Jack cannot make out his face. The two young men freeze on the spot, unsure what to do. The man shouts again, 'Take your stuff and go. D'you hear me? Now!'

The two young men scurry over to their sleeping bags and blankets, huddle them up into their arms along with their bottles and their other few belongings, and rush away as fast as they can. Jack can see the man now and realises it is him, the man on the bus. He stands over him and asks, 'You alright?'

'Yes,' Jack says breathlessly as he sits up, wincing in pain as he does so. His body shakes a bit, the adrenalin yet to subside.

The man does not recognise him. He was so out of it the last time he probably does not remember a thing, Jack thinks. But he does not seem drunk now. Far from it, he appears aware, alert, in control. He kneels down in front of Jack, pulls a pair of half-moon spectacles out of his top pocket, puts them on and starts to inspect Jack's face. There is a little swelling beneath his eyes, his nose is bloody, and there is a small cut on his neck where the knife was held. Then he prods his ribs, Jack flinches. 'They're just bruised, I think,' he says. 'It looks like you'll live.'

'Thank you…' Jack says to him, body still shaking and voice juddering. 'I think you came along just in time.' And the man simply nods. Jack continues, 'I don't know what they would have done?'

'They would've given you a good beating, that's for sure,' he says matter-of-factly, 'and that one might have cut you, but they wouldn't have gone any further than that.'

'Right…' Jack says uncertainly, as he re-plays the young man's parting remark to him, *'I wanted to fookin' kill yer!'*

'I'm sure they wouldn't have done,' the man says again.

Jack looks closely at the man for the first time and is struck by not only his mental clarity this time round but the surety and conviction in his voice. 'Well thank you… I…' he goes on, trying to collect himself.

'Look, it's okay,' the man assures Jack, then turns to walk away.

'No but…'

'I heard you the first time,' the man says firmly.

Jack is perplexed by the man's response. What just happened to Jack, and the man's subsequent intervention, seems almost nothing to him. Jack watches him walk slowly back across the square. He wonders what he is doing over here: he has only ever seen him in West London. Jack sees him settle down on the floor, pull what appears to be a blanket over his legs, then take up something in his hand, a book Jack thinks. Jack gets to his feet. Standing is rather painful. He is not sure what to do. He would like to get himself home and yet he feels that he must at least offer the man something, just to show his appreciation, in spite of his initial reluctance to accept Jack's gratitude. And he is curious once more. Jack feels around in his pocket for his wallet. Still there, thank God. He only has ten pounds but decides he should give him this. He can always go to a cash-point straight after.

Jack approaches him with the money in hand. There, in the dark shadows of the small porch-way of the cathedral's bookshop, he sees the man sitting up reading, with a thick green woollen blanket pulled over his legs, and beside him, a plastic bag full of books and newspaper cuttings, like before. 'I just wanted to give you this,' Jack says, handing him the ten-pound note.

The man looks up, and over his spectacles, and replies bluntly, 'I don't want your money.'

'I'm sorry, I didn't mean to offend you. I just wanted to show my thanks for what you just did for me.'

'I'm okay,' he says flatly.

'I'm sorry, I assumed that living like this, you could do with a helping hand.'

'Living like what?'

'Well... I thought you had very little money... I thought you were...' Jack says, now grasping for the appropriate words.

'No, I'm not homeless anymore. I have a roof over my head as and when I want it.'

'Right...' Jack says puzzled. 'So you live here in Victoria then?'

'No.'

'Where do you live, then?'

'Enough... I'm busy reading,' he blurts out irately. 'D'you mind!'

'I don't mean to trouble you, sorry,' Jack mutters. 'Look, I'll go.' He should not probe any further, he tells himself. It is not right. The man is clearly uncomfortable talking to him. As Jack turns to walk away, he looks up at the cathedral. The man has chosen the perfect vantage point to admire the building from; it looks tall, proud, majestic.

'I'm sorry, I didn't mean to snap at you like that,' the man says, calling to Jack, his voice softer now. 'I get a lot of people who want to talk to me but I don't want to talk to them.'

'Right...' Jack says, turning round.

'But I don't even know you, and well... I'm not being fair,' he says with reluctance, as if he is not used to making an apology but feels that he owes Jack one.

'It's alright,' Jack replies, and smiles at him.

'To answer your question, I live in Pimlico. Joseph, a friend of mine, owns a bookshop there. He's given me a small room at the back. I'm free to come and go as I choose.'

'So what are you doing here then?'

'I come here quite often. I might not be a Catholic but I love the cathedral.'

Then, while the man waits for Jack to say something in return, all Jack can do is look at him vacantly. This encounter feels unreal to him, but the man does at least seem a little more willing to talk to him now. 'So are you sleeping here tonight?' Jack asks as he moves closer to where the man is sitting.

'Yes.'

'D'you sleep anywhere else when not at... Joseph's?'

'I spend a lot of the spring and summer sleeping on the streets. And when I'm tired of people and I want a bit of peace, I sleep in one of the parks... Hyde Park a lot of the time. I really like it there.'

Jack studies his complexion: it is hardy, has clearly gotten used to the cold. He recalls the short winter break he took to Warsaw: it was well below freezing. London, unlike many other European cities, Jack thinks, is definitely kinder to its nomadic and homeless citizens. 'How long have you been living this way?' he asks.

'Over ten years now,' the man says.

'Why?' Jack asks, eager to have his inquisitiveness rewarded.

'I'd rather not talk about it,' the man says bluntly.

'Sorry.'

'No... I don't want to,' he says again, but this time as if almost to himself. His resistance to the idea of answering Jack's question seems less now.

'Okay,' Jack says quietly. The man stares at him now, as if trying to gauge something about him, whether or not he can confide in him, Jack senses. He continues, 'You don't have to say anything if you don't want to?'

'My wife died fourteen years ago,' the man mumbles fast, sounding desperate to get the words out, as if he has not spoken them to anyone in a long time.

'I'm sorry,' Jack replies, his suspicion about his fate finally confirmed.

'After Molly died, it didn't take long. Life instantly took on a very different colour,' he says, now sounding like he has much that he wants to talk about. 'She was a beautiful woman,' he goes on, 'I loved her more than any other. She was so unique, you know, the only one. We used to make love every morning. I'd think about her all the time. She was my life,' he says with tenderness, which prompts Jack to think about Catherine. Yes, he loves her just as this man loved his woman. In fact, Catherine suddenly feels like his whole world, as if there is nothing else beyond her. The man continues, 'I remember when she told me she was pregnant. I couldn't believe it, I was so happy. I was going to be a father. I was going to have a baby boy. I was certain it was a boy right from the start. I wanted us to move house. We found a place in the country. I remember all the wood in the house: there was lots of mahogany and walnut paneling. It'd been rather neglected, but after I varnished it… it looked beautiful. I prepared the nursery… painted it blue, yes,' he says, smiling through his brown-stained teeth. And then he is silent.

'Please don't stop,' Jack urges him.

'Sorry, I lost myself there.' And Jack nods at him reassuringly. He goes on, 'Well I had everything back then, a wonderful wife, a son on the way, and a lovely home. Everything made sense. The world was a good place,' the man continues, 'but then she died… and so did he, my son, before he was born.' And now there is anger in his voice, 'They were taken from me. D'you have any idea what it feels like to lose someone you love more than life itself? No… I don't want you to ever know. It felt like somebody had stuck a knife into me… into my gut… had twisted it round and round, so tightly that the pain would never diminish. I still feel this agony now, to this day. That's why I have nothing now. Grief destroys you.'

Jack immediately recalls the novel he read some months before. How similar the story in *The Purity of Love* is to the one he has just heard, he thinks. The man seems consumed by his grief, just like the novel's protagonist. And yet it is also very different, Jack realises. This man, unlike his fictional counterpart, has not overcome the loss of his wife, and it seems never will. It has been too long. Jack feels powerless to help him. Part of him wants to inquire how the man's wife died, to share his sorrow with him, but another part of him is reluctant to help. Jack rubs his forehead as he tries to think what it would be like for him if he lost Catherine. The very thought of it makes him feel nauseous. He looks at the man again now, and finds that all he can say is, 'You must've loved her very much.'

'Yes I did… perhaps too much.'

'I'm so sorry,' Jack says as he sits down now, only a few feet from him.

The man carries a surprised look on his face now as he stares at Jack, and Jack wonders what is behind this expression, and suspects that he has simply forgotten what it is to experience compassion from someone. He looks vulnerable for the first time. Even when he was drunk and desperate, he did not look this way. His eyes light up as he smiles now. He seems almost grateful to Jack. 'I'm sorry, I didn't mean to become gloomy.'

'You hardly need to apologise,' Jack replies.

'Yes… well, I haven't talked to someone about her for a long time,' the man says quietly. Jack shivers. It is getting colder now. He continues, 'You're cold, you should go.'

Jack wonders whether he should. He grins as he thinks of Sam. He would have a field day if only he could see him now. The idiosyncrasy finally comes to fruition! Yes, that is what he would say. 'No really, I'm fine,' Jack says, reluctant to leave.

'Look here, put your legs underneath this blanket,' he instructs Jack in a paternal fashion, lifting up the other side of the blanket and urging Jack to warm himself.

'Thank you,' Jack answers as he shifts himself up against the wall until he is sitting alongside the man. He pulls the blanket over his legs and up around his stomach, puts his hands underneath, rubs them together, savours the new warmth. 'I don't even know your name?' he continues.

'It's Freddie,' he replies.

'I'm Jack.'

'You look like you're warming up now,' Freddie says. 'You know, I remember my first night on the streets, some time before Joseph offered me a roof over my head… it was autumn. When I woke up, I couldn't move I felt so cold. I had to wait for the sun to rise. It slowly thawed me out.'

'My God… it must've been very hard.'

'The initial humiliation of rummaging through dustbins, looking for either scraps of food or something to read, was harder to deal with than the cold. Passers-by would scowl at me, I remember, and I'd scowl back. Some of them looked away, embarrassed, with pity or shame in their eyes, while others met my look with anger, as if I threatened them in some way,' Freddie says reflectively, then turns to look at Jack who is looking up at the cathedral. 'Sorry, I don't mean to bore you.'

'No, not at all, I was listening, please go on,' Jack insists, increasingly struck by Freddie's growing confidence and lucidity.

'Well… when Joseph took me in and offered me the room, things got a lot easier. He always left some food for me, he still does. It was strange though… because once I was presented with a choice, I'd sometimes decide to live on the streets for a while and fend for myself, like I'd done before when I had to. I still do even now. I'd happily resort to my old days of scavenging. I didn't struggle anymore with my destitution, probably because I knew I had an escape. The boredom left me as well, when Joseph took me in. He offered me an enormous library, a lifetime's reading for any man. Before this, when I was on the streets, I often had a daily battle with boredom. I'd get sick of newspapers and find myself lapsing into dull and obsessive rituals like counting pedestrians or the hairs on my arm,' Freddie says, now smiling to himself. 'Sometimes, I'd go to public libraries and read for a few hours. I found that the best chance I had of being allowed to stay was normally mid-morning and afternoon. Certain libraries were often quiet during these times, and so were prepared to tolerate someone like me. However, when they got busy again, it wouldn't be long before someone near me would complain, and soon afterward, there'd be someone else, until the librarian, however compassionate he or she might've been, had no choice but to get rid of me. Summers were the worst time. As the temperature rose during the morning, the mix of rain, sweat, urine, alcohol and tobacco on my body and clothes became more pungent and toxic. On a hot summer's day, it became a pretty rancid concoction that even had me trying to escape it… and I was its maker! But more often than not, I'd be asked to leave when I got no further than the front desk. I used to try and smarten myself up before I went inside, but the stench of my clothes and shoes usually gave me away. During the winter, the majority of librarians judged me as someone who considered temporary warmth and comfort to be more important than the acquisition of knowledge. And so I was ushered out, back into the cold. But on those occasions when I was allowed to stay, I'd pour over different books with such a passion, like a starving dog that hadn't been fed for weeks on end. I'd gorge myself on philosophy and literature until I was so tired that I couldn't read anymore,' Freddie says, pausing for breath. 'You know, I held a rather romantic notion of my situation back then,' he continues. 'The heart-broken drunk will survive, I told myself. He'll find a way to get by. Part of me didn't really care what I'd come to. So what if I was no longer part of respectable, civilised society. I didn't want to be. I didn't care for it anymore once Molly had gone. And look at me now…' he says, glancing over at Jack's attackers who now hid in a shop porch further down the street, 'I'm the leader of London's dispossessed.'

Freddie seems intelligent and well read, which bemuses Jack somewhat. Jack thinks his mind might have helped him overcome his grief, pull himself together, get himself back on his feet, and reintegrate back into society. And yet it has not. Perhaps his experience of loss was so great that he decided to create a new way of life for himself outside of the mainstream, Jack wonders. Yes, he was forced to re-evaluate everything, develop a different worldview, lead a new life. Freddie just said this himself, that he no longer wanted to be part of conventional society. And yet, he still seems haunted by his grief, a victim rather than a survivor of it. Jack begins to consider what Freddie might have been like before Molly died, and what he might have done for a living. He does not want to ask him this yet as he is reluctant to appear too intrusive.

'Molly was an artist,' Freddie continues, now turning the conversation away from himself towards his late wife, as if sensing Jack's growing interest in him. 'She was a highly creative, sensitive woman. She had the voice of a cherubim angel I'd always imagined existed as a young boy. She was the only person I'd ever allowed close to me… the only one who had a clear view of the kind of human being I was.'

'This is how I feel about Catherine,' Jack says.

'Your wife?'

'No, we haven't reached that stage yet. Or rather she hasn't,' Jack confesses.

'You love her more than she loves you?'

'Well, we haven't been together long,' Jack says defensively, slightly rattled by the bluntness of Freddie's question. 'I'm counting on her feelings changing. She's worth the wait.'

'I hope so, for your sake,' Freddie says flatly, then points to the cathedral. 'And I thought God was dead,' he continues. 'I often wonder whether loving God is like loving a woman. Both require a leap of faith into the unknown.'

'I hadn't thought of it that way,' Jack replies as he ponders this notion, intrigued by it.

'You sure that it's love you feel for her?'

'Yes,' Jack says as he nods his head and looks down at the floor. 'Look, I had better get going. I've got an early start tomorrow.' He gets to his feet.

'Where d'you work?' Freddie asks.

'Notting Hill.'

'What as?'

'An editor and critic. Sounds very grand, but it isn't.'

'Right,' Freddie says plainly, looking away from Jack now and fiddling with a loose button on his tweed jacket. Jack waits for him to say more, but he does not, just sniffs and grunts, clears his throat, then throws an awkward question at Jack. 'You write as well?'

'My own stuff, you mean?'

'Yes.'

'I'm trying to at the moment, but with little success.'

'What about?'

'I have an idea to write a book about love.'

'Fiction?'

'No, non-fiction.'

Freddie is silent again, continues to fiddle with his jacket, a pocket this time rather than a button. Jack wonders whether he should tell Freddie what drove him to start writing. No. 'You should come and see me at the bookshop,' Freddie speaks finally. 'I can pull out some books for you.'

'Right,' Jack says hesitantly, unsure how much the loan of some books can help him.

'What've you read so far?'

'A bit of philosophy.'

'Who?'

'Plato, Aristotle…'

'The usual suspects. You should read some literature. Novelists often understand the nature of love better than anyone else does,' Freddie says, then pulls out a notebook and pencil, scribbles down an address on a piece of paper. 'The bookshop,' he goes on, tearing off the page and handing it to Jack. 'I'm round the back. Come and see me when you're next in Pimlico. I can't tell you when I'll be there. Best just to turn up. If I'm in, I'm in.' Jack puts the piece of paper in his wallet. 'I can see you want to get off, please go. And you don't need to say thank you again, though I'd appreciate a visit some time.'

'Yes,' Jack smiles as he turns away from Freddie and makes his way back to the main road, which is even quieter now, night upon it, stars no longer visible.

# 7

**CATHERINE DROPS** a shopping bag on the floor – she has just bought a new dress – flops onto her bed, and lies there, staring at the ceiling and thinking of Jack. She wears a yellow dress, and in the dark of the room, arms and legs stretched out wide, feels like a shining star in a night sky. It is six o'clock; she has to be ready for seven.

She finally told Jack yesterday she would go with him to his mother's birthday do. He immediately asked her what this meant, typical Jack, and she urged him not to imbue her decision with too much significance. 'I'm free tomorrow night after all, I don't have to work,' Catherine said to him, 'so I can come with you. That's it.' But he is compelled to do this now, she has noticed, to analyse everything she says and does. And so he finds hidden meanings in the tone of her voice and untold truths in the manner of her actions, and then is sure that these 'discoveries' offer vital clues about the future of their relationship. Jack maintains to Catherine that he does this because he has to, since there is often an inconsistency between her speech and action. Yes, there might be, she ponders, but it is also because he is deeply insecure about her.

Catherine jumps off the bed and starts to get ready. If truth be known, part of her is excited about the prospect of meeting Jack's parents. Okay, she is also scared, because she knows she is starting to care for him and meeting them this evening might bring her closer still, but she must be brave, yes. She has really missed him these past few days: he has not been around, doing more work on his book and reading all the time, though she is still rather confused about what he is trying to write. Trust him to draw inspiration from someone like Freddie, she thinks. Jack often seems drawn to suffering, to melancholy at least. But it is strange how he came across him again like that, and he does indeed sound like an intriguing character, almost fictitious.

She reaches for her shopping bag and pulls out the dress she has bought. It is long and white, made of cotton. Catherine holds it up against her body and looks in the mirror. Will Jack like her in this? she wonders. And what will his parents make of her in it? Maybe she should just stick with the one she is wearing … but does it make her look slutty? Catherine is not sure.

Freddie comes to mind again now. It does seem that Jack has become rather fixated with him. After that night outside the cathedral, he talked about little else for the next few days. He certainly holds more than an academic interest in him, she thinks. Jack is drawn to him in some way, but in a manner she finds difficult to articulate. This is in part because he still feels Freddie might have saved his life. 'He had a knife, Catherine, and threatened to kill me,' Jack told her. But his injuries were not that bad, and she considered whether Jack might have exaggerated the incident somewhat for dramatic effect.

The white dress it shall be. Must get a move on, she tells herself now as she hurries into the bathroom and starts to apply some make-up. Catherine is still not sure whether Jack will go and visit Freddie at the bookshop though. She suspects that part of him does not want to through fear that he will get pulled into a relationship, which he then cannot extricate himself from. Jack asked her again on the phone the night before last what she thought he should do, and Catherine told him he should not go just because he feels sorry for him and thinks he might be able to help him in some way. And likewise, he need not go because he feels indebted to him. 'Don't think you can become *his* saviour now, Jack,' she said to him. She knows what Jack is like, and suspects he is carrying around the romantic notion that he can help the poor man in some way, heal his grief, take away his suffering, get him back on his feet again. 'It's not that easy,' she stressed to him. Catherine knows this more than Jack does, how easy it is to make too good a friend of suffering. No, he should go only if he really wants to see him again, for this reason alone, no other, she said to him in conclusion. But Catherine worries now if she was wrong to say this. She has not met Freddie, does not know what he is like.

Make-up done, not too much, she wants to look natural. Must just fetch her white heels from the cupboard. She slips them on. Fetches her coat. Okay, she is ready.

Dinner is in a small Castilian Spanish Tapas bar in Chiswick. Catherine meets Jack outside. When they go inside, she is immediately struck by the restaurant's décor. It has curved white stone walls and a mosaic floor in its centre, depicting a brilliantly coloured dragon. She walks over to the creature and gazes down at its mouth, almost transfixed by it, then hears Jack call out, 'Hi there.'

Catherine looks up to see a man in a dark suit emerge from a small crowd of people who stand at the bar and stroll confidently towards her. He is stocky, of average height, has an air of authority about him. He greets Jack first, shaking his hand and patting his shoulder. Then he turns his attention to Catherine. He does not say anything initially, merely looks at her closely, his observation searching. She is not sure how to respond to him, but he does not threaten her, no, there is a gentleness in his eyes. 'It's so good to meet you. I've heard so much about you,' he speaks finally. 'I'm Jack's father, Theo.'

'And I'm Catherine,' she says softly.

And then, almost impromptu, he wraps his big arms around her slender shoulders, and Catherine, though the level of his affection surprises her, finds herself a willing party to his embrace. As Theo holds her tight, she presses her head against his broad chest, and when he pulls away, she finds herself almost reluctant to let him go, he feels so warm and comforting.

A woman steps forward to greet her now. 'Hi, I'm Ruth,' she says, 'Jack's mum,' taking Catherine's hand, as Theo steps back and returns his attention to Jack.

'Happy birthday. It's a pleasure to meet you,' Catherine replies.

She admires Ruth's hair first, fashioned into a brown bob, then her slender and delicate frame in the swooping tan-coloured suede dress she wears, which gives her a quiet, almost subdued elegance. She invites Catherine to sit down at a large dining table. Ruth takes a seat beside her and both of them stare at a white broken mosaic pattern depicting a cloud, a kind of miniature tribute to one of the features of Gaudi's *Parc Guell* in Barcelona. 'Have you been to Catalunya?' Ruth asks.

'No, I haven't,' Catherine replies.

'You should ask Jack to take you there. I'm sure you'd fall in love with the place.'

'Oh yes, Catherine, I'd love to,' Jack interjects, sitting down beside her.

'I'd rather not go there, to that part,' Catherine says soberly.

'Oh, but my dear… you must,' Ruth insists. But Catherine is silent. 'Your father's Spanish, isn't he. Which region's he from?' Ruth goes on.

Catherine still says nothing. 'Are you okay?' Jack asks her.

'I'd rather not be reminded of my father… that lousy, vile cunt!' she finally says through gritted teeth.

The room is suddenly very quiet as a beautiful solo by Caetano Veloso ends, his final high note trailing off. They wait expectantly for the next song to begin. Catherine looks down at the table while Ruth looks at her son. With the strum of a guitar, Jack takes Catherine's wrist and gets up, as if intent on leading her away from the table to confront her in private, here and now, get out of her why she said this and where it came from. But she will not be treated like a misbehaving toddler, no. Jack has no right to know why she said what she just did. It is her fucking business, no one else's. And so she glares at Jack, her face burning red with anger. It feels hot and puffy. Catherine knows she has not looked at him with such venom before: her threats and tantrums up until this moment have always been playful. Jack responds by immediately letting go of her wrist and looking at her fearfully, as if she has suddenly decided that she has had enough of him.

She turns away from Jack now and addresses Ruth, who is staring at the white cloud mosaic again. 'I didn't mean to offend you… I'm so sorry,' she insists, wiping a tear from her eye.

'It's okay, my dear… really,' Ruth replies quietly and Catherine is immediately struck by the lack of judgment in her voice.

'That was very rude of me. What can I say?' Catherine goes on.

'Look don't worry, you don't need to apologise,' Ruth reassures her.

Theo interrupts them, 'Everything okay?'

'Yes fine,' Ruth replies.

'Well, I think we should get everyone to sit down. It's time to eat,' Theo says. 'Catherine, would you like to join Ruth and I?' he asks, pointing to the other side of the table. 'And Jack, give us a hand will you?'

Catherine nods, stands up and follows Ruth while Theo and Jack approach the bar, calling on different people to take their seats for dinner.

There are about twenty or so people seated round the table. Jack told her that his sister, Sally, arranged most of the evening. She is just as Jack described her: short, slim, feisty and rather beautiful.

'All mum's close friends are here,' Sally tells Catherine as she leans over, introduces herself, then moves her arm around the table like a sniper, singling out different people and announcing their names as if issuing them with ultimatums. There is Gillian, Yvonne, Matthew, Joanna … these are all the names that Catherine can remember once Sally has finished.

Catherine looks over at Jack who is sitting next to Gillian, Bill's mother, big-breasted, plump and blonde. 'Jack and Bill, next door neighbours and very good friends since the age of three,' Sally goes on but Catherine knows this detail already. 'They even ended up going to university together,' she adds.

Then Catherine glances at Theo, who is talking intently to Ruth. She wonders whether Ruth has already told him about her little outburst. However, her speculation quickly ends as Theo turns to her and asks if she is okay, and all Catherine can do is say, sadly and quietly, 'Yes, thank you,' the tone of her voice conveying her guilt clear enough. But Theo does not let her dwell on her misconduct. Rather he just takes her hand and holds it tenderly, his thick set and hairy forearm weighing down on the table, then smiles warmly at her with his sombre brown eyes as Catherine spies Jack looking over at her and his father together.

A giant spread of tapas arrives on the table, ranging from *albondigas* to *boquerones* to *caracoles*. Everyone begins to eat, frantically munching, savouring every mouthful. Catherine sees Gillian spill a large dollop of mayonnaise on her wrist, and watches as she raises it up to her face, glances round the table to make sure no one is looking, then gobbles it down and licks her wrist clean like a greedy lapdog. She is not very hungry and notices that Jack is not either. He looks increasingly tense and preoccupied.

'My son seems very happy at the moment,' Theo says to Catherine, and she instantly recalls what Jack said to her a few weeks ago about his father, that he has always worried about his son's intellectual aloofness and his propensity for solitude. 'He thinks you're good for me. Little does he know,' Jack said to her then, playfully. And he went on to tell her that his father has never applied this kind of scrutiny to the self-assured and outgoing Sally, who has held down a loving relationship for over six years. Unlike how he is with his precious daughter, Jack feels that his father too often treats him, his son, as a patient, assuming a cold, clinical demeanour with him, forever wary of getting too close and not willing to divulge too much of himself.

As Catherine continues to listen to Theo now, it is clear that Jack has inherited his father's intellectual detachment, a mindset that wishes to analyse and understand inner conflict rather than to actually feel and experience it.

The dinner moves on and Jack continues to monitor Catherine's conversation with his father. He has a different look in his eye now, which seems to convey distrust, of his father or her she is not sure, perhaps both of them.

When dessert comes round, Jack stands up to make a speech. He told Catherine he planned to say a few words. As he clunks a silver spoon on the side of his empty glass of sangria, he looks over again at Catherine and his father. 'Ladies and gentleman,' he begins, and his voice starts to quiver, 'well, what can I say? I mean… what can't I say? Yes, that's it. I can't say enough. She's everything… yes… to me… and to all of us.' He nervously mops his wet brow with a chocolate-smeared serviette. 'I had a little speech planned, but I've suddenly forgotten it… sorry, my mind's gone completely blank…' he continues, wiping his forehead again with the serviette, and this time giving himself what looks like a warrior's battle stripe across his brow. Everyone round the table looks at him searchingly, as if all trying to detect the source of his anxiety. 'What I'm trying to say… yes, is that I love you mum!' he says in agitated conclusion as he throws himself down into his seat, then tries to regain his composure by pouring himself another glass of sangria and knocking it back.

The table is uncomfortably silent before the cake appears and Theo initiates a Happy Birthday chorus. Gillian looks at Jack with a kind of bemusement, as if to say she was expecting a lot more from him. 'Well, I fucked that up,' Catherine overhears Jack say to Bill as everyone round the table sings Happy Birthday. 'Christ, I feel like I've really let her down… and everyone else for that matter,' he continues, throwing a glance at his mother.

Then Catherine hears Bill reply, 'Come on Jack, public speaking has never been your forté, has it? You've always been too bloody shy and neurotic when it comes to this kind of thing. Don't worry about it.'

'I know, but I'd planned it, I wanted to say so much…' Jack says, then downs another glass of sangria.

'Look, if it's any consolation, your bumbling approach was rather endearing… in a bumbling kind of way,' Bill says, which induces a smile from Jack's gloomy flushed cheeks.

Then she watches Jack get up and hurry round to her side of the table. Ruth stands up to greet him. 'Thank you for those lovely words, Jack,' she says in her soft and tender voice. 'You okay?'

'Fine.'

'You sure?'

'Yes,' he replies bluntly. 'Look, I'm sorry mum. I just felt bloody nervous as soon as I stood up.'

'It doesn't matter, really… it's not important,' she reassures him.

Jack leans over to Catherine and whispers in her ear, 'I'd like to go.'

'Already?' she asks.

'Yes.'

'You pissed?'

'I wasn't… but I am now.'

'I think we're leaving…' Catherine says, turning to Theo.

'So soon Jack?' he inquires.

'Yes, I need to go.'

'Right… okay,' he says, sounding rather put out. 'Well both of you must come over and have dinner very soon?'

'I'd love that,' Catherine replies fast and instinctively, and is immediately confronted by a look of surprise on Jack's face. He did not expect her to accept this invitation, she knows this, in fact neither did she: it just came out.

Catherine puts on her coat and Theo kisses her goodbye.

'You off?' Ruth asks Jack.

'Yes, but we'll come over for dinner soon. Happy birthday again,' Jack says, as he pecks her on the cheek and drags Catherine away from his father.

'Bye Ruth,' Catherine says, holding out her hand.

'Bye everyone,' Jack shouts as he scurries drunk with Catherine towards the front door, waving at Bill and Gillian, but not leaving them or anyone else time to actually acknowledge his and Catherine's departure.

'He's wonderful… your father,' she says to him as they step outside into the cold night.

A cool gush of whispering wind meets their faces, and Jack sucks at it, as if trying to steady his mind.

In bed, later this same night, after they have sex, Jack kisses her on the cheek and whispers softly in her ear, 'I need you and want you so much… forever and ever.'

She says nothing, gives him the impression that she is asleep. She was surprised by Jack's behaviour this evening. He seemed ever so fragile, needy, as if he was terrified of being on his own again. And the love he professed for her, well … it sounded more like a crippling disease. And when he is like this with her, Catherine struggles to continue seeing him. He agrees with what she says where he should contest it. He condones her secrecy where he should challenge it. In fact, any difference or disagreement is perceived as an enemy of his love. Jack imagines that this congruence will make them inseparable. This is how he will keep her, so goes his wayward logic. But Catherine thinks less of him at times like these.

He caresses her hair with the tips of his fingers now. His strong intellectual self-defence seems to be losing its power. Jack told her that this is what he called on before he met her, when he felt weak, this academic confidence and conviction, but not anymore. She has shown him something else, a world of feeling that he is not used to and does not quite know how to interpret. He continues to try and push their relationship along, to make it something bigger, more tangible. And still, she resists this.

# 8

**JACK IS DUE** to accompany Catherine to a screening of one of her short films. He has to dress up smart for the occasion and is determined to look dashing on her arm: no less will do. To this end, he even plans to get his hair cut. He would go to his local barbershop but there is a salon near to work: he can get dressed in the office, go get his haircut, then meet Catherine up in town straight after. The salon is rather swish and will set him back more than what he is used to paying, but they will do it all with scissors: no clippers here. The place Jack normally goes to, Costa's Barbershop in Shepherd's Bush, has the reverse policy: Costa will only use clippers. He has six different sets plugged into the wall, all with different size attachment comb guides ranging from three to twenty-five millimetres, and he always knows exactly which clipper to use at every stage of the process. He never hesitates, and never needs to resort to scissors.

The salon does indeed provide a very different experience from what he is used to. The receptionist takes his coat, offers him a cappuccino, invites him to sit down and browse through a large selection of glossy magazines, and assures him he will not have long to wait. Costa's offers no such courteous and deferential treatment: in short, the customer is expected to hang up his own coat and keep shtum till his turn comes round. Costa, sure of his impertinence, will have it no other way. Jack looks down at the reading material on offer – *Vanity Fair*, *Esquire*, *Vogue* and *Cosmopolitan* dominate the chic glass coffee table – a far cry from the dilapidated newspaper rack in Costa's that carries a staple tabloid diet of *The Sun* and *The Mirror*. Jack imagines this must be obligatory literature for an up-market unisex salon.

He starts to flick through a selection of magazines. Half-naked women, air-brushed to perfection, flirt with him from the pages, and the words 'orgasm' and 'G-spot' stand out in bold red. Most of the articles seem to be about sex and relationships, and are full of liberal and modern-minded survey opinions that extol the virtues of casual sex. One opinion reads, 'Single people now are entitled, even actively encouraged, to have many different sexual partners.' Another reads, 'It is now estimated that women in Britain today have the same degree of sexual freedom as men do.' A further article concludes, 'For women, the words "relationship" and "commitment" mean something very different these days. Women now are just as likely to be unfaithful as men are. Their powerful sexual needs must be met as well, and they would rather have these satisfied in the arms of a lover than a prostitute – man's preferred choice. Perhaps infidelity should be looked at as something natural and inevitable, and hence acceptable?' Jack stops to reflect on this liberated idea. Nope, he cannot accept it, not at this moment anyhow. In fact, the very suggestion of so much freedom now makes him feel anxious, and he suddenly finds himself pining for a strong conservative voice that will dismiss all these liberal sentiments and ideas. 'The colour technician is ready to see you now,' the receptionist announces.

Jack looks up to see the glamorous young woman, sitting beside him, get to her feet. As he watches her strut confidently downstairs, he notices she has left behind her paper, *The Daily Mail*. On its front page, it advertises a feature about 'The Decline of Family Values in Britain'. Yes, this will reassure him that monogamous, enduring and committed love is still possible. He skips though its pages until he locates the article in question. The journalist begins by making reference to the Conservatives' mission to restore and uphold family life and then goes on to comment on the state of modern relationships and the importance of 'the family unit'. He is sceptical of the sexual emancipation that is celebrated in other parts of the media and laments the decline of family life and values. He makes reference to 'those namby-pamby liberals who try and sell us the dream of sexual emancipation when in fact what they're really selling us is a broken, fractured and unhappy life full of dysfunction, misery and solitude'. He then goes on to attack 'these liberals' for encouraging promiscuity in young people, and for 'portraying monogamy and family life as restrictive and boring': according to 'them', such 'old values are now no more than unrealistic and unattainable ideals'. But according to him, 'family life is still something good, proper and true… the very fabric and foundation of our society'.

'Mr. Stoltz… we're ready for you now,' the receptionist says, temporarily taking her ear away from the phone. Jack puts down the paper, and as he gets up, he hears the receptionist, who is talking to a friend he supposes, say, 'Yeah, I just want him for the sex. I'm not really interested in anything else at the moment, you know.'

No, Jack does not know, he mutters to himself irately, and then wonders whether this is what Catherine says about him as well. He knows their love affair is typical of modern urban life: they fuck a lot. They are obsessed with sex just like everyone else is: the glossy near naked images in magazines, the seedy sex scandals on the front pages of tabloid newspapers, the racy story lines of soap operas, the pornographic titles on sale in newsagents. The modern world is fixated with the prick and the cunt, and everyone strives to be a great fuck and brilliant at fucking. He has got as far as Freud in his reading now, and Jack is sure that he is to blame – well, in part, anyhow. He would have us believe that every man is a cesspit of seething affect and sexual drives who struggles desperately to control these highly charged, conflicting impulses and fears within him: he consciously suppresses them, but he also unconsciously represses them. And Freud judges both action and process, suppression and repression, to be very dangerous, and believes that if a man loses the battle against his powerful sexual urges, then he quickly descends into neurosis, obsession, depression, violence and psychosis. Hence, every man must strive to bring these desires into consciousness. And in order to do this he must drag his childhood trauma out of the dark chambers of his unconscious. Only then can he master his destructive drives. But Jack right now certainly does not feel like his own master as the blonde stylist thrusts his head forward towards the sink in order to wash his hair: far from it, he feels sex obsessed and sick.

It turns out to be the longest haircut he has ever had. Jack has never imagined it could take so long just to cut someone's damn hair. He hurries out of the salon at half past six, wound up and fretting: he only has fifteen minutes to get up to Soho to meet Catherine. He flags down a cab. The traffic on the way up is bad. When they hit Piccadilly, it is clear they are not going anywhere fast. Jack asks the driver to take the back streets. He responds with a series of negative grunts, telling Jack in between heavy sighs that they will be no bloody better than the main road. Fine, Jack huffs, pays him and gets out. He runs up Piccadilly as fast as he can. By the time he reaches the cinema, he is hot and sweaty; his hair, cut short, has not suffered too much from all the frantic exertion, but his clothes have. He tucks in his shirt, hauls up his trousers, re-adjusts his belt and brushes down his jacket. Okay, he is ready now … well, just about. Catherine looks immaculate as he greets her. He feels dishevelled. They walk straight into the small auditorium and take their seats as the lights go down and the film begins.

But Jack is in no mood to watch the film and descends into himself now. He knows that Catherine is familiar with his tendency for introspection. She used to find it endearing when they first started seeing one another and would laugh at how preoccupied he got and quip, 'You thinking again, my little bookworm.' This was his private world, independent of her and the world of practical experience, and she interpreted his escape into the deep recesses of his mind as an important expression of his freedom. But she does not find it so endearing anymore, and has told him as much. Why? Because she feels it is no longer motivated by freedom but by compulsion. And Jack cannot deny this now.

Since he has been with her, it has become clear to him that he used to think too much about himself and the world in general. In this respect, he was part of the Western tradition of analytical thought, the quest for rational knowledge and understanding hailed as the supreme good. Plato might have urged people to pursue the good through metaphysical inquiry and contemplation but Freud insisted that this good is only attainable once people uncover their inner selves: self-knowledge is the cornerstone of life. Jack, like his father, had pursued this Freudian principle with vigour. But then Catherine had come along and given him someone else to think about, and suddenly, the pursuit of self-knowledge and the good seemed far less important. He had someone else to think about, Catherine. And yet this is what she does not like, Jack realises. It is no longer self-knowledge and the good that dominates his thinking, but her.

So as Jack sits here now and the film nears the mid-way point, his thoughts slowly become his enemy. He starts to wonder, first, whether Catherine has grown tired of him. Next, he tells himself she is probably seeing someone else. And finally, he asks himself why she is so reticent, so secretive about certain areas of her life. Where was she last night, for instance?

Oh, he should just give up on her, Jack urges himself abruptly. She will always be elusive, distant. She will never love him. What is the point?

He knows that Catherine can sense what he is doing, that he is not paying any attention to the film. She glances at him occasionally, and he can feel her frustration growing. But try as he does, he cannot stifle these thoughts.

It is not much longer before she has had enough. 'Are you even watching it?' Catherine demands finally, swinging round to confront him.

'What's that?' Jack replies, still lost in the narrative of his thoughts.

'You haven't even been watching it, have you?'

'I…'

'Your head's somewhere else. I know you well enough by now.'

'Where were you last night?' he asks her.

'I can't believe you're asking me this now…'

'I just don't know what's going on with you half the time, that's all.'

'Sometimes, you really can be so bloody insecure and self-absorbed!' she says angrily, then turns back to the screen.

Jack is silent, and they do not speak again until the film has finished. After the screening, Demon, the film's production company, holds drinks across the road in a typical Soho bar, furnished in polished steel with varnished floors, silver chairs and Tiffany blue tables, reflecting the material success and prosperity of its clientele. Jack stands at the other end of the bar and watches Catherine as she talks to two slick and suave-suited men, who both seem more intent upon gawping at her breasts and stroking her hips than telling her what they think about her film. As the ceiling fan above him chops away robustly, Jack, stone-faced and green-eyed, begins to listen to jealous whispers in his head as he guzzles down consecutive beers. Those slimy bastards. Soon, he is unable to contain himself. 'Haven't you fucking told them you're in a relationship with someone?' he shouts at her across the packed bar, and Catherine looks stunned as he marches towards her, pushing past a number of people on route. 'What are you three up to then?' he continues threateningly.

'What are *you* doing?' she asks him incredulously and is met by his angry stare. She immediately attempts to pacify him. 'Guys, this is Jack,' she addresses the two men, 'and Jack, this is Alistair and Mark.'

Alistair grins at her, then looks at Catherine as if undressing her.

'Don't look at her like that!' Jack says, prodding Alistair with his middle and index finger hard in the sternum.

She grabs Jack's arm as Alistair clutches his chest. 'I'm sorry… I don't know what's come over him,' she says apologetically to Alistair, more surprised than offended by his action. 'You okay?'

'Yes,' he replies, scowling at Jack.

Catherine leads Jack away from the bar. 'I hate the idea of other men touching you. I can't bloody stand to even think about it. I'm not just another lover to you, am I… just another man, any old bloke?' he asks her.

'Stop it! You're drunk. You're acting like a twat.'

'No I'm not. Why d'you flirt with other men?'

'Yes you are. And no I wasn't flirting with them.'

'From where I was standing it didn't seem that way. I mean… they wouldn't feel they could stroke your fucking hips if you weren't giving them the come-on,' he insists. Jack is now sure that she was flirting with them more than they were with her. In fact, he now sees a subtext of betrayal in everything she was saying and doing while talking to them. Christ, she was probably arranging to slip away with them this evening, the slut. He continues to shout at her as she leads him outside.

It is a bitterly cold evening. An old homeless woman is huddled in a doorway opposite the bar. Jack notices her out of the corner of his eye; she shivers beneath her inadequate blanket as she stares at a pigeon perched on a railing nearby, cooing at her, like they are engaged in some kind of unique cross-species dialogue. Freddie instantly flashes through his mind. He has not thought about him for some time. Jack goes on, 'D'you want to fuck every man you meet… is that it?' asking this question as if it points to some great universal misogynistic truth.

'Okay Jack, I'm sorry,' she shouts. 'Yes, I was flattered by all the attention they were giving me. Yes, I encouraged them. I'm sorry… really, Jack… I'm sorry…'

When she admits this, he finds himself curiously aroused by the fantasy of her moaning with pleasure in the bed of other men, as long as this never becomes a reality. For he senses that this excitement is more likely to express itself through violence than tenderness. Jack hears the old woman begin to hum – as a freezing wind whips up and blows plucky in her face – like this action will somehow shield her from the cold and his ranting. 'So you want to fuck other men, is that it? Got bored of me, have you?' he asks Catherine like he has not just heard her apology.

'What are you saying? You sound crazy!' Catherine retorts, holding her hands to her face as she tries to block out another gust of wind.

'Well, you've told me so little about your old lovers. How many of them were there? Twenty, fifty, one hundred… what?' he demands, the old woman's humming becoming louder.

'How can you ask me a question like that? You're being an arsehole and I'm not going to answer you. This is precisely why I have the rule of not talking about past lovers.'

'The rule?'

'Yes.'

'Why not?'

'Because it doesn't bloody matter.'

'Well it does to me!'

'Why? Are you concerned that your current lover might be a tart, a whore?'

The old woman's teeth begin to chatter, sporadically at first, then more frequently, and with a deliberate, sustained momentum. Jack cannot help but look over at her. The awful spectacle of Freddie rocking to and fro on the bus flashes before his eyes. 'Is that all I am to you, just another lover?' he asks Catherine.

'What d'you mean?'

'Well… aren't you at least my girlfriend by now?'

'Jack, you sound like a bloody adolescent.'

'I'm trying to establish what I mean to you?'

'No, you're trying to figure out how many men I've fucked…' she says, her face revealing the same kind of enmity it did before at his mother's birthday.

The old woman suddenly lets out an abrupt, indistinguishable cry. Jack and Catherine look across the street to see her bury her head in her blanket. Jack has to get away: he has to clear his head, has to sober up. 'I've got to get out of here!'

'What d'you mean?'

'Look… I'll see you tomorrow, alright?' he says, looking over again at the old woman.

'Where you going?'

'I'm going to see Freddie.'

'What you talking about?'

'Look, I promised I'd go and see him.'

'No you didn't. And who d'you promise Jack? Him or yourself?' she asks.

He does not answer; holds his head down and stares vacantly at the pavement.

She presses on, 'It's been over three months. I thought you'd decided that it'd be more trouble than it's worth.'

'I hadn't decided anything.'

'Okay… but why now?' she says, looking at her watch. 'It's late. It's gone eleven…'

'I know.'

'I wish you wouldn't…'

He interrupts, 'Look, let's talk about this tomorrow. I need to cool off alright.'

'But where are you going?'

'Look, I'm just going to go back to my place, okay.'

'So you're not going to see Freddie now?'

'No. Look, I'll call you in the morning, alright,' he says, pulls up his collar, shoves his hands in his pockets and hurries off up the dark road, head bent down as he presses forward against the wind.

# 9

**JACK RUNS** down a cobble-stone street lined with dingy industrial units. It is pitch black, can barely see anything at all. Slips on an icy patch, falls to the floor. Is this the right place? he wonders. Fumbles in his trouser pocket, pulls out his wallet, rummages through it, removes a piece of paper. Unfolds it, holds it close to his face but cannot read it. Too dark. Scrambles to his feet, runs into the middle of the road. Holds the piece of paper aloft and tries to catch the light from the moon. Yes, there we are, Magnolia Mews. Must check the sign again at the top of the street. Scampers back up, and there in the shadows, he sees it. Yes, Jack is in the right place after all.

He makes his way back down the mews until he reaches a dead end. Where now? he asks himself as he spots a tiny alleyway hidden in the corner, almost concealed by a holly bush. Jack clings to the stone wall and fumbles his way in darkness for what seems like an eternity, until he finally comes to a small porch. He finds himself standing in front of an old oak door. He pauses to catch his breath, and realises he is still not quite sure why he has come here. What does he really hope to gain? he does not know. He must get a grip on himself. What the hell is happening to him? He feels like he is losing control.

Jack knocks. There is silence at first, then all of a sudden the door swings open with a loud jolt. 'It's been a long time,' Freddie says, 'I thought you'd never come. I should have had more faith in you. Well, what are you standing there for? Come in.'

He ducks underneath the hanging branches of an ivy plant, which creeps around the door like an archway, slips on the mossy doorstep and slides inside. Jack imagines that he is on an assault course as he dodges books, journals and newspapers scattered on the floor. Old floorboards creak beneath his feet. He stands in what appears to be a small storeroom at the back of the shop. However, there is a single bed in the corner, made up with a number of thick woollen check blankets. Beside it, notebooks are piled up high on an old bric-a-brac desk, literally hundreds of them. Next to them is a photograph of a beautiful woman mounted in a delicate silver frame: Molly he presumes. She has long dark hair, a slender face and neck. Her expression in the picture is somewhat distant, distracted, as if her eyes conceal a deep sadness. 'Well… here's my roof!' Freddie says smiling.

His accommodation is functional and chaotic. Grey paint has been slapped on floral-patterned wallpaper, which hangs limply from the walls. There is a single small bay window in the room covered by a flimsy plastic Venetian blind. Beneath it, a radiator is hung rather precariously, supported by a single wall bracket. A coarse, pallid brown rug lies on the floor, which conceals the remnants of a dignified pine floor. Jack sniffs. The small room smells of the male life alone, all sense of sweet domesticity long gone: it reeks of pongy socks, alcohol and old rubbish. 'Sit down,' Freddie continues, pointing to an old pale yellow sofa, which has shabby gold-laced cushions and foam poking through one of its arms. 'You want a drink? You look like you need a coffee.'

'Yeah… please. I need to sober up.'

Freddie walks over to a small wash basin in the corner of the room. He fills the kettle, flicks the on-switch, then reaches for the mug that sits in the sink. 'I better get another one if I want one as well,' he says, holding it up, 'I'm not used to guests, you see.' Jack watches as he opens the door to his room and walks through into a small kitchen. Freddie pulls another mug out of the sink and inspects it to see if it is clean or dirty. It is the latter, Jack guesses, as he turns on the tap and fills it with water. Then, rather than the using the dishcloth in front of him, he elects to use the inside of his thumb to clean it. And when he has finished rubbing and wiping it down, he does not rinse it out with cold water. Rather, he just adds a teaspoon of instant coffee. It is not clear how hygienic this method is. 'Coffee mate?' he asks, as he fills the mug with boiling water.

'Yes… please,' Jack replies. 'So this is where you sleep during the winter?'

'Yeah, though I don't tend to actually sleep that much. Not anymore,' he says rather solemnly. This does not surprise Jack at all. The drink probably helps him sleep, but even then, only for a few hours. And this is not sleep in the traditional sense, a period where the mind and body are given time to reinvigorate themselves. Rather, his body most likely just gives in, and his mind has no choice but to accept the body's temporary demise. And Jack is sure that when he wakes, his mind commences work with a renewed vigour, will simply not let him sleep anymore. 'Come through,' Freddie continues, as he summons Jack to follow him. 'Let's get down to the business of why you came to see me.'

'Yes,' Jack replies uncertainly. Still, he does not really know why he is here.

They walk through into the main shop. 'There are more books crammed into this small shop than probably any other small bookshop in the world,' Freddie says rather proudly as he makes a grand swooping circular motion with his arms. 'Look at them all!'

Jack is amazed. The shop floor is small, no more than four hundred square feet, but with a very tall ceiling. Shelves have been built into this space and line the walls, floor to ceiling, and individual bookcases of all different shapes and sizes have been crammed into the middle of the room. It is very difficult to move around inside the shop. At first glance, it appears to Jack that there is no order or system, but upon closer inspection, it is clear that the books – which span countless generations, old and new, dog-eared and pristine – have been ordered and catalogued with great care, dedication and precision. Freddie heads straight for the front of the shop. He clambers up a ladder and reaches for the top shelf. 'Tolstoy. Yes, you've probably read him but now I want you to really read him,' Freddie says as he picks up *War and Peace*, *Anna Karenina* and *Resurrection*, then makes his descent. When he reaches the floor, he hands the bulky volumes to Jack, then becomes excited as he heads off around the shop in search of other books. Jack read *Anna Karenina* as a teenager: it was one of the infinite numbers of books on his school reading list. Freddie goes on, 'Too many people just dip into Tolstoy. You cannot dip into his writing. No, you must let it get inside you, affect you, trouble you, provoke you. This is why he wrote. No other reason! He wanted to initiate thought and change in his readers' hearts and minds. You got that!'

'Yeah…' Jack says sounding rather overwhelmed as he watches Freddie pick up other books.

'Then there's Hardy's *Tess of the D'Urbevilles* and *Jude the Obscure*. He makes his women suffer. They all thirst for happiness in a dark and unsatisfying world. The call of love offers them liberation from the impersonal, indifferent and mysterious forces of the universe. You must read these books in the same way I've asked you to read Tolstoy's. Forget what you were taught about them at bloody university! I had a good dose of Hardy there, I'm sure just as you did. But he meant nothing to me then. I imagine he meant nothing to you as well. But now I want you to really feel what his characters are going through. Experience every event with them, inside them. Stay with them all the way. Don't let it become just a dull, objective academic exercise like before. His writings are worth more than this. Feel, Jack… feel!' Freddie insists. 'And then there's Nabokov's *Lolita*.'

'There's a lot of reading there,' Jack says, staring at the big pile of books in Freddie's hands.

'Yes. Here are men who all write with passion about affairs of the heart. Their central characters are driven by love in all its many different guises and manifestations. Anna confronts high society with the sincerity of her love for Vronsky. Must passionate love of this kind necessarily end in tragedy? Should we condemn the adulterous Jude? Can matters of the heart really be moderated? Love is obsessive, tumultuous and often tragic, but it is also life-affirming and beautiful. Can love be defined in any other way? But can Humbert Humbert's love be described as something beautiful? Is love dualistic and contradictory in nature? You must decide what kind of book you want to write. You must get at the truth of what love is. Be passionate and true. Nothing else matters! Whatever you do, Jack, don't pussyfoot around!' he demands, full of inspiring talk.

Jack is struck by the vigour of Freddie's intellect, how his mind moves restlessly from one theoretical position to another, how it processes ideas and counter-ideas with such speed and clarity. He is desperate to know what he did with his life before Molly's death. He is sure he will tell him soon enough. 'So Freddie, what's your view? What d'you think love is?' Jack asks.

'It doesn't matter what I think,' Freddie answers bluntly.

'Well I'd like to know.'

'Not now. Take these,' he says, handing Jack a pile of six bulky hardbacks. They return to his room at the back of the shop. Freddie holds open a large plastic bag. 'Put them in here,' he instructs Jack.

'When d'you need them back?'

'Take as long as you need, my boy.'

'Thank you,' Jack replies, the manner in which Freddie just said this prompting him to recall two of his former university professors: both were very bright, informed and articulate men. But Freddie seems to offer something more than them, something more tangible, real: he is passionate and intense, and urges feeling above all else. This is what Jack wants now. He continues, 'I… I'd like it if we could talk about your ideas when I return them?'

'Of course. Next time, we'll talk more,' Freddie says, suddenly seeming anxious for his visitor to go. Jack watches him as he begins to pace up and down, nervously rubbing the back of his neck repeatedly. It is like he now feels intruded upon as Jack, this relative stranger, walks around his room, and the shop, and observes everything within. Freddie said himself that it has been a long time since he let anyone enter this place, and it is clear now that he wants his privacy back, right away. 'Yes… well, until next time,' Freddie continues curtly, ushering Jack towards the back door.

'I feel as though I've only just got here.'

'That's enough for today. You've a lot of work to get through,' he informs Jack in a schoolmasterish tone, as if he has just set him an assignment, while pointing sternly at the bag of books he holds in his hand.

'Right…' Jack replies, somewhat bemused, and is immediately surprised by how he is prepared to submit so willingly to Freddie's instructions. He rarely does this with other people: he will normally only do things that agree with his own reason and common sense. He is 'nobody's fool', Jack likes to tell himself, though Sam is always ready to point out that, on occasions, he can be the exact opposite of this. He hopes that this will not be one of these occasions. Freddie's recommendations will not only help his research but will also help him further develop his own ideas. Jack will read everything he has just given him and then will come back and see him.

'I imagine it'll be quite a few months before you come back again,' Freddie says.

'It looks that way,' Jack replies, glancing down at his bag full of books.

As he prepares to leave, Jack spots a picture above the desk, one that he did not notice when he first came in. It is a print of Kees Van Dongen's *Torso – The Idol*. He has not seen it before, and it is one of the most sensual and evocative images he has ever come across: a naked woman, seated, her arms stretched behind her head and her face turned to one side; small pert breasts, a narrow waist and broad hips. As he admires her, he finds his observation working its way down her body towards the bottom of the canvas. The contours of her body are outlined in red, which heighten the woman's sexuality. Her vagina is not visible. The artist merely suggests it, but at that moment, overcome by desire, Jack longs to see this part of her anatomy. He looks up again at her face: it is red and flushed, burning with sexual desire, but is not the same woman's face anymore but Catherine's. Her mouth now seems to be open and it appears that she is looking at him, suggestively, longingly. 'It's an extraordinary picture, isn't it,' Freddie says.

But Jack does not want him to say this about it, about her – Catherine is completely his – and the thought of another man admiring her, possessing her, makes him furious. 'I had better go…' Jack mutters, trying to extricate himself from the fantasy that has just played itself out in his mind.

'It reminds me of my Molly,' Freddie says, glancing down at the photograph of her on his desk, and as Jack looks at her sad face one more time, he instantly thinks of Catherine again. He must finally talk to her, have it out with her.

Freddie closes the door behind him and Jack heads for Catherine's place.

# 10

**IT IS TWO** o'clock in the morning. Catherine sits in the old brown leather armchair in her bedroom, a near empty bottle of red wine beside her. She writes in her journal, has not written in it for sometime, has not felt the need to, until tonight. And now she writes in it with a sort of fury, frantically scrawling her feelings on the page.

Jack said he envied her for this: she writes in her journal with a degree of intensity and passion that he can only dream of when he writes. But this is only because of the rule she set herself. Yes, another one of her damn rules. She decided many years ago that she would never compromise her feelings in her journal: she would express her emotions in their sincerest form. No one else would ever read them and so she was free to do this. And it always seemed to her that the language she ended up using, stripped of all protocol, meant something more than the contrivances of prose and poetry. Often, she chose poor adjectives, her use of tenses was inconsistent and her sentences were incomplete, but none of this mattered. Writing in her journal served a specific purpose: it helped her make sense of things, and whenever she was distressed, she would write, and would always feel better once she was finished.

But now she does not feel any better and she must have been writing for well over an hour. Pages of it. Jack behaved badly tonight, was a jealous fool, and bitterly insecure, but she is prepared to forgive him this – Catherine had been far worse herself in the past. She wishes Jack were here with her now because then she would not be doing this, tearing herself apart. Her thoughts do not make any sense, seem to be coming from outside of her, from someone else. Her journal is not helping her make sense of things, no. She is no longer the best person to judge her inner world, she tells herself now as she stops writing. Someone else can offer her a better insight – a lover, a psychotherapist, God – as long as it is not her mother.

Catherine scans back over what she has written. Alistair was all over her when she went back inside the bar. He asked her back to his place, but she said no. She could not go with him because she just kept thinking of Jack, and she wanted to be with him rather than any other man. Since she has been with him, Catherine has become tired of just sex: fucking is not enough. Jack has given her something else, makes her feel so much more than any other man has.

There is a knock at the front door. Catherine closes her journal, puts it down on the arm of the chair, turns away from the window and looks to the hallway. Is it Jack? she wonders. She stands up excitedly, throws on her nightdress, and walks out of her bedroom and down the corridor.

'Catherine... I'm sorry, I don't know what came over me this evening,' Jack calls through the letterbox as she opens the door.

But she does not want him to know how happy she is that he has turned up like this and so she says rather plainly, 'You're lucky Genevieve's away for a few days. You would've woken her up.'

'Sorry.'

'You still drunk?' she asks as she looks at him standing there, clumsily holding the plastic bag full of books in his arms as if he is cradling a baby.

'Freddie gave me some books to read. The bag broke on the way.'

'Right…'

'No, I'm not drunk anymore,' he says.

'I knew you'd gone to see him,' and with these words Catherine returns to her bedroom and Jack follows her.

She slips off her nightdress and crawls back into bed. He undresses and lies down beside her. She wants him to hold her, but he does not. He lies there and says nothing. She thinks she knows what is coming now. He will tell her he is still struggling with the way she is with him, and that he wants and needs more from her, but this speech will not last long, he will quickly relent, and then they will have sex. And he does just this, begins to speak, and Catherine quietly listens, but then he begins to sound more determined, and Catherine is suddenly not sure what he will say or do next. 'I need to know, see this side of you, Catherine, otherwise it feels like a sham, and that you're lying to me. I need us to really be together, otherwise I can't see you anymore,' he concludes, and Catherine realises at this moment that Jack has at last found the courage to confront her.

Catherine says nothing initially, just gets up and walks out of the room. She returns a moment later with another bottle of wine. She reaches for her glass on the windowsill, spots her journal on the armchair: she has not put it away in its usual place, in the drawer of her bedside table. This does not worry her now. She is more concerned about having a drink. She fills her glass and takes a large gulp. Catherine does not look at him but stands there, naked, looking out of the window.

Jack leaves the room now. He is gone for what feels like a long time. When he comes back, he is holding a glass in his hand. Catherine is not sure what he is drinking. He swigs its contents and groans with discomfort as he swallows. Then he walks towards her. 'I want to hear all about your past lovers… every fucking last one of them!' he shouts, and right in front of her now, she smells whisky on his breath.

'I didn't love any of them,' Catherine replies quietly. 'There've been many… so many I've lost count.'

'Well, I need to know now if I'm just another one of these men, because if I am I might as well get out now,' he demands as she shuffles into the bathroom.

Jack watches her as she plonks herself down on the toilet. The drunken trickle of her urine penetrates the tense atmosphere and she sees his face soften. She gets up, dries herself and walks back into the bedroom. 'You know how I feel about you…' he continues.

'Jack?' she pleads with him.

'You make me want to live more.'

She stares blankly at him, her hands cupped over her ears. She feels small tears well up in her eyes, then water run down her face. Jack has only seen her cry once before, she realises, at his mother's birthday, and then it was only a few tears, which vanished as soon as they left her eye and slid down her cheek. But now she really cries. Tears stream down her face. She suddenly feels different, ever so vulnerable. Jack puts his fingers to her face and caresses her cheeks as her bottom lip, wet with tears and saliva, starts to twitch. 'Take me to bed, Jack. Look after me…' she says, her words slurring off her tongue like a frightened little girl who cannot fathom where on earth her sadness has come from. Jack is silent. Her body trembles. She slings her arm over his shoulder, jumps up into his arms and he carries her over to the bed. He lies her down, then sits beside her naked torso. He strokes her neck, moist with tears; his hands feel so soft. 'I want to want you,' she whispers.

'What?'

'Something hasn't let me give all of myself to you,' she says. 'I'm tired of just fucking. I need to love Jack… be loved…'

'I love you,' he says.

She cannot quite believe this. 'You don't know what I'm really like. If you did, you wouldn't love me. I know many people judge me to be a slut, a whore. I've been awful with most of the men I've been with. They didn't matter to me, because I didn't let them…' she says, now looking at Jack and feeling like she wants his understanding and acceptance. He is silent, lets her speak. She goes on, 'When I left home, I didn't leave out of choice… I'd simply had enough of her. I wasn't sure where I was going. I'd met a man a few weeks before, and we'd got drunk and ended up in bed together. He gave me his address in London. I just turned up on his doorstep, didn't even call first to let him know I was coming. I stayed with him for a month or so, then moved into a bed-sit. That's the longest I've ever lived with a man other than my father.'

'Why d'you have to get away from home?' Jack asks her.

'I can still hear my mother's bitter voice in my ear. She was often so cruel when she was pissed, and the more she got like this, the less I told her. That's when I started keeping a journal, I had to. It was after papa left, left me all alone with her, that's what caused it. He didn't exist after that. I wasn't even allowed to utter his name. 'The bastard', that's all he was. She hated him for being unfaithful, I hated him for leaving me. After he left, I found I no longer had anyone to tell my feelings to. When I told her about them, she just used them against me, they became weapons for her…' and Catherine pauses now as she recalls what she said to Jacob that time.

'What is it?'

'Sorry, I was just remembering what she said to someone. I was eleven or twelve. Jacob, he was my first friend at secondary school. We were sitting in the living room after school. My mother came and sat with us, then said to him, "Don't you think my daughter's beautiful. She likes you. Give her a kiss, go on!" I went bright red, had sworn my mother to secrecy. Jacob hesitated, could see how embarrassed I was, but she just screamed at him, "What's the matter with you? Are you a man or just a sissy bastard with a little fucking prick?" He was only a boy for God's sake. He was so scared he got up and ran out of the room. Jacob didn't talk to me after that for a bit. He told me he felt ashamed even though I told him he had no reason to be. I was so angry with her. I told him that my mother was sorry, though she never said she was. I asked him if we could still be friends, and he said yes, was so kind, so forgiving for someone so young. Jacob and I went out on our first proper date a year later. We decided we both wanted to be more than just friends. We'd entered adolescence after all,' Catherine says and smiles now as she recalls this … their innocent, romantic logic. 'I was so excited. He'd planned to take me to the cinema. He looked so grown up when he came to pick me up, like a man all of a sudden, though he was only thirteen. He kissed me on the doorstep, my first time, I felt all weak. We walked down the path to the front gate, everything was just perfect, but then I heard her. "He only wants to fuck you!" she shouted drunk from the front door. "That's all he's interested in, sweetheart. One of your holes to stick it in! Like all the rest." I can still hear these words even now,' Catherine says as Jack takes her hand. 'My feelings became my own after this,' she continues as she looks down at her hand as Jack holds it, strokes it. Formerly, such empathy and consolation would have angered her, but not now. 'That night, I was sure I heard her cry herself to sleep. I always hoped she was repentant after one of her outbursts. But if she ever was, it was always in the privacy of her bedroom. She never showed her remorse to me.'

'I'm sorry,' Jack says quietly.

'But you know, despite being appalled by her behaviour, I've come to behave like her in so many ways. I'm terrified of being like her, the one person I never wanted to be like.'

Catherine goes on to tell Jack all about her mother and father. Her father, Roberto, left her mother when she was just eleven years old. Eleanor O'Leary has not had a committed relationship since.

## LOVE AND MAYHEM

She refused Roberto a divorce on the grounds of her Catholicism, and maintains this position even now. 'It is almost as if she retains her marital name, Ramirez, because she requires a permanent reminder about the sins of her husband,' Catherine says. After her father left, her mother had short-term flings with younger men but that was it. She never let these develop into anything more. She could stay in control this way, Catherine knows this herself all too well, seduce them with her years of sexual experience, act out all her forbidden fantasies. But her mother took it further than her, probably still does now, used these young men to revenge the misdeeds of her husband the bastard, who, as far as she was concerned, was always more preoccupied with his extramarital affairs than his own wife and daughter. 'I used to watch her through the kitchen window as she groped and kissed different men in the alleyway,' Catherine continues. 'I think these younger men got a kick out of being with an older woman. I'm sure the sex for them was very good with someone mature, and also because she let them do it any way with her. She liked it rough. They often became obsessed with her, romanticising her independent spirit and single-parent status. This strong woman had coped alone against all the odds, that's probably what they told themselves. And the more aloof and indifferent she was, the more they wanted her. But eventually, she'd get fed up with them, with all their "fucking whining" she called it, and they would be left feeling used and hurt. She'd never again put herself in another man's hands, never again suffer the pain of rejection. She'd rather grow old alone and die alone,' Catherine concludes.

Jack strokes her forehead and leans over to kiss it. 'I haven't seen her since I left… nearly sixteen years ago,' she says. 'Jack, I love you, want to commit to you,' and then she leans over towards him and holds him tight. 'Hold me till I fall asleep… don't let go,' she whispers, and he does just this, holds her.

# 11

**CATHERINE FALLS** asleep almost immediately. Jack sits up, puffs out his pillow, lays it up against the wall and watches her chest rise and fall with every breath. He almost cannot believe that Catherine has finally said this to him, that she loves him. Part of him never expected to hear these words, and so he lies here sometime and holds them close to him. He will not think about what she just told him about her mother and father, not now, but tomorrow, yes.

Eventually he is too tired to keep them in mind any longer and needs to sleep. As he leans over Catherine to turn off the bedside lamp, she stirs, mumbles something incomprehensible, then lashes out with one of her arms. Her forearm hits him hard on the cheek.

Jack pulls Catherine onto her front. 'What are you doing?' But her eyes are shut tight. 'Catherine…'

She wriggles her body, and with her eyes still closed, mumbles, 'No, get off me… what's happening to me? No…' frantically shaking her head from side to side as if she is in the grip of a nightmare.

He strokes her hair. It is wet, she is sweating. Then she hits him again, slapping his cheek. He kneels on top of her and tries to restrain her.

'Catherine! What's the matter… what the hell are you doing?' he appeals to her. She part-opens her eyes, stares at him like a petrified child, then averts her gaze. 'Catherine… Catherine…' he continues, shaking her gently, trying to rouse her from her sleep. She does not wake but rather appears to be fast asleep again.

He gets up off of her and moves round to look at her face, which is crushed against the pillow. Yes, she is asleep and suddenly looks very peaceful. He stands up and stares at her body, no colour to it in the dark of the room but only lighter and darker shades of grey.

Then he lies down beside Catherine again, and as he leans over her once more to switch off her bedside lamp, her journal on the armchair flashes red in front of his eyes before there is complete darkness in the room and he can see nothing at all.

Jack finds that though he is very tired he simply cannot sleep but must think about what she told him. He has always known she was concealing something, but he had very little indication that this thing was embedded so deep, was such a great part of her. And now that Catherine has confirmed its existence, he realises that the woman who now lies beside him is altogether different.

He lies awake and tries to ascertain where this violent gesture of hers might have come from, at what point in her past. Jack draws on what Catherine told him about her mother's behaviour and abuse, referring back to the narratives of the particular stories she recounted. He suspects that feelings of shame are at the root of her violence. Eleanor filled her daughter's head with vitriolic Catholic dogma. It was imperative she realise that all little girls come into this world stained by sin, full of lust, and these wicked desires must be controlled and suppressed. How well this element of spiritual control worked for

Eleanor herself is clear enough, Jack thinks. It sounds like, from what Catherine said, that far from struggling to resist the advances of men after Roberto left, she actually revelled in flouting the laws of sexual conduct which she preached to her daughter. She liked it any which way. And so she instilled this fatal emotion in Catherine, a confused spew of sexual and psychological humiliation.

Jack sits up again, leans against the wall. He feels the sudden urge to conduct a rapid and rigorous psychoanalytic inquiry, to encourage Catherine to remember and reflect on all of her painful experiences. Yes, he will unravel her, then help her piece her experiences together into a new, meaningful whole. Then she will be happy. Like the competent analyst, his respected father, he will play the role of psychic detective. He will help Catherine uncover the contents of her unconscious, he will offer her clues and interpretations based on what she tells him, and through this process, she will locate all the causes of her destructive thoughts and behaviour. From this acquisition of self-knowledge, a new Catherine will be born.

And yet Jack knows that there is no assurance that this psychological method will be successful. Though his father is firmly committed to the idea that self-knowledge necessarily leads to greater equanimity and happiness, Jack is less sure of this conviction, though he wants to believe in it now.

He continues to worry about Catherine and does not get to sleep until very late.

In the morning, they are both due at work early. Jack and Catherine sit at the breakfast table, munching on scrambled eggs with brown sauce, and looking out of the pokey kitchen window at the street below; it is getting busy with market traders and early morning shoppers. It is one of those beautiful mornings. The first signs of spring hang in the air: birds are chirping, trees begin to blossom, the sky is cool blue, and the early morning sun sparkles. 'I've never felt such a release,' Catherine says. 'I thought I was losing my mind again.'

'What d'you mean?' Jack asks.

'Well it's happened to me before, but not this time, now I have you. I cannot tell you how amazing it feels to have been able to tell you these things. Thank you, Jack, thank you really. You're wonderful, you know…' she says.

Jack considers asking her what she means by losing her mind, and about what she did during her nightmare: does she remember hitting him? But he decides not to, not now. For she looks at him differently – there is a softness and willingness in her eyes – as though she is a part of him, and he wants to savour this. She has finally given herself to him.

They catch the bus together up to Notting Hill. Catherine has never done this with him, always in a mad rush to get to work. Taking the bus takes twice as long, she always told him. But now she says she does not care, wants to be with him. Just before his stop, on the junction of Notting Hill and Pembridge Road, he kisses her goodbye. As he stands up, she grabs his shirt collar, pulls him close and stares intensely at him, her eyes puffy from sleep and a hangover. Her breath carries the ghost of the night's red wine and tears. She whispers in his ear, 'Let's make a home together, Jack.'

II

# LOVING JACK

# 12

**CATHERINE RETURNS** to his place with several bouquets of flowers, a couple of brightly coloured vases and two watercolour paintings, both depicting rather serene landscapes: these were given to her by Holly, an old friend of hers, and she wants to hang them in Jack's front room now. His flat needs some warmth injected into it, she decided the last time she was here, since it is still very much the home of a bachelor, dour and practically furnished. Catherine looks at her watch. He is due back in about an hour or so. Okay, she had better get a move on.

She heads for the kitchen first of all. Catherine will wash up, then cut and arrange the flowers. Standing by the sink, hands submerged in soapy water, she realises she has never been in Jack's flat on her own, not in nine months. And when she was here with him, she would never let herself stay too long through fear that he got the wrong idea. Twelve hours was probably the single longest period she had spent here. But Catherine knows this is all about to change.

Now she turns to the flowers she has left on the kitchen table. She will put them in the vases she has bought; they will look wonderful, one in the hallway and one in the front room. A collection of lilies and roses. She trims down their stems, arranges them carefully. There, she says to herself as she puts in the final rose stem. Catherine sniffs the air. Ah, that's better, she thinks.

And now the paintings, yes. She wants to put them either side of the oil on canvas that hangs above Jack's settee, a violent and expressive modern abstract. She would like just to take this picture down, but she knows he likes it, God knows why, this image of a man snarling, holding his fist aloft. And so yes, she will leave it where it is. She hangs the watercolours, and they instantly lighten up the place, and the man snarling, well, he is made to look rather less threatening, flanked by two peaceful vistas.

Then she has the idea to put some candles in Jack's drab bathroom. She goes to the bedroom, rummages in her bag for the ones she bought this morning, vanilla and magnolia tea candles. If anything, burning these will get rid of the pungent smell of damp. She looks to the wardrobe now, at the space Jack allocated for her all those months ago – three shelves and part of the rack – and smiles. For him, this was a significant gesture, she knew this: it represented the start of something, the first step on a path, which might ultimately lead them to live together. But she had viewed his gesture with trepidation rather than hope. He had done it after only a few months of them seeing one another, and she acted defiantly, telling him that she was quite happy with her own wardrobe, her own cupboards, her own place. She was still independent of him, of everyone, she insisted. But then a few months later, she started leaving a number of small things – one or two pairs of shoes, some knickers, a couple of pairs of earrings, a few books and videos – and yet she always limited these roaming possessions to the smallest of her allocated shelves. All her things were to be found here, and she could throw them into a small bag, swiftly and easily, if she suddenly wanted to leave Jack, and be gone in an instant. But now she wants her things here, and so Catherine empties the contents of her bag onto the bed and starts putting things on her shelves, filling them until she needs more room.

Jack comes home to find her lying in the bath, surrounded by burning candles. 'Make yourself at home, why don't you,' he says.

'Yes, I thought I would.'

He kisses her on the lips, then walks out of the bathroom and down the hallway. He must have spotted the flowers. She listens carefully for him to say something. But no. He must be in the front room by now, she thinks, judging by the sound of his footsteps. What will he make of the pictures? she wonders. Still, he says nothing. Footsteps again, yes, he is in the bedroom now. All her things, he will probably not quite believe what she has done. She turns to the door and he is staring at her, smiling. 'Well I see you really have made it home,' he says and kneels down beside her now, holding her cheeks and kissing her repeatedly on the forehead.

'It looks a bit better doesn't it… and I've only just started.'

'Yes it does, but you know, it's still a shit hole. It always will be,' he says with a wry smile and with these words she starts to laugh.

'You know, I don't understand how you could ever have bought this flat. It's bloody awful, it's…' Catherine says in between giggles, and Jack can do nothing but join her.

'Perhaps I should sell it?'

'But who will buy it?'

'You know, it was a running joke between Sam and Bill how I even ended up here in the first place. "Only Stoltz could choose such a place," they said. "He must have been afflicted by temporary blindness and deafness." Perhaps they were right? I had an estate agent come round to do a valuation about a year and a half ago, I was thinking of moving then, and she told me without hesitation that the flat has "very few positive selling points", these were her exact words, and could not be situated "in a worse location". Exceptional honesty for an estate agent, I thought. In fact, I almost remember word for word what she said. "It's in a run-down building that backs onto a derelict industrial site, Mr. Stoltz," which let me add now has resisted redevelopment for years, "and is surrounded by ugly iron fencing and plywood hoarding. The view from the front is not much better, a collection of dirty, shabby blocks that resemble gravestones. Your building comprises four flats and yours is on the second floor. There are sitting tenants in the other three, large poor families of six or seven squeezed into flats that are meant to accommodate no more than two, who make a persistent racket… I can even hear them now. And finally, you can always guarantee finding a couple of drunks slouched on the doorstep. It seems to be a kind of meeting point and refuge for all the lost souls of West London, who gather here every day and night to lose themselves in drink. Now who would honestly want to live here?" I think she got it just right,' Jack concludes.

'We could go and live in the countryside together?' Catherine suddenly announces.

'What?'

'Well we could if we really wanted to?'

'There's you hankering after your dreams again.'

'But why not Jack?' Catherine has been thinking about it a lot this past week or so. Okay, she is aware of the seeming impracticality of moving out of London – it would make work more awkward for both of them, and they would see less of their friends – and yet she wants to give it a go, if anything just to remain faithful to her romanticism. 'Jack?' she continues.

The phone rings. 'Let me just get that. Back in a second,' he says and disappears.

Catherine knows that such a move is possible for her now. The film project she has been developing for the last few years with the writer, Dan Gaumont, is now looking closer to realisation. Richard Thomas, her producer, is fairly confident he can secure the necessary finance for *Crisis of Faith*, and has drawn up a provisional schedule, according to which pre-production is due to commence at the end of the year. And if it goes ahead, this will mean that she will no longer be committed to staying in London, waiting by the phone for her next job. Yes, she is almost there, she now thinks. And she also hopes that her reputation has reached a level where if she does move out of London, this will not jeopardise her career and earning power, and if *Crisis of Faith* does not work out, God forbid, and she is not offered another film, well she can always return to the direction of documentaries.

She gets out of the bath and wraps a towel around her waist. Her thoughts turn to the film again now. On the face of it, Catherine knows there is something potentially foolish, and apparently self-indulgent, about its subject matter, the story of a tragic romance between a Catholic nun and a man fifteen years her junior. The heroine is forced to choose between her love for the young man and her love for God. She chooses the former, and goes on to spend three blissful years with him before he dies tragically. After his death, she does not return to the Church – she is now considered an immoral woman led by her passions rather than by her Christian conviction – but lives a quiet life alone, dying herself subsequently, but with no regrets, because she has love in her heart. In defence of its credibility, Catherine is always quick to stress that the script is based on the real life tale of the Renaissance Venetian nun, Laura Querini. But in defence of its objectivity, she is less persuasive. Catherine remembers now what Genevieve said to her during one heated exchange. She accused her of wanting to make the film, first of all, to justify her own bloody promiscuity, and second, to prove that her mother's religion was fundamentally flawed. Yes, Catherine does find it extraordinary that the Catholic Church still insists on celibacy outside of marriage and remains persistent in its view, even in the modern world, of sex as something bad, dirty and unwholesome unless it is for the purposes of procreation. Genevieve maintained that her mission was as messianic, deluded and bloody-minded as the very religion she sets out to undermine and shame. 'You're no better than the fucking Catholics!' Genevieve concluded in a state of profound agitation. And Catherine was forced to concede that her dear friend was partly right. She had got rather carried away, and perhaps the film did risk descending into a rather silly, idiosyncratic rant. She had worked on a new draft with Dan consequently, toned it down a bit.

Catherine bends over the bath as she dries her hair with her towel. She thinks of her other project that she would like to get going – the one that is 'less earnest' according to Jack – but Richard Thomas is fonder of *Crisis of Faith*. Catherine considers its title to be rather portentous, even pretentious, but Richard judges it to encapsulate well the principal theme of the film, and give it a certain gravitas. And Catherine knows that Richard will battle for her to be allowed to fulfil her vision and make a striking and innovative piece of cinema. It is characteristic of the kind of films that he has produced to date, arthouse material that nevertheless can satisfy the commercial palate of a fairly wide audience: this is how he gets his funding. And he is always so ready to stress the project's positive qualities. The love between the nun and the young man is a beautiful portrayal, not depicted as something deviant and sinful but rather as a passionate and meaningful love affair. And the observations about the importance of faith, the dictatorial, oppressive and often abusive conduct of the Catholic Church, and the question of whether or not romantic love can endure such opposition, are astute and affecting. But Catherine must admit to herself that her principal interest in the project continues to be its exploration of the themes of Catholicism and sexuality. She has long ago rejected her Catholic faith, after her father's countless infidelities and her mother's bitter, guilt-ridden sexual indulgence in younger men.

Jack re-appears. 'Who was that?' Catherine asks, wrapping her hair in her towel, which sits on top of her head like an oversized turban.

'My father. He wants us to have lunch with them on Sunday?'

'Great,' Catherine replies without hesitation. 'So listen, what we were talking about before, what d'you think?' she continues, eager for them to carry on where they left off.

'Well I can't just decide like that.'

'Why not? I mean… you said you'd love to do it some day as well. Now is as good a time as any. Your flat is hardly conducive to your writing, unless you claim inspiration from a bleak urban landscape. Think about it Jack, all that peace and quiet, you could read and write all day long.'

'Yeah, I'd get a lot more done, I know this much. I haven't done nearly enough these last few weeks…'

'Well there we are then.'

'But I'm not sure how I'd manage *Detritus*?'

'What about when Sam leaves?'

'He's got the green light for the start of October.'

'Well that's decided then. We're off.'

'Catherine?'

'The only excuse you had was that you might not be able to afford it if you couldn't sell this place. Well you're due for a thirty percent pay rise when you take over from Sam.'

'Yeah okay.'

'And I reckon Sarah would be okay with you working the same days as you are now?'

'You've really thought this through, haven't you. Got it all worked out.'

'Yes,' Catherine says, smiling cheekily.

'Well you've done a good job…' he says, nodding at her,

reciprocating her smile. 'Yeah, I could make it work. I could commute down first thing Monday morning and go back late Wednesday night?'

'Yes.'

'It'd be hard going though…'

'Please…' she says sweetly, sure that he is now only moments away from committing to a life in the country as well.

'I…'

'You'd have me all to yourself four days a week and the peacefulness of the countryside,' she whispers, and Jack cannot but help smile even more at her now as he walks towards her. 'And you could stay here while you're in London.'

'Well it's not as if I can sell the place,' Jack replies.

'Yes then?'

'Yes,' he says finally and embraces her, as she unravels the towel from her head and swoops it over Jack, round his back, then wraps both of them inside it until they are cocooned inside its warm, damp, dense cotton.

# 13

SHE AND JACK decide they have to be within an hour and a half of London by car. Their financial adviser is confident he can secure them a non-status mortgage if Jack is willing to put down his flat as security. He tells them they will find it very difficult to secure a large mortgage otherwise, especially if they confess to the incertitude of their joint income: the film might collapse and the good fortunes of *Detritus* are hardly guaranteed.

And so it is decided. They will use Jack's flat as security for the lender and Catherine will make sure Genevieve has enough time to find someone else to move into her place. They will be out of London by the second week of October.

She and Jack start looking at properties in Oxfordshire and find a place very quickly. They are lucky. It is a beautiful eighteenth-century cottage in the Cotswolds, situated at the base of a synclinal valley. They buy the cottage from an old woman and move in just two days after Jack takes up Sam's old post as deputy chief editor.

Catherine immediately begins preliminary work on *Crisis of Faith*: Richard still has a bit more money to raise but tells her it is as good as on. She elects to work from home where she spends most mornings drawing up her own storyboards, fine-tuning the script, blocking out scenes and testing with her digital video camera.

Meanwhile Jack, when he is not working in London, sits in his makeshift study at home, the second bedroom, and works away at his research for the book. He tells Catherine that the cottage really is his 'perfect work environment'. He can do anything: pace up and down, read out loud, even shout obscenities at himself in the mirror, if he so desires. No longer does he have to appease neighbours, or indeed block them out.

Catherine quickly realises she is not like him when it comes to work. She needs the energy of others and lots of external stimuli, whereas it seems all Jack requires is his beloved books. He thrives off the energy of ideas, which he plays out in his mind like great debates, he tells her. This is never more apparent than when she catches him sitting in his big leather armchair like *The Grand Inquisitor*, judging the merits of an intellectual concept, and assessing its truth or falsehood. He is not far off from finishing 'Freddie's reading list'; this is how he refers to it now, much to her and Sam's amusement. He is working through it chronologically. He started with Tolstoy, and is now close to finishing Hardy. After him, there is just Nabokov.

Jack reads with an even greater passion and energy now, Catherine notices – of the kind that can almost change the shape of things – and seems absolutely determined to stay faithful to Freddie's request. And so whenever Jack picks up one of his chosen books, he repeats Freddie's words several times before he starts reading, quietly mumbling to himself, 'Let it get inside you, affect you, trouble you, provoke you.' This mantra is very important to Jack, though Catherine dismisses it as hopelessly eccentric. 'I can hear you sometimes, you know. You sound barking mad!' she tells him. But he insists that he must remind himself to become fully involved in, and affected by, everything that he reads. He does not want to be detached anymore, he tells her. He wants to work with, and feel, the same level of intensity and conviction that Freddie has shown him a glimpse of.

To this end, Jack starts annotating in notebooks: he is reluctant to write in Freddie's originals. He is determined to record all his thoughts and reactions, and devises a simple system to make the business of cross-referencing – between original texts and his notebooks – both quick and easy, and explains this to Catherine in all its anally retentive detail. He notes all key information on the front of every notebook – author, title, publisher and edition – and the numbers referenced inside each of them correspond to the page numbers in the original texts. Hence, he can always refer back to the originals if his notes are not clear. And then he numbers every notebook, this being his final point of reference. Jack soon begins to build up a large collection of them, and Catherine can always be sure to find one of them lying around somewhere. His notebooks become as precious to him as her journals are to her.

Only Jack, as Bill and Sam continuously maintain to her, would have chosen as his mentor a destitute heartbroken old drunk who lives a reclusive life in the back of a bookshop. 'Really Catherine, Sam and I expected nothing less from him!' Bill jokes with her on the phone. 'It's like he's gone back to bloody school again. I keep on telling him that he's read half of them already!' But this is characteristic of his friend's atypical and sometimes-subversive nature, he tells Catherine. 'He has always sought out experience and knowledge in unusual places.'

There is work on the cottage to be done, and she and Jack decide to dedicate afternoons to it. It is very run-down, distinguished by exposed brick, tatty plasterboard with molding cracks, and chipped paint. They give themselves three months to renovate, decorate and furnish the place before Catherine enters the final stage of pre-production, when she has to be present in London at all times. They also want it to be ready for Jack's parents, who are due to come and stay fairly soon. *Crisis of Faith* is shooting on location in East London, and Richard plans to rent her a one-bedroom property for five months in Bethnal Green: it is better that she stay here than in Jack's flat in Shepherd's Bush since it is right by where they are filming. This period will cover four final weeks of pre-production, seven weeks of principal photography, a contingency pick-up/strike week – where any missing shots or scenes will be photographed, sets broken down and equipment returned – and eight weeks of post-production. Catherine knows this schedule is demanding but nevertheless typical for a low-budget British feature film.

She insists on decorating and furnishing the bedroom and bathroom, and cannot quite believe how excited she is about doing this. Since Catherine left her mother, she has never lived in any place long enough to justify embarking on any serious home improvement. In the bedroom, she paints the four walls different shades of white and cream, then buys an enormous gilt four-poster bed and dresses it in matching bedding. She hangs white silk drapes from the bed frame, which swoop down to the floor like a collection of *haute couture* on display. She lies the gold and brown Turkish rug that she bought in Istanbul underneath the bed, protruding out from either side like a golden eagle spreading its wings. And finally, she mounts a full-length antique mirror at its foot; her mahogany chest, which contains all her journals, is reflected in it, peeking out from underneath the bed. For the bathroom, Catherine finds a big old metal tub rounded with swooping curves; it has brass taps and a beaming white sheen. She installs it in the centre of the room, positioned like a prize-winning contemporary, conceptual art exhibit on display in a modern art gallery. She strips the old floral-patterned bath tiles, paints the walls white and restores the old floorboards giving them a rich deep coat of mahogany wood varnish. A skylight illuminates the bathroom in the day and she lights her beloved candles at night; they bathe it in a faint glow of ochre light and cast their lengthening, burning shadows on the wood floor.

Theo and Ruth come to stay just before Catherine is due to move down to London to start full-time on the film. They arrive late on Friday evening. 'Let me give you the guided tour then,' Catherine says excitedly as soon as they walk through the front door, and Theo is quick to hug her. 'We'll do the downstairs first,' she continues as Jack takes her hand and they walk towards the front room. 'As you can see, Jack's done a terrific job painting it all,' she stresses, 'and his restoration of the original wood floor isn't bad either.'

'I never thought you'd get him to do any D.I.Y.,' Theo says.

'He took a fair bit of persuading, but I got there in the end.'

Then as Theo admires Jack's handiwork in the living room and Catherine says, 'Yes, I even managed to get him to put up some shelves,' Ruth heads enthusiastically for the kitchen.

Moments later, they hear her call out, 'Oh, you even have an Aga. It's just lovely… so cottagey.'

'God, she sounds like a bloody American!' Jack responds dryly.

Then Catherine takes them upstairs. First port of call is the main bedroom. 'This is where you'll be sleeping.'

'Oh it's lovely,' Ruth says, taking it in. 'But isn't this yours?'

'No, we'll sleep next door, mum,' Jack insists.

'Don't be silly!'

'Really Ruth, we'd like you to sleep in here. Jack and I will be fine in the second bedroom.'

Theo pokes his head round the corner of the room next door and peers inside. 'Yes, that's where Jack and I will sleep,' Catherine says, confirming its identity.

'So this is where you're working from at the moment when you're not at the magazine?' Theo asks Jack, looking over at all his notebooks lined up on the desk.

'Yeah, till the study's done.'

'It's like a bombsite at the moment,' Catherine says. 'I'm sorry, we wanted to get the whole place ready for when you came.'

'Yes, it's all Catherine's fault. Inexcusable really!' Jack quips.

'Yes, he's right,' she replies and pinches Jack's bottom.

'It's quiet, you've got a great view. No excuses now not to get on and write that book of yours,' Theo urges his son.

'You know, this would make a perfect nursery,' Ruth says.

'Yes, I said the same thing to Jack,' Catherine replies, joining her in the contemplation of children.

'She's desperate to be a grandmother, you know,' Jack mumbles in Catherine's ear, out of the side of his closed mouth.

'I've gathered,' Theo interjects, holding Catherine's arm, then embracing her, and she feels herself sinking into his arms again, and does not want to let go. She can always feel his psychiatrist's eye probing and searching, trying to get beneath the veneer of contentment and control, and yet this does not worry her, no. She senses that he is aware of her vulnerability, her weakness, and yet he wants to help her, make her stronger, rather than use this against her.

'You're making me jealous, dad. Don't make me get all Greek and tragic on you.'

'Never!' Theo replies brusquely.

Ruth taps her foot on the wood floor, seeming to imagine the playful footsteps of future grandchildren. 'What's wrong with my wish anyhow?' she asks Jack. 'I'd call it a rather healthy desire, wouldn't you?'

'What, patricide?'

'No Jack, your mother wanting to be a grandmother one day, you bloody fool!' Theo rebukes him playfully.

'Of course mum, yes… one day maybe,' he says somewhat

dreamily, looking at Catherine now, and appearing to lose himself briefly in her warm and loving smile. Is he contemplating fatherhood? Catherine wonders.

'Shall we have some dinner then?' Jack says.

'Yes, splendid idea. I'm starving,' Theo replies, patting his son's shoulder, and he looks at him proudly now, Catherine notices, without criticism. Perhaps he is relieved that his often bookish and intellectual son, once described by his daughter Sally as a 'somewhat solitary animal' – she remembers Jack telling her this – has finally found someone that he can share his life with.

Dinner is wonderful, as is the rest of the weekend. Catherine still cannot believe what has happened to her these past few months. She is with someone now, a man whom she can see many years ahead with, and this prospect does not frighten her, but rather calms her. He is a part of her, Jack, makes her feel beautiful inside. She wonders if her father ever made her mother feel this way, and after he had gone, whom did she call on then, her God or all those young men? Now Catherine wishes she had met Jack sooner, why not ten years ago, she imagines. But no, she knows that such thinking is pointless. She was obviously not ready until now, yes, she simply had to wait this long to meet him.

Theo and Ruth leave on Sunday evening. She and Jack stand with them as they look out at the valley, always so beautiful at sunset. The cottage is immersed in the lush vegetation of the valley's base and gracious limbs of rock fold in on it, the fading sun bathing it in sweet red dulcet tones. The sky shines red and orange, and as they look over to their left to the top of the farthest hill, they marvel at what appears to be a lone herdsman leading a herd of camels along a dusty red desert path.

Theo says, 'That looks like…'

'Yes, we know what you're going to say,' Jack interjects. 'But sadly no, it's not a *bedouin* with his herd. In the morning, this dreamlike image will reveal itself to be just a barren oak tree in front of a tight-knit cluster of conifers.'

'Well it looks like a desert scene at the moment,' Ruth says as she walks to the car. 'Theo, we better hit the road before it gets dark, otherwise we won't find our way to the motorway.'

They kiss one another goodbye, then as Catherine and Jack stand on the doorstep and wave them off, she feels compelled to turn to Jack and say, 'I hope that maybe one day my mother might come and stay with us.' She never imagined she would say this.

# 14

**CATHERINE'S TEMPORARY** home in Bethnal Green is a small, functional one-bedroom flat, a typically furnished rented property, painted cream with matching carpets. When Jack first sees the flat, he describes it as the kind of place you want to do no more than sleep in – it has the feel of motel accommodation – and Catherine cannot reasonably disagree with him. For the next five months, when Jack is working at *Detritus*, he will stay with her here rather than in Shepherd's Bush.

He is sure that during this time, he can make some real progress on the book. His role as editor of literature, prior to his appointment as Sarah's deputy, has put him in a strong position with regard to producing a book of his own. He has reviewed many published works of non-fiction and received many article submissions from freelance writers, which help him better gauge the quality of his own work, and he has also formed some strong relationships with a number of publishers.

Jack has just finished Freddie's reading list and has got some way with all his other research as well. He has finished Freud, and plans to read a condensed version of Jung's work, then he just has a bit of Foucault to get through, which he has recently added to the list. He will be in a position to start writing very soon, and part of him looks forward to the peace and solitude that the cottage will offer him while Catherine is in London. There is also less pressure on him, for the time being at least, to continue with his freelance contributions because Catherine is now receiving a higher income since she formally entered pre-production.

During Catherine's first week in London, they struggle to spend any real time together at all. On Jack's penultimate night with her, before he returns to Oxford, Catherine gets home very late and collapses in bed beside him, exhausted after another gruelling sixteen-hour day. She huddles in his arms, seeming to crave the warmth of his body. 'I'll miss you terribly when you go back up to the cottage,' she says to him. 'I feel as though I'm going to be on my own a lot these next few months.'

'Look, I'll be with you every week from Sunday evening through to Wednesday morning,' Jack reassures her. He knows Catherine needs him at the moment, what with the pressure of work, and he suspects that once she starts actually filming, she will need him even more. He strokes her hair and she falls asleep almost immediately.

When Jack wakes up in the morning, Catherine is walking out of the door, on her way back to the production office for yet another marathon day. He calls to her, 'We didn't get a chance to talk last night, you were so tired.'

'Yes, I'm sorry.'

'Well I want to pamper you and take care of you this evening, Ms. Ramirez, d'you hear me?'

'Yes, Mr. Stoltz, I hear you.'

'I want us to spend the whole evening together. I'm going to cook for you and then make love to you.'

'Sounds wonderful.'

'Make sure you call me and let me know how it goes today. I'm sure it'll be okay.'

'It had better be.'

'It will… I'm sure it will.'

'I do hope so. Look, I'll try and get back for eight… okay. Love you, bye,' she says as she closes the door behind her.

Jack gets out of bed. He must be in the office himself fairly soon. He strolls into the kitchen to make a coffee. It is proving to be a very testing time for Catherine, this much is clear to him. Richard and her are due to find out today – just three weeks before the commencement of principal photography – whether their preferred draft of the screenplay will indeed be the shooting script or whether Concept Pictures, the film's sales agent, will insist they shoot an earlier, less contentious draft. It is mad that they have been put in this position so near to the start of filming, though according to Catherine, this is typical of the film industry: it is chaotic by nature. Though they have prepared for the worst – Richard and Catherine have also scheduled for the shooting of Concept Picture's preferred draft – Dan has threatened to resign from the project and pull his name as the writer if the sales agent gets its own way. He has a reputation for his uncompromising nature, Catherine has told Jack, most evident in the work he has written. However, Concept Pictures is in a very powerful position: the company has raised sixty percent of the production finance. The remainder of the money is coming from private equity investment and tax relief schemes. According to Catherine, Richard initially intended to fund the entire production this way. This would have given Dan and her almost total creative control. And yet he was unable to secure all the finance without presales and distribution guarantees. Thus, he was forced to attach a sales agent to the project in order to 'get the bloody film made'.

When Jack gets to the office, all he can do is think about Freddie:

he decided yesterday that he would go and see him. Jack plans to leave at lunchtime and spend the afternoon with him. The expectation of seeing Freddie again after so long gradually builds inside him. It has been almost a year and Jack is not quite sure what he will say. It is not as if he has reached any profound conclusions about the novels Freddie gave him to read. *Resurrection* particularly moved him, yes – despite its Christian anarchism – and he admires Tolstoy's intense and vital commitment to a life of love and faith. He is curious to know now which author's vision Freddie most admires. He suspects that he will tell him it is Hardy's, if only because he is the most romantically tragic and fatalistic of the bunch.

Jack leaves the office at one o'clock sharp. He bundles down the stairs with his plastic bag full of books and hurries down the road towards the tube station. If he gets to Pimlico by half past one that will give him till five o'clock with Freddie, he calculates, after which he has three hours to get ready for Catherine – enough time to go to the supermarket, the florist, get back to Bethnal Green and prepare dinner.

The cobble-stone street leading down to the bookshop looks different in the winter sunshine. It is not that cold a day and Jack worries that Freddie might not be there. He struggles down the alleyway – the books are very heavy now, like big bars of gold bullion – until he reaches the shop back door. He looks at his watch. It is too early to call Catherine. She will most likely still be in her meeting. He will call her in a few hours. Jack clenches his fist and knocks. Just as before, there is a long period of silence before the old oak door swings open. 'The wanderer's returned,' Freddie says as he welcomes Jack inside, 'and with my precious books as well.'

'Yes at long last.'

'Well come in. I thought it'd take you this long.'

'I didn't… otherwise I wouldn't have agreed to bloody read them!'

Jack replies with a warm smile. 'So how have you been?' he asks as he closes the door behind him.

'Me... yes, fine,' Freddie answers brusquely, as he picks up a half-full bottle of whisky that sits by his bed. 'Want a drink?' he continues, as he pours a large measure into a glass.

'No, it's a bit early for me,' Jack issues a prompt reply.

'Fine,' Freddie says impatiently, 'and how are you?'

'Yes, not bad...' Jack hesitates. 'Look, I didn't mean that judgmentally. How much you drink... and when you drink it... well, it has nothing to do with me.'

'I know it doesn't!' Freddie says firmly, then swigs from his glass. 'Look I'm sorry. I've had a bad few weeks. I'm not sleeping at all. I'm...'

'It's okay. Look... I've come at a bad time, I should go.'

'No, that's not necessary.'

'You sure?'

'Yes,' Freddie replies. 'So tell me...' he goes on, 'Catherine, how is she?'

'She's well.'

'Things are better between you now?'

'What?' Jack says, sounding rather bemused, trying to recall what he told Freddie the last time they met.

'You told me that you loved her more than she loved you,' he says matter-of-factly.

'Oh yes... that's fine now. I mean... I think we're equally committed these days...' Jack dithers as he tries to articulate how his relationship with Catherine has developed since their last meeting.

'Good,' Freddie says as he plonks himself down on the old wooden chair by his desk. 'Jack, please sit down,' he goes on, motioning to the settee.

While Jack tries to make himself comfortable on the old sofa –

most of the springs have collapsed – he looks up to see Freddie reach for his half-moon spectacles that hang round his neck, lift them to his eyes, and peer down at him. 'So the books…' Jack says, 'there's some wonderful stuff there.' He waits for Freddie's acknowledgement but it is not forthcoming. He goes on, 'I made sure that I followed your instructions… I really read them, you know.' But Freddie's reticence continues. 'I let the authors get inside me…' Still nothing. All he does is just stare at Jack, with a vacant and detached expression.

Jack suddenly wonders whether he has got Freddie completely wrong. Had he seen something in him before that, in truth, does not exist, and was he right to assume that he might be able help him with his book? Shit, he could have just romanticised the whole bloody thing. Yes, perhaps Bill and Sam were right to take the piss out of him for having faith in a desperate, heartbroken old drunk, and Catherine's scepticism… well this seems pretty justified now as well. God, how could he have been so naïve! Jack berates himself.

'Good… good!' Freddie finally speaks, 'I knew you'd get into them like I urged you to. Not like when you read the damn things at school and university, I bet. I was right about you.'

'What were you right about?' Jack asks.

'Well, I knew that you'd be able to really grasp them, what these men were trying to say?'

'I must confess… I had difficulty with a few of them.'

Freddie stares down at the floor now, as if all of a sudden lost in his own thought. 'All love is, in the modern world, is a series of desperate and fractured encounters,' he says soberly. 'We meet someone, we fuck them till we think we love them, feeding off them like animals in a frenzy of relentless need, but then we tire of them, realising that it is not love we have with them after all, and so we leave them for another distressing, ephemeral encounter with someone else.'

'Who said this?'

'Sorry?' Freddie says, looking up from the floor, as if he temporarily forgot that Jack is here with him in his room. 'There's no point in looking for love in a selfish, violent and hypocritical world,' he goes on. 'They tell us love is the ultimate answer to life's predicament. This is a fairytale, a fallacy, a lie.'

'I can't believe you mean…'

'I would've reached this conclusion if I were Anna.'

'Oh yes… right,' Jack says, confirming this assessment of *Anna Karenina*, and relieved that Freddie has suddenly attributed this bleak philosophy to a fictional character rather than to himself.

'And what d'you make of Hardy? His vision is deeply romantic isn't it.'

'I thought he'd be your favourite,' Jack responds eagerly, now feeling more reassured that he has not got Freddie wrong, has not been duped by him. 'You know… I'm so pleased I read them though. Every sentence seemed pressing and urgent. Maybe this is because I'm trying to build a book out of what I read… I don't know,' he says, gaining in enthusiasm. 'But none of it felt stale. I relished them all, particularly Tolstoy. I must've been too young to appreciate them before, the ones I'd read anyhow… or not alive enough. The whole exercise had been too academic. But this time, it felt so much more than this. It awoke something inside me… really shook me, made me feel alive!'

'Yes. Yes!' Freddie exclaims jubilantly, and gets to his feet. 'This is exactly it! This is what important literature should do, must do!' and he turns to his desk now, pushes the chair aside and starts to rummage through the enormous pile of notebooks, as if searching for a particular one.

'I think I've developed a similar system to you.'

'What d'you mean?'

'Sorry, I was just looking at all your notebooks and it made me think of what my own desk looks like.'

'Right,' Freddie mutters preoccupied as he scrolls down the page of a particular notebook, his index finger moving frantically from right to left. 'Yes, here we are,' he says, then reads aloud, 'It is plain that the object of my quest, the truth, lies not in the cup but in myself… I put down my cup and examine my own mind.' Freddie puts the notebook down and looks at Jack now. 'Proust. Literature is this cup, yes,' Freddie goes on, and before Jack has a chance to consider this, Freddie speaks again. 'Literature makes us ask critical questions, of others and ourselves. Look at Proust in *A la Recherche du temps perdu*. The whole damn thing is a search for the truth. This takes balls, let me tell you, fourteen years of painful self-examination,' and he pours himself another drink, swigs it. 'Proust thinks that love arises only in pursuit of the unattainable and can survive only in an atmosphere of jealousy. What d'you make of this? Can you relate to it? True or false, Jack?'

'I don't know… I…'

But Freddie interrupts him almost immediately. 'Marcel becomes a sadist, locks Albertine up in his parent's house, so convinced is he by his fantasies of her betraying him.'

'I haven't read it.'

'You must!' Freddie replies and drinks again. He is fired up now, wants to talk, tell Jack things. 'And then there's dear old Aschenbach in *Death in Venice*. Don't know the German for it. I read it again recently. Is he right to let himself become a slave to obsessive desire if art has failed to bring him any closer to the truth?'

These have become rhetorical questions now, and Jack feels like a drink, pours himself a whisky. 'At last, he succumbs!' Freddie says, noticing this, then continues where he left off.

Freddie starts to pace up and down now as he continues talking, and Jack feels like he is watching a live performance – a one-man show

– in which the protagonist is trying to make sense of himself and the world around him. His mind takes flight, jumping restlessly from one writer to the next, one idea to another. Jack finishes his whisky in no time at all and pours himself another.

'Eliot says about modern society that beneath the veneer of respectability, there are simply "half-deserted streets/The muttering retreats/Of restless nights in one-night cheap hotels/And sawdust restaurants with oyster-shells," Freddie continues.

His hands move furiously now, like a conductor driving the orchestra of his thoughts to a great crescendo. 'Tomas in *The Unbearable Lightness of Being* says that "attaching love to sex is one of the most bizarre ideas the Creator ever had."'

And on he goes, referring to more writers, more ideas. All Jack can do is listen.

Jack continues to drink and slowly loses track of time.

As Freddie carries on talking, now seeming to use the momentum of his footsteps to drive his thoughts, Jack notices that he is full of passion, poses vital questions, and yet he avoids giving his own opinion. 'But what's *your* view?' Jack finally asks him.

And Freddie is all of a sudden silent. Jack watches as his hands drop to his side, he exhales deeply and slouches forward, head angled down at the floor. It is as if he is a balloon that has just been punctured, all air escaping him. He sinks down, into his chair. The room is darker, the whisky bottle almost empty. 'About what?' he mumbles.

'Well what you've been talking about all this time.'

'It changes from day-to-day,' he mutters. 'On a good day, I'll preach love, but on a bad day, I'll deny it even exists.'

He stares at his notebooks now, strewn all over his desk. He starts to tidy them.

'So… you write yourself then?' Jack asks.

'In my own way,' Freddie replies abruptly.

His elusiveness hangs in the air now and draws out an awkward muteness between the two of them. Just as before, Jack is desperate to discover more about his life but he will not push him to answer these questions, not now, not just yet.

Jack finally looks at his watch: it is seven o'clock. The realisation that he is terribly late does not dawn on him straight away. The alcohol has delayed all his natural responses; it takes a few minutes for a moment of clarity to arise from the foggy haze of his drunken mind. And when it finally does, when it at last comes to him, it does so with all the painful self-recrimination of an alcoholic. 'Oh shit… shit. I'm an arsehole!' he says, heaving himself up off the settee.

'What's the matter?'

'I've got to go. Fuck!'

'What are you doing?'

'I'm really late for Catherine. I'm sorry. It's my fault. She had an important meeting today. I forgot to call her, I was so involved with what you were saying…'

'Right…'

'Freddie, thanks for everything… the book, the drink, all you talked about…' he slurs, picking up his coat and slinging it clumsily over his shoulder. He goes on, 'I… I'd like to buy you lunch just to say thanks. There are a few places in Shepherd's Bush. How about we meet over there?'

'When d'you want to do that?'

'Look, can I call you or something?'

'You can leave a message with Joseph,' Freddie says, handing Jack an old, rather worn business card for the bookshop.

'Right, okay… I'm sorry to leave like this, in such a hurry… it's just that I'd promised her, that's all,' Jack says as he slips the card inside his wallet.

'You go!' Freddie says firmly.

Jack bundles himself out of the back door.

As he runs towards the station, he realises that he is far too late to prepare the romantic dinner he intended to. However, the florist might still be open near the station, he thinks: it might sell gardenias, which Catherine loves so much; their beautiful cream colour, their rich smell, sweet and thick. But no, it is closed. Catherine has always maintained to Jack that she could lose herself in a field of gardenias.

When he gets back to Bethnal Green, Catherine is slouched on the sofa and, it appears, drinking heavily. He can instantly tell what the outcome of the meeting was. She looks sad, weary, as she rubs the middle of her forehead with her index finger in a circular motion.

'I'm sorry Catherine,' Jack says as he sits down beside her.

'Dan's walked,' she says flatly. Dan and her have developed an intense working relationship, which Catherine has thrived off. Jack is not sure what she will do now without him. Yes, he knows she will still be able to do her job, but something will be missing now. She continues, 'I think Concept wanted to get rid of him all along. The two main people there knew that Richard had full chain of title.'

'He owns all the drafts you mean?'

'Yes, so if Dan walks, Richard can still make the film without him.'

'Why didn't Richard refuse them?'

'Well they would've pulled all the money, wouldn't they!' she demands impatiently.

'But I mean… what was so bad about his favoured draft?'

'You know, I've told you!' Catherine shouts at him now.

'I…' he struggles to get his words out. Jack knows that a sustained argument against Catholicism's repressive sexuality ran through it. But was it this, or its treatment of suicide, that Concept objected to, Jack wonders. He goes to pose this question, but she answers it for him.

'They don't want her to die, Jack, they don't want her to kill herself.' Jack recalls now what Catherine previously told him about this part of the script. She and Dan wrote a compassionate defence of suicide, portraying it as a beautiful act, not an ugly sin. 'Concept said it doesn't want to cause offence to the Catholic Church,' Catherine continues, 'and has always been more interested in making a romantic drama rather than a polemical piece debunking Catholicism.' She polishes off her glass of wine. 'I don't know where I'm going with it now…'

Jack does not say anything right away: he is not sure how he can console her. He gets to his feet and heads for the bathroom.

'Why didn't you ring me?' Catherine calls to Jack just before he closes the door behind him.

'I went to see Freddie, to return the books… and well, we had a lot to talk about… he did anyway. I'm sorry, really Catherine, I meant to call you, I lost track of time.'

'I can't believe you forgot. You knew how important this was to me.'

'Look, I meant to call you… I should've called you, I'm sorry. Why don't I order us in some food?'

'It's not about the fucking food!' she shouts, jumping to her feet now.

'Look, give me two seconds alright.' Jack hurries into the bathroom, urinates fast. He exits to find Catherine leaning on the edge of the settee, waiting for him. She frowns at him, her face still full of anger. 'Catherine… I think you're making too much of this,' he goes on.

'How can you say that?'

'Not about Dan, the film, but about me being late.' She says nothing. He continues, 'Look, I've apologised, I'm here now, and I'll listen to you all night… I know how frustrated you must be, I'm sorry.'

'You know what, I don't even want to talk about it I'm so bloody angry with you. Let's speak about it tomorrow night.'

'I'm not here then, you know that.'

'Jack, we have to talk.'

'Let's talk about it now then.'

'I've told you I don't want to tonight.'

'When then?'

'Tomorrow.'

'You expect me to stay in London another night?'

'Yes.'

'Have you stopped to consider *me* in this?' he asks her. Catherine does not answer him but walks through into the kitchen. He watches her as she opens another bottle of Rioja. He continues, 'Catherine, it was important that I see Freddie today. I've spent almost a year working my way through all those books he gave me. This is my project… it's…'

'Jack, I don't think you can compare the two,' she says dismissively as she walks back into the front room.

'And what the fuck does that mean?'

'This film is my professional future right now.'

'The book might become *my* future.'

'Jesus Jack, you don't even have a clear idea as yet of the kind of book you want to write. You've become fixated with this grief-stricken man you met on a bus. You seem to think he holds the key to some kind of universal truth, I don't know… it's bloody perverse, grotesque! I mean, what's he said or done that's so fucking profound? Come on…'

'He saved my life for God's sake!'

'Oh don't be so bloody melodramatic, Jack!'

'You weren't there! They had a knife! Look, even if he didn't save my life, he sure as hell saved me from getting badly hurt.'

'And so because of this you now owe him something?'

'What are you talking about?'

'Well… you've just been to see him again. Why else would you go?'

'He's helping me with my book, you know that…' he insists. 'He's got some… some fascinating things to say…'

'Oh come on Jack! You're a highly educated man who's been taught by some of the leading professors in the country. What the hell are you going to get from this Freddie?'

'There's something there, I tell you. He has an intensity about him that all these damn professors lack. He feels as well as thinks. He's alive, Catherine… really fucking alive!'

'It sounds like he's suffering terribly. Is this what you call "being alive"?'

'Yes he's suffered a lot, he still does, but he carries a dignity inside him.'

'How d'you know this, Jack? What d'you really know about him? You've only met him four times!'

'I'm sure of it.'

'Why d'you need to be sure?'

'Because it sounds like that's a pre-requisite for you.'

'Jack… you know very little about this man? I mean, did he tell you anything more about himself this afternoon?'

'We talked mainly about novels. Look, does it really matter what he did before his wife died… before he started drinking, before he fell apart?'

'Yes, it does.'

'He must've been an academic of some kind. His knowledge of literature and modern philosophy is extremely good.'

'Look, I don't want to talk about him anymore!' she shouts, stamping her foot on the floor now like a petulant child.

'But Catherine…'

'I'm tired, Jack, d'you hear me?' she says, collapsing on the settee.
'Okay.'

'I'm so scared I'm going to fuck it up now. I can't see this draft… it's weak, not as strong. I don't think I'm up to making the kind of film they want me to… it just feels like a stupid, soppy romantic drama now. But if I'm honest with myself, Jack… and this is what's crazy, I wasn't even sure about our preferred draft. Genevieve has always maintained that it smacks of pretension. She said she always thought that I was more astute than *Crisis of Faith*. Well… it looks like she was right after all. For now I'm going to end up making a naff film instead of a bloody self-indulgent one! Richard's assured me that he still believes in the project and thinks that it'll work out okay. But I don't know. You know, I… I really need you with me at the moment.' Jack is silent. She continues, 'Stay with me, Jack… until the film's over. You can write from here?'

'I can't do that, you know I can't,' he says, sitting down beside her and holding her hand.

'But why not?'

'I won't be able to work in this flat. I need my own space, my books… all my things.'

'Don't you love me anymore?'

'This isn't about love, Catherine.'

'What's it about then?' she asks defensively.

'It's about your need, Catherine, what you *need* from me.'

'Fuck you, Jack!'

'Look… this is crazy. I'll still be with you three nights a week. I'll be all yours when I'm here in London, I promise,' he assures her. 'But I must get on with this book.'

'I just want you to be here when I get home late at night,' she says, leaning over and putting her hand on his crotch. 'Just so I can roll into bed beside you and you can hold me and make love to me…' she says, rubbing him through his trousers.

He pulls away from her when she tries to kiss him. 'Catherine… what are you doing? You don't need to do this. Stop it!'

She jumps up from the settee and in one swift motion flies into the kitchen. He listens as she slams drawers and curses out loud. Then he hears the pop of a cork: she has opened her third bottle of wine. He looks up to see her standing in the doorway clutching the bottle by its neck. Red wine drips from her mouth, down her chin, onto her chest; it looks like she has gotten into a fight. She stands there, topless, swinging her bra in her arms like a cheap striptease artist in a grotty working man's pub. Jack wants to confront her, but no, he knows she is being driven by drink now and will not readily submit either to his criticism or to self-examination. 'Why are you so fascinated by him?' she asks, twirling her hair around her fingers, which leads Jack to wonder whether this is a gesture she has made to other men before him.

'Who?'

'Freddie.'

'I've told you.'

'No, I mean aside from his knowledge, what d'you think he can offer you, what is it about him?'

'I think it's because he's let his love for one woman destroy his whole life. His life almost had to come to some kind of dramatic end when she died.'

'Wouldn't you be ruined like Freddie if something happened to me?' she asks softly, standing over Jack.

'Yes, but…' he dithers, struggling with her question, which he knows requires a definitive answer.

'Jack?'

'No… but even when I'm with you, there's a very small part of me which can just walk away. I think that independent, self-sufficient part of me is very important. I think people find it comforting to know that they can stand alone.'

'Well I'm not one of these people, Jack. I don't. Not anymore… since you've shown me what it is to love. What are you saying here? That you could just walk out of my life at any moment…'

'Catherine, I'm not saying that.'

'Well what are you saying then?'

'I'm just saying that this bit of me which no one else can see… well, it helps me keep a sense of who I am. I mean… you have that with your journal, don't you? It's you, it's not for me to see…'

'Yes, but that bit of me still wants you all the time…'

'No… but I'm saying that if I know I can be on my own, that I can cope on my own, then this makes the love I feel for you even stronger. It's like I'm free to choose to love you… rather than feeling as though I must love you, because if I didn't… well, then I'd fall apart… be nothing without you. Don't you see?' Jack says, feeling rather unsure now of what he is saying. He desperately wants to be sure. He wonders whether if he possessed a stronger sense of self – who he actually is and what his life means to him – this would benefit their relationship.

'You'd better be fucking crazy about me, you cunt!' she screams, throwing a glass at Jack. It smashes against the mirror behind him. Catherine rushes to the bedroom.

'Where's this all come from, Catherine?' he demands. 'Everything's been so perfect between us. What are you doing?'

She slams the bedroom door. Jack does not follow her but sits alone in the front room.

He wakes up the following morning, heavy-headed and tired: Jack spent the night on the settee. He sits upright and glances down at last night's debris on the coffee table. Next to one of the empty bottles of wine is a crumpled-up piece of paper, the only new item on the table. He looks at his watch. It is seven thirty. Catherine will have left already, he thinks. Jack heaves himself off the sofa and goes to the bedroom to check. Yep, she has gone. He wanders back into the front room. He will tidy up, then have a quick shower.

Jack goes to clear the coffee table. Wine bottles first, then other bits and bobs. He drops the screwed-up piece of paper in the bin, then hesitates, wondering if there is anything written inside it. He retrieves it and unfolds it; the piece of paper reveals itself as a page that has been torn from a notebook, it looks like. It is Catherine's handwriting. It starts off neat and precise but then becomes more disjointed and chaotic further down the page, and black ink is smeared in one corner making the words barely legible. It appears to Jack that maybe she planned to destroy what she wrote, screwing it up in her fist, but then hesitated once she had committed herself, and subsequently left it here, on the table. He wonders whether this page is taken from her journal. If so, he is reluctant to read it, and yet surely if she left it here, well then it is intended for him. She would not have left it otherwise. Yes, Catherine wants him to read it, Jack tells himself now.

It begins, 'You can't just love me, Jack. I need to be loved beyond reason. I don't feel alive unless I know that we're fully in love. You know what I was like before. I didn't let anyone get to me. And look at me now, I feel completely at your mercy… at times utterly helpless without you. You must love me as much as I love you. You've got to drop down dead for me, like Freddie did for Molly. If you don't love me like this, you're not for me. Totally unreasonable, I know. Throw yourself off this building for me. Do it! Show me you love me. Otherwise, what we've got is shit! Don't be bookish and insular with me. When you're like this, you make me want to scream. I need the desperation and the passion, the breathlessness, the physical ache, the pain that you feel from real desire. I want it so badly not just because I'm romantic. I want it more because with it comes freedom. If you've found what you're looking for, it releases you, free to be who and what you are. I believe this now! You can't be happy without it. I'm too weak to leap without it. Reach out and grab life, Jack. Treat it as a gift. Live it… be free. I don't want your love carved in stone. I want it carved in my fucking heart!' Catherine concludes.

Jack holds the piece of paper in his hand, does not know what to make of what he has just read. How should he interpret, respond to it? She sounds so desperate, as if she had to write these things just to get them out of herself. Better that they be on paper than running riot in her head. Yes, maybe they were just this for her, a necessary catharsis, he tells himself. Catherine could not really have meant some of these things, surely. She cannot expect Jack to give her what she asks of him here. It would be madness.

And yet Jack fears that she *does* actually mean some of them. There is a wildness and extremity to Catherine, he has always known this about her. Yes, she is aware that she is asking for an impossible kind of love, a violent and destructive kind, but she will ask for it anyway. Maybe he can give her this, yes, love her to this extent, like Freddie loved Molly. And perhaps their love is not real unless he is prepared to do just this.

But he cannot stay with her in London. He must get on and write. But he can do both, yes. Jack can still love Catherine as she wants him to, of course he can.

# 15

**JACK GETS** back to the cottage fairly late. There is a message on the answer machine. He presses play, waits, then hears Catherine's voice. 'Hi, it's me, I'm sorry. I came on too strong, that was unfair. I must have freaked you out.' Her voice sounds quieter, calmer than it did last night. She continues, 'You didn't read what I wrote, did you? I left it there, didn't I, for you to see. It must've been too much. I sometimes just have to get it out. You don't need to stay with me all the time. But you must be here with me those three nights. I couldn't bear any less than that. See you Sunday. I love you,' she finishes off. The machine beeps. End of message.

He sits down on the stairs, puts his head back, and lets out an enormous sigh. He knows that Catherine, like him, has a propensity for melodrama: she has to feel the endless longing and desire. However, he is not sure what he wants now that she has revealed herself to him, so needy. Yes, a part of Jack is prepared to love Catherine as much as she has asked him too – he can be just as romantic as her – yet another part of him is not prepared to give this much of himself. He thinks back to when she finally told him she loved him and wanted to be with him, how she was then; Jack found it almost unbearable to see her suffer like this.

He reaches for his phone now in his pocket, dials her number. 'Catherine… I…' he says. It is her answer phone. He waits for her pre-recorded message to finish, then continues, 'Hi, I got your message. Thanks. Look, I love you too, I really do. I hope you're okay now. Call me when you get this.' Then he hangs up, gets to his feet and walks upstairs to the bedroom.

Jack sits on the edge of the bed and stares at the reflection of her mahogany chest in the long mirror, then pictures her journals inside it, this hidden world of Catherine's. He suddenly feels compelled to open it up, just take a peep, read some of what she has written. Jack knows where she keeps the key: it is in the bottom drawer of her dressing table. He retrieves it and pulls the chest out from underneath the bed. As he lifts its lid, he is struck by quite how many journals there are. Jack proceeds to count them, there are twenty-three in all, one for every year since her father left. He listens again to those words she whispered in his ear the first night they spent together: 'Never read my journal…' But now, he wants to know everything about her, all the events of her past. He has to. For since reading what he did this morning, he now feels he does not really understand her again: he is with a woman he does not know, someone who keeps things from him and someone he can never hope to fathom. As he looks at her journals a second time, he realises with striking clarity that now he has the opportunity to really know her. Yes, this is it.

He grabs the first available one and opens it at a random page. The entry is dated 3rd February. It reads, 'A guy came on to me tonight. I didn't do anything. I wanted to though. I feel like this when Jack doesn't adore me. I feel dry and empty. That's when I just want to go and fuck another guy, just to feel adored again.' He flicks forward to another entry, dated 27th November. She writes, 'I worry about what will happen if Jack died, leaving me all alone. I become cold to him when I feel like this. I don't want to make love to him… don't want him to be inside me, touch me, even come near me. I fear needing him too much. I hate this feeling sometimes. It dominates me, controls everything I do. Sometimes, I want to smash our relationship to bits. When I feel like this, I behave badly towards him, I know: I must put doubts in his mind and make him question our future. I always want to tell him I'm sorry straight after. But I sometimes can't help myself. Part of me always feels compelled to test Jack, the relationship, be suspicious… just like my cunting mother. I can never be quite sure, despite how much I want to be. I do try and stop myself, but so often I just don't understand how I feel. I don't want to be like this anymore. But I can't…' Jack cannot read any more of this entry, feels flustered and distressed. He throws this journal to the floor, snatches another one from the chest, opens it at 6th June. 'I wanted him to love me,' she writes. 'Why didn't he? Why did he leave like that? He can't have loved me if he left like that. Ma says he doesn't give a damn about me. If he did, he'd at least come back and see me. But papa's probably happy with another daughter now. She says he's probably forgotten all about me.' She must have written this when she was a lot younger, Jack thinks. He looks for a year but cannot find one: nothing on the cover or the spine. He puts this one down and ferrets around in the chest for another volume. The next one he picks up has no year recorded on it either. He turns to a random page and starts reading: 'It's 30th August and I'm terrified of going mad again. The low periods are unbearable. If I can just keep myself on an even keel, together… then it'll pass, I know it will, like before. I know a part of me likes to indulge the highs. I can completely lose myself in them. I feel like I'm flying, like I can do anything. It's a magical feeling. I become totally lost in my work… I become convinced that I'm creating something magnificent… something that will change the course of filmmaking for years to come. Mad and absurd, I know. Deluded, absolutely. I feel that I'm almost in possession of magical, supernatural powers. I think I can fly. It's a kind of ecstasy of freedom and happiness. But all the time, I'm waiting for the fall, when things suddenly seem not as dazzling… as beautiful. And when it finally comes, I'm completely at its mercy. I just can't stop its momentum. It's utterly relentless. It's intent on dragging me from the sky to the ground, from happiness to despair, from light to dark. I become an utterly hollow and silent woman. I don't know if I could live through another episode. I've had three or four, and got through them… but I don't know if I'd have the strength, the will, to go through another one,' she concludes.

What is this side of her he has just uncovered? Jack wonders. She sounds like she has experienced so much pain. Poor Catherine. He recalls what she told him immediately after she first said she loved him. He replays these words now in his head: 'I thought I was losing my mind again.' No, he cannot face to read any more. Enough. What is he doing anyway? What does he hope to understand about her? Jack closes the journal with a thump. He must get all of them back in the chest right now, lock them up, and return them to their rightful home underneath the bed, out of sight. He should not have read them in the first place: he has broken his promise to her, betrayed her.

And so, in a mad flurry of guilt-ridden activity, Jack returns all the journals to the chest, shoves it back into place, returns the key to the dressing table, then sits back down on the bed and tries to gather himself. He is breathing heavily, sweating, his thoughts race. He vows that he will never read them again. They are Catherine's. He has no right!

As he sits here, Jack's mind churns. First, he worries about her mental state, and then he wonders whether romantic love is in fact a subtle form of madness, a kind of mutual delirium. Does their relationship have to be so all consuming and does he really want the kind of intense love he has with her? It seems that up to this point, he and Catherine cannot co-exist unless one of them craves and needs the other at different times. They found equality in love, but this did not last long. Perhaps there just has to be conflict between them ... they both need a battleground? Maybe they are incapable of inhabiting the adult world as mature and equal lovers? His happiness is inextricably linked to hers, yes, as if the same disease of feeling and neediness contaminates them both. And Jack cannot face this bitter aspect of their relationship right now, which does not constitute the perfection he has assigned it. He needs a distraction, yes, to throw himself into something, to escape into another realm of being. He hopes that the detached and analytical world of the book will provide this.

Jack lies down on the bed, stares at the ceiling and starts to seek solace in the intellectualisations of his book. He has always made recourse to his analytical mind, this trusted part of him, when he has not been able to manage his emotional world, and now is no exception. And so he begins to shape the pain of his feelings into cold thoughts and clinical concepts, and he knows this process of transformation will provide him with the relief he is after. And it does just this.

Over the next few days, Jack begins to write about whether romantic love is necessary to acquire happiness: this is to be one of the key themes of his book. Freddie's fate has forced him to seriously contemplate this question, and it is a crucial one for him to answer. He has a run of three clear days before his mother and sister are due to turn up. First, he considers whether romantic love is more of a hindrance than a gift. Jack knows there are many people who maintain that a full life cannot be lead without it. The absence of romantic love in someone's life confines this person to a destitute and hollow existence: one human life has to be confirmed by another! But cannot God or another kind of spiritual entity serve this function just as well, Jack speculates now, and fulfil this need for another's love. A Buddhist monk is self-sufficient: his existence does not solely depend upon the love of another. Rather, he is guided by the teachings of the Buddha. And then there is a Franciscan monk, who is subservient to God. He finds happiness not from romantic love but from God's unconditional love. For him, life in the service of a spiritual entity is more fulfilling than a life dedicated to loving another human being. And so, as Jack sees it now, romantic love in the West is built around the notion of individual fulfilment. A secular Westerner seeks out a lover who will compliment his ego, enhance his quality of life, increase his personal happiness: the restless quest for personal development and fulfilment drives him forward in his search to be loved, and to find someone to love. On the other hand, love in the East is built around the notion of universal love. A spiritual Easterner is driven less by a nagging desire for personal fulfilment and gratification, and more by the collective will to love, and the collective consciousness for love. The Buddha perceives love as a universal emotion, independent of the self. This love, *metta sutta*, extends to all humanity. And most importantly, it does not rely upon the receipt of another's love: it is not narcissistic, but rather detached, objective and unconditional. Jack wants to know which kind of love someone should ultimately aspire to. And yet he realises he will certainly not get the time to answer this prior to his mother and sister's arrival on Friday evening. He will have to save it for a later date. They are due to spend most of the weekend with him, and he plans travel back to London with them on Sunday. He quietly prays that when he sees Catherine, things will be better between them.

He and Sally spend the whole of Saturday morning cooking, while his mother relaxes in a deck chair in the garden – wrapped in a heavy woollen blanket to guard against the raw blue cold – and reads D. H. Lawrence, her favourite pastime. Jack tells Sally all about his progress on the book and how Freddie has inspired him thus far. His sister, a social worker specialising in the area of mental health, is intrigued to know more about Freddie. From a very young age, she has been passionate about social welfare. She used to throw social statistics across the Sunday dinner table throughout Jack's childhood and adolescence, and the combination of hers and their mother's social consciences represented a formidable force. In fact, Jack's intellectual idealism could never match the collective brute force of his mother's and sister's social and political dinner diatribes, which they fired at him and his father when both of them were least expecting it, as they chomped their way through tasty tender pieces of roast beef. Both women always quoted passages from *The Observer*, as befitted a compassionate mother and her socialist daughter, never *The Times* or 'that God-awful *Telegraph*', as his mother venomously referred to it. Well, their social consciences had rubbed off on him, inevitably. 'Shit Jack,' Sally says, 'He sounds like he's had a terrible time. He's suffering from some kind of mental illness.'

'Why d'you say that?'

'Because a lot of homeless people are.'

'Does a broken heart constitute a mental illness?'

'Jack… from what you've told me about him, Freddie hardly sounds like a picture of perfect mental health.'

'Well… who is?'

'Certainly not you!' she quips. 'Listen, you say he's got somewhere to sleep… but he only uses it during the winter…'

'Yeah, from what he's told me. He says he'd rather sleep outside when the weather's okay,' Jack says as his mother enters the kitchen and the oven timer buzzes violently. The roast is ready.

'Mum, it's all done,' Sally reassures her. 'We're doing everything. Just go and sit down and we'll bring the food out,' she says, pushing her out of the kitchen and gesturing to the fully laid table. Two hours earlier, he and Sally were almost forced to man-handle their mother out of the kitchen after she suggested she was 'quite happy to cook'. The two of them demanded it was now their turn to look after her, after her many years of selfless care and support. Jack proceeds to cut the joint of roast lamb, the scent of rosemary filling the room, while Sally serves the potatoes and vegetables. His mother sits there quietly like a spare tyre, unsure what to do with herself now her children are finally providing for her. Sally plonks a full plate in front of her. She waits patiently until both her children are sitting beside her, and then with her trademark expression, 'This looks lovely' – which no longer even requires a cue – she tucks into her roast dinner. 'You know, a society has got to be judged by the way it cares for its vulnerable,' Sally goes on. She has not finished talking about Freddie. 'I mean… what kind of help is he getting?'

'I don't know, but…'

'Well I can bet you bugger all!' she interrupts Jack. 'Jesus, if you look at Freddie as a case in point, our society is doing fucking awfully. And the bloody government always blames it on drugs!'

'Well yeah, there are a lot of young…'

Sally will not let him finish. 'It's not only just saying no to drugs that keeps you off the streets these days… I mean, Freddie, he's a drinker, isn't he!' she says, on a mission now to prove her point. 'More than a third of London's homeless are mentally ill and in need of help. Who's caring for them? If Freddie's got any chance of getting the rest of his life back, he needs some psychiatric support.'

Jack looks at his mother now as she challenges her daughter. 'Sally, you can't help everyone, you know. Not everyone wants to be rescued.'

'Well, from what Jack's told me about Freddie… it sounds like he could do with a bit of rescuing. I mean… people like him, who spend a lot of time on the streets and drink heavily, are way more likely to kill themselves. And a lot of them are just left to bloody rot and drink themselves to death!' Sally demands, banging her clenched fist on the table. This action causes Jack to bite his upper lip and drop some part-masticated lamb out of his mouth onto the table beside his plate. He quickly scoops it up in his vacant hand and shoves it back in his mouth, swallowing it whole so it cannot escape again.

'Jack, please!' his mother instantly reprimands him for his animalistic eating habits.

'Mm… I…' he mumbles, his lip hurting too much to tell her it was just an accident.

As Sally continues her rant, Jack is left to think about Catherine and what he will say to her when he next sees her.

He returns to London with his mother and sister on Sunday morning. Jack wants to spend as much time with Catherine as possible: she is due to leave for Northampton first thing Monday and he will not see her again until the following Sunday. It is a warm winter's day. They lounge in Victoria Park with the Sunday papers and a picnic.

'I'm sorry again for what I said last week. It scares me when I'm like that…' Catherine says contemplatively while rolling onto her back.

'It's okay,' Jack replies, as he tries not to think about what he has read in her journals. She looks beautiful today: dreamy, almost ethereal, like she has been released from something that has been troubling her. 'You seem a lot better,' he goes on.

'Yeah… I was very angry with myself after what I said to you, how I behaved. I don't know why I felt so… It must be because I hadn't let myself be dependent on anyone else for such a long time. I think I'd started to take you for granted… I imagined you'd always be there.'

Jack nods while Catherine stares up at the cool blue sky, lifting her blouse till it is just below her breasts. She rubs her stomach in a circular, clockwise motion and munches on a chicken drumstick, which she holds in her other hand. As he kisses her stomach and accidentally runs his tongue over her navel – that part of her anatomy, which she does not like him touching – she says softly, 'Jack, I'm going to see my mother again.'

'What?' he asks in disbelief as he tries to process what she has just said, like it has been spoken in a foreign language. 'You've talked to her?'

'No, but I wrote to her and she's just written back. I got her letter yesterday morning.'

'You wrote to her?'

'Yeah.'

'What brought this on? It wasn't because of what happened between us, was it… after I left you like that?' he asks tentatively.

'No Jack, I'd written to her before.'

'Right.'

'I think I'm finally beginning to understand her, you see. I've just felt more sympathetic to her lately… she's been on my mind,' Catherine says. 'I used to hate ma for having her faith. It never made any sense to me when she'd stumble home drunk with another young man on her arm, embarrass me, be cruel to me, then tell me that she was only doing it because of my "bastard father", because divorce was a sin. I never knew whom to be angry with… her, my papa, her young lovers or her God. I had to blame someone back then. But I'm starting to see why her faith was… still is… so important to her, and why she felt she had to impose it on me. She had to feel desirable… she wanted men to adore her, but at the same time she yearned for a kind of pure love, one that was not dependent upon a man but rather a spiritual entity… God. I… I think I'm ready to see her again, Jack… really, I am.'

'What does she say in her letter?'

'She might come to Oxford after the film. I told her about you, you know,' Catherine says now. 'It's funny, but despite everything she's done, I do miss her.'

'Course you do,' he reassures her. 'So how d'you feel about it?'

'I'm a little scared. If we don't make up… what then? What will I do?' she says with trepidation.

'Come on, don't think like that.'

'You know, sometimes she could do the most wonderful things,' Catherine says, speaking almost to herself now as she looks up at the sun. 'I remember one time, I was about twelve, she stopped talking to me. It lasted the whole week… her enforced silence. All she did was make me breakfast before I went to school and dinner when I came home. I'd upset her by telling her that I didn't like her current boyfriend and that he looked at me funnily. She'd got rid of him that same night, but she was really angry with me nevertheless. I tried to tell her I was sorry, but she wouldn't listen. By the end of the week, I was sure she'd never speak to me again, she seemed so furious. And so when I came home on Friday evening, I headed straight up to my room – she hadn't tidied it all week and it was really messy, clothes everywhere – but I couldn't believe what I saw when I opened the door: she'd re-decorated my whole bedroom! It was like a fairytale, the best thing any young girl could wish for, really. She'd bought me a beautiful wooden bed, a big fluffy duvet, new cream sheets, matching curtains, new dresses in my wardrobe, a white dressing table; it was a beautiful white, I remember. She made me so happy that night.'

'I'm sure she will again,' he whispers tenderly in her ear.

They make love that evening back in the flat. Catherine is quieter, more subdued, and Jack wonders whether this is an inevitable consequence of her working so hard or perhaps something more. Beneath her fatigue, there seems to lurk a quiet sadness, he feels, a sense of uneasiness about what might lie ahead.

Catherine leaves for Northampton very early the next morning. She is doing a three-day recce up there; they plan to shoot an interior scene in a Catholic church, one of the few locations in the film outside London. Jack tries not to worry about her reticence. The book will be his distraction again.

# 16

IT IS JUST before sunset as Jack walks up to the magnolia tree that stands at the foot of the garden. On his own in the cottage, when he is not writing, he likes to plod around outside, so beautiful in springtime after the dark winter months when he and Catherine first moved in: then the garden was deprived of light and colour, but not now. The magnolia looks wonderful. Most of the buds are not fully developed, just tight clusters of deep pink. But a few have already flowered, their pink petals opening out as magnolia white, that irrefutable shade of white. Jack pulls a branch down to his eye-line and studies one of the more mature flowers. It seems to him, as he holds a large petal close, that as they blossom, the dusky pink gives way to the white.

Jack wonders now if there are any magnolias at the back of Joseph's bookshop: it is in Magnolia Mews after all. But then he realises that even if there are some there, he probably would not have spotted them since winter has the habit of making even the magnolia look bland and mediocre, and he has not been there during any other season.

What is Freddie doing right now? Jack asks himself. He will probably be sleeping outside on a day like this. Jack smiles as he remembers that he still owes him lunch.

He has thought very little about Freddie, not since Catherine confronted him about his interest in him. She clearly does not like the idea of him seeing Freddie. But Jack is still drawn to him, yes, though he knows that his curiosity is principally founded on the fact that he still knows so little about him. Granted, he holds an enormous amount of pity for the man – and he hopes that one day he might be able to help him in some way – but beyond this selfless, philanthropic instinct, he is motivated by a selfish desire, a restless intrigue to uncover Freddie's life story. He cannot deny this.

Jack decides to make the most of the warm evening. He shall fetch a book from inside. He knows that he spends far too much time cooped up in his study – driven by his inexorable need to be productive, to write a certain amount of words – and the garden, well it offers him closure at the end of every day, a kind of liberation from the intense academic process that he goes through indoors.

He turns on the outside light and settles down in the rickety deck chair, which sits underneath the magnolia, with Sam's copy of *The Purity of Love*: he still has not given it back yet. Jack took it off the bookshelf this morning; it seemed to be the perfect antidote to Hardy's idea of mania, heavy stuff, which he had been writing about the last couple of days.

As he reads it now for a second time, Jack feels his mind open up and his mood lighten. Gold seems to really capture love in its fullness, he thinks, its complex and often contradictory nature. But the work is still passionately optimistic: the hero will endure. The sense Jack gets from this re-reading is that the author simply refuses to let his protagonist be defeated. No, he must win through, though his journey will be hard. This is a far cry from the inevitable tragedy of Hardy's vision, which sees little room for love and hope in a world where people are controlled by impersonal, indifferent and mysterious forces that guarantee their suffering.

Jack is struck by certain similarities between what he knows thus far of Freddie and what he now rediscovers in Leonard Gold's novel. First, the protagonist's wife is an artist as Molly was. Second, he is forty years old when his wife dies; Jack estimates that Freddie was probably the same age when Molly died. And third, the hero of the novel has a love of literature not dissimilar from Freddie's own. Jack has not read anything else by Leonard Gold. He knows he has written four other novels – according to the introduction to the edition he now reads – all of them to critical acclaim, but he has produced nothing since *The Purity of Love* as far as he knows. His abrupt absence from the literary world seems to Jack somewhat irregular and perplexing. It is as if he has all but disappeared.

Jack has the sudden sense he is on to something. He must call Sam. He hurries inside and picks up the phone.

'Listen, I've got a question for you,' he says as soon as Sam picks up, not even giving his friend time to acknowledge him. 'Leonard Gold, the author of *The Purity of Love*, remember, the one I took out of your office… what happened to him?'

'I don't know. Why?'

'I'm curious, that's all. He hasn't written anything since then, has he?'

'You're calling me at midnight to ask me this?'

'Yeah… sorry.'

'Well no, I don't think he has,' Sam says. 'Strange… because he was such a wonderful novelist.'

'That's just what I was thinking, you see.'

'And that's why you've called me? Christ Jack!' he responds with a heavy sigh. 'Look, I'd rather like my copy back sometime, if that's okay,' he goes on. 'You know… I do remember reading somewhere that it was part autobiographical or something?'

'What d'you mean?'

'Well apparently Leonard Gold lost his wife?'

'You sure about that?'

'Yeah why?'

'Well, it… I think it adds to my suspicion?'

'What you going on about Jack?'

'I think that the Freddie I know might be Leonard Gold.'

'You mean your drunken mentor?'

'Yeah, the very one.'

'Oh come on, don't be ridiculous! The Leonard Gold we're talking about was one of the most respected novelists of his generation.'

'What, so it's impossible for him to wind up a desperate old drunk because he was a bloody good writer?' Jack interrupts. 'Jesus Sam, now you're being fucking ridiculous!'

'Well, I mean… come on, it's the stuff of fiction!' Sam replies. 'I don't know… maybe he just left England or something, went overseas?'

'Okay, but if he had, he'd still be getting published over here surely?'

'Well he could've just stopped writing and retired somewhere for God's sake!'

'No, he was only forty when he wrote *The Purity of Love*. Hardly in the position to retire. And why would he, when his work was receiving such high praise… when it was so good.'

'Maybe he ran out of ideas, I don't know?'

'No Sam, it doesn't add up. There's got to be another reason why he hasn't written anything for the last fifteen years. Something must've happened to him.'

'He could be dead?'

'No, I… I'm sure…'

'Look, I'll tell you what I think. You're spending too much time on your own at the moment and your imagination's gone AWOL!'

'Ha… ha, very funny. Look Sam, if I find out that Freddie really is Leonard Gold, then we'll see who'll be laughing.'

'Yeah alright Jack.'

'Look, I got to go. Speak soon, yeah,' Jack says hurriedly and hangs up the phone. He ferrets around in his wallet for the business card Freddie gave him. Picks up the phone again, dials the number. What is he doing, it is gone midnight. He will call first thing in the morning, when the shop opens.

Jack wakes very early, unable to sleep anymore, and counts down the hours till opening time. He rings 'Joseph's' at nine on the dot.

'Hi, this is Jack Stoltz,' he says impatiently into the phone, not giving the person on the other end of the line time to speak. 'I need to…'

'Joseph's,' a man's soft, eloquent voice interrupts him. It is as if the man has not heard him.

This must be Joseph, Jack thinks. 'Yes, hi… this is Jack Stoltz,' he says again. 'I'm calling to leave a message for Freddie.'

'Yes?'

'Can you ask him to call me?'

'Yes.'

'I… I'd better give you my number then,' Jack says hesitantly, somewhat struck by the man's reticence. 'D'you have a pen?'

'Yes, go on,' the man says, as he proceeds to write down Jack's telephone number, repeating every digit back to him as he does so.

'Yes, three,' Jack confirms the final digit.

'Fine. I'll have him call you.'

'Thanks.'

'Goodbye,' and with this final word, the man hangs up the phone and the line goes dead.

Two weeks go by and Freddie does not call. And so, when Jack is next in London with Catherine, he decides late one evening while still at work that he will go by the bookshop before returning to the cottage. He is sure to catch him there, he thinks; the weather has been awful and the forecast for the next few days is not much better. Yes, he will get out of work early tomorrow and stop by Pimlico on route to Paddington.

Jack leaves the office and picks up a takeaway on his way back to Catherine's. She has promised him that she will be back earlier this evening, by ten o'clock at the latest. He feels like they have grown apart since she has been in London. Though they have continued to spend three nights together each week, most of this time has passed with both of them asleep. Catherine is always exhausted and normally has just about enough energy to peck him on the cheek as she clambers into bed and collapses beside him after another relentless day.

It is approaching eleven and there is no sign of her. The food sits on the table getting cold. The telephone finally rings. It is Catherine. 'I'm sorry, I'm not going to be back till much later,' she says.

A man laughs on the other end of the line – then Catherine mumbles something out of earshot of the mouthpiece – and Jack's mind instantly leaps to the words in her journal about her wanting to go with other men when she feels distant from him. He knows that she continues to miss him terribly when he is in Oxford. 'Well what time then?' he asks her impatiently.

'I don't know, Jack. Why don't you go to bed? I'll get back as soon as I can.'

'I bought some food in for you.'

'I'm sorry.'

'I just want to see you. I feel like we haven't spoken for ages.'

'It's been me all this time whose wanted to see more of you,' she whispers into the phone as if trying to conceal her words. 'I've longed for you Jack, but you haven't been here.'

'We've been through this… and anyway, you're at work constantly. If I was in London full time, we'd still hardly see each other.'

'But we'd see each other more than we are at the moment.'

'Look, I have to work, just as you do. This is how it is.'

'I know…' she says, her voice drifting off all of a sudden, the tone of it puzzling.

'What's wrong?'

'Nothing.'

'No, you sound like there's something wrong. Catherine please?'

'I'm fine,' she says quietly.

Jack hears the man's laughter again in the background. 'Who's that with you?' he asks angrily.

'Jack, don't be silly…'

'Listen, just get home when you can, okay!' he says abruptly and hangs up the phone.

Jack leaves the flat soon after: he is unable to sleep, his mind preoccupied with thoughts of Catherine. As he walks, the lugubrious sky assumes a foreboding aspect, masses of cloud grouping then dispersing. These wet-looking clouds file for rank, their status determined by their size. Then large and small seem to merge en masse as the rain begins to beat down, heavy and violent. He does not have an umbrella with him, is not even sure where he is going, just needs to clear his head. Jack feels like Catherine is drifting away from him … and he from her.

The havoc of the rain around him forces him inside a black cab. Jack clambers inside, soaked through. 'Pimlico, please,' he says to the driver without thinking. But does he really want to go, he asks himself as soon as he has spoken these words, and right now … tonight. But then why was he so sure a moment ago? Jack does not know what to do.

'Where to in Pimlico?' the driver asks.

'Magnolia Mews,' Jack replies without hesitation. It is decided.

The journey is quick. The taxi speeds along, its black bulk battling the rain that pounds its roof and windscreen. The driver follows the river all the way. Jack sits in the back, on the edge of the seat, flustered and shivering. Warm air blasts him and the rain on his face slowly becomes sweat as droplets drip down his chest and spine. His fingers tremble as he brushes back his small soggy fringe pasted to his forehead. The cab swings into the mews, under a small arch, as if darting for cover. It bounces down the cobblestones until it reaches the end. Jack bales out of the cab and ducks underneath a magnolia tree, which stands at the foot of the tiny alleyway that leads down to the bookshop. He reaches the back door and knocks on it. Nothing. He stands there, cold and shivering. Freddie must be here, he thinks. Where else could he be for God's sake, in weather like this? He knocks again, but this time fiercely. Still nothing. Is he avoiding him? No … maybe something has happened to him. He will try the front of the shop. A small iron-gate near to the back door provides access to a pathway, which leads down the side of the building. It is padlocked. Jack clambers over into complete darkness, and hands to the wall, feels his way down the path until he reaches the front of the building. It is just as he has imagined it – small, quaint, Dickensian. An old Victorian street lamp lights up part of it. He backs into the middle of the road to get a proper look just as a red bus comes hurtling towards him; it has to swerve to avoid him, its brakes screeching, its horn sounding and its engine throbbing as it careers past him. The window display is slipshod, the sheer volume of books inside taking preference over any sense of careful marketing aesthetic or design. The books are what matters: all else is insignificant, mere surface gloss, deceit. 'Joseph's bookshop' is painted in white gothic lettering on the shop's front. Jack looks up to the first floor window. There is a light on. Maybe Joseph lives upstairs, he thinks. He approaches the front door, bangs on it several times. Waits. He looks up as another light comes on and an indistinguishable face peers through some net curtains. Jack ducks underneath the small porch as the rain gathers momentum again and cascades down. His head pressed against the door, he hears the sound of slow footsteps descending a creaking staircase. Then the door opens and a distinguished-looking elderly man peers through the darkness. Jack struggles to make out his face clearly in the low light.

'What do you want?' a gentle, mellifluent voice inquires.

'Is it Joseph?'

'And who might you be, young man?' he says, unwilling to confirm his identity.

'I called a couple of weeks ago. We spoke, I think. My name's Jack… Jack Stoltz, d'you remember? I left a message with you for Freddie.'

'This is a rather strange time to call by,' he replies, lifting up his wrist slowly, then looking at his watch. 'It's almost midnight.'

'Look, I know… I'm sorry. I thought he'd be here that's all. I didn't mean to wake you. I tried the back door. There was no answer. I was worried that maybe something had happened, you see…'

'No, as far as I know, he's okay. I saw him a few days ago. He comes and goes as he pleases. That's the arrangement we have.'

'Yeah I know… he told me. Look, I'm sorry, but I do really want to speak to him. Did you tell him I called?'

'Yes.'

'Well I'd be very grateful if you could tell him that I called by this evening. Could you give him my number again and ask him to please get in touch with me as soon as he can? You see… I promised I'd buy him lunch. He helped me… in more ways than one… yes…' Jack says, struggling to articulate why it is that he suddenly needs to speak to Freddie so urgently.

'Yes, I'm Joseph,' the old man says warmly, now choosing to verify his identity as he steps out of the darkness and into the light of the street lamp. He is a gracious looking man in his late sixties, tall and thin, with slightly sallowed cheeks, wears a paisley dressing gown over matching pyjamas, and holds a pipe in his hand. He continues, 'And yes, I'll tell him you called by and ask him to call you. I gave him your message when you called before. I don't think he's been very well lately. He might be going through another one of his bleak spells. He has them.' Jack fumbles in his pocket for a pen and paper in order to write down his number again. Joseph interrupts his search. 'I have it already. You gave it to me last time. I don't need it again. He'll be in touch when he wants to be, when he's ready, I assure you. Now, if you'll forgive me, I'm an old man who wants to get back upstairs to bed. Goodbye Jack,' he says as he turns around, then closes the front door behind him.

# 17

**SHE AND JACK** have a champagne breakfast at Café Nouveau in Chipping Norton, about five miles from the cottage, to celebrate her homecoming. The film has not gone the way Catherine wanted it to. 'It's nothing like it could've been,' she says to Jack as she sips from her cup of coffee.

'I'm sorry, Catherine,' he says.

'I should have gone with my instinct when Dan left, and walked away then.'

'No, but I think Richard was right when he said that you should compromise and do it anyway. It's your first film after all.'

'Yes, but what a first film…' Catherine says hesitantly as she sits back in her chair and loses herself briefly in her relentless analysis of what went wrong. She fought to the very end to downplay the safe romantic aspect of the drama, and the edit she screened Concept Pictures a month ago was indeed sexually explicit. But Concept, true to bloody form, judged it to be unfaithful to their approved script and overtly hostile to the Catholic Church, and subsequently, ordered her to make changes. And then Catherine learnt that the company's fucking president happens to be a prominent member of America's Catholic community. Christ! It was then that she had to accept she would never get her own way.

'You okay?' Jack asks her.

'Sorry, I lost myself there,' Catherine says.

'You've got to stop beating yourself up about it.'

'Yeah I know, but I can't. It just makes me so angry that the whole thing has ended up becoming such a shoddy process of euphemism and… concession. Yesterday, I just turned in something they wanted, that I knew they wouldn't object to.'

'D'you bring this edit with you?'

'No, but I have my one, for what it's worth.'

'I think you'd got too close to it. You knew that anyway. It was like you were trying to prove a point by making it. And they were never going to let you do that. And if they had, then you wouldn't have come across well…'

'I know. What was I thinking? I was just being a silly pretentious little cow!'

'Catherine, don't,' Jack says, and she realises that she must try and be kinder to herself. 'So when she's coming anyway?' he continues.

'Who… my mother, you mean?'

'Yeah.'

'Within the next month or so, I think. She said she'd let me know exactly when. You know, I never thought I'd say this, but now I think I'm actually looking forward to seeing her.'

'What you going to do now? Perhaps you should just take some time off?'

'I don't know. It depends how it's received and whether I get an opportunity to do another film. I don't have to work for at least three months. I've got enough money in the bank to last me. I feel like I need a break, I'm knackered at the moment.'

'Yes you should rest, you need to.'

Catherine leans over the table and holds his cheek, cupping it in her hand. 'Jack, I will see more of you now, won't I?' she asks. 'Both of us have been busy, I know… but I'm finished with the film now. I want to be with you again.'

'Yes, so do I.'

'I can't wait!' she says excitedly.

But they do not have more time together. Almost as soon as she is back in Oxford, Jack comes home with the news that *Detritus*'s circulation is down significantly. He tells her that he must support Sarah and Jonathan Goodhart, the magazine's publisher, as much as he can, otherwise he shall be out of a job. Sarah and Jonathan are having a lot of pressure put on them by the magazine's philanthropic owner, Geoffrey Bloom. Circulation has fallen by seven percent in the last four months since February and Bloom wants to see a twenty-percent increase over the next six months, otherwise he will have to reconsider his investment.

And so Jack starts to work a four-day week in London, much to Catherine's dismay. He tells her that he and Sarah plan to try and attract contributions from established and well-known writers, actors, academics and even politicians. This goes against *Detritus*'s founding principle of encouraging new writers and undiscovered talent – Catherine is quick to remind Jack of this – and yet she knows that in light of Bloom's tough circulation review they have little choice. She is also aware that this change of tack is consistent with the tenets of modern magazine culture, where the notion of celebrity is everything. If publishers do not have the money to recruit famous people to write on their pages, then they will make celebrities out of the writers they already have. According to this new press culture, the contributors' names which appear in big, bold and colourful print on the front cover – and the sizes of their accompanying byline photos – are far more significant than the actual quality of their writing and what they inform the reader about their chosen subject. Catherine is deeply sceptical. But according to Jack, Bloom wants *Detritus* for his public reputation more than anything else. He will not kick up his heels at this change of marketing and editorial tack. *Detritus* is kudos for him, nothing more. Up until this point, he was happy if it just broke even. But now he wants to see some profit.

And so while Jack is working ever-longer hours in London, Catherine spends her days lying in the garden, usually in the same place – her favourite spot – the small patch of lawn near the top, which is flanked by pink and blue hydrangeas and her beloved gardenias. The sun gives her skin a gentle brown hue. She sleeps a lot during this time, needing to recover her strength after all her hard work on the film. But she also finds herself writing more in her journal now – she has to – and it is full of her fantasies, of sex with strangers, anonymous sex to fill that hole inside of her: she feels this a lot now in Jack's absence, fears that their love is dwindling.

As the days draw near to her mother's arrival, Catherine begins to agonise over the arrangements for the weekend. First, she spends hours pouring through different cookbooks, trying to find 'the right' meals to prepare, even though she is doubtful what this 'right' constitutes. She is not sure what her mother will like. Salmon, yes, she remembers that ma used to cook this for her as a special treat when she was a girl, though she always knew that it was ma rather than her who was passionate about fish. Catherine would rather have had frozen hamburgers out of a packet and a big bowl of oven chips. Second, she contacts the local church for details of Sunday services: her mother never failed to miss Mass on Sunday. And third, she maps out the routes of several walks she wants them to make. This is all very unlike her, she knows this, she has never planned her personal life in this ordered manner, with this level of forethought, but now she feels compelled to. Everything must be just right for ma. It has to be.

How will she look, what will she be like now? Catherine wonders. Ma was always obsessed with the idea of dying in a state of sin. This only happened after papa left. Once he had gone, whenever she met a new man, she would indulge herself in the bedroom in every conceivable way, then drag Catherine to church straight after to seek penance. It had been compulsive: this action of casual sex – fucking for fucking's sake – immediately followed by contrition. It was as if, by making confession, she would somehow be made virtuous again … that is, until the next time. Like mother like daughter, Catherine now thinks. Her need was like her ma's before she met Jack, as strong … and yet after sex, she was not driven to God but rather inside herself, to self-contempt. It is not as bad now that she has Jack: she is no longer throwing herself at men she hardly knows. Catherine always got angry with herself after, not because she felt she had sinned – God no, she has always refused to believe in that crap – but because she had not been able to control her feelings, her desires, in the first place. Catherine has always wished she could find relief another way. Sex is a quick fix … but the vulnerable feelings always return.

# 18

'JACK, IT'S FREDDIE.'

'Freddie?'

'Yes, Freddie,' he says slowly and deliberately.

'No, sorry… I know it's you, it's just a surprise, that's all. I didn't think you were going to call. It's been some time. Listen, hang on a second,' Jack says, as he puts his hand over the mouthpiece and addresses the young woman at the counter. 'Look, I'm sorry, I've got to take this call. I'll just pop outside. Be back in a moment,' he assures her, puts down the bottle of wine he is holding, then hurries out of the off-licence. Jack has promised Catherine he would pick up some booze while in London – some good stuff for Eleanor – at the place near to the office, which has a unique selection of reds, particularly Riojas. He might even find a bottle of Catherine's favourite stuff here, a *Luis Cañas Reserva.*

'So…how are you?' Jack continues awkwardly as he steps outside.

'Fine, fine,' Freddie replies succinctly.

'I called by the bookshop about two months ago. Joseph told you, I presume.'

'Yeah,' he answers.

'Well… what have you been up to? Are you okay?'

'Fine,' he says, issuing yet another laconic reply.

'Right…' Jack replies hesitantly, unsure where this tense and strained exchange is heading.

There is a prolonged silence. Freddie finally speaks. 'I went through a black spell, Jack, but I'm out of it now,' he explains. 'Enough of that. So tell me… how are you, the book, Catherine?'

'Okay. Things are alright.'

'The book must be coming along… I hope so.'

There is another difficult pause in the conversation. Jack's curiosity has been quickly reinvigorated. He wants to confront him on the phone right now, ask him straight out if he is Leonard Gold. But no, this is not the right time. He will wait until they meet. 'Listen, d'you still want to do that lunch I promised you?' he asks.

Freddie does not answer right away, as if carefully considering the invitation. 'Why not,' he says finally.

'Well when are you free?'

'Tomorrow?'

'That's good for me. I'm free for lunch before I head back to Oxford.'

'Tomorrow it is. In Shepherd's Bush?'

'There's a place opposite my flat. Café Magic. D'you know it?'

'I do. I'll see you there,' Freddie says, then hangs up the phone, and Jack goes back inside the shop to pay for the wine.

Café Magic is an old diner, a former government-subsidised restaurant that now operates independently. It still promises 'A Great Quality Meal At A Cheap Price', as the banner reads in big gold letters in the window, and it keeps to its word. Bachelors, spinsters and the elderly frequent it: people on their own, who do not have anyone to cook for them anymore or have never had anyone, who need the comfort of a meal which tastes home-cooked, and who cannot afford anything else. As Jack sees it, the café is the ultimate personification of pragmatism: it consists of rows of old rickety chairs and lop-sided school dining room tables, the place built around the central ethos of sustenance rather than indulgence. Jack enters to find Freddie sitting in the corner, sipping on a black coffee. 'Hi,' he says, shaking Freddie's hand and sitting down.

'Jack,' Freddie replies, nodding. 'So you really do live right opposite, don't you.'

'Sorry?'

'I saw you through the window,' Freddie says bluntly, pointing to Jack's front door across the street.

'Oh yes… right,' Jack replies as a frumpy waitress approaches the table, hands him a menu, then hurries off.

'So tell me… why the urgency?'

'What?'

'You came by the bookshop that night. Joseph told me you were very anxious to see me.'

'Yes I was…' Jack replies, struggling to confront him.

'Why Jack?'

'Are you Leonard Gold?' he blurts out.

'Can I take your orders, gentlemen?' the waitress calls to them as she returns to the table. Jack looks at Freddie expectantly.

'The chicken for me, my dear,' Freddie says to the waitress, seeming to ignore Jack's question.

She proceeds to ask both of them a series of questions about what they want to eat and drink. It is no simple matter of just picking one dish off the menu. No, every meal comes with a choice of different salad, vegetables and potatoes. She methodically goes through all the different options. And then there are drinks to order as well, which prove to be yet another unusually complex and prolonged affair. When she has finally finished – it seems to Jack that she must have written a short essay on her waitress pad – she waddles back to the kitchen. Then the two men are alone again. Jack stares at Freddie and waits for him to answer. Freddie holds his head down and stares at the place mat on the table, which carries a rather ugly, sentimental portrait of Queen Elizabeth II. He speaks finally. 'Yes Jack… I'm Leonard Gold.'

'Leonard Gold the novelist?'

'Yep.'

Jack shakes his head from side to side.

Leonard continues, 'Why d'you look so surprised?'

'Well, because…'

'Because of the state I'm in now. Is that it?'

'No, it's just…'

'It's okay. I'd be thinking the same thing if I were you,' Leonard says quietly. 'When Molly died, I really did lose everything as you can see.'

'Why, Freddie?'

'I wanted to be anonymous. It was the first name that came to me.'

'I read *The Purity of Love*. It's one of the most beautiful books I've ever read. The writing's exquisite. I can't believe I didn't realise sooner.'

'Why should you have done?'

'Well I don't know. It's just I read it right before I met you. I got it off a friend of mine. And then when I read it a second time, after I knew about Molly… knew more about you… well, it suddenly came to me who you might be.'

'I wrote it the first year after she died.'

'Your way of trying to come to terms with her death?'

'Yes… though it didn't quite have the desired effect,' Leonard says.

'No, you can't say that!' Jack assures him. 'Just to give people a book like that to read, a book that well-written, with that much compassion…'

'Thanks.'

'You know, I read it a second time after a gruelling spell on Hardy. You offer your reader such hope.'

Leonard shuffles in his chair now, seeming uncomfortable all of a sudden, as if something Jack has just said has upset him. He makes a rather ominous growl as he clears his throat. And then he scratches the back of his neck irritably, signals for another cup of coffee. 'Why are you interested in me?' he asks.

'Sorry?'

'Why have you befriended me? I need to know. Is it because of who you suspected I might be, a former esteemed novelist?' he asks wryly.

'Leonard, what are you talking about?'

'It's Leonard now, is it? No longer Freddie.'

'Freddie, Leonard… it doesn't matter.'

'Is it because you think you owe me something after I helped you that night outside the cathedral?'

'No, it's not just that. Look, there was something about you that intrigued me. It was your intensity, passion… your…'

'What, how much I've suffered, you mean?'

'No, it was what you seemed to know, what you know about…'

Leonard cut him off mid sentence again. 'You mean all those books I gave you to read?'

'Well yes…'

'Jack, I wouldn't have read these in the way I did had Molly not died. Don't you see?'

'Yes, I do. Just as you wouldn't have produced that exceptional novel.'

'Christ Jack, I produced that damn book to try and get over her death! It was nothing more than this. It wasn't for art's sake. I just fucking needed to do it!'

'But surely it helped you… it was worth it?'

'What d'you think? D'you see a wiser man now some fourteen years later?'

'I don't know. I mean… I didn't know you back then. What've you done since writing *The Purity of Love*? Have you written anything else?'

'Yeah, quite a bit. But I can't get it published. Why else would I be living like this?'

The waitress puts down a fresh cup of coffee and Leonard grabs at the handle like he needs to drink right away. His hand shakes as he clumsily sucks at it, too hot to drink. He then goes on to tell Jack about how his writing has been affected since Molly's death. A cocktail of alcohol and sleep deprivation propelled his professional decline, Leonard explains, though it is not clear which one has done him more harm. He says that when he sits down to write now, he follows very little routine. The order and precision he used to apply to his work has vanished. He used to always follow the same routine when he prepared to write. He would sit upright in his enormous black leather swivel chair over a beautiful walnut desk, switch on his old word processor, brush his hand over his old leather desk mat, turn on his desk lamp and angle it at the keyboard. Then he would lean back, hold his arms up in the air, lift his knees toward his chest and arch his back, stretching his body like a cat waking from a deep sleep. Only then would he be ready to write. But now, his work method is fractious and chaotic, Leonard tells Jack. He wishes it was not. He says that when Molly was alive, he would often write at night when he could not sleep. On occasions, he felt very isolated up there in his study at the top of the house – everything was so still, so quiet – but the act of writing was very comforting. He used to write through his feelings of loneliness and constantly remind himself that the most precious thing in his life lay asleep directly beneath him, his dear Molly. Often, after a period of great concentration, his uneasiness and solitude would pass, to be replaced by feelings of tranquility. But his self-criticism immediately became severe when Molly died: it was as if he had lost the one person who could moderate his criticism of his work and himself. And so, according to his critical mind, all of what he wrote thereafter was 'shit, bad, and weak'. As Jack listens to him now, it seems that Leonard's harsh self-estimation has played a large part in driving him to despair. For he sounds like he considers himself to be unlovable now.

Their food arrives on the table. Leonard's chicken looks delicious: it is golden brown and deep-fried. Jack's water-logged plate of spaghetti Bolognese, however, has the appearance of something rather less inviting and palatable: the pasta is soggy and over-cooked. He takes his first reluctant mouthful as Leonard's knife cuts through a piece of mouth-watering chicken breast, then smears it in thick, ambrosial gravy. The Bolognese sauce's taste and fragrance has a hint of being seasoned with a rather unconventional ingredient. Jack winces as he swallows. 'That bad taste in your mouth is probably cigarette smoke,' Leonard says through a large gob of cabbage. Jack notices that he eats like a man who has not eaten a square meal in days. He shovels down a whole roast potato, barely chewing it. 'The chef here has an eighty-a-day habit,' he continues. 'The times I've been here, I've never seen him in the kitchen without a fag hanging out of his mouth,' he concludes, wiping a globule of gravy from his beard.

Jack peers round the door to the kitchen. Lo and behold, the cook stands over the grill, chomping away at the end of a cigarette butt, drawing out the last bits of nicotine from the small residue of tobacco. 'You look hungry,' Jack says.

'Yep starving,' Leonard replies. 'I often forget to eat. I've never really been any good at looking after myself.'

When Leonard has finished wolfing down his lunch, he goes on to explain to Jack what happened to him after Molly's death. *The Purity of Love* had made him very little money. Neither had any of his previous novels. Yes, he was well respected in literary circles, but this was – and still is to this day – a rather small circle; Jack knows this all too well. However, Leonard was well on course to securing a happy and reasonably prosperous future for himself within this diminishing world of book lovers. But when Molly died, the course of his future changed dramatically. *The Purity of Love* did not achieve in personal terms what he hoped it would: he had construed it as a necessary catharsis that would heal his grief. But no, he was still desperate after writing it. Subsequently, Leonard began to drink heavily and flitted away most of the money he had. His growing inability to write – his mind muddled and distorted by a constant stream of booze and grief – forced him out of his home and into rented accommodation: he was not able to keep up the payments on his mortgage. He proudly and doggedly refused the help and support of his friends and literary colleagues. And he had no family left. He said no to a back-to-work scheme, which forced him lower down the social security ladder into grimy bed-sits. During this time, he produced sporadic pieces of work but nothing in publishable form. His alcoholism eventually forced him onto the street. Then about five years ago, he found refuge in the bookshop. Joseph was a great admirer of his novels and agreed to take him in. 'And well… that is it,' Leonard says, concluding his story.

'What are you going to do now?' Jack asks.

'I'll just carry on as I am.'

'Can't I help you in some way? I mean, if you were to stop drinking, get back some financial independence, get some of what you've written over the last decade published…'

'It's not that easy.'

'But with your ability, your mind… why not?'

'I…'

'You need help, Leonard… professional help!' Jack urges him.

'Life's very complex, Jack!' Leonard responds forcefully. 'I resisted the attempts of my old friends to explain my decline in psychoanalytic terms. You know… I'm suspicious of any kind of judgment that ascribes me a pathology. My decline, my "tragedy" as people refer to it… is grief, grief,' he repeats this word very deliberately to give it emphasis. 'This thing cannot be reduced to the confines of a specific psychiatric disorder or mental disturbance. It's part of the human condition. It's life… just life!'

'Look… I just want to help you, that's all.'

'Listen Jack. I'll always fight any attempt you make, or anyone else makes for that matter, to label or categorise my experience and its effect on my thoughts… my behaviour. You hear me?'

'Okay, forget what I said before about the professional help, but surely you'd accept *my* help.'

'Well look, you've bought me lunch… and I'm very grateful for this.'

'You know what I mean? I mean… what d'you want now? What will make you happier, make your life easier?'

'I've been on my own a long time. This is difficult for me… I haven't shared my life with anyone for many years.'

'Well Leonard… I'm here if you need me,' Jack says. 'You have my telephone number now. If you just want to talk or you fancy lunch again, just call me.'

'Thanks Jack, thank you.'

'Look, I've got to go.'

'You haven't got time for pudding? I recommend the spotted dick. The jam roly-poly is very good as well.'

'No really… I must get back to Catherine.'

'She needs you a lot, doesn't she,' Leonard says matter-of-factly.

'Well… yes she does,' Jack replies, slightly taken aback by Leonard's observation.

'Yes, the needs of love, the needs of a woman,' he utters. 'Be careful she doesn't take you away from your book!'

'Yep,' Jack answers, Leonard's remark making him feel slightly uncomfortable. He continues, 'I haven't seen her all week and her mother's due to come at the weekend. It's the first time she'll have seen her in seventeen years. It's a big thing for Catherine. I'm sure you understand…'

'Wish her my luck. Families are difficult beasts at the best of times.'

'I will,' Jack says, leaving fifteen pounds on the table, more than enough to cover the cost of their lunch and Leonard's proposed dessert. 'Listen, take care, and remember what I said. If you want to call, then please do.'

'Right, okay… I will, thanks,' Leonard replies as Jack pats him on the shoulder and hurries out of the café.

When Jack gets back to the cottage that evening, he finds Catherine up to her neck in flannels, paint and white spirit when he opens the front door.

'What are you doing? he asks her, but she just smiles softly at him, seeming reluctant to give anything away. 'Let me guess,' he goes on, hastily making his way upstairs to the second bedroom. Yes, his hunch is right. She has decided to decorate it prior to Eleanor's arrival. A few weeks before, they had finally finished the study, and Jack had re-located his work to its intended home.

'It's got to be just right for her. I know what she's like,' Catherine says to Jack as he stands in the doorway and admires her work.

'Catherine... it's been a hell of a long time. She might've changed.'

'I hope so...' she says.

He admires the room, which looks so beautiful in its white simplicity. Catherine has bought new bedding, a small ornate dressing table and a beautifully carved stool, and long linen curtains that hang gracefully from the ceiling, flowing onto the new-fitted carpet. Everything in the room is white; so lucid, delicate. 'You've really gone to town. You've re-done the whole room. I'm gob-smacked. It's a complete transformation.'

'She'll love it, won't she?'

'Yes... yes, she will, of course she will,' he assures her. 'Look, are you sure you want me to be there when she arrives? I've been thinking... it'd be better if the two of you at least spent the first night together on your own.'

'No, you must be there... I want you to be! I'll feel better... safer with you there. You can always give us some time on our own on Saturday and Sunday.'

'You sure? She mightn't be comfortable with this. I mean... she's never even met me, and the two of you... well, you have so much to talk about.'

'No, I've told her you'll be there but we'll have some time on our own to talk. I need you when she first arrives, please. She says she's quite happy with this, really... I wouldn't say so otherwise,' Catherine reassures him as he sits down on the bed.

'Okay,' Jack replies, taking her hand, and she kneels in front of him, then lies her head in his lap. He gently strokes her hair as the room grows dark and night falls.

# 19

**MA ARRIVES** on Friday evening. When Jack opens the front door to let her in, she does not embrace Catherine right away. Rather, she just stares at her daughter, as if sizing her up after so many years apart, and Catherine is made to wonder whether this is what she will look like twenty years from now. Ma still has long black hair like her, no signs of grey, and a narrow waist, long legs and swaying hips – her black satin dress clings to her body – all those defining characteristics that Jack found so attractive in her … yes, Catherine thinks. There are only two features that distinguish mother and daughter apart, and Catherine is aware of these now as she stares back at her: ma's complexion is paler in its pure Gaelic origin, and her eyes, rather than Catherine's striking brown, are piercing green. They are the same height but ma wears high heels now. She tilts her eye-line down to meet Catherine's. 'My darling…' she says as she stares at her, observing her daughter as if a stranger.

'Hi ma,' Catherine replies nervously, expectantly, as she waits for her mother's next move. Ma … ma, she voices this word a few times to herself, never imagining she would utter it to her mother's face again.

Ma raises an awkward smile as she puts her hand to Catherine's face and gently kisses her cheek. 'You look so different,' she says.

'Do I?' Catherine asks. 'It's been so long… too long…'

'Yes I know,' she says sadly. 'You look older.'

'Ma, we haven't seen each other for over seventeen years.'

'That was your choice, darling, not mine!' she snaps back.

'Ma, not now, not like this, when you've just got here.'

'I'm sorry… I'm sorry my darling,' Eleanor says softly, then runs her fingers through her hair, brushing it back just as Catherine always does. Her crucifix, on a silver necklace, swings forward and rocks against her chest.

'Ma, this is Jack,' Catherine says.

'Hi Jack, my daughter's told me all about you,' her voice softens now as she turns her attention to him.

'Hello Eleanor. It's good to finally meet you,' Jack replies.

Ma smiles delicately, her eyes holding on him. 'So…' she says, turning to Catherine again, 'are you going to let Jack show your mother around your home?'

'Yes, why don't I show your mother where she's sleeping?' Jack interjects. 'Catherine re-decorated the spare bedroom just this week. She was determined to get it done in time for you. It looks fantastic, it really does!' he says, clasping Catherine's hand supportively.

'Well, I can't wait to see it. Shall we go?'

'Yes, I'd better finish off getting the dinner ready…' Catherine says, turning and hurrying back into the kitchen.

'Yes darling,' ma acknowledges her daughter's action, in a way that suggests they have never been apart, and then Catherine watches her as she admires herself in the full-length mirror, smiling seductively at her reflection, which possesses a kind of wearied voluptuousness, before following Jack upstairs.

'Doesn't it look just wonderful?' Catherine overhears Jack say to

Eleanor. She cannot concentrate on the food now. She is simply too preoccupied with what is going on above her.

'It's very white isn't it,' she hears ma say rather dismissively.

'Yeah, I think that's what makes it so special,' Jack replies.

'Yes,' ma says, and then Catherine cannot hear anything and wonders what she is doing now. Catherine walks out of the kitchen and into the hallway. 'I'd like to see yours and Catherine's room,' she hears ma say.

'Sure… okay, it's… just over here,' Jack responds uncertainly, thrown off guard by the manner of her request.

'So you let Catherine decorate. She's got her mother's taste,' ma says, and Catherine imagines her looking around the room now, scanning its decoration and contents, her gaze full of scrutiny.

Then there is another lull in the conversation and Catherine moves closer to the stairs, takes hold of the banister and tilts her head slightly.

'I don't know why she's still got that fucking black panther!' ma suddenly blurts out, and Catherine is immediately convinced that she has not changed one iota, is still as damn volatile and unpredictable as she was before. She continues, 'When's she going to get it into her head that it was her father who ruined everything for her… everything.'

And Catherine does not want to listen to anymore now, feels flustered, huffs out her frustration, stomps back into the kitchen.

She has been slaving over the stove all day, following each recipe with the utmost care and precision, eager to create the perfect meal for ma. And for what? Catherine asks herself angrily. No, but … she has just got here, and needs time, this is what Jack told her. Catherine must be patient.

She lays the Parma ham on top of the rocket leaf. Just the fresh figs to add … and the starter is ready. She should see how the fish casserole is getting on: it will probably be just right by now. Catherine fetches the oven gloves, removes the dish from the Aga. The smell hits her when she lifts the lid … onion, garlic, white wine; it infuses the air. The casserole is meant to sit for a bit before serving. She will leave it on the hob. Okay, the dessert, she should quickly check the refrigerator one more time. Three bowls of raspberry and mango sorbet sit there. Catherine is rather proud of what she has done here, has never made sorbet before. What about some mint? she thinks. She quickly fetches a stem from the garden, washes it under the tap, picks off three leaves, then garnishes each bowl of sorbet with a single leaf. Voila.

'It's ready,' she calls to Jack and ma.

Ma saunters into the dining room. Catherine has lit it with candles, which burn gently all around the room. Jack opens a bottle of Rioja and asks ma, as she takes her place at the head of the table, whether she would like to taste the wine.

'What is it Jack?' she asks.

'It's a Rioja.'

'No, I don't drink Spanish wine, not anymore!' she says bluntly.

'Ma…' Catherine pleads with her, and when her mother refuses to acknowledge her, she feels compelled to get out of the room, away from her, otherwise she might say or do something she will later regret.

In the kitchen now, she paces up and down, staring at the stone floor, rubbing her forehead as if trying to pacify herself. She looks up to see Jack, shakes her head. 'Jesus, she hasn't changed at all!' Catherine exclaims. 'I thought she had. In her letter, on the phone… she sounded different, like she had. But no, she's still off her fucking rocker!'

'Catherine, look… you've got to give her time. You know that. I don't think she really means it.'

'How can you say that! She knows exactly what she's saying. I heard her upstairs as well. She's fully aware how bloody cruel and out of order she can be. I'm not prepared to make excuses for her anymore, Jack. I made too many when I was growing up.'

'Just give her a bit more time, Catherine. You can't dismiss her right away. This is so important to you… you know that, just…'

'Yes, you're right,' she says, trying to rouse her spirits now.

'You're sure about this, aren't you?'

'I am, yeah. Look… I wouldn't have made contact otherwise, I know that. I want her back Jack… in my life again,' she speaks hurriedly, wiping her cheeks and gathering herself.

'It's okay. We've got some other wine we can give her that's not Spanish,' Jack says smiling, then heads back to the dining room. 'We've got a French red here, Eleanor. How's that?'

'Yes, that's better… thank you,' ma responds quietly, as if her momentary segregation has given her the time to reflect on and confront her unreasonable behaviour.

'There we are,' he says, popping the cork and pouring her a glass.

She immediately takes a hefty swig. 'Thank you, Jack, yes that's a lovely wine,' she says while Catherine lays the starters on the table. 'This looks wonderful… really,' she goes on.

The conversation is stilted at first as they all commence eating. Mother and daughter are still not quite sure what to say to one another. Catherine attempts to break the deadlock. 'Ma, I thought we could go on some walks. Jack and I often go together. It's so beautiful round here. The weather's supposed to be good all weekend.'

'I only have heels darling.'

'I can lend you some shoes. Aren't we the same size?'

'No, your feet are bigger than mine.'

'Well, we can always pick some up in town.'

'Alright then… but I wish you'd told me.'

'I'd planned it as a surprise for you. That's why I didn't say anything,' Catherine appeals to her.

'That was very thoughtful of you… thank you darling. Yes, I can buy myself a pair of shoes tomorrow,' ma says, striving to be conciliatory, receptive to her daughter.

'Great ma. I'm looking forward to it, just you and me. Jack might join us on Sunday,' Catherine says, placing her hand next to ma's and secretly hoping that she might reach out and hold her hand, just show her that she still cares for her, still loves her.

'Good… good,' ma says, smiling at her but unable to reciprocate her daughter's affectionate gesture.

Jack and Catherine take the empty plates through to the kitchen and fetch the main course. Catherine returns to find ma helping herself to more wine, and she finishes this glass by the time they serve up the casserole. She has a greedy thirst like her, Catherine thinks.

Ma drinks more and more as the dinner progresses. She starts to reminisce about her days with Catherine. She tells Jack that she used to read her daughter romantic fairytales when she was a child to help her sleep. But it was not only just these fairytales, however, that ma subjected her to, Catherine now recalls. There were also the old movies as well. In fact, ma made her watch so many of them that they became a fundamental part of her childhood. At times, it seemed to Catherine that her mother was intent on bringing her up on nothing other than a staple and wholesome diet of 1950s and early '60s Hollywood movies, the ones that always played on Sunday afternoons, the romance of a bygone era. They were always of a sentimental variety, morality tales overloaded with Christian teachings. Doris Day's sanitised screen image of sexual purity and innocence was always preferable to Dietrich's complex, provocative and androgynous sexuality. Ma loved these splashy, fantastic spectacles, and they were good, clean, unambiguous romantic fodder for Catherine. Never mind what the mother was getting up to when her daughter was out of sight.

Catherine watches as ma becomes increasingly tactile with Jack.

LOVE AND MAYHEM

The merrier she gets the more she holds his hand, the more she strokes his head. He looks over at Catherine, unsure how to respond to her mother's infamous penchant for younger men.

'D'you have anything I can see?' ma suddenly addresses Catherine.

'Sorry?'

'Of the film, Catherine, the one you've just finished… the one you told me about in your letter.'

'I was thinking I could show it to you on Sunday just before you go,' Catherine replies, reluctant to talk about it so soon. She is very aware that her mother might not react well to it, in particular her own edit, which she plans to show her. She wants them to talk first, to try and understand what happened between them all those years ago, before she shows her anything of the film.

'Oh no, I'd like to see it sooner than that. You can't make me wait that long,' ma persists. Catherine says nothing. 'You said it was about a Catholic nun who struggles with her faith,' she continues, slurring her words.

'Yes.'

'You've got me intrigued.'

'That's good, ma,' Catherine says, still keen to steer clear of the subject until the time feels right.

'Well what happens to her then? I mean… what's the story?'

'She meets a man and falls in love.'

'It's about a nun falling in love?' she says, sounding bewildered by the notion.

'Yes.'

'That's absurd… ridiculous!'

'Look, can I get anyone another drink?' Jack interjects.

'Ma, the heroine's exploits are based on a true story,' Catherine says purposefully.

'Well it sounds highly improbable to me.'

'You might not believe this ma, but there've been quite a few nuns who've had sex on the side. When Dan and I were putting together the script, we both read a heap of archive material about what a particular group of nuns got up to in Renaissance Venice. It wasn't difficult for them to get out of their convent and break their vows. In fact, there must've been nuns all over the Christian world who also struggled with chastity… and there still are, I'm sure.'

'Nonsense,' she insists.

'Ma, even if you don't believe me about the old Venetian nuns… you've got to accept that all nuns must find their vows pretty difficult. I mean, surely this is inevitable. You can't ask a woman to deny a fundamental, innate aspect of herself? A woman's sexuality doesn't vanish as soon as she enters the convent. It stays with her. A nun is still a woman. She must still yearn for physical intimacy, yearn to be with someone.'

'So…'

'Well, this is what the film's about. Laura, the heroine… must decide what's more important. Her sacred vows to the Church or her love for the young man. She…'

Ma interrupts, 'Her vows to God you mean.'

'No, the Church. We all know the Catholic notion of chastity is a man-made construct.'

'The word of God is not man-made!'

'But how can you demand that a woman give up her sexuality?'

'These women choose to give it up. They must live with their decision!' she says angrily, and Catherine is made to wonder whether ma resents them for their abstinence.

'No, it's a condition imposed on them if they want to get closer to God. They're told that if they're sexually impure… defiled, whatever the hell this notion means, then they'll never get close to Him.'

'Well of course!'

'What so you can only get close to God if you're pure and chaste?'

'Yes!'

'Well you can't be that close to God then!'

'What did you say?' she shouts.

'Ma, you of all people must realise this can't be right. Yes, people do choose celibacy, but they choose it freely. It's not a condition of their faith, their worthiness. They find it for themselves. Look at the *Silacarini*… you know, the Buddhist nuns. Many of these women choose to ordain later in life. They come to it only when they're truly ready to relinquish their sexuality. I mean, they're giving up an enormous part of themselves. There's no force or compulsion here. Rather, it's conceived as some kind of liberation. They're not just told to be rid of it like in Catholicism. Can't you see that ma, this fundamental difference?'

'Darling, I don't want to talk about this anymore. Let's talk about something else,' she says as she returns her attention to Jack. She places her hand on his, then leans over seductively, inviting him to admire her cleavage in her tight-fitting dress. She is pissed now. Ma whispers in Jack's ear, 'You know, Catherine used to have such chubby cheeks when she was a little girl… all bloated and puffy. Poor darling,' she says condescendingly. 'And then, as a teenager, she had these podgy legs that made her look boyish.'

Jack does not respond.

'What did you say ma?' Catherine asks her.

'Jack and I were just sharing a little joke, my darling.'

Jack pulls his hand away from hers.

'Ma… can't you see what you're doing, what this is all about… what it's always been about?' Catherine says frustratedly. 'You've put yourself in this position where you can't win. You don't have sex, you're miserable. You do have sex, you're made to feel guilty and ashamed. That can't be right!'

'Catherine, not now… not here in front of Jack!'

'Look, I'm going to leave you two alone,' Jack says, getting up from the table.

'No you don't have to do that,' ma says, reaching out and holding his hand, but he pulls it away. Jack kisses Catherine, then promptly leaves the room.

Catherine continues, 'Look, I'm sorry… but don't you see, can't you see? I was never angry with you for having affairs with all those men…'

She interrupts, 'I didn't love any of them. They never meant anything to me.'

'Why did you bother to have relationships with them then?'

'Because I got lonely sometimes alright,' she says angrily.

'Exactly. Don't you see… you needed a man to love you, be with you, make love to you… I understand that ma. You don't have to apologise!'

'It was never about love. It was lust, plain and simple. I was with all these men for their dicks, nothing more. I just needed a good fuck!' she says bitterly.

'Ma, it was your bloody hypocrisy that drove me away, your cruelty… not your need to have sex. I mean, for Christ's sake, you've been all over Jack ever since you got here, and yet at the same time, you try and defend the virtues of sexual abstinence. It's preposterous, coming from you of all people… you must see that?'

'Me of all people?'

'Oh come on… you've always liked it rough, haven't you?' Catherine demands impatiently.

And then they are both silent.

Ma sits back in her chair and places both hands on the table in a judicial fashion. Catherine strokes the tablecloth with the tips of her fingers.

'So when are you two getting married then?' ma asks.

'Marriage isn't important to us.'

'What d'you mean by that?'

'We're happy together. Isn't that enough for you?'

'What about children Catherine? You're not as young as you were. It might be too late for you soon.'

'I've always wanted children. I just never felt ready.'

'So you're ready now?'

'Maybe soon.'

'And what about Jack? He might get bored of you… like that father of yours.'

'Did he get bored or did you drive him away?'

'What?'

'You heard me.'

'How dare you say that? He cheated on me, you know that!'

'Did he?'

'What d'you mean?'

'Well, I never saw any of his lovers.'

'You wouldn't remember anyway. You were too young!'

'I was eleven when he left.'

'Yes, you were just a child.'

Catherine stares searchingly into her mother's eyes. 'There weren't any, were there?' she asks matter-of-factly.

'What?'

'All these lovers he was meant to have had…'

'He was a cheat, your father!'

'They never existed, did they?'

'Of course they did.'

'You needed a reason for his departure so you created one.'

'No Catherine…'

'Better that you paint papa as the sinner rather than yourself.'

'No!'

'Did this help you justify your own sexual appetite, is that it? I mean… now you had the moral licence to seduce any man that came your way. Your husband had been obsessed with sex, he'd enjoyed innumerable affairs, and now that he'd gone, well… you could follow his lead.'

'You've gone mad.'

'You needed to construct a fantasy in your mind. Better this than confess to your daughter that your husband had simply had enough of you… of your incessant need.'

'How dare you!'

'He just couldn't take anymore of you…'

'You stupid little bitch!' ma says coldly.

'Where is he now?' Catherine demands.

'If he really loved you, your "papa"…' she says, cruelly mimicking the way her daughter refers to her father, '… then he wouldn't have left you!'

Catherine stares at her mother with an enigmatic blend of sadness and contempt, then lashes out, reason and control abandoning her as she lunges across the dinner table and slaps her hard across the face. A glass smashes on the table. Jack barges through the door to see what is going on. There follows an excruciating silence, as the room seems to stand motionless in time, the candles still burning redly in the low light. Tears well up in Catherine's eyes, watery black droplets running down her cheeks. Ma sits there stone-faced: her blank stare fixed on her reflection in the mirror, her face conveying a sad nescience. Then she mutters, 'I loved him, loved him so much… more than any soul in the whole world… and he left me, he fucking left me… and I became a filthy slut, a whore, and I still can't get over him, even now after so long.' Then she stands up, walks out of the dining room, and head bowed, makes her way upstairs.

Jack immediately turns to Catherine: she still sits at the table. 'Catherine?' he appeals to her.

She says nothing, just holds a piece of broken glass in her hand, twirling it between her thumb and index finger as if it possesses the calming and consoling power of a rosary. She turns towards the front door as the floorboards on the stairs creak. Ma stands in the hallway with her bag. Blood starts to seep from Catherine's fingers. As she looks down at the bloodstain on her white skirt, she hears the front door slam shut.

# 20

**IT IS SIX** in the morning. Jack sits at the grey slate bench in the garden, sure that Catherine is finally asleep. He was up the whole night with her: she barely stopped crying after Eleanor left and finally drifted off in his arms at half past five, just as the sun began to rise through a bank of black clouds. Then Jack retreated downstairs, out into the garden. Unable to sleep, he now gazes at the early morning skyline: black becomes blue and red becomes yellow, a welter of flailing colours mixing and separating. He prays that Catherine will not sink into a depression now.

Again, Jack wonders what it is they actually have together and how much they really love one another. He does not want to contemplate these questions, not at the moment – she needs his support not his doubt, his conviction not his apprehension, his compassion not his ambivalence – but he is unable to suspend the critical dialogue that has begun to expound itself in his mind. First, he thinks back to what Catherine wrote that time, which demanded his love for her be not 'set in stone' but 'carved in her heart'. Leonard had given Molly this kind of love, and its subsequent loss had destroyed him. And then he recalls how afraid he used to be of losing Catherine. This fear made it very easy for him to love her, but now that he is sure she will not leave him, he feels this love fading.

He has felt so much pressure from her these past few months, in fact ever since she started work on the film. She suddenly came to need him so much more, and though he wanted to support her throughout this period as much as he could, he was also determined to commence writing. Leonard's words, 'She needs you a lot, doesn't she,' come to the forefront of his mind now, and then he remembers what he said immediately after this: 'the needs of love, the needs of a woman… Be careful she doesn't take you away from your book.' These words now seem to contain a certain element of prophecy: Jack planned to write today while Catherine and Eleanor spent the day together. Not anymore.

No, he must stop this. He is tired, worn out, has to try and sleep. Jack takes himself inside, back up to bed.

But when he wakes up later on, he immediately begins to scrutinise his relationship with Catherine in the same manner and with the same vigour. It seems that he simply cannot stop himself now. And so over the following weeks, while Catherine throws all her energy into making their relationship better, Jack throws all his into making it worse. He finds himself pulling away from her, backward like a beaten stray dog that cannot trust anything but itself. The book becomes his insular world now, a kind of permanent distraction. He spends hours in his study, writing and rewriting. He approaches each new chapter with a kind of fanaticism: his arguments have to be clear, convincing, irrefutable; his concentration and effort must be absolute. Jack forces himself to work in two five-hour blocks, with a half hour break for lunch in between. He has to be wholly focused and dedicated to it.

During those small periods when he is not writing, Catherine attempts to talk to him about her father: she wants to see him again now, and so called her cousin Sylvia, her father's side of the family, not long after Eleanor left. She is determined to find out what really happened between them, and tells Jack she is now sure her father is not like her mother said he was. Her cousin helps her track down his address and phone number in Barcelona. She calls the number repeatedly but there is no answer. Perhaps he has moved somewhere else? Jack speculates. It might require a trip out there? Catherine wonders. She tells him she must summon the courage to go, sooner or later, and find him. But more often than not when she is talking to Jack about all this, he is not really there: no, his head is somewhere else, wrapped up in the ideas of his beloved book. He knows it will not be long before this becomes intolerable for her.

Jack returns home late one evening to overhear Catherine on the phone in the kitchen. She sounds a little drunk. He does not call out to her as he normally does when he opens the front door, but rather says nothing, gently closes the door behind him, stands perfectly still in the hallway and carefully listens to what she is saying. 'You know, I really hate his fucking book now!' Catherine says. 'The way he is with it, it makes me want to scream. I think it's pulling us apart. I know that sounds funny, but that's what it feels like. I had the same uneasy feeling about Freddie, but he's not around anymore. Jack seems different now, or is it me? He didn't look at me the other night when we made love. I feel like he's avoiding me, like he knows a big secret about us that he wants to tell me but can't...' she says, and then is silent. The person on the other end of the line must be talking now, Jack thinks. But before he has time to contemplate who it is, Catherine speaks again. 'I feel as though if I can't trust him then I can only hate him... I can't talk to him about her, that's why I'm talking to you... I think I just need to get back to work, then everything will be okay... Yes, you're right... Of course I still do!' Catherine says, and then is quiet again. Jack waits. He is sure she is still on the phone. He has not heard her put it down; it must be the person on the other end of the line talking again. Who is she speaking to? Genevieve, maybe Dan, or perhaps someone he does not know, another man? Jack picks up on individual words in the conversation and tries to ascertain what she means by them. The 'her' that she just referred to must be her mother. But what about when she said 'still do'? Is she saying that she still loves him or someone else, the person she is talking to? 'Yes, bye… bye,' Catherine says finally and hangs up.

Jack waits a few moments before he opens the front door, calls out her name, and then slams it shut. He performs this deceitful, surreptitious act without even thinking. It comes to him almost instinctively, as if he possesses an inner cunning that he has not formerly been aware of. As he walks towards the kitchen, a soap opera scenario plays over in his mind: the jealous husband listening in on his wife's conversation, just waiting for the right opportunity to expose her deceit. When he enters the kitchen, he sees Catherine sitting in her panties and bra, legs up on the table, sipping on a glass of red. She stares at her reflection in the mirror and in the low light of the kitchen, only half her face is visible, the other half just a dark and brooding shadow. The bottle of Rioja is almost empty. 'Hi Jack, I was just thinking about you. We'd better fuck now,' she says, opening her legs, pulling her knickers back, stroking her wisp of pubic hair and pouting her lips. He says nothing. She goes on, 'I know you'll want to be asleep soon. Don't want to break that precious routine of yours.'

'I need to work, you know that,' Jack says defensively.

'This isn't about your work. It's about you, your withdrawal from me, your growing inability to even talk… listen to me.'

'The magazine's taking up a lot more of my time at the moment. I've no choice. It has to work. If it doesn't, then how do you propose we pay the mortgage? Remember, you haven't worked for two months now.'

'Bollocks! I've still got money left over from the film, you know that. Anyway, this isn't about your work at the magazine. It's about…'

He interjects, 'I can't simply just drop the book.'

'When you're not in London, your head is permanently inside it. There's no room left for anyone,' Catherine shouts. He is silent. She looks at him expectantly.

'I think you need to get your teeth into another project,' he speaks finally. 'You need to work again. You've spent too much time on your own in the cottage.'

'I'm the problem then, am I? Okay, and if I did this work, are you telling me that it'd be better between us, that suddenly we'd be happy again just like that?'

'No, but it would help.'

'What, so you've got even more time to wallow in your thoughts about the bloody nature of love!'

'What d'you suggest we do then?'

'Look, when we're together, I want you to be with me, really with me. You're always inside your own head, looking for answers. They're not enough, Jack! I need more from you. I feel abandoned. There's something wrong between us. We've got to see whether or not we can work it out.'

He knows he has the opportunity to be open with her now, to tell her exactly how he is feeling. But he says nothing, suddenly finds himself incapable of bridging the widening gap between himself and Catherine, the disparity between his knowledge of what is driving them apart and his ability to address the problems in their relationship and begin the process of reconciliation. Catherine does not say anything more but quietly leaves the room.

Jack goes to his study and slumps in his chair. Leonard immediately returns to the forefront of his mind, and he listens to his words again now, 'the needs of love, the needs of a woman… Be careful she doesn't take you away from your book.' Why did he say this to him? Jack wonders. Perhaps Molly took Leonard away from his work. He has the sudden sense that this might have some bearing on Molly's death, and what happened to Leonard subsequently. And now that he has posed this question, he cannot let go of it. Thoughts of Catherine instantly vanish.

Leonard told him he had difficulty getting his work published after *The Purity of Love*. Why was this? Jack assumed this was because of his worsening grief and alcoholism. But perhaps there was another reason as well. He recalls now what Catherine said to him, that he was 'hopelessly naïve and innocent' in his initial assessment of Leonard – a sad and passionate man who has never recovered from the loss of his wife – and that there was most likely 'another side to the story', which cast Leonard not solely as a tragic romantic victim but rather as a 'decisive perpetrator of his own fate'.

Jack turns to his computer and switches it on. He proceeds to run a search on the web. Taps in Leonard's name. Hundreds of thousands of items are found. He scans through a few of them. One refers to 'Leonard Gold Chartered Accountants', another to Elmore Leonard's *Gold Coast*. He narrows his search to the words, 'Leonard Gold' plus '*The Purity of Love*'. This time, the search engine offers up fewer keyword matches. As he randomly scrolls through them, he comes across one item that reads, '*The Purity of Love*, Leonard Gold's decline…' He clicks on it and it takes him to an article in *The Observer*. Written some twelve years ago, it appeared in the Home News section. Jack reads the first line, 'Leonard Gold, the renowned novelist, has been convicted of indecent assault.' He pauses, struggles to process what he has just read, continues. 'But serious questions are already being asked about how the prosecution used Gold's fiction to make their case. They relied heavily upon a new book the novelist was working on at the time of his arrest, which was 'lewd and cruel in its treatment of women', according to the prosecuting counsel, John Osmond, QC. After reading extracts from it in court, Osmond asked, 'Ladies and gentlemen of the jury, what would a woman make of this book? Well I think any woman would hate it, because Gold seems to hate all women.' Jack stops reading this piece, returns to the list of items found. He looks for another newspaper that picked up the story, needs further confirmation. Locates an article that appeared in *The Daily Mail*. The journalist here was unforgiving of Leonard's conviction. In fact, as far as he was concerned, 'the content of his new work, which was made public by the case – the story of one man's descent into misogyny – is proof enough of Gold's guilt,' he wrote. 'I will not quote here any of the passages which Mr. John Osmond, QC, read out in court,' he went on, 'but suffice to say that they are nothing more than vile pornography, written by a rather wicked man.'

Jack feels breathless now, does not know what to do. Part of him wants to learn more about what Leonard actually did, but another part of him feels he knows quite enough already.

Then the phone rings, Jack answers it, and it is him.

# 21

**HE STANDS** at Speaker's Corner. The spell of good weather has gone. It is wet, muggy, humid. Streaks of grey cloud charge along the tops of buildings and showers break out at sporadic intervals: they cannot be predicted. It is ten past one and Leonard is late. Jack shuffles on the spot, expectant and watchful as his eyes constantly scan the area directly in front of him. Questions invade his mind like bolts of lightning: where is he? Does he suspect that Jack already knows? Maybe he will not show? What should he say to him? Should he just confront him right away, have it out with him? Jack feels like he has been duped. He thought Leonard was someone else – a romantic, an idealist, an intellectual – but not this. There is a tap on his shoulder and then a voice, 'Jack.'

'Leonard?' Jack replies, turning round to confront him, stunned by his presence even though he is expecting him.

'So how are you?' Leonard asks rather soberly.

'Okay. Listen, let's find somewhere to sit down,' Jack says, flustered.

'Right, we can go to one of the Arabic cafés on Edgware Road.'

'Fine,' Jack issues a curt reply.

It is not far. They walk in silence and say very little to one another as they push past shoppers and tourists at Marble Arch, and the sporadic bodies of *London Evening Standard* vendors jabbering 'Stan'ard' like wild predators emitting cautionary growls, loaded with aggressive intent. They head up Edgware Road and go inside the first café they come to, a small Lebanese place just off the main street. A few men lounge around inside, reading one of the Arab dailies published in London, and blowing out plumes of perfumed smoke from their *hookahs*. They sit down and order tea right away. Jack is unable to contain himself any longer, leans over, asks accusingly, 'Why didn't you tell me about your conviction for indecent assault?' Leonard does not answer him. Jack continues, 'Who was she, this woman?' Still nothing. Jack persists, 'I have a right to know.'

'You have a right do you!' Leonard bellows. 'And who gave you this right? Who? Who!' he demands, his whole body shuddering.

'You did. Because you made out you were someone else.'

'What are you talking about?'

'You didn't tell me who you really were… you lied about your name.'

'I didn't lie. I told you I changed it because I wanted to be anonymous.'

'Well now I know *why* you wanted to be anonymous.'

Leonard runs his fingers over the laminate wood of the table, and with his other hand strokes his beard, scratches his chin. 'She was a prostitute,' he says quietly, almost to himself. 'I went to her after Molly died.'

'What did you do to her?'

'I lost it… I forced myself on her.'

'How long d'you spend in prison?'

'Nine months.'

The waiter approaches the table. Jack and Leonard fall silent. He places a beautiful coloured-glass teapot, two small ornate glasses and matching saucers on the table. He pours the tea and offers them sugar. When he is done, Jack immediately resumes his cross-examination. 'I thought you were a romantic. The man I met outside the cathedral, the man who gave me all those wonderful novels to read, the man who wrote *The Purity of Love*… this man was…'

'Jack, don't be so bloody naïve,' Leonard interrupts him. 'So I'm not the great romantic you thought I was.'

'Leonard… this isn't about my naïveté, this is about you not being honest with me, you pretending to be someone else,'

'I didn't tell you my real name because I knew that once you knew this, you'd find out what I'd done… what had become of me… and you'd reject me. This has happened a lot since I did what I did. And in light of your current reaction it would seem that my intuition was right.'

'Leonard, I haven't rejected you yet. I just need to know more… before…' Jack hesitates.

'Before what? Before you can decide whether or not you're still prepared to maintain some kind of relationship with me. Is that it? I must be thoroughly vetted, uncovered, scrutinised.'

'It's not…'

'And am I entitled to examine you in the same way Jack?'

'Look I'm sorry, I didn't mean it quite like that, okay. I'm not here to pass judgment,' Jack concedes.

'Why are you here then?'

'I'm curious Leonard… and I've grown fond of you, you've helped me in some way. Look, we've been through this before!' Jack says impatiently.

'Yes.'

'All I know is what I got from a couple of old newspapers.'

'Which ones?'

'*The Observer* and *The Mail*.'

'The latter was one of the most savage.'

'They said that you were writing another book at the time.'

'Yes.'

'What was it about?'

'Well what they said it was. It was the story of a man who all but gives up on the notion of romantic love. With the end of his marriage, he decides he does not want to marry again, has no intention of forming another meaningful relationship with a woman, and would rather just use the services of prostitutes as a means to fulfil his biological drive and need for sex. And so his relationships with the opposite sex become purely practical. He enjoys the women he pays to sleep with but he does not become attached to them. They are objects to fulfil his desire, nothing more. However, when he meets the prostitute Celia, he finds that he suddenly yearns for meaning and substance. Here is a woman he can finally love. But when she rejects him, he hits her in a violent rage. The book ends with him making a resolution never to love a woman again.'

'What you said to me before, that all love is, in the modern world, is a series of desperate and fractured encounters driven by need… and that there is no point in even looking for it. Is this what *you* believe?'

'If a woman whom you loved more than life itself was taken from you, what would you believe?'

'Leonard, you can't write off love just because of what has happened to you. You can't be this simplistic.'

'Why not?'

'It's inhuman. I mean… what about all the love affairs that endure. Are these worthless as well?'

'Who knows? You'd best consider this question for yourself. I have something I'd like you to read,' and he passes over a small red notebook to Jack. 'This is where I'd got to with it. I suspected that you'd found out about me so I brought it with me.'

'You still haven't told me how Molly died?'

'She was drunk… very drunk. We were fooling around. She fell off a balcony. It was a terrible accident.'

Jack does not read the red notebook right away when he gets back to the flat but launches himself into another bout of web research: he must know the whole story now.

The next thing he comes across is the allegation made by an old girlfriend the day after Leonard's conviction. His lover five years before he met Molly, Juliette Beart claimed she left him because 'his moods were unmanageable', he was 'often arrogant and dismissive', and had 'raised his hand' to her on one occasion. She said no more than this and the public was left to speculate as to what 'raised his hand' actually entailed. Had Leonard Gold been physically violent to her? Either way, the seed of doubt was cast, and Leonard's reputation tarnished further, whether he was guilty of this particular allegation or not.

Then to make matters worse, Jack discovers an hour or so later, a former friend, Damien Webster, came forward and insisted that Leonard regularly visited prostitutes. In fact, he had been to one not long after Molly died, which Damien referred to as 'callous, perverse and distasteful'. Webster went on to say that since Molly had died, Leonard had 'become increasingly prone to angry, violent outbursts', and it was his inability to control these fits of rage which made their continued friendship impossible. 'When he was drunk, I feared for my own safety, let alone the safety of others more vulnerable than myself,' his former friend stated. These words were of course fatal, this much is clear to Jack. Not only had Leonard just been convicted of indecent assault, but he had been portrayed by a former lover and friend as a violent brute and a plausible threat to women. How on earth could he recover from this?

The picture is becoming clearer to Jack now as he sits here engrossed in another man's life, doing all he can to make sense of it. He opens the red notebook and what he finds inside is a kind of diary – only about forty pages or so – a record of one man's thoughts and feelings. A lot of it is barely legible, and those passages that he can read mostly describe – in monotonous, painstaking detail – lurid sexual acts. It is as Leonard described it to him, one man's rejection of romantic love and his descent into nothingness.

Jack can see that after Molly's death Leonard became increasingly impatient with the establishment, with the world around him. *The Purity of Love* did not provide the catharsis he had so hoped for: this sublimation of his grief in his work was ineffectual, he still suffered terribly. Consequently, it seems, Leonard's pronouncements became more radical, and in turn his admirers became fewer. His writing began to define itself as aggressive, forceful and intrusive at this stage; it sought to directly challenge accepted and conventional mores of decency and taste. This is what the contents of the red notebook, the work he was writing prior to his arrest, was all about! Leonard was crying out for someone to hear his pain, but few listened since he had done such a damn good job of alienating them.

The final thing Jack finds on-line is an interview Leonard gave, he is not sure quite when, in which he was quoted as saying, 'Literature must be a profound examination of the self. It must be an attempt to grapple with one's true nature and the true nature of man in general. Literature must not only convey that which is amenable and beautiful. It must also convey that which is difficult and ugly.' *The Daily Mail* journalist had most likely read this as well when he wrote his devastating piece. Jack remembers now what he wrote: 'Leonard Gold sees in himself something ugly and misogynistic and, it seems, has sought to apply this to all men.'

Jack lets go of the mouse and leans back in his chair. He is not sure if his mind can absorb any more new information today: it feels heavy, overloaded. He looks away from the keyboard and down at *The Purity of Love*, which still sits on his desk: he has not put it back on the bookshelf since last reading it. This wonderful book, Jack thinks, elevates love, the Greek notion of *eros*, above the libido, and propounds the view that man's essential desire is to relate to, to cherish and to adore a woman, to enter into a deep and beautiful union with her and commit himself to this end. But now, it would seem, Leonard has come to completely reject this romantic view of man's aspiration to love as a façade, a fabrication, a perversion of the truth. For him, man's only master now is desire, the unstoppable energy of sexual desire. This drive is raw, selfish, chaotic and unpredictable; it resists being moderated or civilised; and it does not want to be turned into something it is not, namely romantic love. It is not adult and mature by nature and it should not be made to be. Rather it is animal, childlike, irresponsible. A man in the grips of his libido wants to have sex with a woman regardless of who she is.

# 22

**JACK CONTINUES** to be remote, preoccupied with his book, and so here she is, in the garden, forced to write in her damn journal, desperate to capture the depth of feeling she can no longer experience first hand with him. Catherine wants to feel high again, to have that feeling of flying through the air: so magical, beautiful, brilliant. There is no sign of autumn. It is warm, bright; the air is still. The sun beams nonchalantly in a clear blue sky. She now has not worked for over three months, has been offered a number of documentaries, but has turned them down. She is developing some ideas with Dan, is due to direct a short film he has written – having finally received funding for it – at the end of November or early December. However, she is in no mad rush to get back to work. Her head is moving somewhere else now: Catherine has begun to think about having a baby.

For her, this is about creating something, bringing something into this world other than a bloody film – something living, innocent. What is a film at the end of the day? she asks herself. It is just a roll of celluloid or a silly bit of videotape. And Jack's precious book, well, this is nothing more than a collection of words on a page. Catherine is sure this is what she and Jack need, a focus, a thing to share and love. She wants it to be like it was when they first moved into the cottage. She will never forget this period it was so perfect. Jack, this man who made her feel more adored, who filled her with more love than any other man. She refuses to lose what he has showed her, will continue to love him no matter what. She will not let herself become like ma, no never! But he must not make her wait too long. She waited too long before.

Catherine looks up towards Jack's study now. There he is, engrossed in his world of ideas. She knows he is becoming increasingly worried about *Detritus* now: the last edition did not perform any better despite his and Sarah's bold initiatives. He has agreed to cover the whole mortgage this month and the next, until she formally returns to film production after her sabbatical. He looks up from his screen now, out of the window, at her. She gets to her feet and calls to him, 'It's like an Indian summer out here, Jack. It's wonderful, you must come outside.'

'Yeah okay, I'll be out in a sec,' he replies, and she is taken aback, did not expect him to agree to her request. She was getting ready for his usual barrage of, 'I need to work!'

'Okay,' she says excitedly.

'Let me just finish this bit.'

'Let's go for a walk, Jack. We haven't done this for so long.'

'Yes… good idea.'

'I'll just put my shoes on,' she says as she runs up the lawn, and inside the cottage.

Jack emerges from his study. 'I've had a good day,' he calls to her. 'Just finished the seventh chapter. I'm more than half way through now.'

He seems different today, peppy, almost light-hearted, thank God. She does not know why. Perhaps he wants what she wants now? Catherine wonders. Dear old Jack, forever taking life too seriously. He has been so sombre of late. But not now, and she is instantly aware of what she has been missing as he stands at the other end of the hallway and beams a broad smile at her. 'Ready?' Catherine asks.

'Coming,' he replies as he slings his pullover over his shoulder and bundles down the hallway towards her.

She and Jack walk down the valley. Catherine wears a sarong and a silk blouse. She removes her cardigan and wraps it round her bare waist. Her blouse has an open back, and she can feel the sun on it, then Jack's arm as he puts it around her waist, caresses this part of her. They do not speak to one another. She does not feel the need to, and senses that Jack does not either.

Their doubts about their future together seem to vanish as they make their way towards the woods; he is different with her. The man she walks alongside now, he loves her, and she knows he always will. It is as if he has suddenly had enough of the endless questions, thoughts, notions, ideas about love, and just wants her, Catherine.

She takes his arm and leads him into a dense patch of woodland. They make their way through thick, scattered shrubbery. The sun filters through the trees, forming shafts and pools of light all around them. She and Jack find a clear patch of deep green grass in the shadows. They lie down side by side, flanked by foxgloves with their tiers of magenta bells. The air is perfectly still. They look up at the small-leaved lime tree above them. 'It's so quiet,' Catherine says. 'All I can hear are the birds.'

'Yes it is.'

'I feel wonderful today Jack. It's funny but I don't know why. I just feel happy, happy to be alive.'

'I love you, you know. I might not have shown it very well lately… but I really do,' he says.

She stands up and removes her blouse and sarong; she is not wearing any underwear. Catherine stands over him, naked. A tear runs down Jack's cheek, and she thinks she knows where this is from. Perhaps he has been reminded of what Catherine is to him. He undresses, a rather sublime image in the woodland, and she sits on top of him. She makes love to him slowly, tenderly. And after, they just lie wrapped in one another's bodies, skin touching, lips kissing.

In the silence that follows, Catherine wonders whether she might have conceived.

Jack leaves for London early the following morning and kisses her tenderly, in a way that he has not for many months. He has come back to her, yes. She held this awful sense that once he thought he had her, had won her heart, then she would be reduced to nothing more than a habit in his mind.

Papa comes to her again now. Catherine managed to get hold of one of his neighbours the other day, Viuda Garcia – Sylvia had tracked down the number for her – who told Catherine she did not know where her father is. He has a villa in the countryside and often goes there for long periods, sometimes months at a time, but this time it seems longer. And yet, she does not know him very well, Widow Garcia conceded. Catherine was not able to get anymore than this out of her: her English was poor. Sylvia called her again on Catherine's behalf – her Spanish was near fluent – but Widow Garcia offered up no more information other than the fact that Señor Ramirez keeps himself to himself. He is a quiet man … a private man, she stressed. However, she assured Sylvia that if she heard anything, anything at all, she would let Catherine know right away.

Widow Garcia is a rather difficult, unreliable old woman, and according to Sylvia, Catherine would benefit from finding someone else out there that knows him better. Perhaps she should get on the phone to Sylvia right now and see if she has any ideas about whom else she could call. But no, she does not feel compelled to do it at this moment, not now that Jack has come back to her.

# 23

'SO… WHAT d'you make of it?' Leonard asks him as he sips on his whisky and peers at Jack through his spectacles, perched on the edge of his old wooden chair in the back of the bookshop.

'I don't know what to say. What I read was very bleak… and to be honest, I didn't read much of it… I think I'd heard enough when you told me what it was about,' Jack replies as he struggles to find a comfortable spot on Leonard's dilapidated sofa.

'Yes, it's bleak… but I didn't write it to entertain. I wrote it to try and get at something.'

'At what?'

'The truth.'

'The truth?' Jack inquires bluntly. 'Well it's a pretty subjective one you reach. I mean, it's just one man's point of view.'

'My point in writing it was I didn't think it was. I thought it was representative of quite a few men.'

'You think all men loathe women, is that what you think?' Jack asks.

'Is that what I thought, you mean. I wrote this book twelve years ago Jack.'

'Okay, is that what you *thought* then?'

'Let's discuss it first!' Leonard says firmly.

Jack gathers himself, then speaks. 'Well look… I can't accept your protagonist's view that libido is all there is…' he says, 'that feelings of love are merely illusions in the mind.'

'My character concludes that sex is just about release. It's a physiological process and nothing more. Pent-up energy and fluid are discharged, they build up again, and then need releasing again… and so on.'

'Yes it is just this but it's also a lot more as well. I mean, what about when you have sex with someone you love? Catherine and I had sex yesterday and it was wonderful… it was so much more than what your character says it is.'

Leonard wriggles in his chair and frowns, seems almost uncomfortable at the mention of her name. Jack waits for him to respond. He finally speaks. 'My protagonist would say that libido is a quantitative and not a qualitative thing,' he says. 'A man might often think he feels something greater for one woman than for another, but in reality, he doesn't. His biological need has simply duped him into thinking he does. The object of his desire is less important than the amount of sexual energy and fluid he has stored up inside him.'

'Come on Leonard… what you're saying here is ridiculous!'

'What my character is saying you mean.'

'Well what are *you* saying then?' Jack asks.

Leonard fixes his stare on him.

Jack manages to calm himself, then continues, 'Look, I didn't mean to shout, it's just that… sex is often no good at all even when you haven't had it for ages. I mean… most of us don't fall in love with one-night stands, do we? Surely you can't agree with your character's view here. You loved Molly. I'm sure sex with her wasn't like sex with other women. It felt better, deeper, more real… you enjoyed it more… because you loved her,' he insists.

'Yes, I might've done. But she's gone now, hasn't she!' Leonard rebuffs.

'Let's keep to the work, okay,' he goes on, irritated, eager to regain control of the exchange. 'With the failure of his marriage, my character's compelled to re-evaluate what love is. He wonders whether it's just about being gratified and fulfilled, having one's own needs met. It's a lot easier to love someone when you get your own way with them. He goes on to have sex with lots of different women rather than just committing to one as he'd done with his wife, and his life is no less rich, fulfilling…'

'Leonard, his life ends in bloody despair for God's sake!'

'But is it any less valid, less true because of this?'

'What're you talking about?'

'I'm talking about how his life changes, how he decides to be faithful to his desires, not to moderate or control them… how he'll not be swayed by the majority consensus… how he comes to view love as something else.'

'But Leonard, this majority might say that your protagonist ends up a cruel, pathetic and deluded bastard. Okay, he might be determined to get to the bottom of his masculinity, his soul, whatever… and he might, as a consequence, become more faithful to his innate desires as a man, a human being… but this doesn't warrant the reader's respect and admiration, and it doesn't necessarily bring him any closer to the truth, whatever the hell you think this is. I mean… he just ends up a misogynist… and why, because he couldn't make his marriage work. His failure's made him angry and bitter, that's it… and all he's got left to do now is take it out on vulnerable women!'

'And I could say in his defence that the majority of people are simply reluctant to confront the ugly truth that he represents. He'd say that all us men have it in us, Jack, to hate women, and he has the honesty to express this part of him however awful it is. Most of us dare not express this part of ourselves for fear of rejection.'

'Is that why you assaulted that woman then?' Jack says accusingly, unwilling to distinguish anymore between Leonard and his fictional creation.

'Maybe it is?'

'And what about *her*, Leonard, what you did to her, how you made her feel?' Jack demands.

'I'm still living with what I did… to her. But this is something that *I*…' emphasising this word, 'that I must struggle with,' Leonard insists.

'What are you getting at?'

'I was judged by an angry mob after I did what I did to that woman. It was a frenzy of moral outrage. Why?'

'Because of what you'd done Leonard.'

'But I hadn't done it to them. *They* were not my victims.'

'Yes, and…' Jack presses him.

'I'd awakened something inside them Jack.'

'What?'

'Most people are usually more than willing to judge and condemn *someone else*, and some will even delight in this person's subsequent suffering, as long as it is not their own!'

'I don't know about *most* people.'

'Well it seems that way. Most of us have a formidable appetite for other people's sins: the tabloids are testament to this. Surely this inclination is more than just simple curiosity.' Jack is silent now. He knows Leonard has more to say. He continues, 'Me, Leonard Gold, the noble writer, was suddenly labeled a sad and pathetic man, a hater of women. I was dismissed as bad. But if only there were more people who were willing and prepared to really look inside themselves. I think you are.' Jack looks over at the bottle of whisky on the table; suddenly, he craves a drink. Leonard goes on, 'Most people won't acknowledge the duality of the human psyche because it exposes an aspect that is dark and sinister. It doesn't sit well with a more singular, undivided, benevolent vision of human nature. But this incompatibility doesn't make this duality a lie. Far from it, it should offer the majority of people another way of looking at themselves, and others.'

'But your creation is ultimately full of hatred. How can this be seen as something good, constructive… laudable?'

'My protagonist hates people who are so convinced of their own virtue that they criticise and judge him for his lack of it.'

Again, Jack looks over at the whisky. 'Can I get myself one?' he blurts out as he reaches for the bottle.

'Go ahead. You'll find another glass by the sink. You'd better rinse it,' Leonard says. Jack does not bother. He pours himself a large measure, gulps it down. 'What I tried to get at, and what I'm still trying to get at, is the contradiction, you see,' Leonard presses on as Jack pours himself another whisky right away. 'And this incongruity is so important because it reveals what man really is. My protagonist doesn't only hate but loves as well, doesn't only destroy but creates as well. He expresses *all* of his humanity,' he says, pausing briefly to catch his breath. He continues, 'Oedipus unwittingly killed his father and married his mother. When he realised what he'd done, he went mad and cut out his own eyes while his mother hanged herself. He wasn't wholly bad or exclusively evil. No, course he wasn't! He was a man who battled with his passions, with all of his humanity. He was true to what it is to be a man, what it is to be human. Don't you see!'

'Of course I do Leonard. It's all in the *Poetics*, and in Freud and Jung… the shadow self and all that. Look, none of what you're saying is new. I've heard it a thousand times before!'

'Yes but how many have actually *lived* this life rather than just bloody pontificating about it, huh… and which of us live it now, today… which of us really have the courage to explore it? Come on!'

'And *you* do I suppose?' Jack asks him soberly as he takes another large mouthful of whisky, screwing up his face in discomfort as it hits the back of his throat.

'That's for you to decide,' Leonard says, then rushes to the front of the shop. Jack listens to the commotion of books thumping the floor and thudding against one another. Then he hears footsteps pounding towards him on the wood floor. 'Here we are!' Leonard announces, standing over

## LOVE AND MAYHEM

Jack in the manner of a schoolmaster again, arms outstretched, holding four big books as if he is displaying a magnificent trophy. He drops them into Jack's lap. 'You have some more reading to do if you really want to get at what love is,' he goes on. 'There's Schopenhauer, Nietzsche, Camus… and of course, we mustn't forget Sade. No doubt you know their ideas, but I want you to read them in the same way that I asked you to read the novels I gave you.'

Jack sits here, overwhelmed by Leonard, anxious to get away from him now. Yes, he has read Nietzsche and Camus, and he is familiar with the others' ideas, but does he really want to read them again, and why. What is Leonard really offering him, for God's sake? Just a mish-mash of other people's ideas! His mind might, at one stage, have been capable of original, groundbreaking thought, but not now, after all the whisky he has consumed over the past twelve years.

But whatever it is Leonard wants Jack to know, he clearly has not finished. In fact, it now seems he will stop at nothing to make Jack see the world the way he, and a few select others, see it. 'According to Schopenhauer, man is driven by a blind and restless will. He'll stop at nothing to exercise it, to fulfil its wants and needs…'

'I don't think I can accept this view.'

'Why not?'

'Because of the existence of love. There are many people who are selfless, who put other's needs before their own.'

'Yes, granted. But are they happy?'

'Yes, I think they are. They realise that happiness can be acquired through sacrifice rather than a blind allegiance to the "yearnings of a restless will".'

'But are they being *truthful?* Are they not living a lie, just deceiving themselves? Are these people denying what it really means to be human?'

'This is a massive assumption you're making!'

'The whole history of ideas is a long and great series of assumptions. Thought can only evolve through supposition and generalisation. Look at what Sade said for instance. He maintained that we're all selfish creatures in pursuit of the maximum amount of enjoyment.'

'But where does all this self-gratification *lead*?'

'To "the hell of our desires", in Camus' words.'

'Yes…'

Leonard smiles perplexedly at Jack as he takes another swig of whisky, at this moment seeming to give credence to the rather irresponsible notion that happiness does indeed lie at the bottom of a bottle. 'Here are men who all confirm that love exists in polarity with hate. You must get at the truth, Jack, otherwise why even bother to write the damn book! If you conclude like Sade that we want to subjugate other human beings rather than love them, then say so. Maybe we can't be happy unless we're allowed to dominate? Or you might think like Camus that we can only find happiness if we harness these destructive desires, fight them in ourselves and make them a force for good. D'you want to show love in all its fragmentation and absurdity, or d'you want to show its harmony and interconnectedness? This is a vital question! You must delve inside your *own* heart. Examine yourself. Be truthful. What is it? What d'you really think love is, deep down in your belly?' he shouts passionately, then slumps back down on his chair and throws his head back.

Leonard sits in the chair, limbs splayed like a rag doll, looking exhausted. He does not say anything else now and the room quickly becomes very still.

Jack sits there and listens to Leonard as he starts to breathe gruffly through the silence.

And when his breathing evolves into a deep, grumbling snore, Jack picks up the books he has just been given and quietly leaves the shop.

# 24

**IN THE MORNING,** Catherine runs downstairs and calls to Jack in his study, 'Just popping out. Won't be long.'

'Where you going?' he asks.

'Just into the village.'

'Can you pick me up some headache tablets? We've run out.'

She does not answer him right away, and so Jack asks again, 'Is that okay?'

Perhaps she should tell him? Yes, she should, goes into his study and blurts out excitedly, 'Look, I can't keep it to myself any longer. I'm late.'

'What?'

'I'm late, my period's late,' and she looks to him to say something but he says nothing. She goes on, 'I think I'm pregnant, Jack.'

'Right,' he mumbles, shaking his head.

'Jack, we might be having a baby…'

But he is speechless now, just looks at her blankly, then turns away.

'Jack?' she continues, appealing to him.

'I…' he mutters, and it is immediately clear to her that he does not know what to say. He was not meant to respond this way to such potentially wonderful news, no.

'D'you hear what I just said?' she asks, even though she knows he did, of course he did, how could he have not.

'Yeah,' he replies. 'It just came as a bit of a surprise, that's all.'

Catherine finds herself immediately seizing on the tone of his voice: it sounds flat, almost dispassionate. 'You sound like you don't care?'

'Course I do… it's just such… an enormous thing. I thought it wouldn't happen this way… that we'd plan it first, talk about it, you know…'

'I thought you'd be delighted…' she says, and her words trail off to nowhere.

'Catherine, I'm happy, course I am. I didn't mean to come across like that, I'm sorry…'

'You needn't apologise… if that's how you really feel?'

'Look, I'm happy about it… really!'

But she knows he is not, and sinks to the floor now, sliding down the back wall. 'I want a baby Jack,' she says tearfully. 'I've thought about it a lot since I came back from London. I need something more in my life than just bloody pictures on a screen, the whirl of images inside my head…'

'Why didn't you tell me?'

'I was scared to when things weren't good between us. But we've been happy together just recently… really happy, haven't we?'

'Yes we have.'

'Well then it's good news isn't it?'

'Look, d'you know you definitely are?'

'Well no, not for sure. I was on the way out to get a test.'

'Let me go,' he says as he stands up, takes his jacket from the back of the chair. 'I'll get it for you.'

'Isn't it for us?'

'Yes… of course it is. Look, I'll be back as soon as I can,' and with these words, he is gone.

Jack has offered to go because he needs to think, needs to be alone, does not want her judgment. This is typical of him. He runs when he cannot face something. And she can picture him now in the car, fretting over the eventuality that she is indeed pregnant, looking at it from every bloody angle. God, why must he do this, and now more than ever, question, analyse, dissect everything.

Catherine looks over at his desk, at a pile of books. From where she is sitting, she tries to read one of the spines but cannot make it out. She clambers to her feet and walks over to the desk to see what book it is; it is Nietzsche's *Collected Works*. Jack has been reading again the last month or so, approaching each new book as if it were a mission, working with a greater intensity than ever before. It is like he is an addict: for he seems to derive the same kind of relish and gratification from his work that a junkie derives from his next hit of smack or a drunk from his next can of booze.

She reaches for one of his notebooks on his desk, opens it, begins to read. 'There are certain men that are terrified about becoming the object of a woman's love,' Jack writes. 'According to this type of man, a woman's love brings with it so much expectation and responsibility that his fear slowly transmutes into irritation, and before he knows it, he finds himself in the unwelcome position of being needed and wanted all the time. Thus he begins to resent the woman who loves him.'

Catherine is quickly convinced that he is writing about himself. He is one of these men, is starting to resent her. She puts down this notebook, takes another one, opens it, scans one of its pages as if searching for more incriminating testimony. His words will indict him, confirm his unreliability, his untrustworthiness. Christ, has he just strung her along all this time? Yes, maybe ma is right.

She reads on, 'When a romantic man first falls in love, he feels that he's suddenly discovered his true self. It's as if he's found his way home at last. Everything the woman says and does seems to bring him closer to his core identity. He locates a person who, to his surprise, is hopeful rather than despairing, genuine rather than insincere, benign rather than malevolent, and selfless rather than selfish. The woman helps him locate the positives in himself. She holds up a mirror for him, and he begins to like what he sees. Here is someone who helps him confirm his identity rather than scrutinise and negate it.'

Yes, this is exactly what she has done for Jack. She has made him less shy, awkward, neurotic, introspective. He is happier with her than without her. Encouraged, Catherine continues. 'However, as this man's love fades, so his self-image wanes as well: the less he loves his woman, the less he loves himself. We'd all like to believe that self-esteem is something we can objectively nurture in ourselves, independent of others: we don't need the encouragement of others to feel good about ourselves. But is this really possible? For when we look closer, we see that our sense of self is based both on our perception of others and their perception of us. We, like them, are looking to bolster, and feel better about, ourselves. People are more likely to compliment us if we compliment them. Likewise, they're more likely to criticise us if we criticise them. Hence, we're motivated by self-interest. To this end, we'll deceive ourselves into thinking that our self-image can somehow be verified objectively. Someone tells us that we're a kind and sensitive person, and therefore, we are just this. But they didn't see how cruel and insensitive we'd been just moments before. Hence, the judgments of others don't always provide reliable data about our true character. This awareness begs the crucial question: perhaps we can only love ourselves when we love others? Hence, doesn't it follow that we love others only so we can feel better about ourselves? And so, is romantic love merely a trick of the weak and insecure ego, a deceptive kind of self-love? Rather this than sit in our room alone, as Pascal observed.'

No, Catherine says to herself, enough. She does not want to read anymore. Jack does not really believe what he is writing here, surely, this cynical logic. He cannot. It leads to appalling selfishness. She tosses the notebook to one side, reaches for another one. Opens it. Jack has scrawled across the top of the page, 'Freddie's right about this. I'm sure he is. There is a tendency in man to...'

'Catherine, what are you doing?' Jack says as she looks up to see him standing in the doorway holding the pregnancy test in his hand.

'Jack?' she says, her voice full of panic. 'I... I didn't hear you?'

'Obviously not. Why are you going through my notebooks?' he asks her, his voice loaded with recrimination. She does not answer him. It is now her turn to be elusive. 'Catherine?' he continues.

'You're still seeing Freddie aren't you?' she demands, holding the notebook aloft in her hand, waving it in the air as if she holds the crucial piece of evidence to confirm his betrayal.

Jack swipes it violently out of her hand, looks at its front cover, reads the date scrawled on it, then shouts, 'This notebook is over a year old!'

'Don't fucking lie to me, Jack! I can tell when you are.'

'And what if I am?'

'Those are *his* bloody books, aren't they!' she says, pointing at the pile of books behind her on his desk.

'Catherine, I never told you I wouldn't see him again.'

'Can't you see, Jack, how he comes between us?'

'No I can't.'

'We argued about him before.'

'That wasn't about him. It was about you wanting me to stay in London.'

'No Jack, it was about *this man* coming between us.'

'Catherine, you're being irrational.'

'You've changed the more time you've spent with him. You've become more gloomy, pessimistic…'

'What you talking about?'

'This book you're writing. It's become less hopeful, more melancholic… you must see that!'

'No.'

'You're being dragged down by a mad, bitter old drunk!'

'You haven't even met him. How can you judge him in this way? What d'you know about Leonard?'

'Leonard?'

'Yes, it's Leonard not Freddie.'

'What you going on about?'

'The mad, bitter old drunk you're referring to is Leonard Gold, the novelist. He was a fabulous writer, Catherine.'

'And he's instrumental to your book is he?'

'Well…'

'Even if he affects our relationship?'

'That's unfair.'

'Is it? I mean… why? For what Jack?'

'You know why, Catherine. You know what I'm doing it for!'

'No I don't!' she screams.

'I'm just trying to get at the truth Catherine!'

'The truth? You sound like a bloody lunatic! What is this, Jack… this word. What does it fucking mean?'

'What do we really have between us, Catherine… what do we have? Is it love?'

Catherine snatches the test kit out of his hand and dashes upstairs to the bathroom. She slams the door behind her, bolts it shut. Takes out the absorbent strip, urinates on it, then without so much as looking at it, lays it on the ledge beside her.

Waits.

The wait is long. She hears Jack downstairs in the kitchen: he puts away the clean dishes. She listens closely to the rattle of plates piling up on one another, the clunking of mugs as he stacks them in the small cupboard, the chiming of glasses in the drawer. A door slams, then the pipes groan as he turns on the tap, fills the sink. The squirt of washing up liquid as it leaves the plastic bottle. New soapy water. The tinny jangle of cutlery as he shakes the bowl, knives and forks thud against the plastic, a dull sound.

He is doing anything to keep his mind off what she is in the process of discovering up here, on her own.

Catherine leans over now, tentatively looks at the strip. It is not only wet with her urine but her blood as well. She tosses it to the floor and begins to sob.

Cannot hear anything now other than her short, disjointed gasps of breath, the mucus in her nose and throat.

And when she stops crying, the house is very quiet, no sound at all.

Catherine turns, leans over and ferrets for a sanitary towel in the small wicker basket on the shelf behind her.

# III

# LOVING ONE ANOTHER

# 25

**SHE AND JACK** are asleep in bed when the phone rings. It is late, about one in the morning. Catherine rolls over to pick it up. 'Hello…' she says, then continues curtly, '… right, yep, hang on a second,' and thrusts the handset into Jack's open palm.

She jumps straight out of bed, and irritated, storms into the bathroom, slams the door behind her. She stares at her reflection in the mirror. What is Sarah doing calling him at this time? Catherine has found it almost impossible to talk to him since he said what he said. Why does he feel the need to doubt it, why? If he wants to question it, test it, push it to its limit, then so be it … she will do the same. He does not need to do this, no.

Christ, how many other women will he have to fuck before she stops loving him, ten, twenty … and how many other men will she have to fuck before he stops loving her? Is this what he wants them to do now, fuck around, go with different people?

Stop this … Catherine tells herself as she takes hold of her face, looks to the mirror again.

But no, she cannot calm down, does not want to.

She takes off her bra and knickers, struts back into the bedroom. Begins to parade naked in front of Jack: he is now deep in conversation with Sarah.

Frustrated by his lack of interest, Catherine jumps up onto the bed and stands over Jack, peering down at him. She takes her breasts in her hands and pulls her nipples. He waves his arm, shooing her away, off the bed, but Catherine ignores this gesture. Instead, she begins to rub herself with the tip of her middle finger before she slips the whole finger deep inside her, then says, 'Are you fucking her, you arsehole?'

Jack forces his hand over the mouthpiece and looks at Catherine in disbelief. She just stares blankly at him. He puts the phone back to his ear and says, 'Sarah… listen, sorry… I've got to go.'

'Yes, Jack had better go now. His woman needs fucking!' Catherine says.

Jack tries to ignore her as he struggles to wind up his conversation with Sarah. 'I'm sure it'll go okay,' he says. 'We've worked damn hard. We all deserve it, remember that. Good luck with him. I'll call you at midday when you get out of there… okay, bye,' and with these words, he hangs up the phone, looks up at Catherine and asks coolly, 'What the hell was that about?'

She does not answer him but just pulls back the duvet and tears at his boxer shorts, yanking them down his legs. Then she clambers on top of him, grabs his flaccid penis and begins to move her fingers up and down its fleshy shaft. 'Come on, Jack. Can't get it up anymore, eh?' she shouts, then slaps him hard across the face.

He clutches his cheek, which turns red right away, looks sore. He grabs her by the arms. He is hard now – now that she has hit him – and he pulls down on her shoulders as he forces himself inside of her.

Catherine wriggles her shoulders free of his grip, pins him down by his wrists, but holds him there, inside her. Leans over and kisses him first. Finds that she wants to bite his lip but also touch it tenderly. Then she proceeds to thrust away on top of him, intent only on pleasing herself.

Jack lets her come, then grabs her shoulders and pulls her off of him. Catherine falls onto her stomach, and he clambers on top of her, forces her legs apart, enters her. He begins to pound away military-style like a soldier doing press-ups: she has not been fucked like this in a long time. 'Harder you bastard, harder…' Catherine screams then winces in pain. Her desire to be fucked by Jack is now indistinguishable from her desire to be hurt by him. But before she is able to get hold of this thought, he comes inside her.

He rolls off Catherine and lies on his back, sweaty and out of breath. She gets up and walks slowly towards the door. In the dark of the room he does not look real. She thinks that he might just vanish to another place, and she would not stop him. No, she would let him go.

Jack opens his eyes now and stares at her. They look at one another sharply, but say nothing.

# 26

**WHEN HE** is next in London, he arranges to have dinner with Sam. He has not seen him for some time, what with all the trouble at *Detritus*.

Jack turns up to the restaurant fairly drunk – which is unlike him, he knows – and as the evening goes on, he finds himself needing to drink like a man who wants to forget everything. Dear Sam is very conscious of quite how much his friend is putting away tonight – he has always been terrible at hiding such chummy concern – and conveys his disapproval with the occasional disparaging look, but does not actually *say* anything until the end of dinner.

'Come on. Let's get another drink!' Jack says as they stand up to leave.

'No Jack, let's get home.'

'Sam, we're in the heart of Soho, look around you…' he says as they step outside.

'You've had enough.'

'What you talking about? Come on…' Jack slurs as he stares at a neon sign just down the road, which carries the pink silhouette of a naked woman.

'You alright Jack?' Sam asks him.

He knows that this question is pointed, is concerned less with his physical state right now and more with how he is feeling inside since they last saw one another, how things have been with Catherine, and how things are at the moment. 'Yeah fine. Couldn't be better!' Jack says buoyantly. 'Why?'

'I don't know, it's just... I haven't seen you like this before.'

'Like what?' Jack asks, staggering down the road towards the neon sign.

'Well... you know, this drunk, this...'

'Oh come on... just one more drink,' he says with all the monotony of an alcoholic as he takes Sam's arm and leads him down the street.

'No, really Jack. I'm done for the night.'

Jack stops underneath the naked woman. 'How about in here?' he persists, pointing through an open door that leads into a club. 'Just one!'

'I really think you've had enough,' Sam urges him. 'Why don't we jump in a cab?'

'If you don't want to come in, I'll go in on my own.'

'Jack...' Sam appeals to him, 'in there, they'll take all your money.'

'No it'll be fine.'

He knows that Sam is reluctant to leave him on his own, the state he is in. 'Look, I have to call Jude first,' he says frustratedly, 'just to let her know I'm going to be a bit late.'

'What?'

'I have to let Jude know.'

'Jesus Sam, she's got you on a fucking tight leash!' he quips back, not giving himself time to appreciate quite what he is saying, quite how offensive he is being.

Sam does not rise to his provocation. He probably attributes his poor behaviour to the drink. Forever the gentleman! Jack has never been so outright rude to him. But as he dials Jude's number, he gives him that look, which Jack knows all too well from when he used to work with Sam, when Sam was his boss, the look which says very firmly, 'We'll talk about this tomorrow, Jack. Alright!' He speaks into the phone now, 'Hi, it's me. Look, I'm sorry I'm late… I'll be back soon.' He hangs up, then turns to Jack and says, 'Just one okay, and then I'm going to take you home.'

The club is big inside; it has high ceilings, imitation chandeliers, a black marble top bar, and gigantic curvaceous settees. Mirrors line the walls and even make their vanity-driven quest onto the ceiling. There are young women everywhere. They all wear tiny garments of clothing, beachy and transparent, which leave little room for the imagination.

He and Sam sit down near the bar and survey the floor. A waitress takes their order. Most of the women appear confident and brash as they parade themselves along the bar, the stage, and in between tables. They know the power they hold over their male clientele, a seemingly desperate collection of lonely and frustrated men who are searching for the sexual intimacy and release of a pre-packaged kind, tipped off by a twenty-pound note wrapped round a G-string.

Jack watches Sam as he looks over at a fat man to his left who slouches on a red leather couch – slack-jawed and drooling, his stomach bulging over his trousers – while a young naked Chinese girl, probably no more than nineteen years old, rubs herself up and down the man's thigh. He stares at her genitals, as if this space between her legs is filled with infinite possibilities. 'You want to touch me, don't you? I shaved it just for you. You like it like that, don't you?' she says to the man.

Their drinks arrive. Jack now finds himself almost transfixed by the Chinese girl's hairless vagina, which makes her look very young indeed, almost prepubescent. She catches Jack's eye, winks at him and he looks away, embarrassed. At that moment, Jack feels as needy and hopeless as all the other men around him; like them, he craves the tender touch and smell of a woman's body, the 'healing powers of her bosoms, her buttocks and her vagina', in Leonard's words. He read this in the red notebook, and now remembers the rest of it almost word for word: 'When men are sad and lonely, they all yearn for a naked woman to take away the pain.' Then Jack takes a swig of whisky, slumps forward on the couch and stares down at the shiny red carpet. 'You okay?' Sam asks him.

'I was just thinking about Catherine…' he says.

'What about her?'

'Oh I don't know…' Jack mumbles, then looks up again and returns his observation to the Chinese girl, who continues to dance for the fat man.

'I can feel you're hard now…' she teases the man, then smiles at him and cackles. A new song comes on. 'You want another dance? Yeah…' she whines at him as she thrusts her arse in his lap and grinds away at his penis trapped beneath his trousers. 'Oh it's big,' she mutters.

The man lets out a sudden sharp moan, then thrusts himself forward and sits upright, elbows on knees. 'I better go to the bathroom,' he grunts as he slips a note into her hand, then sheepishly shuffles away. Jack is not sure whether the man has just ejaculated in his trousers or whether he plans to masturbate in one of the toilet cubicles.

A tall Russian blonde girl walks up to Jack and forces one of her long bare legs between his crotch. 'You look lonely. You want me to dance for you. My name is Lolita,' she titillates with a mischievous but vulnerable smile as if trying to assume the aspect of Nabokov's adolescent heroine, then pulls her stomach in to accentuate her cleavage. Jack looks up at her. She must be almost six feet, early twenties, he thinks, with an enormous cleavage and round hips, a far cry from her fictional namesake. He nods awkwardly as she removes her black lace knickers and slings them in the air without any attempt at graceful seduction. Then she theatrically sweeps one of her legs, Broadway-style, in between Jack's legs, and rubs her open-toed stiletto against his groin.

'Look, let's get out of here,' Sam says, taking Jack by the arm and pulling him towards him. 'You don't need this.'

'What you talking about?' Jack slurs. 'It's just a bit of a fun Sam. Don't be so melodramatic.'

'That's rich coming from you,' Sam replies just as another girl appears beside Lolita and thrusts her crotch in his face now.

'You want a dance like your friend here?' the girl asks Sam, then strokes his groin. 'He likes Lolita, I can see…' she murmurs, smiling at Jack, '… and I think you like me, don't you,' she says provocatively.

'No I'm okay really…' Sam answers, as he sits upright, turns away from her crotch and addresses Jack again. 'Come on, let's get out of here. You're pissed and I don't want to leave you here on your own. They'll take all your money… and I'm worried about you getting home, the state you're in.'

'Leave him alone baby,' Lolita says to Sam. 'He's happy here, I can tell.'

'She's right. I am happy here,' Jack replies.

'You don't need to be doing this,' Sam goes on.

'What does that mean?' Jack shouts back. 'Jesus Sam, don't get all holier than fucking thou on me!'

'Look, I'm off okay. If you want to stay, that's fine,' Sam says resolutely. 'You alright to get yourself home?'

Jack nods yes, then mumbles, 'Why don't you stay for one dance?'

Sam shakes his head and with the words, 'I'll call you tomorrow,' he gets up and leaves.

Lolita, still standing naked in front of Jack, kneels over, kisses his cheek, licks the tip of her finger and rubs her clitoris. 'Ooh, oh yeah… yeah. I'd like you to rub it too, but it's against the rules, you know…' she toys with him.

Jack quickly becomes aroused and he feels his heavy heart lighten as Catherine and Sam vanish from his mind. Lolita has a near perfect body and her physical beauty astounds him; she consumes his consciousness. But at the same time, he is very aware that despite her wondrous femininity, which appears to him almost like a divine apparition – as he sits here staring intently at her genitals – he is responding to her as a sexual object, the embodiment of a male fantasy, rather than a thinking and feeling woman, and part of this aspect of depersonalisation excites him, and makes him recall some of the passages he read in Sade's *The Adversities of Virtue*. Jack imagined that this self-awareness would make him feel rather ashamed, uncomfortable, even cruel, but no, it makes him feel free. For he enjoys the fact that all around him now men are almost being encouraged to look at women in this way. There is no emotional attachment.

Lolita turns round, slaps one of her buttocks, then begins to rub the hole in her arse. Jack becomes very excited and shuffles in his seat. With her other hand, she strokes his penis through his trousers. Jack finds himself glued to her sexual organs, which he explores in extreme close up. He feels an intensity of pleasure he has not experienced before. But before he has time to really savour this new-found feeling, the song ends. Lolita pulls her hand away from his penis, removes her finger from her arse and turns round to face him.

'You want another dance?' she asks.

'Yeah, don't stop… please,' he pleads with her.

'That will be forty pounds now.'

'Okay,' he answers curtly, as he takes her hand and puts it back on his penis.

When Jack gets back to the flat, there are two messages on his answer machine. He does not listen to them right away. He blunders drunk into the kitchen and fumbles around in the cupboards for a half bottle of gin: he is certain it is lurking somewhere amidst all the jars and tins of food, the bottles and cans of drink. But he cannot find it.

Jack pulls a piece of paper out of his pocket, clumsily straightens it out with the palm of his hand and stares at it, first with mischief, then with panic. Lolita has scrawled down her number. She told him that if he felt horny when he got home and wanted sex, he should call. She finishes up in the club at two o'clock, and can take a taxi to his place, be with him in no time at all. She charges one hundred pounds for half an hour, and one eighty for an hour. What should he do? he wonders.

He slumps on the settee and imagines Lolita sitting on top of him, her broad hips wrapped round his waist, but the sudden clang of the telephone disrupts his fantasy. Jack keeps his eyes firmly shut and battles to hold this image in his mind: he does not want to lose it. And yet he now finds himself staring at a damp patch on the ceiling; the discoloration of its surface gives it the appearance of a disfigured heart shape, its edges blurred, bleeding brown and green, seeping outwards into a contemptuous shape devoid of love. And its stench amplifies its deformed aspect. He still will not get up to answer the phone. On the fourth ring, it diverts to the machine. He looks at his watch. It is very late, past two in the morning. It has to be Catherine. The caller rings off without leaving a message.

The fantasy has by now slipped from Jack's mind. He is not able to conjure it up again. He begins to listen to the rumble of passing cars outside, then watches them throw their headlights on the walls and ceiling. Finally, he gets up to listen to the messages on the machine: he will do this before deciding whether or not to call Lolita. He presses play. The first is from Catherine. She plans to leave early for Edinburgh to start work on the short film; she will not be at home when he gets back to Oxford. Jack presses pause, puts his hand to his mouth, and takes a deep breath. What on earth is he thinking? He loves Catherine. What is he doing even contemplating having sex with someone else? He turns and catches his reflection in the mirror now; his shirt collar is smeared with lipstick, his shirt drenched in sweat, his eyes bloodshot. He reeks of booze and tobacco. Jack gives himself the look of self-contempt, a look that any heavy drinker has given himself a thousand times. He presses play again. The second message is from Leonard. He needs his books back urgently.

# 27

**HE SITS** in the Irish pub opposite the office. Jack is due to meet Leonard to return his books. The single work that has impressed him most is Camus' *The Rebel*, a study of man's rebellion in the twentieth century and the terrible destruction that ensued. As he turns to the preface and goes to re-read it, he is interrupted by Leonard's sudden arrival. 'You got time for a drink?' he asks Jack, thumping his fist down on top of the pile of books. Jack jumps in his seat, looks nervously over his shoulder at the imposing figure of Leonard looming above him. He continues, 'You're twitchy, aren't you! Someone after you, eh?'

'No, it's just…' Jack struggles with his words.

'You want that drink then?'

Jack glances at his watch. 'I've got to be in Paddington in half an hour,' he replies. 'I've got time for a half though.'

'Good,' Leonard says as he makes his way to the bar.

'No, Leonard, let me get these.'

'I'm a poor man, but I can afford to buy us a couple of drinks.'

'No, I didn't mean it like that. It's just, well… my way of saying thanks for the loan of the books, you know…'

'Pleasure, but these ones are on me.'

'Alright,' Jack replies. 'So why d'you need them back so urgently?'

'I've been working on something…' he says intensely, '… as you've probably guessed from all those notebooks on my desk. Well I've nearly finished… but I need to go back over some of my sources.'

'Right…' Jack replies. 'You don't want to lose the flow.'

'Exactly!' Leonard shoots back. He seems fired up, manic, on edge.

'So what's it about?'

'I think it's the most important work I've ever written… but I'll not say anymore than this at the moment. I want you to be the first person to read it.'

'Right,' Jack says reservedly. Though part of him is excited about the prospect of a new work by Leonard – it might be another striking and affecting piece of writing, of the kind he used to produce so routinely – another part of him is very wary.

Leonard hands him his drink and the two men sit down. 'So… who was your favourite?' he asks, pointing at the books.

'Camus,' Jack replies.

'So you've settled on the side of romantic optimism.'

'A loveless world is a dead world.'

'Sade has something exceptional though!' Leonard declares, switching to his preferred writer.

'Only if you regard the unleashing of instincts even to the point of criminality as a good thing,' Jack states soberly.

'This "unleashing" you talk of… it isn't this. Man's natural instincts shouldn't be "leashed" in the first place. Man should be free to satisfy himself. He can only find liberation through the fulfilment of all his desires.'

'Even if this freedom leads to cruelty and abuse!' Jack rebuffs. 'You know, Leonard, a Buddhist would say the complete opposite. Personal liberation can only be found through harnessing one's desires.'

'I've never been one for austere spiritual practice!' Leonard issues a blunt reply as he shoots back a whisky chaser. 'You got time for another?'

'Yeah… just one more,' Jack replies. He no longer has to get back to Oxford this evening to see Catherine: she will not be back for another two weeks. He can always stay in London and head back tomorrow. 'Same again?' he continues and Leonard nods in acknowledgement. Jack makes his way to the bar and watches Leonard while he waits to order: it is getting busy now. Leonard perches on a small stool and thumbs through the Schopenhauer volume with his characteristic intellectual ardour, and as he skips from one part to the next, it seems to Jack that he knows the book inside out. Jack finally returns with the drinks. Leonard downs the whisky before he has even touched his beer. 'So much for a whisky chaser,' Jack says flatly.

'Yep,' Leonard replies gruffly, then emits a deep, hoarse growl as he clears his throat. 'So tell me, how's Catherine?'

'Yeah, okay… she's okay,' Jack replies.

'You don't sound very convinced.'

'I'm not. I don't know why I said she's alright.'

'What's wrong then?'

'Where do I start? I mean… now I've called my love, our relationship, into question… since we last met, since what I've read… I don't…'

'Since *we* last met?' Leonard asks with keen interest, sitting upright, arching his back, and having to adjust his eye-line now to look at Jack.

'Well yes,' Jack responds impatiently.

'And how has this affected things?'

'Oh come on Leonard!' Jack demands incredulously. 'I mean, how can you ask a question like that? You're the one that bloody posed it in the first place!'

'Yes, right,' Leonard says softly, looking down at Jack.

'Catherine… she wants a child. I don't know if I do. I wish I wasn't having all these doubts, these thoughts about other women.'

'Other women?'

'I went to a strip club last night, got pissed, spent too much money. I was desperate to…'

'And you don't know what to do now?' Leonard asks.

'No, I mean… I know I love Catherine more than I've loved anyone, but I don't seem to be able to give her what she needs. She really loves me… and yet this somehow isn't enough. And the moment I questioned our love, she became angry, despondent. For well over a month we've barely spoken. I don't know what's happening between us?'

'Jack, you do know. You decided to test the relationship, to see what you have together.'

'But what am I seeing, what have I discovered?'

'That maybe love is not what it seems… that perhaps it's something else altogether,' he says, the orange light of the lamp behind him suddenly making his face appear more wizen, his skin more swarthy. 'Jack, is it possible you've clung to Catherine all this time and told yourself that you love her when really you're just bloody terrified of being on your own?'

'Where you going with this Leonard?' Jack asks defensively. 'I mean… I've heard this before. And anyway… the same can be said for anyone. People need companionship. I spent quite a few years alone before I met Catherine… and yes, I got bloody lonely sometimes, course I did… and there were times when I wanted someone else in my life.'

'So you've just settled then, is that it?' Leonard quips. 'This isn't love!'

'What is then?' Jack fires back.

'What I had for Molly!' he shouts. 'You've got to ask yourself what is the point of your love if it's only about bloody submission, sacrifice, compromise… an act born out of weakness… an inability to stand on your own!'

'Where the hell's all this come from? And anyway… how can you maintain that *your* love was more real?'

'It was, but not anymore… not now.'

'What you going on about?'

'The love I felt back then crushed me, Jack. It fucking crushed me!' Leonard says. 'This kind of love is no good. I've finally realised, since meeting you… yes, that it was never going to last forever, no, that was an illusion. You'll lose it, the love you feel for Catherine, just as I did. If she doesn't die sooner, she'll die later. You might as well leave her now Jack!' he continues, talking fast now, his mind racing, ideas convoluted, reasoning unclear.

'Leonard… what are you saying? Stop this, this is crazy.'

'No!'

'This is no reason to leave someone. I mean… I could be the one who dies sooner!' Jack insists, looking into Leonard's eyes, trying to hold him to one line of thought. 'I could drop down dead tomorrow for all I know.'

'You're making excuses now for your indecision!'

'No I'm not!' Jack says. 'I'm just trying to show you that what you just said is ridiculous and cowardly. Don't even enter love because it's only going to end. Just look out for yourself instead. No, this can't be right.'

'I gave everything to Molly, Jack, to the extent that I had nothing left when she'd gone. I don't want you to fall apart like me.'

'But you just told me moments ago that the love I have for

Catherine is less… that it isn't comparable to the love you had for Molly.'

'I said it *was*, but not anymore!' Leonard shouts. 'Past tense, Jack. Now I think differently. I've changed my view. And I'm asking you to do the same. You must consider your feelings… your love, just as I've done!'

'Leonard… I don't have to do anything. I mean, this is mad, absurd.'

'And your idealised love isn't, eh?'

'You're assuming that my relationship with Catherine is just like the one you had with Molly, that it'll suffer the same fate.'

'Jack, you still want to love Catherine in the manner you loved her when you first met her. Such love is unsustainable!'

Jack sighs heavily, sits back in his chair and stares at Leonard now as if he is a stranger. 'What's happened to you Leonard?'

'*The Purity of Love* was just fantasy!'

'So you're telling me that the small red notebook is your reality now. The man you wrote about who has lost all feelings of love, who can only have dispassionate sex with prostitutes. Yet doesn't he wish for more? Don't *you* want more than this as well?'

'Jack Stoltz, the great romantic, the defender of true love,' Leonard replies wryly. 'We need more drinks! Doubles this time!' he announces as he marches over to the bar.

The barman pours him a whisky and he knocks it straight back, then signals for another. He turns round and glares at Jack, holding up his empty glass. Leonard has thrown down the gauntlet and Jack is compelled to follow. This is less about each other's tolerance for drink – Jack is fully aware that Leonard can drink him under the table – and more about who will submit to the other's argument, the other's will. Leonard returns to the table, downs another double – Jack does the same – then he stumbles off to the toilet.

Jack slumps in his chair and takes the opportunity, in Leonard's absence, to compose himself and prepare for the next onslaught. He is not gone long. Leonard marches back, still clearly in defiant mood. 'So tell me, Jack, what's she like in bed?'

'Who?'

'Catherine.' The alcohol has, by now, dispelled any notions of restraint and respect.

'Leonard, please... don't!'

But Leonard continues, 'I bet she's beautiful, just as Molly was, and a bit wild, like Molly as well. They sound the same... they really do. Both fucking needy!'

'It seems that *all* women are needy to you.'

Leonard glares at Jack through red cheeks and dilated pupils. Jack takes another big swig of whisky. 'I bet when you have sex with Catherine now... it's mechanical, detached, you feel like strangers,' Leonard says. 'It's become an anaesthetic for both of you. It prevents a confrontation, the need to face up to the absence of actual love. You fuck, then fall asleep. Better that than not fuck and lie awake. At least you can unload, eh Jack.'

Jack shakes his head from side to side, and hands under the table, clenches his fists. 'What d'you know about our relationship?'

'I think I know enough. Call it a sixth sense!'

'You've said enough now, okay. You're drunk, I'm drunk. Let's leave it!'

And yet Leonard is still not finished. 'I bet your relationship with Catherine is so bad now that when she won't fuck you, you're reduced to wanking surreptitiously underneath the sheets while she lies beside you, wide awake, listening to your pathetic, adolescent schoolboy fumblings. I'm sure at times like these, you feel utterly enslaved by your libido. It holds you captive, you need to discharge. And then follows the inevitable anti-climax. But don't worry, let me assure you,

Jack, it's the same for all us men. We all live with the sex maniac inside us, the constant nagging itch of our libido. We all need to fuck! And so after you've come, you lie there, quietly hyperventilating, trying to conceal the consequences of your orgasm, as you mop up the dead semen on your stomach with an old tissue, before shoving it behind the bed-board or in some other seemingly discreet location. You've had the release, you've discharged, but now you don't know what for. Part of you begins to wonder what just gripped you. Why did it seem so pressing, so urgent? You expected a greater reward. The end didn't justify the means. And so now you're full of self-contempt, and yet you can't but help get excited about the next time, when you just need to come again.'

Jack slouches in his chair now, feeling out of it, and stares at Leonard through blue and bleary eyes. He struggles to find the energy to challenge him now. 'You mustn't have any illusions about sex and love anymore,' Leonard continues. 'Sex is just fucking. Us men need it and want it most of the time, the discharge. Fucking someone else will help you understand this. Modern man will do anything in the pursuit of fucking, anything just to get laid. Sex today is all about technique, performance, release. It has no spiritual or emotional substance. When we fuck, we fuck objects. Modern women, in the rich world, offer nothing other than their candy-coated appearances. They're fixated with their hair, their nails, with fashion, makeup, perfume, moisturisers… the list is endless. These common obsessions have lumped most of them into a contemporary vision of dull and vacuous femininity. They've become a type, lost their individual beauty, no longer seem real but rather fake, superficial, plastic, and appear like they might pop or burst at any minute. They all share the same emptiness. There's nothing left to do but just fuck them. And once you've fucked one of them, you've fucked all of them. Love and relatedness are no longer possible. You might yearn for real passion, real intimacy with Catherine, the sensation that when you make love you become one with her. Well, this doesn't exist, it's the trick of your libido, a mere fantasy in your mind, nothing more.'

Leonard seems to make no attempt to inhibit his abuse now. The alcohol rushes through him, driving him on, making him spit and sweat as he leans forward on his stool and leers at Jack. 'It's gone stale with her, admit it. It happens. I can see you don't like the thought of fucking someone else behind her back. But you can't trust women. They twitch their cunts and us men come running. You must be careful. You give her your heart and she'll break it. She's doing it already. Spread yourself, Jack. You're a ball of unfulfilled desires. Relieve the itch. Don't try and control the uncontrollable. Fuck some other women!'

'No Leonard,' Jack says, making himself sit up now, and rubbing his eyes, desperate for him to shut up.

'What about last night then? I mean… it seems like you want to? You just didn't have the balls. I know a place you can go to. It's not far from me. It's in Victoria,' Leonard says as he tears a beer mat in half, scrawls down the address. 'There are a few girls there, some pretty ones as well… different shapes and sizes, fat and thin, black and white, young and old. Only forty quid.'

Jack puts his hands on the arms of the chair, pushes himself to his feet. 'Look, I'm going,' he mumbles and walks towards the door.

'Don't go,' Leonard says, the tone of his voice changing now like the snap of a finger and thumb, as if he suddenly cannot bear the thought of Jack leaving him here on his own.

'I'm going,' Jack says quietly.

'Right, don't forget this then,' Leonard says in conclusion as he gets up from his stool, wobbles and thrusts the torn beer mat in Jack's inside jacket pocket.

# 28

**JACK HAS** booked a table for them at a restaurant called Souq, which specialises in North African cuisine. Catherine suspects this is his attempt to rekindle the exquisite contentment they experienced, the serene love they felt, two and half years before in Morocco.

He called Catherine during her first night in Edinburgh and told her he did not want to lose her, insisted they meet as soon as possible, wanted to know when she was free, even said he would come up and see her there. They had planned to spend the whole time apart, but not now. She said she was happy to come to him, and so here she is, back in Oxford for the weekend.

Catherine wonders now as she and Jack walk from the car towards the restaurant what motivated his sudden phone call. Perhaps he had spent the night with another woman and it had been no good, or perhaps he had talked to Sam over dinner – she knew he was catching up with him – and his friend had warned that he was in danger of throwing everything away?

It is strange that he called then though, Catherine thinks, as she looks over at him now, on that night, because she might have been in bed with another man. She had dinner with one of the actors, James Neill: he is young, only twenty, and he flirted with her all evening and wanted to come up to her room at the end of the night. Catherine told him she was with someone, someone she loved … and someone who loved her, and that she did not want to be unfaithful, no, and could not be even if she wanted to be, and yet this beautiful young man looked at her with such curiosity and wonder in his eyes, and made her feel adored again, and when he embraced her at the end of the evening, she held him close to her bosom and did not want to let go of him: she felt like an animal clinging to him for warmth, and at that moment, wanted him inside her, yes … but then Jack had come to mind.

They enter the restaurant and its décor is very authentic. As Catherine walks down a low-lit corridor with Jack, golden lanterns make a seemingly symmetrical path out of the asymmetric walkway and bounce rich and warm yellow light off the battered stone walls onto a musty terracotta floor. White cotton drapes envelop the ceiling and fold onto the grey walls. Then they go down a claustrophobic stairwell, Catherine goes first, clinging to a banister that is richly crafted out of brass into sultry three-dimensional odalisques. At the bottom of the stairs, she ducks down underneath a low archway and is hit by a soft red light bouncing off the walls of the cavernous dining area, which makes her feel like she has just entered a forbidden place.

A pudgy head-waiter greets her, then gives Jack a crazed grin through turgid and protruded lips as he inspects Catherine while she removes her pink cashmere scarf and long black overcoat to reveal a tight-fitting silver sequin dress. The waiter looks her up and down – she can feel his eyes all over her – his mouth part open, his complexion porous and greasy. 'Come with me,' he drools, clutching Catherine's overcoat and touching her back with his hairy fingers as he leads them to the table. Jack does not retaliate, defend her as *his woman*, and part of her wishes he would, just beat his chest, warn this man off. He would have done this before, but not now. The head-waiter returns to his position by the entrance, and then with heavy-lidded eyes, he stares back at Catherine now and grunts from his rebarbative mouth like the caricature of an elderly sexual degenerate but without the long mackintosh. He smirks at her as he chomps on pistachio nuts, spitting the shells with pinpoint precision into a crystal bowl positioned next to him on the bar.

Sitting on hand-woven arabesque cushions and resting their elbows on a low wooden table, she and Jack smell fresh Moroccan bread wafting through the air, accompanied by the sweet spice smells of cumin and ginger. Jack leans over to Catherine, brushes her long hair back and hooks it behind her ears. He stares at the black jewel choker around her neck, then looks deep into her eyes as if searching for something, a resolution of their unhappiness. His eyes sparkle and she catches her reflection in his dilated pupils. Catherine smiles at him, he takes her hand. 'Thanks for coming down,' he says. 'Look, what do we need to do to make it right again?'

'You need to be sure about being with me.'

'And you need to want less from me.'

'What d'you mean?'

'Catherine, I feel as though I don't make you happy. You live life at this extreme emotional pitch.'

'What you saying?'

'Well I feel that you're never quite satisfied. I know how unhappy you've been in the past, how there are some things you'd rather keep to yourself, not even share with me…'

'How d'you know this?'

'Oh Catherine!' he demands abruptly, losing his cool, as the head-waiter looks over. 'I only have to see you scribbling away in your bloody journals to know when there's something wrong.'

She screws up her face and scowls at Jack as the head-waiter instructs one of his waiters to approach the table to diffuse the mounting argument.

A very handsome young Moroccan man walks towards them. 'Is everything okay, madam?' he asks Catherine. She looks up at him and smiles, and he in turn blushes, and then stands there, says nothing.

'Look, we're fine okay. Thank you. Bye,' Jack says impatiently, urging the waiter to leave them and allow them to continue talking. He walks away and Jack continues, 'You were so sad after things didn't work out with your mother. I felt powerless. Nothing I said could ease your pain. And I felt as if you resented me for this failed reconciliation, as if somehow I could've done something…'

'Of course not,' she interjects.

'Let me finish,' he insists. 'I've always felt an enormous pressure loving you. Your beauty, passion, intensity… I feel as though sometimes I just can't match them. It's as if they want too much of me. D'you understand?'

'It's not me that wants too much of you. It's your book… Leonard.'

'You lose yourself in your work as well. And Leonard… I don't want to talk about him anymore.'

'But he's so much of the problem. This man has got inside you. He's changed you.'

'Let's forget him.'

'Well you haven't.'

'I have now.'

'What?'

'Look, I saw him the other night, he was awful, he was… look, I can't tell you. Let's just leave it.'

'What did he say?'

'He's a bitter old man, let's leave it at that.'
'So you're not going to see him anymore?'
'No.'
'I can't tell you how happy that makes me feel,' Catherine exclaims, and she has the immediate sense that things will be okay now between her and Jack. 'I knew he was coming between us… I could feel there was something bad about him, about your relationship with him.' Jack nods. She continues, 'So what about the book now? What'll happen to it without Leonard?'
'It'll be fine.'
'Course it will.'
'I'm not far off now.'
'But really Jack, I think everything will be okay now that he's gone. I mean… you sound better, more optimistic about us, you don't doubt our future together anymore.'
'Yes, but…'
'But what? Everything should be okay now!'
'Catherine, I can't simply forget what I've been through with Leonard, what I've written about, what I'm still trying to write about.'
'I'm not asking you to.'
'Well what are you asking me for then?'
'All of you Jack.'
'What does this mean?'
'You know.'
'I need a bit more time Catherine… not yet.'
'When Jack?'
'I can't say at the moment.'
'Where does that leave me?'
'Please be patient with me,' Jack says as the young waiter approaches the table again.

'Are you ready madam?' he addresses her.

'For what?' Catherine teases, smiling seductively at the waiter, but at the same time wishing she did not feel the girlish compulsion to do this anymore, play petty flirting games with a young man she does not even know, games full of silly innuendo, and she looks at Jack now as he grips his serviette in his hand and wrings it tight. He probably wishes it were her neck, Catherine thinks. Yes, he would like to strangle her right now. The waiter blushes yet again. 'Yes, we are. Thank you…' she continues.

Catherine asks for *tagine* of lamb while Jack orders the waiter's recommended house speciality, conger eel. While they wait for their food, she rubs her ankle up and down Jack's leg and sporadically massages her breasts. Then she sweeps her hair back and cannot help but look over at the young waiter and smile at him once more. God, she thinks, I am behaving like an older woman now, who feels rejected by her husband and will do anything for the affections of another man. And with this rather embarrassing thought in her mind, her eyes narrow as she turns to Jack and says, 'You asked me for total commitment back then… and I opened my heart. I gave it to you, gave you all of me.' He continues to hold his serviette in his hand, which he massages now, rubbing it on his knee. 'Look at me,' she continues. But it seems he cannot, and so Catherine again looks over at the young waiter, then winks at him out of the corner of her eye.

'Go on, you can fuck him now!' Jack shouts. 'Go back to your old ways, be with another pretty boy. You'll be in control of this one as well until you suffocate him with your idea of love, till he can't give you anymore even though he wants to more than anything else.'

She glares at Jack and he looks away guiltily, and she knows that this can only mean one thing. 'You've read my journals haven't you?'

'Catherine?'

'Don't fucking lie to me!'

'Yes,' he says quietly.

A long silence follows.

The young waiter watches them from the bar. 'I'm sorry,' Jack continues as Catherine begins to cry.

Her tears last a long time, and she is almost bemused by this, has not realised quite how much sadness is stored up inside her.

Their food arrives and they eat in silence and do not look at one another. This passionate meal, intended to rekindle something between them, now feels contrived.

When they get back home, they lie in bed together like two corpses in a mortuary, side-by-side and cold.

Catherine cannot sleep and so stares out of the window; the sky is drilled with stars, and the round moon stands gracious, glowing and conscious of its ephemeral beauty. It seems to her that neither of them knows how to bridge the gap between their increasingly disjointed worlds. She will not stay the weekend, Catherine thinks. She will return to Edinburgh tomorrow.

# 29

**AND SO** the next day, while Catherine makes her way back to Edinburgh, Jack heads for London.

He takes a train to Victoria and sits in a pub just down the road from where Leonard has told him to go; he holds the torn piece of beer mat in his hand and stares at the address.

It is early, only eight o'clock. He looks around at all the single men sitting by the bar – men without women – and imagines that the place where he plans to go will get busier later, after these men have left the pub at closing time. Following an evening of drunken banter inside, they will no doubt be disturbed when confronted by the stillness of the world outside – no music, no chatter, no warmth, the cold night will confirm their solitude – and so these men will drag themselves to the same secret place that Jack is going to, underground, in a basement, in search of warmth, intimacy ... sex.

Jack feels edgy, wonders what it will be like, what he will do if she asks for more money than he has on him – he has a fair bit more than Leonard said, just in case – and what he should say to her, what he should ask for?

He orders another drink from the bar. Drinks it fast. Talks himself up, assures himself he has nothing to fear. Takes a deep breath. Okay, he is ready.

The place is just a very short walk away. His heart beats fast; he fights to steady his breath. It is on a residential street, just off the main high street. The gate down to the basement is open. He walks down the stairs. Rings on the bell. Nothing. Then the porch light goes on. A woman in her early thirties answers the door. She is small, white, maybe only five feet three or four. She wears a pair of jeans and a white T-shirt. She stands in the doorway and just stares at Jack. He says nothing. Does he have the right place? he wonders. Then without saying a word, she gestures with her arm for him to come in. He walks tentatively into the hallway and gazes down a long corridor.

'You early,' she says. 'My name is Carolina. What can I do for you?' She sounds Hispanic, Latin American maybe. Jack is silent. 'Am I okay?' she continues. Still, he says nothing. She goes on hesitantly, 'We have other girls later, if you want.'

'Sorry, yes…' Jack says, finally reclaiming his power of speech, '…you're fine.'

'What you want?' she asks, and before he has time to answer she continues, 'Forty for straight sex, or you want to do by half hour or hour. Seventy for half, one hundred and thirty for whole hour.'

'An hour please,' Jack says.

'Okay, you want to take your time, good… we go to nice room at the back then,' and she nods through an open door at an older woman as she takes Jack's hand and leads him down the corridor.

The bedroom is not as he expected it. He thought it would be bare, functional, run down. Perhaps the other ones are, but not this one. The room possesses a quiet, subdued charm. The bed is dressed in red and pink sheets, a few paintings hang on the walls, a small wooden dressing table is adorned with flowers; there is a crucifix on the wall and a few other Christian artifacts are scattered about the place. 'You like drink?' she asks.

'A beer please,' he says, sitting down on the bed.

She returns a few moments later with a can and a glass full of ice. 'Sorry, beer is warm. I have some ice though.'

'Thanks.'

'You pay me now?'

'Yes of course,' Jack says and he hands her the money.

'Take off your clothes, make yourself comfortable. I come back very soon,' she says as she closes the door behind her.

He strips off down to his boxer shorts and sits nervously on the edge of the bed.

She returns moments later wearing a pair of black lace panties and a red silk dressing gown. She walks over to her dressing table, sprays some perfume on her legs and arms, then switches on the stereo: *salsa*.

Her hips swing seductively as she walks towards the bed and stands over him. He sniffs her arm. 'You like?' she asks.

'Yes.'

'Relax. Lie down on your stomach. I give you massage first.'

Jack turns over and lies on his front. She removes her panties and gown. 'I take these off,' she says gently, tugging at the elastic on his boxer shorts.

'Yes…'

She removes them, then squeezes some oil onto the backs of his legs and begins to massage them. Her hands move slowly, gently, over his calves and inner thighs. Then she takes his feet and massages them, first the soles, then between each toe. He lies flat, head pressed hard against the pillow, desperate to relax but still feeling tense. Next she sits naked on top of him, straddles his arse and pours oil onto his back and shoulders. She begins to rub them. 'You tight. Relax…'

'Yeah,' he mumbles.

Then she asks him to turn over. Jack rolls onto his back and she takes his limp penis in her open palm and caresses it with her free hand as if it were a dead rodent. He stares at the ceiling, embarrassed, unable to look at her. 'It's okay,' she says sweetly, as if she fully understands his anxiety at that moment. She begins to rub her body up and down his, slowly. One of her bosoms touches his chest. He smells her perfume: so sweet. He feels her leg brush against his, the skin soft, smooth. Jack glances down her body as it moves on top of him, her eyes exploring his physique. Her head moves slowly up his body until it meets his. They stare at one another, then she kisses him tenderly. He feels a great surge of blood rush to his penis. She smiles at him as she reaches for a condom on the side table, takes it out of its packet, inserts its tip in her mouth, places this on the head of his penis, then rolls it down the hard shaft with her tongue and lips until his whole penis is inside her mouth. Jack watches her lips move up and down its body, slowly, exquisitely. Then she stands up, licks her finger and inserts it in her vagina. She squats down, easing herself onto him. It does not take long: she is wet already. Her breasts are small, round. Her skin is a gentle white. He rolls her over and gets on top of her. They kiss, finding each other's tongues. He withdraws and lifts her up. She rolls over and gets on her knees; he enters her from behind. Her buttocks are small, compact. Jack loves the touch of them against the insides of his thighs as he penetrates her. He wants to look into her eyes again. He pulls out and sits down on the bed. She clambers on top of him. They hold onto one another tight. She squeezes her arms around his back and thrusts away, trying to have as much of him inside her as possible. Then she rolls off of him and lies there, out of breath, gasping, fulfilled. He has not come and yet strangely he does not mind.

'You want to come?' she asks, leaning over now and taking his penis, which is still hard.

'No, I'm okay. That was wonderful.'

'Really?' she asks.

'Yes, it was,' Jack says as he sits up on the edge of the bed.

She gets up and stands over him, between his legs, holding his head to her chest. He puts his arms around her waist and holds her. He feels comforted, grateful. Again, it is not what he expected: he feels as if he has just made love to her even though he does not know her. He feels liberated, free … yes. He never thought it would be like this.

# 30

CATHERINE RUNS down the hotel corridor towards her room: she is late. She fumbles for her key, hurries inside, flings her bag on the bed and rushes into the bathroom. There is a knock at the door. It must be him.

She takes out her lipstick, quickly applies it. She called James on the train on the way back up to Edinburgh – she could not bear it any longer – and arranged for him to come straight to her hotel.

He looks so handsome now as Catherine opens the door. He seems even taller now, over six feet; he has cut his hair for the part, into a crew cut, and he is unshaven, wears a thick silver chain round his neck.

Catherine wastes no time and kisses him right away, runs her hand over his head, strokes his cheek.

Then she pushes the door shut, pushes him up against it. Reaches for his belt buckle, loosens it, unbuttons his flies, grabs his penis.

'Don't say anything,' she says.

She pulls his trousers down his legs, then yanks down his boxer shorts. She is wearing a skimpy cotton dress – was planning to put something else on. She wears no underwear, and so without any hesitation puts her hands on his shoulders and lifts herself up onto him.

'I should put on a condom…' he says.

'No, don't. I want you like this.'

And with these words, she takes his penis and forces it inside of her.

'Take me to the bed,' she tells him.

He carries Catherine over. She pushes her bag onto the floor, and he lies her back on the mattress. She lifts her legs in the air, until they are parallel with his upper body, then says, 'I want to feel every bit of you.'

He kisses her tenderly now: she does not want this from him. 'You're…' he goes to speak.

'Don't say anything… please,' she insists.

He reaches the point of climax quickly. Catherine can feel he is about to come: his thrusts quicken, he groans increasingly sporadically, with more spontaneity and less control.

'I'm coming as well…' she says, feeling the rush inside her now.

Then he slows, his body twitches, convulses, his arms tense, he clenches his teeth … and comes.

And she finally lets him speak as he mumbles, 'Yes,' and says this word a few times, and Catherine holds him tight, wrapping her legs around his torso and holding him there.

# 31

**JACK LEAVES** the basement flat in Victoria and slowly makes his way back to Shepherd's Bush.

He does not get back till late, gone one in the morning, and finds a large tatty package jammed through the letterbox: a bulky brown document size envelope wrapped in a plastic carrier bag. Jack tries to wrestle it out of the tight slot but it will not budge, and so he jams his foot against the door and tugs hard. It finally gives way, and when it does, he flies backwards, with the parcel clenched to his chest, and bangs his head against the wooden banister at the foot of the staircase. He feels a golf ball lump swell on the back of his head, and as he prods around the wounded area with his fingertips, a surge of pain pulses through his body, and suddenly infuriated with the cause of the accident, this damn package, Jack flings it against the opposing wall.

Okay, he tells himself now as he sighs heavily, picks himself up off the floor, and drags himself up the stairs and inside his flat. He slumps on the sofa and removes the large envelope from the carrier bag. He tears it open and pulls out a manuscript. Jack glances at the title page. It reads, *The Unreasonable Man*.

He just stares at it initially. After the way Leonard was with him, part of him wants simply to refuse to read it. Why on earth should he? Jack asks himself.

Wind rushes through the bottom of the bay window now and the pages of the manuscript flutter, then fall open at a particular page. Jack looks down and begins to read, choosing a spot at random, near the middle of the page. 'I often feel like a wild animal, a blind force that isn't interested in reason and order but unreason and chaos. I want to demolish everything: people, ideas, truth. Smash them all to bits! This is the real drive of man; his need to create, dominate. They think I'm too noisy. They find my ways difficult. They're afraid of me. And so they try and punish me, for my curiosity, my conviction and my hope for something better from this fucking mediocre world! Rather this than confront all of their humanity, their demons as well as their angels, and the innate chaos all around them. Who is this "they" I refer to? Well, it's the assembled masses I see before me, every uninspired and unfulfilled last one of them who doesn't know how to bloody live. But I'll not let them make me bland, apathetic and disappointed. No, they can't make me brain-dead. They can try and alienate me but I'll never join them! They make me out to be in cuckoo land, off with the fairies, a little bit crazy, sick in the head. And just because I think with my head and feel with my heart.'

As Jack reads on, it is not clear to him how much of it is specific to Leonard's actual thoughts and experiences. *The Unreasonable Man* seems to be a rambling first-person record of one man's experiences, ideas and aspirations as he strives to understand his essential nature and mankind's in general. The work seems to be part philosophical, part political, part psychological, part sociological and part anthropological: a hybrid piece in that it embraces so many different rubrics and disciplines. And the writing style is disordered. As Jack sees it, the main thrust of the protagonist's argument, most of which appears to be lifted

# LOVE AND MAYHEM

from Nietzsche and Freud, is that despite the pretence of reason and compassion, man at his root is fiery, irrational and conflicted. He is driven by primeval and powerful forces, which wrestle to determine and control his life. He has a constant lust for power and paradox. And faced with this essential nature, love cannot win.

It becomes increasingly clear to Jack as he continues to work his way through the manuscript that Leonard has contrived certain passages as wild and raging polemics against all those people who rejected him after his criminal conviction. And some of these passages appall him while others fascinate him, if anything, due to the sheer force of their vitriol. The fictional world of the book is degenerate, insane and worthless, and the protagonist's behaviour – unfettered and unbalanced – reflects this twilight reality of unreason, a place where the opposites of pleasure and pain, desire and torture, have become one and the same thing. Jack can see that Leonard has worked hard to encourage the reader to admire his hero, though he knows that this admiration can never extend to love. According to Leonard, we should admire his creation because he is simply more honest than the other men around him are: he is not a wimp or hypocrite but is determined to express all of his humanity, good and bad. But Jack finds it difficult to even respect him let alone like him. His voice is too often arrogant and vicious, seeming to revel in the horror of his world's irrationality. 'I'm fucking God. I do whatever I like,' one chapter begins. 'Fuck everyone else, d'you hear me? I do things my way. I am the truth. I live in an age that's lost its bearings, that's completely fucking lost, blind to its true nature, its purpose. There's moral cynicism everywhere. There's a great confusion of values. Families are disintegrating. And sexual antagonism is rising. No one around me knows what love is anymore. Whether we're murderers or not, we're still pushed, all of us, by the irrational side of life.'

Jack knows that the majority will dismiss *The Unreasonable Man* and its author as mad and bad, and stop reading after the first few pages, but a minority – and a very small one at that – will probably read on, driven by a curious mixture of horror and fascination. As far as Jack can ascertain, Leonard seems to be proposing a kind of intellectual and existential radicalism, not dissimilar from the ideology propounded by his chief figure of inspiration, Nietzsche. 'An individual is only worthy if he possesses a rigorous intellect and a passionate heart!' the protagonist declares at one point. 'He must struggle to understand the world, must thrive on intellectual argument, must develop his own ideas, must formulate his own principles, and must defend his own truth with vigour and courage. Man must re-invent himself in this new image: otherwise his existence is meaningless and he might as well kill himself now, right now!' And yet, the more Jack reads of *The Unreasonable Man*, the less convinced he becomes. Beneath all the grand, apocalyptic rhetoric of the protagonist – Leonard Gold's very own *ubermensch* – Jack feels that Leonard simply does not have a clear idea of this new way of being he is proposing. If someone realises it in this world, will this person suddenly be free from all previously held moral illusions and live in a permanent state of happiness and fulfilment? No, he will not, Jack is sure of this. Rather he will be as troubled and conflicted as before. One only has to look at the fate of Nietzsche himself, Jack thinks. His rebellion drove him to madness and despair. In this respect, Leonard's pedagogic vision is almost suicidal.

As Jack nears the end of the manuscript, he recalls how Leonard referred to *The Unreasonable Man* when he last saw him: he thinks it might be his 'most important work'. No, not at all. The ideas do not hang together, they are not that original, and they do not stand up to scrutiny. And the book's structure is ragged and the whole thing is poorly written. In short, it does not come close to *The Purity of Love*. At this moment, it seems to Jack that Leonard has written *The Unreasonable Man* for himself alone: he never intended for it to be read by anyone else, that is until he, Jack, came along. The work represents nothing more than Leonard's relentless need to express the conflict inside him, which he has not been able to resolve for all these years. And so it seems this is yet another bid to solve it through his work – those hundreds of notebooks – and yet even here he has found no resolution.

When Jack finally finishes reading it, he cannot sleep. It is almost six in the morning. He lies awake, tossing and turning.

He gets up late. It is ten. Jack has only had a few hours sleep and is exhausted; his mind feels like it is weighed down with heavy bricks and cement. He walks into the living room, and the first thing he sees is Leonard's manuscript on the settee. He cannot make it into work, not today, and so calls the office and tells them he will not be in, then heads straight back to bed, but just as he is closing the bedroom door behind him, the doorbell rings. He shuffles sleepily across the floorboards to see who it is, and as he turns the lock, the door is pushed hard from the other side and Leonard barges past him, inside the flat. He is drunk already. 'So my manuscript, you've read it, I presume?'

'Leonard, what are you doing?'

'What d'you think? I'm here to talk to you about *The Unreasonable Man*,' he says matter-of-factly as he plonks himself down on the settee.

'You can't just storm in here unannounced at ten o'clock in the morning and demand to know what I think of what you've written.'

'But you're allowed to intrude on me, is that it? Or have you forgotten those times when you just turned up on my doorstep, needing to talk to me? I didn't turn you away!' Jack struggles to say anything in his defence. Leonard goes on, 'Right, now we've got that bit of hypocrisy cleared up, I want to hear what you think.'

'After the abuse you hurled at me last time, the way you were, I thought that was it.'

'What you talking about? I haven't even got going yet,' he now says with a sardonic smile.

'What so you're planning to be even more abusive?'

'Oh stop bloody moaning. I'll say what I think, alright!'

'Even if it means being an arsehole?'

'Jack, you knew what you were getting yourself into.'

'What?'

'You're beginning to realise that what you and Catherine have isn't quite what it seems.'

'You seem bloody determined to drive us apart.'

'No Jack. I only want you to be truthful about what you have with her... whether it's really love or not?'

'And what the hell does it have to do with you! I mean... what stake d'you have in my future with Catherine?'

Leonard is silent and looks closely at Jack now while stroking his beard, as if trying to convey a calmness of mind even though there is little evidence of such. 'I want to hear what you think of *The Unreasonable Man*. This is the accumulation of five years work.'

'I don't know where to begin.'

'Did it shock you?'

'Yes.'

'Why?'

'It's so extreme... so...'

Leonard butts in, 'Before, if I thought someone was an arsehole, I referred to his or her character as "questionable". But now I call an arsehole a "fucking arsehole". They used to admire me because I was always polite and reasonable... what I said conformed to their standards of opposition and criticism. In other words, I was prepared to flatter where I should've criticised, diminish where I should've emphasised. I was treading on bloody eggshells, scared to offend, to voice what I really thought. Well... I'm not afraid anymore, no. And this is what they won't be able to accept… still can't accept. These wankers… perpetually whipped up into a frenzy of self-righteousness. They can't tolerate anyone that challenges literary and moral orthodoxy. And I have now moved so far away from what should be said, what is deemed acceptable, that I am marginalised, cast out… And all because I seek to tell it how it really is… with no graces, formalities, constraints… blah, blah, blah. That's all I can and shall ever love now… the truth!'

Jack does not say anything right away, and Leonard, agitated by Jack's lack of response, is driven to ask him another question, 'What else, Jack? Come on, what else d'you think?'

'Well, I think your hero's terribly conflicted,' Jack says.

'And you're not conflicted, eh Jack? One minute you're telling me that Catherine is the love of your life, the next you're banging some cheap dirty whore in a …' and Leonard waits now for Jack's acknowledgement that he did go to the basement flat in Victoria after all, and all Jack can do is look away. Leonard continues, 'I knew you had. Listen, if infidelity weren't good, it wouldn't exist.'

'If everyone lived by this reasoning the world would be an upside down place.'

'Well it'd be better for it. The sooner people realise the way the world *really is*, the better. There are no authoritative independent criteria to determine that one belief system is any more valid than another is. Life has no ultimate meaning. There's no absolute truth, no enduring substance to the world. No one can reliably know anything, anything at all.'

'Leonard, if you believe in nothing, if nothing makes sense, if we can assert no value whatsoever, if everything is permissible and nothing is important… then the adulterer is neither right nor wrong, what I did last night means nothing… wickedness and virtue are just accident or whim.'

'Yes, perhaps this is it Jack? We've all been duped into virtue when it's merely an illusion? I mean I was!' and he stamps his foot now, gets to his feet. 'I won't be inhibited from expressing my passions, fulfilling my desires.'

'Even if you end up bloody assaulting someone!' Jack shouts. 'And who are "they"… this enemy of yours?'

'Jack… "they" are the majority of my literary contemporaries, the majority of Londoners, the majority of Englishmen, the majority of Europeans… the consensus.'

'So you believe in nothing then?'

'Judge for yourself.'

'How can you say this?'

'I believe in my own worldview Jack, that love is merely a series of desperate and fractured encounters. We meet someone, we fuck them till we think we love them, feeding off them like animals in a frenzy of relentless need…' and then he suddenly begins to speak quieter, his words seeming to trail off to nowhere, '… but then we tire of them, realising that it is not love we have with them after all… and so we leave them for another distressing… ephemeral…' and then he stops mid-sentence as if he has finally had enough of these words, as if he has spoken them, and written about them, so often that they no longer hold any meaning for him.

'You put these words in your character's mouth,' Jack says. 'They weren't meant to be your own.'

'Well they are, they are now. You see, I don't think I can believe in the goodness of this world anymore.'

'But who's to say your view is the right one?'

'No one, other than me.'

'You're hiding behind gross intellectualisations, and this somehow justifies your indifference, what you did to that woman. We live in a loveless world do we? So what were all those feelings of love you had for Molly, were these just illusions as well, were you completely unaware of her as an individual human being? Did it only matter that she was a woman with a cunt?'

'Yes, yes...' he mutters, 'it would seem so...' but he now sounds as if he does not quite know what he is saying anymore as he scratches his chin incessantly.

'Well now you do sound like a bloody misogynist? It'd seem that they... your detractors... were right all along.'

'No, Molly was different!'

'So you hate all women apart from Molly?'

'She was the real one, the true one... don't you see!'

'You didn't need to turn your back on everyone after she died. Your life has become a relentless justification of your victimhood. You've given your grief this powerful intellectual defence that no one, least of all me, dare challenge. At any price, you must defend your precious anger. And now, it seems, you want me to suffer as much as you've done. I'm to be the next Leonard Gold, another bloody victim!'

'No.'

'Don't you see that your long, self-imposed exile from love is destroying you. You don't believe in love anymore because you don't have it anymore. If Molly were still alive, then you'd still believe in it. I think you still long for it, but you've nowhere else to go, you're at a dead end.'

Leonard drops his face in his hands, rubs his cheeks, mumbles to himself, and looking at Jack now, Jack suddenly feels terribly sorry for him and wants to help him. 'What's happened to you? Are you going through another one of your black spells? You're drinking heavily again, aren't you?'

He gets to his feet. 'I have to go,' Leonard mutters as he hurries over to the front door and is gone before Jack knows what to do or say next.

# 32

**SHE AND JACK** arrive at the Stoltz family home in Chiswick armed with carrier bags full of Christmas presents. Catherine has elected to wear a beautiful red dress with white polka dots, appropriately festive in colour and design: she is determined to enter into the spirit of things.

They walk down the driveway. The last few days, she has felt herself spinning out of control again. The feelings have been dormant for so long – it is as if Jack's love has successfully contained them – but with the dwindling of his love, they have returned with a new impetus. Catherine has to tell him, yes, but when is the right moment, she asks herself, as they near the old oak front door.

A large holly bouquet tied to the doorknocker with a flame red bow draws her attention. It seems that Theo has finally let festive superstition and sentimentality into his household, Catherine thinks. Jack has always made much of the fact that, as a child, he was never given a 'proper' Christmas, and that this was not solely on account of his father's Jewry. No, Theo is immensely sceptical about all religious festivals, Jewish ones included. In fact, this deep suspicion extends beyond the festivals to the very religions themselves. And he makes no exception for Judaism. According to Jack, his father has long ago given up waiting for the real Messiah. Rather his faith resides firmly in the material world, the world he can understand empirically and analyse scientifically. And so it is Ruth who has always tried to bring some festive charm and jollity to the occasion, and it seems she might have had some success this year as Catherine now looks up at the gleaming white mistletoe, which hangs from the porch lamp above, and feels compelled to say, 'It looks beautiful.'

'Yeah,' Jack replies quietly, and she can tell his mind is on something else, certainly not the mistletoe.

'Jack?' she asks softly. But he does not respond. 'Jack!' she blurts out.

'What?' he shouts back, startled.

'I can't hold this in any longer. I can't…' and she knows now that she simply must tell him.

'What is it Catherine?'

'I slept with someone else in Edinburgh.'

'What?'

'Yes I did… I'm sorry,' she says breathlessly.

Jack looks away as if he cannot bear to look at her – the slut who has slept with another man – and then the front door swings open to reveal Theo standing in the doorway with big open arms. 'Hi, it's wonderful to see you,' he says, stepping forward and wrapping his arms around Catherine.

She rests her head on his chest and closes her eyes: Catherine feels all of a sudden very peaceful. Then he lets go of her and greets Jack in familiar fashion, patting his shoulder and shaking his hand.

Jack immediately makes his way to the downstairs toilet and Theo says to him, 'We'll be in the living room,' and as they walk towards it, and then inside, and then over to the big black couch that sits proudly in the middle, Catherine can picture Jack now, in the toilet, alone with his thoughts of her betrayal.

'Jack, is that you?' she hears Ruth call out.

'Yep, hang on a second,' he shouts back. 'I'll be right with you.'

'Where's Catherine?' and Ruth's voice sounds nearer now, she must be in the hallway.

'Where d'you think?' Jack replies dryly.

'Talking to your dear father I suppose. The two of them are always inseparable when they see one another,' and Catherine cannot help but smile when Ruth says this as she looks at Theo now, completely absorbed in the drink's cabinet in the corner of the room, blissfully unaware of everything else – like father, like son.

'Where are Sally and Michael?' Catherine hears Jack ask.

'They're upstairs,' Ruth answers. 'Can you give them a shout for me? They've got something they want to tell us all.'

Jack's footsteps in the hallway and then, 'Sally!' he calls, as Catherine imagines that this is just as it was when he was a boy, calling up to his big sister to tell her that mum wants her.

'Coming!' she hears Sally shout back, then the sound of Michael and her bounding downstairs moments later.

'Let me go and get mum,' Sally says excitedly.

Theo sits down next to Catherine on the couch, hands her a glass of red wine, her favourite, a *Luis Cañas Reserva*, and she recognises it instantly, and finds herself starting to cry. Theo holds her hand, says nothing: it is as if he instinctively knows what is happening to her again. Then hearing the brisk, chattering voices of Sally and Ruth in the hallway, Catherine dabs her eyes with a tissue and tries to regain her composure.

Ruth enters first, embraces her. She sees Theo look at Jack now, a harsh look. The pop of a champagne cork as she turns to see Michael filling glasses and Sally distributing them.

'Hi Catherine,' Sally says as she hands her a glass, pecks her on the cheek. 'Can we all raise our glasses?' she goes on, her eyes sparkling now, her smile broad. 'I'm pregnant, everyone, and Michael and I are finally getting married.'

Michael and Sally embrace for what seems like an eternity, while she and Jack try not to look at one another across the room.

# 33

**HIS FATHER** retires to his study after lunch, to sit in his auburn leather armchair and snooze for half an hour, Jack supposes: this has been his ritual after a bout of excessive eating for as long as Jack can remember.

He waits five minutes or so until after his departure, then gets up himself from the dinner table and wanders down the hallway. As he walks past his study, Jack expects to find him here, true to previous form, fast asleep. But to his surprise, he discovers his father sitting bolt upright on his imposing matching leather sofa, like someone who has no intention of sleeping at all, almost as if he is expecting somebody, Jack, to be precise.

His study is full of books that creep up on mammoth shelves all the way to the ceiling. Jack remembers now that as a young boy he used to watch his father make the climb to the top of the stepladder in order to refer to one of his beloved books, and this ascent was always far more heroic and worthy of Jack's admiration than the workings of his father's analytical mind as he elucidated a psychoanalytical concept or explained a psychological theory.

Jack enters now and sits down in his father's armchair. It is higher up than the sofa, and he has chosen it for this very reason: he hopes it will help him maintain a certain distance from his sometimes-overbearing father. But his father immediately pats the vacant puffy pillow next to him on the sofa, summoning his son to sit beside him, assuming the paternal role rather than the position of clinical adviser and mentor. Jack pretends not to have noticed his subtle gesture and stays put.

'I wanted to talk to you,' he says, looking at Jack, anticipating an immediate reply. It is not forthcoming, and so he continues, 'About Catherine.'

'What did she tell you?' Jack asks defensively.

'You must know how unhappy she is at the moment.'

'This is between Catherine and me. It's our relationship.'

'Are you still working all the time?'

'I have to.'

'Like father, like son,' he says with a wry smile.

'Look, I'm not proud of being work-obsessed, alright,' Jack insists. 'I know that's part of the problem.'

'And yet you continue to put your work, the book, before her,' Theo says. 'Why is that, Jack?'

'You know the state that *Detritus* is in. Bloom is about to wind it up at any moment.'

'Does part of you feel that your love can't endure the problems before you and Catherine?'

'Don't bloody pathologise me and treat your own son like a damn patient!'

'I'm not Jack.'

'Well come on then, give me your analytical judgment. I'm waiting…'

'Look, all I want you to see is that you've got a choice here. You could leave *Detritus* now and just concentrate on your freelance work. You have the contacts and the reputation to earn enough money this way.'

'Catherine's only done one piece of work since the film. One of us has to have a stable income.'

'You could generate an income through freelance work. Why don't you put the book on hold for a bit?'

'I can't do that. I've had to neglect it recently because of all the trouble with the magazine. If anything, I need to get back to it, give it a lot more attention.'

'Even at the expense of your relationship with Catherine? And what about this damn fellow Leonard?' he says.

'Look, I'm not involved with him anymore okay. I've been through this with Catherine.'

'But why Jack… why have a relationship with someone like that?'

'What d'you mean? You don't even know him. Have you any idea how judgmental you sound! And I'd expect a little more compassion and understanding from you of all people.'

'Not when they threaten my family, Jack. Look, all I want to do is try and help you rectify your relationship with her. She loves you with all her heart. You really prepared to let this go?'

And his mind begins to throw up difficult questions now, ones which he would rather not have to try and answer. He looks away from his father, as if hoping this action will somehow halt the dialogue that has begun in his mind, but it does not. Can he really throw her love away? he asks himself. But there again, maybe Catherine does not love him as much as his father thinks he does. She has been unfaithful. Jack is sure she omitted this small detail when she confided in him just now, and he seizes on this thought, voices it, 'She's fucked someone else!'

But his father does not react to this revelation how Jack expects him to. Rather, he just stares at his son purposely. Jack goes on, 'She's always wanted other men… she wrote that in her journal… but only when she thinks I don't truly love her.' Still, he says nothing. 'But I do show her my love!' Jack insists, and with these words his own infidelity comes to mind. Should he tell her what he has done?

'Stop it, Jack, will you? Enough!' his father says, finally breaking his silence.

'Well what are you telling me here? To love Catherine more? To appreciate her love more? D'you know how I feel?' he asks, remonstrating wildly with his hands.

'Look, just be honest with her Jack, with yourself. If you want to fully commit to her, then do it. It can't be done half-heartedly. You must decide what you're going to do!'

Jack studies the three vertical creases on his father's forehead. 'I don't know, d'you hear me. Have I got to be sure about it?'

'She wants to have a child with you. When it's about someone else's feelings, someone else's life, yes you do have to be… have to know what you bloody want, especially with Catherine!'

'Look, our relationship has nothing to do with you,' Jack sputters again in his defence.

'Jack, she's told me very little about what's going on between the two of you, okay,' he says. 'But she did tell me a little bit about what's going on inside her. She's losing a grip on things, she's losing herself Jack.'

And Jack recalls her journal again, her fear of the madness returning, and she does seem strung out now, all restless and preoccupied, and yet she has always been like this, he thinks, ever since he has known her, sometimes volatile, all over the place, and then perfectly calm, almost serene. But maybe it is more than this now.

'Look, I'm going for a walk okay,' he suddenly announces, getting to his feet, needing to think and be on his own, and so leaves his father sitting here.

He sets out for Chiswick Common, the walk that his mother always encouraged Sally and him to make on Sunday afternoons after a big roast lunch. The dreaded questions fast come to mind again, and Jack knows he must not avoid them any longer but must try and answer them. He finds that many of his thoughts are skewed, born of guilt and self-recrimination. Is it right that she now seems to love him more than he loves her? Maybe he will love her more in a month's time and she will love him less? But is he strong enough to be on his own, should he decide to leave her? Perhaps, deep down beneath his fear, he loves her more than she loves him? Jack, at this moment, is seeking a final truth about their relationship, about *his* feelings for her and *her* feelings for him.

Then his mind turns to Leonard. He wonders how happy he and Molly really were. Was their love as beautiful and complete as Leonard depicted it? He thinks about how Molly died. And then he considers what Leonard would be like now had he met someone else, had he managed to find love again. But then, maybe it is impossible to find such love again in a single lifetime?

No, this is mad, he must not think about him anymore. Enough! He just cannot help Leonard: he does not want it.

Jack must not be afraid, must help Catherine. Yes, his father is right, he must decide. She really needs him now. Jack must get back what he is in danger of losing. He loves her, yes, always has, always will.

He hurries back to the house to be with her.

# 34

**IT IS** Boxing Day and Jack has been so different with her these past twenty-four hours. He has been present, yes, right with her as opposed to off somewhere else, inside his own head, inside the world of the book. They made love last night for the first time in ages, and it was wonderful. It felt like they were new lovers again.

Catherine does not understand this, after what she told him: it is as if Jack has just forgiven her. He has said nothing about it. She raised her infidelity with him again when he got back from his walk but he quietly shushed her, told her not now, and then embraced her. Perhaps this is because he has done the same thing, Catherine wondered then. And yet the thought of his infidelity did not make her angry either, and it does not make her angry now.

She can feel herself coming up, yes; everything seems brighter, better, more exciting, and she does not want to spoil this feeling while it is with her.

'I'm sorry Catherine, for everything,' he says to her now as she stands in the kitchen and prepares a cafetière of coffee, pushing down the plunger.

'What's that?' she asks, turning her head to look at him as he leans against the kitchen sink.

'I was unfaithful too. I should've told you yesterday.'

'I thought you were,' she says, and does not feel the need to probe him any further.

'Look, I… I went to…'

She interrupts him. 'I don't need to know the details.'

'But I feel… I feel I owe you a full explanation.'

'You don't, Jack.'

'But…'

'Did I give you one?'

'Well no…'

'And d'you want me to?'

'Not really, no.'

'There we are then.'

'But surely we must talk about it?'

'Why must we?' she asks.

And he smiles at her, and this seems to say it all: it was about sex, the need for it, Catherine thinks. And for now at least, both she and Jack are able to see sex and love as two very separate entities.

'Catherine, I want to be with you, I want all of you…'

'You sure?'

'Yes.'

She stares intently at him, his eyes luminous and dazzling. 'I don't know what to say,' she says.

'You don't have to say anything.'

Catherine throws herself at Jack, and he opens his arms, and she sinks her face into his woollen jumper, aware of nothing else but him. 'What's brought this on?' she whispers in his ear. 'What made you decide?'

'I've always known.'

'I thought he'd won.'

'No, never.'

'You're lucky I was prepared to wait.'

'I know.'

'It felt like a battle sometimes between him and me,' she says.

'I felt like he was pulling me apart.'

'But you're okay, Jack. We're okay.'

There follows a brief silence between them before Jack gently pushes Catherine away from his chest and asks, 'Are you really?'

'Yes I'm fine,' she says. 'Why shouldn't I be?'

'Well, you seem really up today, almost euphoric…' he says, looking at her with concern now, as if struggling to articulate some feeling he has about her.

'I am. And now after what you've just told me, I feel like I can do anything Jack. Yes… it's going to be wonderful. I'll be the happiest woman in the world, and you'll be the happiest man. I love this world Jack, I really do!' she declares, throwing her arms in the air and Catherine suspects from his look that she has overdone it now, shown him quite how over the top she is feeling. But Jack does not say anything more, not for the moment.

She stands underneath the magnolia tree in the garden, legs slightly apart and firmly planted to the ground, and arms in the air, Catherine waves them in time with the gentle breeze and her long thin cotton dress shimmies around her ankles. She thinks about Jack's news this morning: *Detritus* is finally at an end. He seems to have taken it very well. It was fast becoming inevitable. 'Bloom's patience has finally run out,' he said to her this morning over breakfast. 'It must have been one of his New Year's resolutions.' Well, Jack has no choice now but to pursue his freelance writing. This will give him more time with her, Catherine thinks, and this prospect excites her. He will only have to make a few trips to London every week and the rest of the time he can work from the cottage. She is optimistic about everything at the moment: in fact, she is almost incapable of responding to events – be they good or bad – in any other way.

The last few days, Catherine has felt like she is flying: she is happy all the time. And she feels like this now as she squints her eyes, peering through the branches at the blue above her, flying through the sky, over a lush landscape and towards a big city. And suddenly she is in the city, gliding above streets and people. She dives down and then swoops up again, up the side of a very tall building … yes, a skyscraper. Up and up like a bird.

Oh … she, Catherine, can do anything, absolutely anything. The whole world is hers. Everyone is beautiful. She loves them all. She wants to help everyone in need, care for them all. Life has become a daydream, a carnival of magical colours, everything so bright and clear, wherever she looks. Catherine does not know why she feels so elated, so wonderful, powerful: it does not make sense. But she does know she must savour this high while it lasts: she has secretly been longing for it for some time. She stared at herself in the mirror when she got up this morning and did not quite know who she was.

Catherine puts on her headphones now as she looks at the sky again, blue, so blue. She feels like she is going inside the music, feels it so closely she becomes it. Personal identity gone. She is a soprano's voice. The pluck of a guitar string. She is so free. It feels like an orgasm; it is unstoppable. She is higher than she has ever been before, Catherine thinks. She knows she is flying too high, like Icarus she is too close to the sun. Her fall is inevitable, but she does not care. While she feels this good, may it last as long as it can.

But during the weeks of mania that follow, she begins to struggle to curb her restlessness. Catherine starts to work with an extraordinary intensity, and at times finds herself so absorbed in her new project that she is not capable of thinking about anything else. The here and now of her art is all that matters. She works fourteen, sixteen hours a day, and often late into the night, and she develops a mantra to urge herself on, which she finds she sometimes says to herself repeatedly, 'I must create, express,' as if it possesses mystical powers of artistic creation. And yet she is happy, serenely happy, and is reluctant to break the spell.

# 35

JACK IS IN his flat in London. He plans to finally sell it now that he no longer needs to stay there during the week. Plus, he and Catherine need the money. He, of course, does not expect to get a good price for it – it remains, rather stubbornly, one of the most undesirable flats in London – but at the same time, Jack knows he will rather miss the old place: the derelict view, his noisy neighbours, the drunks on his doorstep. For him, it has always possessed an almost implausible (to everyone else at least) off-beat charm.

He has hired a van to take all the old furniture down to the skip. However, Jack has typically not realised how long it will take him to get everything ready for when Sam turns up. He is due to come straight from work and give Jack a hand lugging everything downstairs. The doorbell goes. Jack looks at his watch: it is six already, Sam's here, and he has only managed to get half of it ready. 'What you been doing old boy?' Sam says, walking inside, looking around the place. 'Head somewhere else as usual, eh?'

'Yep, something like that,' Jack confesses.

'Your mind still on that book of yours?'

'Yeah, but I think I'm almost done with it.'

'Great news, Jack. When can I have a look at it?'

'Soon Sam… soon. But I warn you, it's a bit of a mess. Lots of thoughts and ideas, but its structure's all over the place. It's a hefty, chaotic thing that needs sifting through, re-ordering… you know…'

'So… you finally discovered what love is?' Sam asks.

'No, but I know when it comes, it's…' Jack replies, searching for the appropriate word.

Sam interrupts, 'I can edit it for you, if you want?'

'Yeah, you could. You'd be a braver man than I. There's a lot of work there I can tell you. I've decided to take my mind off it for a bit. I need to get on with earning a living. But when I'm ready to get back to it, then maybe, yes… we'll talk about it. I'd love you to help me with it, give me your thoughts,' Jack says. 'For the moment anyway, I want to give my time to Catherine.'

'Your darling Catherine!'

'Yes Sam, my darling Catherine,' Jack responds in a deadpan tone.

'Look, I don't mean to be a prat,' Sam concedes. 'You seem a lot happier again, you really do.'

'Yeah.'

'So it's come back?'

'It has,' Jack says with deep contentment, of the kind he knows his friend rarely sees in him.

'You know, without sounding like a…' Sam looks for the right noun, cannot find it, then blurts out, '…look, I think there's always been something extraordinary between the two of you.'

'I hope that's extraordinary "amazing" as opposed to extraordinary "irregular". I'm not sure if the latter would constitute something good.'

'The former,' Sam says. 'Look we better get on, otherwise we're going to be here all night.'

The majority of the furniture still has to be dismantled so they can get it down the narrow staircase. Two hours later, he and Sam are finally ready to haul everything down; it proves gruelling work. They dump everything at the skip first – Jack drives like a maniac to get there before it closes – then go on to Sam's new flat. For as long as he has known him, Sam has always had his eye on his dressing table: it is by Heal and Son, made around 1900, in mahogany, with a glossy French-polished finish. In fact, it is quite valuable, except for some damage to one of its drawers. Jude loves it as well. She told Catherine that they would convince Jack to part with it one day. Well, he has finally given in to their interminable pleading. 'Consider it payment for helping me out,' Jack says to Sam as they haul it into the lift and take it up to the twenty-third floor. He can tell that Sam is rather excited about showing him his new place. The flat overlooks the Thames and it is almost at the very top of the tower. 'Catherine would love it up here,' Jack continues as he plonks his end of the dressing table down and scans the place. It is open plan, bright and spacious, all glass and light.

'We got it off you at last!' Jude exclaims.

'Yes,' Jack answers as he heads straight for the big windows overlooking the river.

'There's a balcony as well,' Jude says excitedly as she follows Jack, throws her arm affectionately round his shoulder and leads him outside.

'My God, I've never seen London look so incredible!'

'Yeah, it makes it look like another city from up here,' Jude says.

Sam follows them outside. 'You feel on top of the world, don't you!' he says.

And Jack nods, overwhelmed by London's panorama as he glances at the illuminated buildings on the other side of the river, different coloured lights casting their reflections over the water. 'What's that there?' he asks, pointing with his middle finger.

'I thought you'd recognise it. That's where the infamous Leonard Gold saved your bloody life!' Sam quips.

'Course it is, yes. I'd completely lost my bearings. I didn't realise we were so close.'

'What's happened to him?' Sam asks.

'I don't know,' Jack says. 'Let's not talk about him.'

'Sure, no problem,' Sam replies. 'So listen, when are you and Catherine going to come over for dinner?'

'I reckon we might be able to do next week sometime. I just have to check with her.'

'Just let us know,' Jude says.

Right at this moment, it begins to pour with rain. It seems to come from nowhere: one minute the sky beams a dark blue, the next it bellows black cloud and beats down heavy rain. 'Christ, I'd better go. I've got to drop the van off and get back to Oxford. I promised Catherine I'd get home tonight.'

'It's late. You can phone her. Why not stay here?' Jude says.

'No, I'd better go. Look, if I leave right now I'll be back around midnight.'

'You sure?'

'Yep really. But thanks away,' Jack says and hurries to the door.

'Don't forget about dinner next week,' Jude calls to him.

'I won't!' he exclaims as he dashes into the lift.

Jack speeds back towards Shepherd's Bush. As he nears the van rental drop-off point, he remembers he has left one thing back in the flat, a bag of journals that he planned to take with him back up to Oxford. He should go and get it now, then drop the van off.

It is dark and visibility is poor as he turns into his street. Outside his flat is deserted, as if the rain has banished everyone indoors, even the usual brethren of drunks, bar a solitary figure who sits huddled on his doorstep. And though Jack cannot make out the person's face right away – the head is bent downwards to the pavement – as he pulls up on the other side of the road and parks the van, he knows who it is, that it can only really be one person, that it must be Leonard. Who else would be sitting in a downpour such as this on his doorstep?

Jack stays inside the van and stares at him for a few moments, unsure what to do. He cannot leave him like this. He is drunk again, he supposes, and must be soaking wet. Jack does not want to take him inside the flat, but he knows he can at least get him out of the rain and back to the bookshop: otherwise he is likely to catch his death of cold. Jack jumps out of the van and calls to him through the beating rain, 'Leonard… come inside the van.'

'No!' Leonard shouts back.

Jack hurries across the street towards him now; the rubbish and grime on the tarmac make it slushy underfoot. 'What are you doing?'

Leonard stands up to confront him. 'Is Catherine dead?' he screams.

'Look Leonard, if you're desperate again, I'll help you, okay. I know what it's like…'

'How d'you know, Jack!'

'Oh come on, Leonard. Enough of the self-pity. D'you want my help or not?'

'How d'you know?' he asks again.

'We all have to go through it, the hard times. I've been very low before, Catherine as well. Christ… she might be about to go through it again. But we get through, don't we.'

'She sounds just like my Molly, prone to bouts of bloody melancholy and despair.'

'Sounds like you as well.'

'No I don't get melancholic anymore, I just get fucking angry,' Leonard counters. 'You know, Jack, she needed so much, too much, all of me… I couldn't give it. Just couldn't.'

Jack recalls her beautiful face in the photograph on Leonard's desk: her long dark hair, her slender face and neck. 'Isn't that what love is?' he asks.

'No!'

'What happened to her?'

'I told you. She was drunk. She fell off a balcony. You know that!'

Jack is now unconvinced by this explanation. Her expression in the photo: distant, distracted, those sad eyes that seemed to convey something else. She died another way, in a way that Leonard will not tell him. 'I don't believe you,' he says.

'What?'

'You heard me.'

'Why would I lie about this… about this of all things?'

'You didn't tell me about what you did to that prostitute.'

'That's bloody different!'

'How is it? You didn't tell me because you were worried what I'd think about you if I knew. Isn't this the same?' Jack says, then puts the same question to him again. 'How did she really die?'

'How dare you!' Leonard says, spitting now. 'You stand here before me as some kind of fucking judge. What can you claim to really know about me, about what's really going on inside me?' Jack is silent. 'You can't. No one can really know what's going on inside someone,' he continues. 'You were a naïve prick when I met you. Your head was stuck in the clouds. You were pathetically innocent. You believed in that silly fucking thing called love. The idiocy of your faith. Where would you have been had I not intervened that night outside the cathedral? In intensive care most likely, that's where. I've told you things, made you feel things. Without me, your book would be bloody nowhere. And this is the thanks I get. I'm doubted, I'm criticised, I'm judged.'

'You're miserable, Leonard. Can't you accept that there are people who've tried to help you? Your friends, literary colleagues, Joseph… Their willingness to help had nothing to do with your literary reputation. Rather, they just cared about you. They wanted you to stop drinking, get your life back together again. Don't you see that? And me as well, Leonard. Yes, I count myself as one of them, I wanted to be your friend. But as long as you continue to hate this world you'll be miserable. You need help for God's sake!' he insists, now reaching out to hold his hand.

It seems to Jack as he looks at Leonard at this moment that he is experiencing himself in desperate isolation, not as a whole person, but rather as someone who has split in two, his self wildly disoriented, his will almost paralysed. Leonard has reached a point where he is no longer able to identify with other people. Suffering is his rule of life now. The boundaries between victim and perpetrator, good and evil, right and wrong are blurred. And yet he does not have the courage to take his own life. Leonard pushes Jack's hand away violently. 'Who's going to help me? A psychiatrist?' he quips. 'Is he going to help me know myself? Because to really know oneself is extremely difficult. Some would rather kill themselves, kill others or go mad than find out who they truly are? How much self-knowledge can a human being bear, huh? I was labelled a filthy piece of shit after my conviction. I became an enemy of so-called civilised society. Why? Because I'd expressed what the majority suppress. They still fight me now, the way they stare at me… they treat me as their enemy, little realising that they're fighting themselves. What I express about women is in every man and what I express about men is in every man. They said I could never have loved Molly after what I'd done to that woman, that

I must hate all women… and probably always have. I'd treated Molly badly… that's what they alleged… and I'd treated subsequent women even worse. I treated them all like pieces of meat. Holes to fuck! I saw them as either aggressive predators or passive strangers…' he rattles on, whipping himself up into a frenzied state.

'Stop it, Leonard, just stop it. Where's this all going? Why can't you just stop fighting?' Jack pleads with him.

'Listen Jack. I'm against a world that's pissed me off, that's wronged me. Molly shouldn't have died. They shouldn't have judged me as they did. This is what I'm still rebelling against, and will continue to fight against until I die. I'd rather die on my feet than on my fucking knees. D'you hear me?' Leonard demands.

Jack now sees before him a man who has come to reject everything. Born out of his malignant solitude and alienation is a philosophy of despair. Listening to and watching his agony, Jack senses a terrible sickness in him, in his heart, his soul. Like many others before him who rejected all other principles but desire and power, Leonard has been driven to the brink of madness.

Leonard presses on, 'How much can you take, Jack? How much pain! You know, I'd hate Catherine if I were you… for putting you through all that misery, and for what?' he splutters, these words exploding like coughed-up phlegm from his mouth, rambling and bilious.

'No Leonard… no.'

'Can't take it anymore, Jack? Had enough of me, have you… had enough of her?'

'Something else happened to Molly didn't it?'

'Not that again.'

'Yes Leonard.'

'You're obsessed with this.'

'How did she die?' Jack persists.

'I told you!'

'Tell me again.'

'Why would I have made it up?'

'Because you can't handle how she really died. You feel responsible, don't you! You feel as though you could've done more to help her, stop her doing what she did. You loved her, yes Leonard… it's obvious you did, but she couldn't carry on could she?'

'Shut up, just fucking shut up!' and with these words, tears start to roll down Leonard's cheeks. He wipes the rain from his forehead, scratches his chin repeatedly, sniffs, grunts, coughs.

'You loved Molly but your love wasn't enough,' Jack says. 'You couldn't help her.' Leonard's face is pale now; he looks lost. 'She killed herself, didn't she. She threw herself off that balcony, didn't she. She didn't fall. And you made a fantasy of her death. You could only accept it if it was an accident.'

'No.'

'And deep down you still resent her for what she did even after all these years. The happiness she's deprived you of… the guilt she's made you feel. You wonder whether you could've been a better lover, a better husband, a better friend. These questions have tormented you for too long. You've come to see her as weak, as you have all women. You've come to hate the very thing you once loved and cherished. Can't you see?' Jack appeals to him.

'Yes she threw herself off!' Leonard shouts. 'Why did she do that? She said nothing to me. I had no clue, no sense. Her own bloody secret world, which I was granted no access to! If only she'd spoken… said something. Why?' he mumbles through sobs as the rain continues to beat down.

And all Jack can do now is stand here, drenched and exhausted, as Leonard pours out his pitiable life. He does not try and intervene anymore.

And when Leonard finally stops crying, he scurries away, without even looking at Jack.

He looks at his watch, wipes the mist from its face. It is late now and Jack will not be able to get back to the cottage this evening. He does not want to go back to Sam and Jude's, no, he would rather be on his own, and anyway, it is gone midnight and he is reluctant to disturb them. He decides the best thing to do is drop the van off now, get some sleep in the flat – the floor will have to do – then catch the first train back to Oxford in the morning.

Jack runs back to the van and hops inside, finally finding shelter from the rain, which has not let up in the slightest. He is wet through and dreams of a hot bath: he will have one in the flat. He rummages for his mobile phone on the floor, calls Catherine. 'Hi it's me. Look… I'm so sorry. I got held up… I…' he says breathlessly.

'What's happened?' she asks.

'It's okay. It just took a little longer than expected to move everything out, really. I've just dropped Sam off. Look, I'm going to spend the night at the flat and head back tomorrow.'

'Oh right…' she says, quiet and subdued, her voice trailing off.

'You okay?' Jack asks, concerned for her now, the tone of her voice worrying him.

'I'm fine. Why?'

'You sure?' he asks again, and his question is followed by silence. 'Catherine? Catherine… please…'

'No Jack, no. I'm feeling mad again,' she says.

'I know.'

'I don't know what's happening inside of me…' she continues, as if she has not heard how he has just responded. 'I didn't want to tell you. I thought it would be the final straw if I did.'

'I know,' he says again.

'What?'

'When I read your journals it was all there. I know how you can get sometimes, it's okay.'

'Have you talked to Theo?'

'Yes I spoke to my father.'

'I don't understand why I feel like this Jack. I mean… we're so very happy at the moment. I feel so much love from you. It doesn't make sense. I wish I wasn't… I…'

Jack interjects, 'You don't need to apologise for how you feel. But you must talk to me now, you must tell me how you're feeling, otherwise I'm lost, I can't help you.'

'I don't want to burden you.'

'I want you to burden me. I mean… I've burdened you with enough of my crap, come on!'

'You'd told me that I needed too much of you.'

'No Catherine, not while you feel like this. You can have as much of me as you want at the moment.'

'But I don't want to inflict all my misery on you, Jack. That's not fair, that's not what you do when you love someone.'

'Nonsense!'

'I can't believe it's come to this. I never would have dreamt it,' she says softly.

'What?'

'That we'd both be like this again after what we've been through.'

'Yes.'

'I was meant to hate you by now.'

'Yes, you were,' he says. 'Look, I'd better get some sleep. I'll see you in the morning.'

'Okay,' she murmurs.

'Okay,' he whispers back.

# 36

**CATHERINE PUTS** the phone down. The high is slipping; she can feel it sliding away, going down, right down. She is angry at it for leaving when she was on the cusp of something magical, something true. Yes, her creation is flitting away as well. Beauty disappearing, phantoms returning. She cannot bear to go as low as before, but she has Jack, and he will be back soon, in a matter of hours.

Before he called just now, Catherine tried papa again on the same number, but still no answer. He is not back from the countryside, if that is where he has actually gone. Widow Garcia is of little use – she has not tried her in ages – and Sylvia says she cannot help her anymore either and recommends she just go out there.

Yes, Catherine thinks, she should do just this, get on a plane right now and go and find him once and for all.

She runs to the bedroom and starts to fill a rucksack, throws things inside it with little forethought: a skirt, a dress, some sandals, three pairs of knickers. Why three pairs? Catherine asks herself, but cannot answer this question. But she knows she must not give herself too much time to think. And so to the bathroom, her wicker basket of things – toothpaste, toothbrush, daily moisturiser, perfume, tampons – she empties its contents into her bag. Her passport, yes, and her wallet. What else? Catherine wonders. That will have to do. To the front door. Oh, she should leave a note for Jack for when he gets back. *Gone to Barcelona to find papa. Don't worry. Will call you when I find a hotel. Love you, Catherine.*

Now she is in the car and driving to the airport; she will be there in no time. Catherine still does not know if she is doing the right thing.

She parks the car, hurries to the departures lounge. Airline desks everywhere: she must buy a ticket. The first one she approaches does not even fly to Barcelona. But the second one does.

Catherine boards the plane and hurries to her seat. The plane is cramped and noisy. A young girl sits in the seat in front; she screams and her mother tries to comfort her. Her cries are piercing, obstinate. Catherine feels an impulsive urge to shout back at the distraught child, give voice to the chaos in her mind.

She hurries to the toilet, and once inside the tiny cubicle, Catherine stares at herself in the mirror. She imagines smashing the bathroom to bits: the toilet seat, the sink, the soap dispenser. Her thoughts race, as if a monkey is chattering wildly, nonstop in her ear; and this monkey will not let up. She has to get out of here.

Catherine makes it back to her seat as the screaming young girl in front looks at her sympathetically. The girl cannot be more than four or five, has blonde curls and big blue eyes, and stares at Catherine now as if she understands that something is wrong inside of her and that she needs help.

She grabs her Walkman and presses play, the music begins, and then everything is still. The singer's voice, all dreamy, and the smooth sound of the saxophone take Catherine somewhere else. A brief respite, yes.

# LOVE AND MAYHEM

The plane lands in Barcelona and Catherine takes a taxi from the airport to Gracia. She found out from Sylvia that when papa left England all those years ago, he chose to settle in a small, modest flat that overlooked the *Sagrada Familia*. According to Sylvia, he has always adored this building and would talk about it at any available opportunity.

As the driver weaves his way through the back streets, the whole city comes alive and long repressed memories of her childhood come flooding back. When papa left home all those years ago, ma so successfully obliterated his life and image that Catherine only remembered small biographical details about him. He used to run a small art gallery where he hung and sold his own work, as well as the work of a handful of other artists who lived in the area, and ma used to model for him; he used to love to paint her. But beyond these few snippets of his life, Catherine retained almost no memory of him. What was he like as a man? Well, she did not know.

But now, she begins to visualise him again: his tall slender frame, his soft brown eyes, his wavy black hair, his carefully cut short beard. A picture begins to take shape in her mind of her ma and papa standing in the sea and embracing one another. They are a beautiful couple: ma's pale Gaelic complexion set against the dark skin of her Hispanic husband. They look blissfully happy together. Then a very young girl no more than three or four years old enters the scene. She wears a pair of pink bikini bottoms and paddles around in the shallow water, keeping a close eye on her parents in between chasing small crabs that dart in and out of the sand. Catherine has never remembered this far back.

Papa lives in a tall apartment building. She asks the driver to stop here rather than take her on to a hotel: she only has a small rucksack with her after all, and she can find a place to stay later on, depending what happens with papa. He is on the tenth floor, number 1017.

Catherine gets out of the lift and walks tentatively down the corridor. His apartment is at the very end. She is finally here and can barely bring herself to knock on his door. She stares at the wood, real oak, she thinks. She wipes her hand across it, then runs her nail through the grain. Oh, she is just procrastinating. Come on! Catherine tells herself, then takes a deep breath and knocks.

Nothing. She waits a few moments, then knocks again. Still no answer. Catherine immediately begins to panic and remonstrate herself. God, she has rushed out here in a distraught state with no forethought at all, has merely acted on a whim, a nagging need to see her father. What on earth was she thinking?

Catherine looks at her watch. It is one o'clock, midday back home. Jack will be worried sick. The fire exit at the end of the corridor is ajar. She pushes it open and peers down a rather flimsy-looking black metal platform that leads to a stairwell, which spirals all the way down to street level. Catherine steps onto the platform; it feels relatively safe. She notices the windows to her father's flat, then looks out across the city skyline to confirm the view of the *Sagrada Familia*. Yes, she can see it perfectly, and from this vantagepoint the cathedral in all its *modernista* eccentricity looks like a kind of heavenly, fairytale confectionery palace. She peeps through the first window: it is his front room, Catherine presumes. But she cannot make out much inside: the sun shines voraciously straight down and its bright glare makes her investigation impossible. She resolves to wait until the sun moves over head; she knows she will not have to wait long. And so Catherine removes her jacket, spreads it on the floor and lies down. She is tired, feels the need to rest for a bit and soon falls asleep.

She wakes up to the sound of two birds squabbling just above her. One of them flies low then has to flap its wings vigorously to avoid hitting Catherine, who is forced to raise her arms to shield her face. It manages to fly away while the other remains perched on the windowsill above, looking down now as if scrutinising her. The sun has moved some way overhead. She has been asleep for well over two hours.

Catherine gets up and gazes sleepily through the window to the front room. She can make out an oil painting of the cathedral on the back wall, which hangs next to a striking portrait of a beautiful young woman with long black hair and piercing green eyes. The young woman looks straight out of the canvas and her stare is full of passion, as if she is in love with the artist painting her. It is an exquisite picture. Catherine finds herself momentarily transfixed by the young woman's expression; it is ma.

There are also many other paintings lined up against the walls, she is eager to see more, and so edges along the platform to the next window. Catherine begins to form the impression of a man who leads a simple life, on his own, surrounded by his paintings and memories. And when she comes to the bedroom, she finds a single bed, a small leather armchair and a print of Picasso's *Guernica*, which hangs on the back wall.

All this is a far cry from the image ma painted of him, a hedonist with an insatiable appetite for different women and the good life. Then she notices a picture on the bedside table of a small girl; it is she, Catherine.

Her inspection is suddenly disrupted by the hysterical cries of a woman behind her, *'¿Qué estás haciendo?'*

'What?' Catherine replies, swinging round to confront her inquisitor and losing her footing on the metal grill. She falls to the floor and one of her legs slides over the side of the balcony. It is a long way down. She immediately grabs hold of her stray leg and pulls it back towards her body then clambers to her feet.

*'No, no, ¡es peligroso!'* the woman shouts, then lets out a heavy sigh.

'Yes... I know I shouldn't be out here. *'Ya lo sé... vale...* it's just... I...'

*¡Ven! ¡Ven!'*

Catherine climbs off the metal platform and returns to safer ground inside the building. The woman, she is old and thickset and wears a long black dress, promptly slams the fire door behind her. 'You the English girl, *sí*, the one I spoke to on *teléfono*?' she asks soberly.

'Yes... yes, that's me,' Catherine replies.

'You come for... *Señor* Ramirez?'

'Yes, Roberto Ramirez. He's my *padre*. *Viuda* Garcia, *sí?*' Catherine says, holding out her hand. But Widow Garcia is suddenly silent and does not offer her hand. 'Is he still in the countryside... *campo, sí?* Do you know how I can find out where his cottage is?' Catherine goes on, at this moment wishing she has a sufficient grasp of Spanish.

'*No*, I don't, look...' Widow Garcia struggles with her reply, and Catherine is not clear whether her reticence is due to her poor English or whether it is on account of something else.

Then the front door to the flat opposite papa's creaks open and Catherine turns round to see a distinguished looking man in his sixties walk towards her. '*Antoni, esta es la hija de Señor Ramirez,*' Widow Garcia continues, uneasily, breathlessly.

'Catherine, *me llamo* Catherine,' she says, holding out her hand to Antoni. He wears baggy beige linen trousers and a matching shirt, his silver hair is shaved close to his scalp, he has deep olive skin.

'Hello,' he replies, taking her hand. 'It's a pleasure to meet you at last.'

He must know him, yes. Papa must have told this man about her, his daughter. Antoni's voice is gentle; he sounds like he has a very good command of English. 'You know my father?' she immediately asks the question, cannot contain herself.

'You and I need to talk. Please come into my flat,' he replies, gesturing with his arm towards the open door. *'Vale, voy a hablar con ella,'* he says to Widow Garcia now, nodding at her.

*'Bueno, bueno,'* she mumbles in response as she looks at Catherine with deep sadness in her eyes, then wobbles off down the hallway back to her flat.

'What d'you want to tell me?' Catherine asks Antoni as he closes the door behind her.

'Please sit down,' he says, motioning graciously to the settee. The room is full of reds and browns, wooden antique furniture dominating the space.

'It's about my father, yes?'

'Can I get you a drink?'

'D'you know where he is?'

'Please sit down, Catherine?' and again points to the sofa.

'Something's not right.'

'Catherine, please?'

'Look… why don't you just tell me what you know?' she demands, feeling agitated now, sure that he is concealing something, and so stands tall, clenching her rucksack in one hand, gripping the handle tight.

'I'm sorry, Catherine.'

'For what?'

'Your father died… he died a fortnight ago.'

'No,' she mutters quietly to herself and goes to sit down.

'I'm sorry.'

'Look, I've got to go…' she now says, standing up straight, moving away from the settee, then Antoni, making her way towards the door. 'I've got to get out of here.'

'He was a good man,' he calls to her.

'Why did he leave me then, huh?' she turns round and shouts at Antoni, this man she does not even know, but she must express her anger to someone.

And he stands here and says nothing. What can he say after what she has just said to him? And Catherine watches him sit down now, bring his hands to his head and wipe his face, as if he is wiping it with a wet towel. He closes his eyes and breathes in deeply, in between his fingers, momentarily losing himself in his own contemplation – perhaps he is thinking of his times with papa – before he exhales deeply, pulling himself back to the present, to Catherine. 'Look, I'm sorry,' she continues. 'Did you know him well?'

'Yes.'

'How did he die?'

'He had a heart attack. It was sudden.'

'I missed him…' she says quietly and begins to cry, and finally allows herself to sit down on the sofa.

'He told me all about you. He said it was the hardest thing he ever had to do.'

'He left me all alone.'

'He told me he couldn't cope anymore.'

'What d'you mean?' Catherine asks, though she suspects she already holds the answer to this question, and yet she needs this man to confirm it.

'He loved you very much, he still loved your mother, but he felt he'd reached a point where the only way he could get through life was on his own.'

'On his own, I don't understand… you say he loved us, and yet what he did, that wasn't love?'

'Look, I can't speak for him, I'm sorry,' Antoni says and looks away now, towards a painting which hangs on the wall, one of papa's, Catherine guesses.

'Well why are you speaking for him then?' she demands, pissed off with this man who seems to have so much affection for papa, who seems determined to try and excuse what he did.

'Your father was not what you think.'

'Well what was he then?'

'He…'

'What… dependable, supportive? Come on, he wasn't even there!'

'He… he struggled with your mother.'

'Ma always told me he'd abandoned us, that he was a bad man who screwed around all the time, who didn't give a shit about me!'

'No, that's not fair, Roberto wasn't a bad man. He was just too sensitive… she, your mother, overwhelmed him, needed too much of him. Yes, he ran away, he shouldn't have left you like he did… but it wasn't for the reasons your mother told you.'

Catherine just stares at the cathedral now and from this aspect it looks slightly different. She becomes engrossed in its spires, which go up and up like they are in search of something. 'I must go to it,' she suddenly announces.

'What?'

'His church. He loved it, didn't he?'

'Yes, he adored it.'

'I must go now then,' she insists, gathering up her rucksack in her arms as if cradling a baby and going to leave for a second time.

'Have you come straight from England?' Antoni asks, trying to dissuade her from departing quite yet.

'Yes.'

'Well where are you going to stay?'

'I don't know. I don't need to be here anymore, not now,' she says, pulling open the front door.

'How did you know where to find him?'

'I got his address and number from my cousin… and I spoke to Widow Garcia.'

'Well I wish your cousin had given you my number. I could've called you and told you what had happened.'

'Yes… but it's too late now,' Catherine says. 'You know… I just wanted him to hold me,' and with these final words she darts out of the flat and heads for the lift.

'Catherine, come back please,' Antoni shouts. 'There's so much he'd like you to know… so much more.'

'I must go…' she calls to him as the lift doors closes.

But what else does she need to know? He is dead, that is it.

Catherine feels delirious now, a labyrinth of images and reveries flitting around inside her head, seeming to move from clarity to obscurity like bolts of lighting. She tries to interpret these mental pictures and discern their significance, but they are too evanescent, real and unreal at the same time. Her heart throbs, beating like a barrel drum, the sound of it reverberating in her ears. Catherine feels completely disassociated from the external world. Her madness has sculpted its own florid phantasmagoria.

She dashes out of the apartment building, and with no forethought or deliberate intention, finds herself charging towards the cathedral like a small balloon at the mercy of a great wind. She feels as if someone else other than the Catherine she knows is carrying her along now, like she has been possessed by another entity, which wants to show her things she has not seen before and make her feel things she has not felt before. And in no time at all, she is right here, outside the cathedral, head slung back, eyes fixed on its massive spires.

Catherine embarks on a whirlwind tour of the building, first to the *Nativity Façade*, then the *Passion Façade*, then the *Belltower of St Barnabus*. The equanimous part of her knows that a building such as this should be observed slowly, methodically – there is so much to be taken in – and yet the unbalanced part of her is not interested in such measured and thoughtful appreciation. And so she charges around between cranes and spires in a near frenzied state, and barges into people, knocking some to the ground, and when they confront her to explain her behaviour, she screams obscenities at them. Thankfully, most of her abuse falls on deaf ears: they simply cannot understand what she is saying.

Then she hurtles towards an image of Christ on the cross, falls to her knees to genuflect, and looks up at the man before her; he is almost naked, bleeding, in pain. Catherine is suddenly overcome with sadness and wants to embrace him, and so scrambles over the brass railing and flings her arms around Him. A man who witnessed her earlier outburst approaches her and takes her arm, but she shrugs him off, then bolts outside again. She has to get back home.

Catherine hails a taxi and tells the driver to take her straight to the airport. Once there, she makes a frantic phone call to Jack, telling him that she is sorry, that she did not mean to worry him, that everything is happening too fast, that she cannot get a flight till ten, that she loves him, that she wishes papa was not dead, that she did not buy a return ticket because she did not know how long she would be here for, that she needs him now more than ever.

Her flight is delayed and while she waits, her grief sets in and plays a carousel of different sorrows. She prays for his resurrection, imagines he is alive again, blames ma for driving him away, blames papa for being so weak, and finally blames herself. God, she should have gone to him sooner.

When Catherine finally boards the plane, it is packed, and again, she has to endure the cries of small children and the screams of parents as their tempers flare. She tries to steady her mind by reading but this is a futile exercise, then tries her Walkman but this does not help either, and lastly goes for something simple, just closes her eyes, but finds that when she does this, her head spins evermore wildly.

Her thoughts are convoluted now, moving too fast, chasing one another like wild hares in every direction, scarcely perceptible. The exclusive poles of logic and sentiment feel sandwiched together inside her mind, and her thought sequences, well they are repetitive and tedious, a melting pot of reassuring words, radical ideas and despairing thoughts continuously wrestling with one another for dominance. Madness, for Catherine it is a kind of infectious uncertainty or schizophrenia. She is suffering to think and thinking to suffer. And so she sits here for the remainder of the flight, eyes part open, vision blurred, hyperventilating, praying that her mind will just give her a little peace.

Jack is there to meet her at the other end and Catherine senses right away that he wants to tell her how angry he is with her for leaving like that. But at the same time, he has the look of someone who knows that normal reasoning cannot be applied to her at this moment. And so he says nothing, just takes her straight home.

Then back at the cottage, Jack takes her upstairs to the bedroom, undresses her while Catherine sits exhausted, her feet dangling off the edge of the bed like a small girl's. Then she lies down in his arms and falls asleep almost immediately.

# 37

**SHE PACES** up and down the living room, feels so alone, as if solitude itself is attacking her, gnawing at her chest, and she cannot quite believe the sheer bloody size of this feeling, its morbidity astonishing her. Oh yes, she, Catherine Ramirez, is full of self-pity now, she knows this, and quite rightly hates herself for it.

Catherine searches the room, the view outside, her own mind, for a spark of joy, something to look forward to. She wants to discover a new reality now: the whole world seems like an illusion. She looks over at her journal on the coffee table. Even this has become fucking dull, monotonous, just as she has become to herself.

'You bore me Catherine!' she screams at the top of her voice. 'D'you hear me, you miserable cunt, you fucking tedious old cow! Go on, surprise me, be bloody miserable again, why don't you!'

It used to make her feel better, the act of writing, but not anymore. She swings round to look at herself in the mirror and her face does not seem real, and so she tugs at her cheeks, then pulls her hair until she wants to scream. Who is this person, an impostor? Catherine asks. Yes, no one can assure her otherwise. Maybe she is living behind a glass wall? Her pupils look bigger and blacker, as if a demon has possessed her and is trying to impose itself from within, forcing its way outwards until there is no semblance left of her, and this demon possesses all those characteristics she detests in herself.

Catherine turns to face the window now. The sky is clear blue, sunlight strong, but she cannot appreciate the day's beauty. She needs love, loves Jack more than anything, but she cannot live like this. Catherine has to make herself see blue again, has to try and fly again. These dreadful feelings will not beat her. Love is fundamental, of course it is, there is nothing more important, it should permeate everything. Without it, there is nothing. She will love this world not loathe it.

It is Thursday, and she and Jack are due to have dinner this evening with Sam and Jude. They have put off this dinner for far too long. Dear old Sam, he will make her feel better, and *she* will make herself feel better. Why doesn't she cook for them all? Catherine thinks. Yes, she will call Sam right away.

'I'm so looking forward to seeing you,' she says to Sam as he picks up the phone. 'It's been too long. Listen, I've had an idea, I want to cook.'

'What?'

'I want to make dinner. I want to make a *linguine ai frutti di mare*. I'll buy the mussels, clams and squid fresh from the market… it'll be wonderful. And the wine, yes…'

'If you're going to do all that, then I must get the wine!' he butts in excitedly.

'You and Jude do like it, don't you?'

'Yes of course we do.'

'Jack adores it.'

'Right, that's settled.'

'What time are you and Jack back from your meeting?'

'About seven-thirty, eight. Probably nearer eight though. The guy we're seeing goes on a bit.'

'What about Jude?'

'She won't be able to make it before eight either.'

'What were you going to do for dinner then?'

'What d'you think? Takeaway, that's what. What else is there?'

'Right, well you're going to get home-cooked food tonight!' she says adamantly. 'I'll pop by the office and get the keys off of you. When you all get back, dinner will be served!'

She has done this several times before, and Catherine knows Sam considers it to be part of her devil-may-care attitude: whenever she is seized by a particular idea, she must carry it through, no matter what.

And so three hours later, she goes bounding into Sam's office. 'Right, I'm off to buy the ingredients,' she announces. 'The keys?'

'Here we are!' he says, tossing them to her.

Catherine jumps up and catches them in one hand. 'See you soon!' she exclaims and skips out of the room.

# 38

**HE AND SAM** get back to the flat just before eight. They walk towards the kitchen area without calling out Catherine's name.

Jack looks at all the ingredients carefully lined up ready to sauté and cook – the *marinara* sauce, fresh cleaned seafood, chopped garlic, olive oil and *linguini* – while Sam inspects a wonderful Mediterranean salad she has put together with *romaine, roquette, frisee* and *lolla rossa*.

He thinks about what Catherine has been like the last couple of days. She has seemed in better spirits, more grounded, and though they discussed the possibility of her talking to his father again if she felt the need to seek professional help, Catherine assured Jack that this was not necessary at the moment. A period of depression was inevitable after she has been so high, but she has got through it before and will get through it again. He made her promise, however, that if she changed her mind, she should inform him immediately. Help is at hand if she wants it.

And yet now Jack notices, despite this initial semblance of order, that there is a plethora of culinary utensils and a jumble of pots and pans, many of which seem utterly irrelevant to the meal Catherine is preparing, and then as he watches Sam stroll nonchalantly onto the balcony and look out over the river, he is made to wonder whether she is not getting through her black spell as well as she would like him to believe she is, and that perhaps she has simply done a very good job of concealing the full extent of the mayhem in her mind.

Jack goes over to the dining table. There is a pile of plates, some cutlery, and Catherine's journal, which lies open. And now, he has an even stronger sense of what she might have gone and done. The mind on the brink, though it fears stepping over the line into the unknown, into the abyss of unreason, is also excited by this prospect, and Jack has the dreadful feeling that Catherine might have just found it irresistible.

Now everything happens very slowly. Sam beams a warm smile as he turns to him and says, 'I do love this view, you know,' but Jack is charging towards him, and as he steps onto the balcony, he pushes Sam out of the way and throws his head over the side of the building.

'What the hell are you doing?' Sam shouts, confounded by his actions, and taking him firmly by the shoulder.

But Jack is motionless now, just stares straight down. And there she is, Catherine, sprawled out on the ground. Her body lies just behind the perimeter wall, a few feet from the water's edge.

Jack is silent at first, too shocked to summon any intense emotion. The only thing to come out of him is a strained whimper as his body trembles. He stares at Sam, the whites of his eyes glistening through tears, then walks inside in a daze and slumps on a chair by the dining table.

He looks down at Catherine's open journal. Her writing is frantic, scrawled and barely legible. He begins to read, 'Dear journal, this is my last entry… and this is for you as well, Jack. I no longer need to hide this from you anymore. No more secrets, not now. At last, I've had enough of them. I finally know what I have to do to find peace, to be free. And strangely, the thought of this doesn't frighten me. In fact, it empowers me. My mayhem has left me now that I've decided what to do. Its cessation lies in my decision. It might be the wrong one, but please respect it, this I ask of you. Jack, I've always felt more love for you than I did for anyone else. And I know you've loved me like no other as well. You've made me so happy, thank you. I don't do this to spite you and punish you: I'm not angry with you anymore. No, I do this to set you free from my mayhem, but also to set myself free. You see, I've had enough… not of you, but of the need, the constant ache, the desperation. I love you Jack, but now you must let me fly, I must fly… fly…'

Catherine said to him the day after she got back from Barcelona that a small part of her 'welcomes the madness with open arms and indulges it'. This mind of hers was taking her somewhere else, yes, towards the twilight of unreason, a haven of stormy, unbroken, intense emotion. Here, she told him, feelings 'explode forth', simply unwilling to heed the warnings and recommendations of a reasonable mind.

And Jack sees now, as he clutches his stomach, that Catherine has been taken to the same place as Leonard, and yet in her mayhem, amidst all her terrible pain, a deep love in her heart was still present, active.